D0298005

GOLD TOWN

GOLD TOWN

RITA CLEARY

SUNSTONE
PRESS

SANTA FE

The events, people, and incidents in this story are the sole product of the author's imagination. The story is fictional and any resemblance to individuals living or dead is purely coincidental.

Jacket Illustration by Faith Delong

Sunstone books may be purchased for edcational, business, or sales promotional use. For information please write: Special Markets Department, Sunstone Press, P.O. Box 2321, Santa Fe, New Mexico 87504-2321.

First Edition

Printed and bound in the United States of America

10 9 8 7 6 5 4 3 2 1

Library of Congress Cataloging in Publication Data:

Cleary, Rita, 1941-
    Goldtown: a novel of the American West / by Rita Cleary.—1st ed.
    p. cm.
    ISBN: 0-86534-241-5
    1. Frontier and pioneer life—Montana—Fiction.   2. Gold mines and mining—Montana—Fiction.   I. Title
    PS3553.L3916G65   1996
    813' .54—dc20   95-35518
                                                        CIP

Published by   SUNSTONE PRESS
               Post Office Box 2321
               Santa Fe, NM 87504-2321 / USA
               (505) 988-4418 / orders only (800) 243-5644
               FAX (505) 988-1025

To the
Montana Ghost Town Preservation Society
that our heritage may not vanish.

Chapter 1

It was a long ride up the gulch, past the diggings and the tailings, the slashed treestumps, the ugly little huts and the hillside pierced and pock-marked with pick and shovel. The aspen and pine must have been beautiful. They were gone now. Garnet Creek must have been beautiful too, running clear and cold off the mountains, but now it was eddied and muddied with the dross of flume and rocker. The gold diggers had dredged it out of its comfortable bed, strained and sluiced out its riches and poured the worthless sludge back in. The rocks were still there. But even they were nude, stripped of the mosses and lichens that had clothed them, or covered by ugly little warts of huts and dirty tents. Gold-seeking was a scourge upon the land, a barbed whip that flayed the earth. Just like Georgia. Lee Cameron remembered. General Sherman had flayed Georgia to the bone, rent the skin from her back, like an overseer flogging a captured slave. Cameron could never go back.

It was midday in Varina. The mountains beyond the town rose to the great willowy clouds hovering over the peaks and sweeping skyward to the firey sunball at their zenith. Their beauty made the devastation all the more horrible. Lee Cameron squinted at the sight and swallowed hard. His mouth was dusty dry. He repressed his painful memories, forcing them down to the very depths of his soul. He had come for the future, not for the past. He was a seeker like all the rest. Impatiently, he waved a farewell to the freight wagons and his unsavory bullwhacker companions, spurred his pony, and loped on ahead to the town.

It was safe to ride toward Varina. Not so safe to ride away. The road agents saw to that. Greedy for the yellow dust, they preyed on all who tried to leave like vultures upon carrion. But Cameron had no thought of leaving. He nodded to the muckers and panners as he passed but they did not turn from their toil. An occasional grunt was the only welcome he received.

Varina was a hungry town, grey and dust-covered, not pretty even from a distance. She would welcome the stores the wagons brought and she would pay. Her citizens crowded the street awaiting the flour, coffee and sugar and eggs that the oxen hauled—especially the eggs. Loving hands had packed them gently in sacks of flour so they would arrive whole. Eggs were worth more than gold. Flour too. Cameron knew—if he had invested in a barrel of eggs packed in flour, he would be a richer man today. He had helped unload the flour and eggs at the wharf in Fort Benton and had heard the stories. Flour had run low last winter when snow choked the passes and ice froze the river. There had been riots. Regulators had seized and distributed what small supplies existed. Prices had soared to ninety dollars a sack. Normally one pound of sugar cost sixty cents; a pound of bacon forty cents; a shot of whiskey twenty-five. There was money in Varina, Cameron was convinced, more than enough to restore the fortunes of one itinerant gambler.

Gold dust was the legal tender, worth double its value in government bills. Men hoarded it and spent it foolishly. They measured it in pinches and carried it in rawhide pouches called pokes. Lee Cameron carried two pokes in the lining of his old coat, the grey captain's coat he had worn thin these last few years. He had been lucky since the war. He'd used his wits and he'd only cheated Yankees. The riverboats and gaming tables had employed him eagerly. Varina would employ him too and lavish some of her riches on him. He would be one of the lucky few. For the rest, life was hard.

Gold mining was not easy. Lee Cameron spotted several miners knee deep in icy creek water. They heaved shovelfuls of muck up onto sludge piles shoulder high. They built dams and dug trenches to divert the creek. They hammered together flumes and rockers. They watched the blood turn blue in their fingers and the muscles of their ankles contract in the cold water of the spring thaw. They felt their tendons strain and their joints crack with every slam of pick on bedrock. Even now in the full luster of sunshine, when they checked the riffles in their boxes for every tiny flake and gripped the cold metal of the wet pan, they shivered.

Lee Cameron was not one of them and would never be. He came with another purpose. He'd suffered his losses like all loyal sons of the south—the War Between the States had left him destitute. Now, in early 1867, like many southerners disgusted with Reconstruction forced upon them by the Northern Democrats, he left his home. The old plantation system was dead. He parcelled out his last acreage among his remaining slaves and headed west. He came up the Missouri River to the territory of Montana. He'd heard of Varina. It was a Confederate stronghold and he was hungry for life and wealth and belonging and hungry for love. He would find friends here and he was looking for someone.

He'd almost given up. Then he'd heard she had come up the Missouri too. She'd disappeared from St. Louis and changed her name. Some said she'd married. He didn't know for sure. Before the war, he'd met her. Her name was Emma LeClerc then, of the LeClercs of Baton Rouge. Now she was Emma Dubois. She was young and beautiful and he would've changed her name to Cameron except for the war.

He stopped to inquire. A grizzled, frowning face looked up from a ditch that almost spanned the road and eyed him before answering. "Emma Dubois! What you want her fer? You need a stake you want to talk to her. You don't look like a moneyed man to me."

Cameron realized too late that he still wore his Confederate dress coat. The captain's braids still hung raggedly onto one sleeve. The three gold bars were tarnished but still decorated its stand-up collar. He rode astride his old Cavalry saddle and the initials C.S.A. still labelled his canteen. The sweaty miner looked at him with cold suspicion.

"I'm an old friend...from Georgia."

"Mrs. Dubois ain't from Georgia! Yer a thievin' Reb, like the rest of you Davis men. Come barkin' an' snarlin' at my heels! Want to steal my claim! Want me to fill it in and git outta yer damn road! That's what you want! Think you'll whup me like yer goddamned slaves! Git off a my land or I'll blow you from 'ere to hell!" He dropped his shovel and pulled an old revolver from his waistband.

Cameron bristled. His Navy Colt was wrapped carefully in his bedroll or he might have called the bluff. His rifle hung in its scabbard but he hadn't cleaned it in his rush this morning to be up and on the road early. Besides he'd seen enough killing. He bridled his anger and waited.

He phrased his next question with careful civility. "Then maybe you can direct me to the Citadel Saloon?"

The Yank pursed his lips and turned back to scrubbing the riffles in his sluice box. No Georgian would get help from this man. Cameron clamped his mouth shut, balled his fist and rode on. He slipped his arms from the old grey coat, rolled the old Captains' braid inward over his canteen and tied both over the pommel.

The next miner was more willing and he was a Reb like Cameron. He stood up to his hips in the cold mountain run-off and looked up at Cameron through baggy, watery eyes that perched over a dripping nose. He spotted the dress coat hanging over the saddle and spoke before Cameron had framed his own words. His voice droned languidly with the rolling inflexions of the deep south. "Was you with the Sixth?"

"Nineteenth Georgia, General Archer."

"Figured." The old soldier stared sadly away at the mountain, looked back at Cameron and reorganized his thoughts. Cameron recognized the symptoms of a man whose bitter memories fused with the good. He waited for the man to speak.

"Once, I had a coat like that misself an' a hat with a plume. Used to think hell was goin' to heaven with the Yanks. I was a young man then, an' whole. Chancellorsville's what got me this." The miner held up his right hand. The hand was white except for the last three fingers. These were reddened stubs. "Canister blew the reins clean outta my hand an' killed the best horse I ever owned. Doctor said there warn't a thing he could do. Fingers was amputated already. He poured some Tennessee lightnin' on't, stanched the blood with a brand from the fire and sent me back to the front. Hurt like hellfire. Lucky it warn't my whole hand. I can still pan." He held up the cold metal pan between thumb and forefinger.

Cameron spoke up, "I missed Chancellorsville. Fredericksburg's where I got mine, me.... an' General Jackson."

"Great man, Tom Jackson. The devil's work done 'im in; 'twas one of our own." The miner shook his head and looked back at his mangled hand. "Folks around these parts think Injuns got me.. I keep tellin' 'em, Injuns is a thievin' bunch but they'd have lifted my hair, not my hand. 'Specially now with Gen'ral Meagher raisin' an army. "Meagher of the Sword", they calls 'im. Hot-headed Irish Yank if ya ask me. Terrible combination, Abolitionist an' Irish! No tellin' where he'll stop. Injuns is mad as hornets, I tell ye...an' they're sendin' Meagher to burn out the hive. Them Injuns'll swarm and sting!"

Lee Cameron sat his horse patiently. The man's speech trailed off. He looked from his hand to Cameron and held it out. "Glad to meet another Reb....Name's Farnsworth."

"I'm Lee Cameron. I'm looking for Emma Dubois."

"You'll find friends in Varina... An' then there's some ain't so friendly. Mrs. Emma lives on Jones Street. That'd be the street below Warren to the north, low down along Sunshine Creek. Left turn off Jefferson. Only house with a porch. You'll find it easy. She can afford paint. She could afford to live on the hill, but folks won't let 'er... Looks like a woman's place all right. She painted it green. Did the job herself!"

Cameron found Warren, then Jefferson and Jones. The house with the porch was there and the porch was painted bright emerald green. Lee Cameron stopped his horse across the street. It was a large house by frontier standards, twenty feet wide at the front and extending back about forty feet. There were glass windows with curtains and a white bench on an ample roofed porch that spanned the width of the house. She had done well. "Emma's Boarding House", the sign read over the door. This was hers. A handsome black girl in bright red gingham swept the last remnants of afternoon dust from the floorboards. The front door was open.

Cameron wiped the sweat from his brow, swung his leg over the cantle and dismounted. He was trail-worn and dusty, unshaven and tired, but a powerful curiosity drew him forward. He dusted off the dress coat and shoved his arms into the sleeves. It was the last remaining piece of his dashing captain's uniform and that was how she would remember him.

"I help ya, mista?" The black girl spoke up. "You lost?"

"Rachel, it's me, Lee Cameron." His voice rattled. Rachel was a former slave who must have stayed with her mistress after she was set free.

The girl's white eyes widened. She stepped back as if she'd seen a ghost. "Captain, Mr. Lee, we thought you was dead!" She stuttered the rest, "The missus be right inside that door. It's open. You kin see her yisself."

Cameron nodded, stepped up and tracked dirt over the clean porch. With his hand on the door jamb, he stopped again and took off his hat. One more step and he was turning the pages back five years. They were not happy years.

"She be right there." The black girl backed away hesitantly.

He stepped quietly through and closed the door behind him. A strikingly beautiful woman in dark blue silk sat at a wide mahogony desk. A carved sofa and tall armoire lined the wall facing her. Her silver-framed spectacles perched delicately above an aquiline nose and framed dark blue sparkling eyes. Black hair was piled high in a knot on top of her head and held there with silver combs. Wisps of

11

curls that had escaped the combs dotted the pale nape of her neck. Cameron's first urge was to reach out and touch them. Then he realized his own inadequacy. Instead he wrapped his knuckles tightly around the brim of his hat. She was as he remembered her, only older, fuller, more beautiful.

She heard the door click and looked up. Her head snapped back rigidly. The spectacles dropped to the catalogue she'd been reading. Cameron recognized it immediately—Wilson and Finck Company of San Francisco. It was the professional gambler's bible: how to keep the odds in your favor—he had one too.

She folded the spectacles and put them gently into a velvet case. "What are you doing here?" She recognized him. "You look dreadful. You've aged."

In his haste to see her, he'd forgotten how he looked. He smoothed his matted beard and ran sweaty fingers through his shaggy brown hair. He was a handsome man, tall and lithe, with a fine classic profile and liquid brown eyes, but now the sweat and dust of the trail lined the creases in his face. His grey coat hung crookedly from his shoulders, the weight of gold tugging and bagging it to the right side.

"I've been looking for you. It's been a long time. You're no different. You're still beautiful." He'd rehearsed every word but they didn't come out smoothly. Hearing himself, he sounded so foolish. Silence. The years fell away like old pieces of flaking skin. The devastation, the battles, the crushed hopes and final defeat, faded into some vague warmth when he looked at her.

She spoke again. "Looking for me?...That was five years ago when you left.... August...'62....I cried every night."

Cameron marvelled at her directness. How could he tell her he had cried too? He was not a man who bared his heart freely. He stood there like a prisoner convicted, waiting for his sentence. She continued, "Not a letter, not a trickle of news, no word of your whereabouts." Her lips drew back into a pencil line. Was she angry or compressing some deep emotion into stiff rigidity? "No inquiry as to how we were faring. Five years is a long time. I gave you up..."

He listened dumbly like a faithful mongrel cowering at his master's rebuke, without knowing what heinous act he should be sorry for. He bowed his head. His fists tightened around the broad brim of the planter's hat and wrenched it back into a tight corkscrew.

Shouldn't she have jumped up to welcome him, smile, at least asked him to sit down? Lonely, embattled, he had dreamed of this reunion. He had lain in agony, near Fredericksburg, the stubby roots of a giant oak grinding into the small of his back, stabbing pain each

12

time he tried to move, the pound of cannons and thousands of rifles beating a steady tatoo in his head, recalling him from the brink of unconsciousness. He had seen her in his delerium, floating over him like a protecting angel. It was an image he carried with him still. He knew he should turn, walk back out the door, but something in what she had said anchored him to the floor.

"You're ruining your hat...."

He was a few moments collecting his thoughts. "You said 'we'?....Who else?"

"I bore you a child."

Her words thundered through his head, worse than the booming crash of artillery. His eyes closed and his neck arched back. An incredible sadness gripped him. His hand swept up to hide his face and he shook his shaggy head as he would dust from a old carpet. The hat fell to the floor. When he started to speak, the words tumbled out, "I'm sorry. I didn't know." He stopped abruptly, stupidly. It was a pitiful reply. He was good at campfire stories and the banter of the gaming table, but deep feelings stuck like glue somewhere down in his chest. He nodded his head again and his dark hair fell forward into his eyes. He brushed it backward with a single swipe and looked dolefully right through her.

She was sorry for him then and softened her sharp tones. "She's a beautiful little girl. I named her Marie." Her voice held the last syllable. She removed a golden locket from around her neck. "The nuns had her picture wrought....She has your eyes." Slowly she reached out and handed him the open locket.

He reached to take the locket and touched her hand. He looked down at the tiny golden oval, flicked it open and stared into the great serious eyes of a young girlchild, so beautiful, so like her mother. Memories frozen by years of war, flooded back. Emma LeClerc had been only eighteen years old when he left. And he had been twenty-six, a captain, Nineteenth Georgia, Army of Northern Virginia, C.S.A. The officer's braid and gold Captains' bars glittered golden against the grey wool coat and the dark brown waves of his hair. He rode tall and straight in the saddle with the gentle hand of the expert, on a thoroughbred horse. He carried his father's gold watch. His grandfather's saber rattled at his side and in his broad-brimmed hat he wore an ostrich plume. Romantic and dashing, he'd swept her off her feet. Now the horse was dead, the watch smashed and the saber's golden hilt melted down for a cause and a system defeated. It was a war he didn't fully understand but he supported it anyway through loyalty to his father, his family and the red clay Georgian soil on which he was born.

He still had his six-foot height and classic profile but now the contours of his face were covered with beard and his dark brown hair was snarled and dull and lightly salted with grey. There were wrinkles in his brow, a squint to his brown eyes and a hunch to his broad shoulders. His boots were scuffed and his hat lay crumpled on the floor. Like his plantation home, his family, his inheritance, all gone. He'd wandered these last few years, first to Nashville, then to St. Louis, then lured to the great Missouri River by the swoosh of the side-wheelers, the promise of gold, the vague hope of restoring his fortunes and a chronic hammering in his heart. It was in St. Louis that he'd heard she had married and come upriver. But no one had told him about the child.

He'd found her. Once on the river, it hadn't been that difficult. Men remembered a beautiful woman and the tragic death of her husband en route, where no help was available. She had prospered, ran a business, wore silks and lived in her own house, a painted house. By old standards, this was no life for a lady. But the old standards were as dead as the hopes of the Confederacy and she had survived better than he. And she had a daughter—his daughter. The thought engulfed him like sticky quicksand and he floundered. Words choked back in his throat. A daughter! And he had no claim to her!

In the dim light, he held her gaze. He weighed each word and coughed them out, "I loved you. I'm truly sorry." At least, he was honest. There was nothing more to say. Wearily, he turned to go. He shouldn't have come.

Her lower lip quivered. It was his eyes that held her and the terrible sadness there to which she responded. But she could only speak to his back and her voice stopped him as he retreated. "Wait! I was sick. I couldn't earn my keep. Dubois was kind. He married me. But everyone knew that the baby would come too soon. People stared. I couldn't set foot on a respectable street in Baton Rouge. I went back to St. Louis, away from the war."

Her words circled like a fog in his brain. Dubois, the other man. That was his name. She didn't call him by his first name. Mrs. Pierre Dubois, that was her name now and Dubois would be the surname of his daughter. Lee Cameron swallowed hard and turned his sad eyes back upon her. He spoke softly. "You have respect here. You married Dubois."

She could not meet his stare and looked down to the catalogue. Her fingers worked the dog-eared corner of a page, the cardplayer's fingers used to the motion. "No, not here either. I run a dance hall. You know what that is—only one step above a brothel. And now Dubois is dead. The respectable ones do not accept me. The toughs I want no part of. I am alone."

He understood. He'd drawn his last paycheck in Confederate dollars, rusty-colored, worthless scraps of paper now, kindling for the fire, where value was placed in gold. He had to eat. His gambling was all he knew, that and horses and how to fight a war. Family, position, the War had ended all that. He could breed horses but that needed an investment that he didn't have.

"You could marry again."

"I tried marriage with Dubois. Once was enough. Thank God I can write and figure and pay my own bills." She lifted her chin. He remembered the independence and fierce southern pride, the liquid fire in her eye.

He turned and looked down at her catalogue. The ink was smeared. A tear? Like him, she would never admit it. She was too proud. He'd brought only grief. Gently, he prodded, "Where's the child?"

"A convent. In Saint Joseph. I still have a few friends there. She went downriver years ago... The nuns took her in, and I pay all her bills. There was no place for her here." Her mouth snapped shut. "She is well cared for. She will be respectable."

Her knuckles were white where she gripped the edge of the page but she appeared composed and met his gaze. She'd missed the child, like he'd missed her, he knew. He began to see how terribly isolated she was.

He stooped to retreive his hat, "If I can be of any help, I'm at the Citadel. I'll be working there." He was talking at her now, delaying the moment of departure.

Her answer was curt, filled with pregnant tension. "I have a business partner. He's been a great help—Daniel McGillicuddy." She raised her eyebrows and arched her shoulders backwards in the proud gesture he remembered so well but her last words seeped gradually like ice water from a glacier. "Together we own the Citadel."

It was a cruel dismissal. She hadn't meant it that way. She certainly did not need him now but deep down she was glad to see him, glad he had survived, and she would have treated him more kindly, but he was so dirty—he should have waited before visiting her. He should have cleaned himself up and prepared what he would say and given her some warning that he was coming. She watched him shake his head as if to dismiss all the painful should-have-beens. He turned and with a slight, chivalrous bow, walked out the door.

Lee Cameron was glad to escape. Rachel was still outside, busily sweeping the porch. She drew back when he passed, but she'd probably witnessed his humiliation, glued her ear to the keyhole and heard every word. He hurried down the steps into the dusty street.

He hoped now he wouldn't be fired. Emma Dubois could ruin him. McGillicuddy had just hired him as dealer earlier that month when they met in Fort Benton and he needed the work. He needed good clean gold dust. His IOU's weren't worth much. It was Saturday, payday at the mines. The Citadel would be busy tonight. Cameron unhitched his horse and leading the horse, climbed the hill to Warren Street. There he found the Mayfair Livery on the west edge of town. For half his stake, he stabled the horse. The Plantation House was only a short walk across the street. But the clerk wanted gold, not paper. Cameron found another hotel, the California House, cheaper. It fronted on the Brewery and smelled like beer, but it wasn't the smell that annoyed Lee Cameron, it was the dirt.

Chapter 2

E mma Dubois closed the door. He was gone. He had been gone for a half hour now and still she had not regained her composure. She'd convinced herself Lee Cameron was dead. With death, there was no betrayal and no self-recrimination. His reappearance was a rude shock. She hadn't treated him kindly, not even courteously. That was not like her. He had changed so. He was so gaunt, unkempt, and dirty. It repelled her a little. But he was just off the trail and there was a deeper quality she sensed, a new depth, a shy hesitancy and humility that peeked her interest. And there was pain. Where had he been? What horrors had he witnessed? What suffering had he endured? And why had he come here? She could not shake the vision of his haunting eyes. She sat pensively staring at the blank inside of the door that had closed so quietly on the broad expanse of his back. A turbulence welled up within her, like a rush of tide when the moon is full. She had not moved since he'd left. He had aroused the old memories, the old emotions and old regrets. She should have been more patient and more kind and now she wished he had stayed longer. Emma Dubois stood up and walked outside. Rachel had not come in. Where was Rachel? The porch was empty. Its shiny greeness assaulted her eyes. The street was empty too. Its grey dust lay dead, undisturbed, like her own heart these last few years, until the spring wind swept up the lifeless grains into a whirling cloud.

She crossed the street to the creek. Sunshine Creek meandered quietly down through the willows and cottonwoods to its juncture with Garnet Creek and now, in mid-afternoon, sun and shade dappled its water. No dredging muddied this stream. It ran clean and cold from off the frozen cirques in the high peaks. Rachel's father-in-law, Dad Long, and husband, Jimmy Long, worked at the sawmill drilling pipes from the straight trunks of lodgepole pines to bring its pure drinking water into Varina. It was a back-breaking job.

Emma listened to the rush of water, stooped down and scooped a handful to her lips. She held back a tear. Why couldn't life flow as smoothly and clearly as the pristine waters of Sunshine creek? Why must its goodness be wrung out and sullied like the banks of Garnet Creek? Why had Lee Cameron come back? She hung her head and covered her face with her hands.

Laughter from around back of the house interrupted her thoughts. A clatter of hooves and squeak of harness sounded harshly. A four stall barn and carriage house was there, home to McGillicuddy's bay gelding. Emma composed herself and walked there now. Rachel was hitching up the horse. She was an excellent driver and it was her duty to exercise and feed the bay every day. Midge and Gertie usually went along. They were Emma's boarders. Rachel lived with her father-in-law, Dad Long, and his son, Jimmy, her husband, next door. They were poor blacks, former slaves and they did not live in the same houses as whites. Like Emma, whose business ventures were on the border of propriety, Midge and Gertie and the Longs were not permitted up the hill in the more respectable part of town. They looked forward to these outings for the mountain scenery and fresh air.

When the girls went out alone, Emma worried for their safety. Vigilantes had hung most of the murderers, but there were mountain cats, bears and wolves all along the perimeter of the gulch. Worse were the lonely and often brutal miners who lived like hermits and hardly ever saw a woman. To Emma, miners were all a little crazy.

"You have a rifle?" Emma reminded the eager girls.

"Jimmy's Henry an' its loaded."

Rachel slapped the horse's rump with the reins. He stepped out eagerly as the buckboard swayed up the Sunshine Creek Road. The girls giggled happily and Emma wondered what would happen to them all without Daniel McGillicuddy. She would have to speak to McGillicuddy about Lee Cameron. He was best sent downriver the sooner the better, before emotions became too intense, before too many painful memories surfaced. She'd have to tell McGillicuddy who he was. Rachel knew. For now, Emma shelved her worries and walked back to the front of the house.

A man stood on the porch. She hadn't seen him come. Her first impulse was to think it was McGillicuddy or Cameron—the sun threw a haze over his silhouette and she couldn't see him clearly. He was too tall for McGillicuddy, too clean for Cameron. He had no whiskers and wore a hat, one of the new and popular Stetsons, not the flat, rumpled plantation type like Cameron's. When he spoke it was with an oily courtesy and the stench of whiskey and tobacco on his breath.

"Miss Emma, I have to speak with you." He smiled and his yellow teeth protruded like the worn incisors of an old horse.

She was surprised. He stood on the porch two steps above her. She looked up squinting into the sun at his back. His features were shadowed and undefined.

"Speak your business, Mr. Ervin. I'm listening." He deserved no courtesy, sneaking up as he had. She did not trust Spud Ervin.

"No need for the whole town to hear. We can go inside." He swept his arm toward the door. She looked up and down the empty street. The girls were already five hundred yards up the creek road, well out of earshot. Warily, she stepped past her visitor, across the porch, through the wide doorway to her desk. A Remington .44 single shot lay in the top drawer.

Spud Ervin followed her and sat down without being asked. He leaned back with the smug defiance of wayward youth. His jaw worked tobacco in a steady circle. His eyes stared. They belied youthful innocence. They were deeply recessed and looked out as if from behind a mask, beadlike. He was young and would have been handsome except for his eyes.

She sat within reach of her desk. "Yes, Mr. Ervin."

Slowly he rolled the wad in his cheek and spat a long stream into a brass spitoon.

"My pa, Sime Ervin, sent me." There was a challenge in his directness.

"I know your father." Or did she? Sime Ervin lived like a hermit and was hardly ever seen on the streets of Varina.

"He says you're settin' on his claim. He's filed claim on this land an' you're operatin' your boardin' house on his property."

"I beg your pardon, Mr. Ervin. I bought this lot from Tom Younger who had it when they laid out the town grid. Your father knew Tom. They were partners, two of the four men who made the first strike here and started the rush to Varina... What is it you want? There is no gold worth claiming on this side of the hill. This parcel was purchased, deeded, sealed with witnesses and registered at the land office and mining district, and it is not for sale."

"I'll explain Ma'am." He glared at her condescendingly. "According to the original city grid that my pa an' his friends laid out for Varina, this here property where your house stands was platted by my pa. I

19

have the deed right here." He pulled out a yellowed piece of paper. "If you want, I'll read it to you."

Emma reached for the paper. "I can read thank you, Mr. Ervin." She placed her spectacles on the end of her nose.

The deed was a parchmentlike paper, about fifteen inches square, inscribed in an elegant hand. She read carefully, "...in the Alder mining district, on the Sergeant Lode, city of Varina..." It outlined a claim beginning at a stone marker four inches square and extending north, east, south and west in a set number of degrees and minutes. A rough map was drawn at the bottom of the page. It was registered in the land office at Varina, in October of 1863, and signed by Sidney Edgerton, the newly arrived magistrate of Idaho Territory before the inception of the Territory of Montana. It assigned the said property to four men, one of whom was Simon Ervin, another of whom was Tom Younger.

"I have never seen this stone marker."

"My pa says its under your house."

Young Ervin continued. His tone was patronizing. "It's like it was in Californie in '50 and these last few years in Idaho Springs—that's in Colorado not Idaho Territory—and now here. A man strikes gold where the vein apexes—that means surfaces Ma'am. He has a right to follow that vein, underground, even beyond the surface boundary of his neighbor. The Sergeant Lode apexes under your boarding house. You understand Ma'am?"

"I understand that your father is only one of four claimants. Tom Younger, from whom I purchased this house, is another. I was told you father assigned his share to Mr. Younger in a transaction subsequent to this deed."

Spud Ervin was surprised. He hadn't expected this kind of incisive, rational resistance from a woman. She could read and write and she had a fair understanding of property rights and mining law. Spud Ervin fell silent, rolled a cigarette and lit it.

"My house is not your house, Mr. Ervin." She almost laughed, but the hard lines in Ervin's face stopped her.

"My pa has his rights, Ma'am, according to this deed." His face went rigid. "My pa wants to look again, for this Seargeant Lode. It apexes Ma'am, right under your house, here." He pointed to mark on the map at the bottom of the page. "He'd have to set powder charges... blast."

"Mr. Ervin, if the lode were here, if it existed, your father and his partners would have found it years ago."

20

She moved toward the door but he would not be dismissed so easily. His voice assumed a sharper edge, "No, Varina grew too fast and built right over the lode. It could run in all directions, under these very streets. It runs under your house."

She knew it was some kind of hoax. She knew how fanatic miners were about claim jumping, about moving in on someone else's claim, and Sime Ervin was more fanatic than most. But this was Spud and Spud Ervin was not a miner. What was Spud Ervin? He was an unruly, tow-headed kid or used to be, a colt unused and untrained to the bridle. He'd filled out this past year and now looked the man, clean-shaven and well-dressed, a little too well. But he was still wild. He loafed around town with Curly Shaw and some other young louts, playing poker, creating mischief, fighting, shooting and betting on anything that would run or fight. In St. Louis, Emma would have called him a rowdy or a thug. Here, he was merely considered an annoyance and a parasite. And everyone knew who his father was.

Emma drew her shoulders back and countered, "Just what do you want, Mr. Ervin?"

"Favors." He stubbed out his cigarette on the sole of his boot and threw it on the carpet.

She stooped to pick it up and made sure it was really out—fire was a terrible danger in a boom town. "Surely, you're joking, sir." She was about to laugh again but the challenge in his cold blue eyes and curling upper lip stopped her.

"No, Ma'am." He stood up slowly and deliberately, in one stride spanned the few feet between them and put his bony fist under her chin. "I first saw you, Ma'am, I was a boy. I been watchin' you these last years. I'm a man now, Ma'am, an' lonely for a woman. Too young to be lonely. Too old to be patient. I ain't never had the favors of a beautiful woman."

She froze. So that was it. He took his hand away.

"Think about it, Ma'am. I say so, my pa don't contest your property, or if'n he does and the gold assays out rich an' you sticks by me, I build you a fancy house, like them up the hill—in the respectable part of town." He got up and walked to the door. "You think on it, Ma'am."

Emma thought she'd rather see her house burn to cinders than acquiesce to the demands of Spud Ervin.

Chapter 3

The Citadel was busy when Lee Cameron entered. McGillicuddy seemed no wiser. The air stank with sweat, whiskey and smoke. Men streamed in to the clink of glasses and slap of cards. They paid a dollar a shot for whiskey and fought for places at the bar. Midge and Gertie circulated among them. They charged a dollar a dance—in clean dust. You pinched it out of your poke and if you didn't trust your neighbor's pinch, you carried a pair of hand scales in your pocket.

Cameron's long practiced fingers dealt the cards and measured the winnings. He had a quick mathematical mind, trained by necessity—gambling was what had kept him fed and clothed these last few years. But the game demanded his total concentration and it could be dangerous. A pearl handled Navy Colt hung at his hip. He needed his gun on a night like this when liquor flowed freely and the face of a card sealed a man's fate. He sat with his back to the wall. The night air was chill even inside, and he wore the grey greatcoat with his meager wealth sewn in the lining between the seams. To all of these men, he was suspect, a stranger. But there were other southern sympathizers here, other bits of old uniforms, more grey than blue.

The play was good. He started with two young hired men eager to foil the shaggy newcomer. He won. As the stakes grew, miners and shopkeepers replaced them. A younger man in a new Stetson, the kind of hat just recently made popular in Colorado, looked on with a bevy of friends. He was broad of shoulder yet thin, blond and handsome in a raw-boned sort of way except for his eyes and mouth. His lips were thin and straight and worked round and round with the constant motion of his jaw. His eyes were icy, deep blue and hard like tiny stones at the base of deep holes. They were set wide on each side of his head. He tilted the hat back and fumbled with a gold watch chain across the front of his vest. His hands were clean, not chapped and red like a miner's or permanently grimed like a freighter's. He had the ugly habit of spitting every few minutes into the sawdust on the floor. To Cameron, he appeared somewhat of a blusterer, overdressed and out of his depth.

"You can outfox the hairy Reb, Spud." A red-curly-haired onlooker baited him.

"I could at that, Curly, but Blackbeard the Greyback ain't invitin' an honest Union man to play." A greyback was a louse, also a Confederate soldier. Cameron stiffened.

"That's cause you'd clean 'im out, Spud, pick the nits right outta 'is mane." He flared his nostrils like an animal and sniffed. "Hey, don't you Rebs ever wash?"

Cameron's eyes flashed bolts of anger at the red-headed man but he held his temper. It was his first day on the job. He forced himself to ignore the taunt. "It's an open game—everybody's welcome."

"We'll stake you, Spud." The red-headed man was over-eager.

"I got my own stake, Curly." Spud Ervin puffed out his chest, pulled back a chair and sat down. "I got nothin' to lose an' a whole lot to win—send some of these thievin' Rebs racin' for the canebrakes, like a bunch a coons runnin' from the hounds tails curled under their backsides!" He was grinning now, but the grin, instead of lighting his youthful face, exposed yellow teeth and pulled the skin taut across the angular bones of his jaw. "I hear Johnny Reb likes coons...He eats 'em fried, along wit' possum an' boiled snake, probably rats too like them yellow-skinned Chinese!" They laughed.

Cameron grit his teeth and sucked in his cheeks to contain a surge of anger. He snapped each card he dealt. Spud Ervin raked in his cards.

"Name's Ervin," he announced. He was grandstanding, inflating his prestige. "The boys call me Spud, but you call me Mr. Ervin, Reb." He looked around for approval. The laughter came only from his own companions.

Cameron sat immobile and let the insults drip off. He'd seen this kind in the army—young whelps who belittled others to inflate their own prowess. They usually fled under fire. Spud was showing off to the young men and to the ladies and eyed them lasciviously.

Cameron answered Spud with stiff decorum. "I'm Captain Leland Cameron C.S.A." His voice lingered slightly on the rank. He used his full name. His patience was wearing very thin. He pointed to an aged, white-bearded miner opposite to draw attention away from himself and added flatly, "We've been callin' him 'old man'."

Spud looked at the old man with contemptuous bravado. "You already died an' gone to heaven, ole man?" He laughed. "Just how old are ya?"

The old Irishman didn't take offense and defused the conversation. "Older than Methusallah, and wiser and richer for it. Name's Lysaght." White hairs poked out like wings over his ears, but the top of his head was bald. He grinned, exposing the dark gaps of missing teeth. The old man's eyes bulged innocently, like an owl's. He knew how to bluff. And he knew how to count his winnings. He used a Chinese opium scale and measured every bit of gold to the last grain. This one knew how to survive in the gold fields and he brushed off the taunts of Spud Ervin like so many gnats.

The play ebbed and flowed. The old man's owl eyes fairly lit up with glee, and his lips worked feverishly. He was having fun. But Spud's eyes hardened and the grin disappeared. He spat a stream of juice on the floor and ran a wet tongue over parched lips. Curly melted away on the arm of a bargirl and Spud was on his own.

The stakes were high. Two men folded, pushed out their chairs and got up, but the old one and Spud held on. The old man, Lysaght, played with the abandon that comes from having won fortunes and lost them and won them back again, but young Ervin was careful and tense. Cameron studied him carefully, through narrow, impassive eyes. Spud Ervin would resent his losses. He was losing now.

Lysaght asked for one card. Cameron turned the card up.

The old prospector worked his lips, rubbed his bald pink pate with his free hand and continued to bid. He spoke in a quiet brogue. The white beard bounced on his chest below twinkling grey eyes. "I raise ye two hundred."

The younger man waited, motionless and alert. His laughter was gone. His face stiffened in concentration. "Two cards." He swept a wet tongue again over his upper lip, hungrily this time. Spud's eyelids veiled his pupils. He looked down toward the cards. Slowly, he turned up the corners of his two new cards, and held them greedily against his chest with his other three.

"Two hundred...." He met the bid, paused, "And raise five. More gold than you'll ever see in yer treasury, Reb, or was you one a them rich slave breeders?" He sat back and bit off a new chaw.

Cameron knew he was deliberately being baited to confuse the deal, upset the game, ignite emotions. He met the bid quietly and the play returned to the old man on his left. They waited.

The grey eyes flicked in an arc from left to right. The old man pulled out a ragged cloth, dug deep into its folds and pulled out a nugget the size of an egg. "I be neither Reb nor Yank but a poor son o' the old sod, and this be my wager, and this.." He dug deeper into his pocket. "be the assay report... four pounds six ounces, 2 pennyweight of gold solid, at 12 troy ounces to the pound, worth one thousand U.S. dollars." He smacked his lips together carefully tucked his opium scales into his pocket, pushed the nugget to the center of the table, and grumbled as an afterthought. "Me scales won't weigh it. It be too heavy."

Silence struck the onlookers. Spud Ervin frowned as the attention he craved frittered away. Everyone in the saloon wanted a look. The largest nugget ever unearthed in Varina weighed 44 ounces. Lee Cameron glared at the old man but he was staring gleefully at the younger one as if he knew what the youth's reaction would be.

Cameron spoke up, "You sure you want to do this, old man?" The old man's clothes were ragged and stained. He looked as if the nugget was his last earthly possession.

"Lysaght's me name, Captain...There be more where that came from, I should live long enough to spend it all. You weigh it. God be me witness, I tell ye true." Cameron signalled for the house scales and McGillicuddy himself brought them over.

Lysaght was still staring at Spud Ervin and smiling through his beard, but he addressed Cameron, "Tis a handsome soldier like yisself should win it God willin'. Buy ye a night a bliss with fair Madame Emma." Now the old man leaned farther toward Cameron. "She be choosy, that one, and expensive...very expensive."

Cameron drew his shoulders back indignantly. Now Lysaght provoked him and he balled a fist over his folded cards as if to squeeze back the tension. The expression on his face was as flat as the cards upon the table. Instinctively, he glanced at Spud Ervin, caught the reaction. He smelled a rival like a hound smells a bitch in heat. He rapped his fingers on the table like a nervous drummer going into a battle for the first time and felt like smashing the white whiskers into the old blarney's teeth. Had she sunk so far? She said she ran a dance hall and saloon, not a brothel. But they were the same in the eyes of many. In one way he was relieved: according to Lysaght, very few men could afford her.

Daniel McGillicuddy came up with the hand scales and presided over weighing the nugget like Solomon seated in judgement. A crowd gathered to watch as McGillicuddy placed the nugget on the tray and added weights to its counter. He called for more weights. The nugget lay still, even with the additional weight. McGillicuddy's voice rang with authority. "You men willing to take this old man at his word, the house will." They all nodded.

A thousand dollars was the bid and the game was now the focus of a congregation of onlookers. Cameron sucked in his cheeks as was his habit to retain outward calm.

The grin had faded from the face of Curly who stood in silent anticipation and Spud Ervin's mouth froze in a cruel frown. He clutched his five cards with fingers that wrapped like talons around their prey. A shock of blond hair tumbled over his eyes. There was a barbarism in Spud Ervin, in the taut muscles and the angular jaw, more like a renegade horse than a colt, the kind that never tamed and would charge the corral gate. Now Spud stared glassily at his cards but at the same time seemed to scrutinize the entire room. One by one, he studied each card, caressed it and placed it face down on the table. Finally, he tilted his chair back, hooked one thumb in his belt and rubbed his gold watch with the other. As he drew his brows together, his eyes faded into his head.

Suddenly, he snapped at Lysaght, "I'll call your bluff, old man...." Then turning to McGillicuddy, "You know my father, Sime Ervin?" He spoke presumptuously over Cameron's head. "You know the value of claims around here?" He pulled a worn piece of rawhide from his pocket, in a reckless ploy to upstage the old man. "This here's the deed to the Cleopatra mine.... worth an even thousand easy and more....my pa thinks the mother lode's in that mine... What you got, old man? I call."

"Hold on Spud, your pa know you have that deed?" McGillicuddy's remark was meant to calm, stall, to give time to consider, but Spud Ervin heard it as the voice of the superior, the slap of the cane on the backside of a naughty child. Spud heard rebuke and insult. McGillicuddy meant appeasement. And Spud didn't like the way McGillicuddy pronounced his name. Spud's face stiffened and reddened. The blood pumped at his temples. His jaw froze and his eyes receded further. He flung back his head: the boyish mockery had vanished. This was a young stallion ready for combat and waiting to wrest command of the herd. McGillicuddy seemed not to notice but Cameron had seen it before on the battlefield in the undisciplined raw recruit, unused to taking orders and too eager for blood. Unpredictable, they were the most dangerous because they put not only themselves but whole battalions at risk. Lee Cameron would watch Spud Ervin very closely.

"It's mine, Daniel." Spud Ervin spat the name. No one ever called

McGillicuddy by his complete first name. Only good friends called him 'Dan'. Spud slapped the rawhide down defiantly. There was a puff of gold dust. Conversations stopped in mid sentence. How careless he was with his gold, blowing it away in the back-draft of his sweeping motion! In Varina, gold was always treated with great reverence and youth always deferred to age. Not so for Spud Ervin.

McGillicuddy lost his patience. He stroked his impeccable mustaches and commanded, "You wager it, you play it, boy." He nodded at Cameron and Cameron met the bid.

Now all eyes turned to the weatherbeaten face of the miner. "Call." The word spurted like a sheet of flame that whistled from between the gaps in the old man's teeth. His lips had stopped moving. He turned his cards face up. Three kings.

Young Ervin relaxed. The corner of a lip turned up. He turned over his cards—flush, spades, king high—and leaned over to rake in his winnings.

Lee Cameron sat quietly guarding his hand. Now he turned them over. Four queens! He reached over to stay young Ervin's hand.

The younger man's head snapped back. "Dirty Reb! Don't you touch me!" He threw up his arm suddenly, thrusting Cameron's hand into the scales. Weights and gold dust clattered across the table.

"Four of a kind beats a flush, boy. Cameron wins." McGillicuddy calmly recited the rules of the game. Cameron rested the tips of his fingers on the edge of the table, apprehensively. The onlookers drew back.

Spud Ervin had been so absorbed in the old miner and his nugget, at his perceived threat to his own importance, that he hadn't detected the challenge from Cameron. He struck out now like a coiled rattler. "Cheat me! Look up your sleeves under that Rebel rag!" He grabbed Cameron by his coat's lapels and pulled. Cameron jumped free, hand on his gun.

"He's armed, Spud, don't touch 'im." That was Curly, the redhead again. Cameron heard the voice off to his right. Miraculously, McGillicuddy appeared next to him obstructing any opportunity of crossfire.

Cameron swept his hands in a half circle, palms up. "All these people and McGillicuddy here are my witnesses. I've played fair."

"Like hell you did! You're a lyin' Reb an' yer bluffin' now with that gun, like you was bluffin' with them cards? Not on me you don't!" Spud reeled and toppled the table and all its wealth to the floor. It was a foolish diversion and now in a fury, he reached for his gun. The bullet winged the bartender's ear and shattered the mirror behind him. But

Lee Cameron had sensed the danger. He was up now, ducked and reached too and he was an old soldier, cool under fire. He fired late and not to kill, but accurately. The bullet from his Navy Colt slammed through Spud Ervin's hand, deflecting off the barrel of Spud's own gun to tear a gaping furrow from wrist to elbow in his right arm, carving out the flesh and shattering the bones of the forearm. Ervin's gun clattered to the floor. Spud stared unbelieving at his own spurting blood and shards of bone. Blood spattered the Cleopatra deed and soiled the bright flecks of gold dust that flickered yellow in the gaslight in the sawdust on the floor. The nugget glowed with streaks of gold where it lay, like a bronze daisy in a bed of red flowers under the summer sun.

The old prospector sat unperturbed. "Ye never bets what ye can't afford to lose, what's-your-name? Spud? Spuds are potatoes in Ireland..." He shook his white head. "Today, Spud, 'tis a piece of yer arm. The saints be kind ye lost no more." The old prospector put his hands on the table, tilted his chair back and lifted one bushy brow, "And tomorrow?" He got up from his chair and walked through the blood and dust to the bar. The glittery gore stuck to his boots.

McGillicuddy stripped his string tie from around his neck, and wrapped it tightly around young Ervin's biceps to stop the flow of blood. Garrity, the bartender grabbed a towel to dab his bloodied ear and sop up the mess that puddled on the floor. He would profit from the evening's episode—he would wash out the gold dust from the towel later. The nugget and the deed he wiped off and handed to Cameron.

Cameron hadn't moved. He was still standing beside his chair. He blew the smoke from his Navy Colt, put it back in its holster and righted the table. He would reload later. The deed and the nugget he wiped off and placed in his pocket. It was a disturbing start at the Citadel. He had almost killed a man.

Young Ervin was in shock, his face white, his jaw hanging open. He would feel the pain later and he would live, probably maimed for life. He stared wild-eyed at his own flesh and blood on the floor and cursed like a bullwhacker. "Thievin' bastard...Steal my mine! I'm comin' back! Inch by inch, I'll feed yer balls to a rattler .... He was still screaming like a cat in water when Curly took his good arm and pushed him out the door. McGillicuddy went with them. "Your pa's not going to take kindly to all this. Let's go see Doc Lubbock."

Chapter 4

Nerves settled and the play resumed except for Cameron and the old man. Cameron could feel the tension across the back of his shoulders and down his spine. Not since the war had he shot a man. It sickened him and brought back the stench of blood and smoke, the shriek of shells and the screams of the wounded. He braced himself and started toward the bar. He needed a drink. The old prospector was there and he walked over. "Here's your nugget back, old man. I don't want winnings I earn with blood. Word gets out I shoot to win, nobody will sit in on my game."

He'd said it light-heartedly but the old man frowned. "Ye be sayin' ye did not win it honestly, that the young firebrand was right? Ye cannot give it back. They'll think ye cheated boy. Sure'n Daniel McGillicuddy's games be fair, ye cannot cast a doubt on him or yourself. 'Tis yours, me boy, if ye want to uphold your good name."

"I've no name to defend, old man, not since the war. I won it as fairly and I'll win again. You're no card player, old man. You made it easy. Here, take it. Buy a meal. Buy a horse."

The old man stiffened. "I'll burn in hell, before I'll take your charity. Pat Lysaght earns his keep. I'm too old to get rich. 'Tis gold brought the curse on me. Killed the best friend I ever knew. The little demons be plaguin' me ever since." He reached over and closed Cameron's fingers around the hunk of gold. "'Tis yours now...I'll not be needin' it. Ye won it fair. Dan McGillicuddy'll fire ye fast for givin' away his winnin's. Lord willin', 'twill bring ye better fortune than I."

The image of Emma at her ledger flashed through Cameron's brain. Maybe his luck would change. He smiled, then chuckled. "Buy you a drink old man?"

The old prospector's face brightened at the mention of whiskey. "Now that be truly chivalrous!" He turned to the bar.

"Not here. In the back room. I don't feel comfortable with your nugget in my pocket." He put an arm over Lysaght's shoulder and guided him to McGillicuddy's office.

This was a small room at the back of the saloon where McGillicuddy slept. It was dark and warm. A small fire glowed in a pot-bellied stove. A cot and a rolltop desk spanned one wall and two narrow chairs, a table and a safe crowded into a corner. The rest of the room was piled high with casks of whiskey. A door led to a back alley. There was an oil lamp, a decanter of brandy and glasses on the desk. Cameron struck a match to the lamp, helped himself to the brandy and poured a glass for his friend.

The old man smacked his lips. "Delicious! Imported. This McGillicuddy, he's a fine judge of spirits!"

"He can afford it with what I earned him tonight." Cameron poured out a second glass for them both.

The old Irishman eased himself into a chair. "We be havin' a private libation, seems I ought to know ye better."

"Cameron, Lee Cameron, lately of Saint Louis and Fort Benton, formerly of Athens, Georgia."

"Cameron, 'of the crooked nose'. Did ye know your name has a meaning? And ye be such a handsome lad at that, Lee-of-the-crooked-nose!...I'm Patrick Lysaght from Blackhawk, that be in Colorado, from Placerville in Californie, New Orleans before that, and from me far-off and beloved County Galway before the British bastards put a price on this old bald head...." He lifted an index finger like a careful teacher, "A fighter I was 'til I threw a rock at King George, his loathsome majesty. They wanted to hang me." He thrust out his hand. Cameron grasped the callused palm and they shook heartily.

Suddenly, the door flew open. "Daniel McGillicuddy, I have to speak to you." The voice was Emma Dubois' and she was upset.

Cameron and Lysaght jumped to their feet. Her slender form stood silhouetted against the darker interior of the saloon. She had flung her hooped skirts through the open door but was still looking back toward the gaming room. She turned abruptly and spotted Cameron. "You again!"

"I work here...."

"Where's McGillicuddy? I didn't see him."

"He's escorting a client to see the doctor."

She frowned. She knew there'd been a shooting. The tips of her eyebrows crimped over the bridge of her nose. "Who?" was all she asked.

With the poise and disdain of British nobility, Lysaght jumped in to defend his companion. Clearly he liked to talk. "I believe his name was Ervin, Madame. Young brazen lout. The cards betrayed him and the devil himself possessed him. My friend here, Mr. Cameron, unfortunately had to shoot him, or he'd be fearin' the Lord's judgement for himself. Only by the grace of the mighty God, is Mr. Cameron still alive."

"Who are you?" She looked down her nose at the wizened old man.

"Permit me to introduce mesself Ma'am." He swept into a low bow. "Patrick Lysaght of County Galway, Ireland, lately of Blackhawk...and my handsome young friend is Mr. Lee Cameron, Captain, C.S.A." The exaggerated decorum did not impress Emma Dubois. She turned on Cameron, eyes flashing. "After you shoot a man you drink to his health?" Cameron had hoped she hadn't seen the shooting.

Lysaght explained, "A bit o' brandy, Madame, settles the nerves and renews his trust in his fellow man."

Cameron swayed slightly toward her. "Would the lady care to join us?" The brandy had made him bold.

"I don't drink, and I don't like shooting. It's bad for business." Emma Dubois' voice cracked like dry kindling.

Pat Lysaght chimed in again. "'Tis a great pity, Madame, that ye cannot enjoy a wee refreshment. Lee here has been a distinguished and brave warrior. The spirits warm his heart after a fair fight like campfires in the snows of winter, and the ministries of a fair lady would lighten the weight of the battles that he bears upon his soul." He elbowed Cameron. "I am always most solicitous of the wishes of a bee-ew-ti-ful lady, especially when she's incensed. A lady never angers. Ye ken, Lee?" His eyes twinkled. Was he deliberately infuriating her? No. Cameron suspected strongly that he was trying to matchmake and he laughed. Lysaght turned back to Emma. "If milady would grace our fair table, me handsome young friend would be overjoyed and, as for mesself, I might even go to church of a Sunday to say a prayer for ye both!"

Cameron had risen politely when she entered but now stood snickering at Lysaght's performance and smiling down on her. Lysaght stayed where he was, holding out her chair. Both were mildly, happily drunk.

But Emma Dubois heard only mockery in Cameron's laughter and condescension in Lysaght's lilting brogue. She erupted. "You're drunk! Out! Get out of my office the two of you!"

"'Tis Mr. McGillicuddy's office, Madame." Lysaght's glassy smile hinted a casual ridicule and the certainty that neither he nor Cameron had listened to a word she said. Emma's anger boiled to fury.

Cameron addressed her now with the same affable drunken decorum. "Madame Dubois, I think you should put this into the safe. I

31

don't know the combination." Cameron placed the nugget squarely in the center of the table. Emma's eyes spewed sheer invective. She didn't even look at the nugget.

Carefully, Cameron handed the two glasses to Pat Lysaght, picked up the brandy bottle and with Lysaght at his heels, sauntered amiably out the door.

When they were ensconced at a corner table, old man Lysaght proposed a toast. "To the fairest lady of Varina, may her incensement disperse like the silvery dew in summer's breeze and her beauty endure like the tresses of gold that shower these fair streets with riches."

His words rang out loudly in the crowded room. The miners had themselves a good laugh and Cameron poured Lysaght another drink.

"Old man, where'd you learn to talk like that?"

"Tis the brandy, Lee. And the poetry... We Irish love poetry. An' sure as your crooked nose, I still have an eye for pretty ladies."

Pat Lysaght took a long, slow gulp. His crinkled eyes clouded over. "Beggin' your pardon, Lee, but the brandy does jog me old brain. I wasn't always old, ye know." He sniffed and wiped his nose on his sleeve. "I used to have quite a way with the ladies...but they're a breed I'll never understand. She is beautiful that one, isn't she? Brings me back. I knew one like her once. What do ye think set her to stormin' so?"

Lee Cameron put both palms down on the table. "Me. I knew her in Saint Louis.... I loved her and I left her."

"Not smart, Lee, leave a beautiful woman."

"I had no choice. There was the war." Cameron looked off distantly into the dim light.

"Do ye love her still?" Cameron's gaze did not swerve. Pat Lysaght's watery eyes seemed to comprehend. "Ye do, don't ye?"

"I won't answer that, old man. I've had too much brandy." Pat Lysaght poured him another.

Together they finished the bottle and staggered off down Warren Street, Cameron to a narrow cot in the California Hotel and Lysaght to his blankets and tent, if he had one. A brown dog followed him from the door of the saloon. At the corner of Missouri, Lysaght and the dog turned uphill.

Cameron wondered who would sleep better. The hotel was cheap and Cameron knew his sheets would not be clean and free from vermin. He didn't go back to the hotel. He stopped and turned back to the Citadel Saloon and sat in a dark corner, following Emma longingly with his eyes, and thinking that Pat Lysaght was the first friend he'd made in Varina. Finally, he let his head fall to the table and slept.

Chapter 5

McGillicuddy wanted to be far away when Sime Ervin found his son, and learned where the shooting took place and who did it. Now he walked over to warn the sleeping Cameron.

"You know who that young ingrate was, don't you?"

Cameron awoke with a start and stared.

"You better wake up and stay awake... Sime Ervin finds out you shot his only son. He's a vindictive man...Can't hurt to go on down to the Doc's and see how the young'un is doing."

Cameron nodded and got up. He walked dutifully up Jefferson to Doc Lubbock's. Spud was asleep—the doctor had had to pump whiskey into him and get Con Garrity, the brawny bartender, to hold him down while he amputated his arm at the elbow. It was a thankless job and now the doctor wanted to talk. He offered Cameron more whiskey which Cameron refused, then poured himself a healthy shot.

"Ugly wound that one. Nothing a doctor can do...How'd it happen?"

When Cameron explained, the Doc rubbed his red eyes and shook his head. "It's Sime's fault you know, not Spud's. My job would be so much easier without the Sime Ervins of this world." The Doc did not approve of Sime Ervin and proceeded to tell Cameron why. Sime Ervin cared more for his gold than for his own flesh and blood. Doc Lubbock hadn't even sent for Sime when Spud came in. He knew where Sime was—shovelling and chipping and mumbling his calculations of how much his gold was worth or where the richest ore lay hidden. Sime rarely left his dugout. Someday he'd probably die there and no one would miss him. No one really had to deal with Sime. But they had to deal with his son. Grudgingly, Sime gave Spud enough to live on and to buy fancy clothes. Spud lazed aimlessly all over the streets of Varina and Highland and usually spent more than he received. His creditors had to brave his father's wrath to collect. But Sime always paid. Of late, Spud was developing a very arrogant and belligerent streak. He deemed himself unquestioned heir and self-proclaimed defender of Ervin riches. He was an angry youth. He had no mother and he'd lost his father to the frenzy for gold. He was not going to let anyone steal his inheritance and he let everybody know it. Now he had lost the Cleopatra mine and looked the fool in front of Emma Dubois. Worse, he had lost his right arm because of Lee Cameron.

Lee Cameron listened carefully. The Doc's words were easy and friendly, but Cameron sensed the warning. The father was a miser, selfish and grasping, but the deprived and neglected son was dangerous.

The conversation made him uncomfortable and Cameron found an excuse to leave. He volunteered to bury Spud's severed arm. He wrapped it in canvas, and headed down Jefferson to Jones, but it was dark and he had no lantern, so he stopped just short of unfamiliar territory, in the alley by Emma Dubois' barn, where the soil was soft from the animal dung. There he dug a shallow trench.

It was very late when he re-entered the Citadel. The clientele had thinned. He walked in and sat down at a table to watch a faro spread. The bartender brought him a brandy and he settled in and lit a cigar. He needed company after his evening chore. He could never have been a doctor.

Suddenly, McGillicuddy came in through the swinging doors. Cameron hadn't noticed that he was absent.

"Daniel!" Emma nearly screeched. Cameron jumped. Had she seen him? She was even angrier than before he'd left. She must have been waiting for McGillicuddy all this time.

"Emma, now why startle a man?" McGillicuddy puffed his cigar.

"I've been waiting hours, that's why."

McGillicuddy pulled himself up to his full five feet two and reluctantly strode toward the office. Emma Dubois followed and slammed the door. Her voice was shrill and the partitions thin. You could hear every word she said on the other side of the gaming room.

"Why did you hire Lee Cameron?"

McGillicuddy took his time before answering. The question rankled. He was never a gambler himself but he did have a sense of people and always hired shrewd, intelligent and honest dealers, amiable bartenders and a sprinkling of tough peace-keepers. The combination worked.

This sense of people was the source of his success. In the past, Emma had always respected his judgement and not interfered.

"Met him in Benton. Watched him play. Clever fellow and as fine a looking chap as I've known...personable...a bit daring. I like that in my business....our business. And he's a Reb. He fits in around here."

"Do you know who he is?"

"Should I?"

"He is Marie's father."

Lee Cameron cringed. Everyone at the bar and at the gambling tables was within easy earshot. Fortunately it was late and only a sprinkling of players remained. Of those, many were consumed in their own conversations and seemed not to have understood.

McGillicuddy's voice tried to soothe. "You don't want him around? He's a good dealer."

"He shot a man."

"Spud Ervin had it coming. None of my other dealers had nerve enough....Neither did I. Arrogant brat, struts in here like a pidgeon, calls me 'Daniel' to my face. Tell you what." Here McGillicuddy hesitated again. "You never told me anyone but Dubois fathered your child. I take it no one else knows about this.... I like Cameron. I'd like to see him take on the Ervins and I think he will....I keep your secret.... You let him stay."

"That's a bribe."

"No, I didn't hire him with any intent. You told me your secret of your own free will. Cameron'll probably make his strike if he's lucky and get rich or go broke like the rest and go back stateside and maybe get killed going...Tell you what, I can raise his percentage and maybe he'll leave all the sooner... How old is Marie? Six? Seven? She's fine with the nuns and you've a profitable enterprise and even wealth. Cameron can't touch you...I gave my word. I don't go back on my word. But I can keep a secret." Mc Gillicuddy had made up his mind. It was a question of honor. Lee Cameron would stay.

McGillicuddy's voice turned fatherly. "Why the fuss? Do you still love him, girl?" There was no answer.

The door opened and Emma emerged. The shadows of the oil lamps threw harsh lines across the delicate structure of her face, but not a twinge betrayed her emotions. She eased herself into a chair, oblivious to all in the room. Her mind had stopped at the thought that Cameron could be killed trying to leave Varina. She thought he'd been killed in the war. She'd wept over that. Death was so common. Good men left the diggings, rich. They went to restore fortunes of wives and families, never to be heard of again, waylaid by thieves, dead, not even buried, fodder for the wolves and worms. This should not, would not happen to Lee Cameron. McGillicuddy just didn't understand. Yes, she still cared for Lee Cameron. It was just that she dared not hope. So many times before she had hoped for love, husband, family, and her hopes had crumbled in the ashes of war. Love him? She had to sort all that out.

Suddenly, she looked up and saw Cameron looking at her. "You heard?" He nodded. She rose majestically, smoothed her skirts and walked regally out through the door of the main saloon. The longing stares of lonely miners followed the curve of her bust across the smoky room. Cameron followed alone.

McGillicuddy watched them go, dumbfounded. Emma had never asked him to dismiss anyone before. What was it about this man? And how quickly she had retreated. He thought back to his first meeting with Cameron in Fort Benton. McGillicuddy had made that trip to assure that his yearly stock of whiskey would arrive undiluted and on time and at full weight. He went every year to Fort Benton when the Missouri steamboats came in. He had to be there himself. Shippers were notorious for skimming the whiskey barrels and making a handsome profit in the Indian trade. As usual, the barrels were late coming upriver and he had waited in Benton. He was there when Cameron stepped off the boat. Cameron cut a fine figure even then, stinking and unwashed after weeks on the river. He'd worn the same shabby C.S.A. captain's coat he wore when he arrived in Varina. McGillicuddy thought back to his first meeting with Cameron in I.G. Baker's store. Cameron was a tall man and knocked his head against the low door frame. He'd been entertaining his acquaintances with a wild story about a steamboat race up the Missouri. It was a true story. Cameron had made book on the race and won. He was willing to take risks. McGillicuddy admired that in a man. But it was the yarn-spinning that endeared Cameron to the Irish in McGillicuddy. Cameron fascinated his listeners. The sidewheelers had raced neck and neck all the way to Dauphin's Rapids. Later that same evening, Cameron arrived at the Overland Hotel with a red and white barcloth wrapped around his head looking like a swordsman from out of the Arabian Nights, and McGillicuddy bought him a drink. That's when he heard the rest of the story and offered Cameron a job. When Cameron arrived in Varina, McGillicuddy was good for his word.

How was he supposed to know that Cameron was Marie's father? Her last name was Dubois. Emma was a puzzle to him, an independent and resourceful woman twenty-five years his junior. Were he younger, taller and better looking, he probably would have courted

36

her. As it was, he was content to be friend and business partner. She had needed him in Fort Benton and he had helped her selflessly without demand. He had counseled and she had listened to his advice and prospered but she had never confided in him. He realized now how little he knew of her. He had never seen her angry before. She had always been headstrong but her violent reaction to Lee Cameron baffled him. Suddenly, the idea that was simmering just below the level of his conscious thought broke through.

"Love. Dammit!" he swore out loud. "She does still love him." He had so startled himself that he almost dropped the cigar from between his teeth again. His own experience with this emotion was limited to a few infatuations a very long time ago. He did not want to deal with it now. If they could just hold on to the status quo for a few more years they could retire in luxury to San Francisco or New York. Surely, she could see that. He put out his cigar, slid the iron bolt in his door, lay down on his cot and tried to sleep.

Chapter 6

Sime Ervin sat huddled in an old rocker, at a table near a smoking stove. He lived in a dugout on the mountain. He'd lived in the same dugout since he and three other Kentuckians first discovered gold in Garnet Creek. He was a Union man. His companions all had southern sympathies but they had one aim in common: to stay out of the army, any army. So they went west. The other three had tolerated anti-social Sime because he was the only one who had prior experience prospecting and understood rocks. He had followed the gold strikes first to Colorado, then to Idaho where the three others had dug him and his young son out of a cave in. They nursed him, brought him to Montana, and he told them where to look. They all struck it rich: Varina was their bonanza. But Sime was always the fourth, the extra. With their riches, they had left Varina or died trying. Now Sime was the only one left. His living habits were plain. He was a loner. He lived in the earthen house on top of this first claim with his son, a Chinese cook and his gold. Two mine workers, a foreman/retainer named Curly Shaw—Spud's caretaker—and two half-breed Indian fighters named Hump and Worley who lived in a spacious bunkhouse nearby. They had better quarters than their employer. Hump had injured his back in a fall from a horse and was named for his deformity. No one knew where Worley got his name or if Worley was his real name. No one cared. These two guarded Ervin's gold. The Chinese, a young girl in her twenties, Sime had purchased from her father for six hundred dollars. It was a high price. She was a pretty girl.

In the early days of Varina, Sime Ervin had survived a murderous attack by road agents. The four men had tried to ship out their gold.

Thieves had waylaid them, killed one and the two surviving partners had thought Sime dead too. They fled. He had looked dead. His horse had been shot from under him and he was pinned beneath, spattered with his dead horse's blood. For hours he lay in the dust and blood without help. But his partners stayed away. After dark, he pulled loose and fled. He never forgave them for leaving him.

And he remembered his attackers. They had walked up to finish him off, but he played dead and they assumed he was dead. He had become a vigilante and saw to it that they hung. But beyond his own narrow interests he had no concern for the law, especially when the law demanded time and sacrifice. No on had helped him. He simply hadn't shipped any more gold. He hoarded it. And he had no concern at all for his son.

Today, he owned six claims and interests in several more. He was forty-four years old. His hair had whitened since the ambush. A thick beard hid most of the expressions of his face. He trusted no one. His dark, beady eyes were set far apart and seemed to operate separately, as if he were looking two places at once. His son had inherited the same shifting gaze. You never really knew what held his attention. He kept his gold with him, buried in the empty shafts beneath his dugout, guarded by the two gunmen, Hump and Worley. He paid them handsomely. In gold. He demanded total loyalty. His foreman, Curly Shaw, was his eyes and ears in Varina. It was an easy job. Curly loafed about town, gambled and whored with young Spud and brought Sime a newspaper once a week. Hump and Worley kept all trespassers off his claims.

Tonight, Sime sat munching a chunk of roasted venison, reading his news and scribbling figures on a scrap of paper. Curly had not returned. Nor had Spud. The boys were staying out later and later. Sometimes they didn't come home at all and spent the night in saloons and whorehouses. Sime Ervin knew it was time to find something more secure for his son to do but he didn't know what and he didn't trust him any more than a stranger.

He thought of Hump and Worley. Worley was asleep on a cot in the bunkhouse and Hump sat guard on the mine shaft. Why couldn't Spud be useful like them? Spud couldn't sit still long enough to pan a claim much less guard one. He was always moving, always jumping from one thing to another, always getting into scraps.

Now Sime Ervin was estimating the cost of shipping his wealth to St. Louis. It was something he probably would never do, but he loved to calculate the risks. There were several ways he could do it. He could send it by stage via Helena and Fort Benton, then by steamboat down the Missouri to Westport and on to St. Louis. Or he could ship it with a wagon train south to Salt Lake, then east to Corinne, Utah, where the Union Pacific Railroad had stopped its construction. Or he could outfit his own wagon train and follow the new Bozeman cut-off via Forts C.F. Smith and Phil Kearny. Each had its drawbacks. The Missouri River would fall in about a month depending on snow melt and rainfall and all boats would be beached until the following spring. Worse, reports circulated that the Blackfeet were camped dangerously close, between the Yellowstone and Fort Benton. He didn't trust the Mormons in Salt Lake any more than the Blackfeet, and he had even less confidence in the Irish thugs who were building the Union Pacific—they were worse than both road agents and Indians. Finally, last winter, along the Bozeman Trail, Red Cloud had massacred seventy-eight U.S.Army regulars under the command of Captain William Fetterman. The Montana Post reported the Bozeman Trail closed. Just a few weeks ago, the Post reported John Bozeman himself killed by Indians. Sime Ervin had read the articles. Immediately he dismissed this route. It was too dangerous. The riverboats via Fort Benton were probably the safest way, but he would have to move fast, by the end of July at the latest. His son, Spud, could accompany the gold to St. Louis. He could probably recruit enough extra guards from the units Governor Meagher had formed and then disbanded to fight Indians. Meagher had raised a sizable army. Ervin needed a small army. His time was very short. The river was falling.

Now he sat phrasing a telegraph to several possible recruits. Curly would wire them in the morning. It was a difficult task. Sime's schooling had been sporadic and he had never quite learned to spell. Mr. Hugh, in the new telegraph office, charged a dollar a word. Sime Ervin made sure there would be no extra words. His quill scratched the paper softly in the dim candlelight. Worley snored steadily in his sleep. Outside, a horse stomped. Then came the patter of a horse cantering. Curly had returned. It was too early for Spud.

Sime got up and walked to the door. "That's too good a horse to run over them rocks. Want 'im to come up lame?"

Curly ignored the rebuke. "Bad news, Mr. Ervin, Spud's been shot."

"Dead?" It was a blank question, without emotion.

"Naw, he'll live....but I heard Doc Lubbock had to take his arm off."

"Which arm?"

"The right. His shootin' arm."

"We'll see. My boy kin defend 'imself." Sime spat a stream of tobacco juice onto the dirt floor. "How'd it happen?"

"Gamblin'." Curly hesitated. Sime Ervin waited. "I heard he lost the Cleopatra to some Rebel card shark just arrived from off the river." Curly waited for Sime to anger and blow but whatever it was Sime felt, he wasn't exposing it.

"I gave 'im that deed this morning." A pale reddishness crept up from beneath his beard and spread across his brow. He didn't tell Curly that Spud was to deliver the deed to the assayer.

Curly continued. "I come as soon as I heard the news. It happened in the Citadel, McGillicuddy's place. Feller named Cameron did it, a new dealer, almighty calm and careful with a shooter."

"Where's Spud now?"

"Doc Lubbock's keepin' 'im fer the night."

"In the morning, you go get 'im. Bring 'im home."

Nothing more was said. Curly turned in. Sime Ervin didn't go to town for his son. He went back to his chair and stared at the orange coals in the grate.

Chapter 7

Dawn came early in Varina. Daniel McGillicuddy was the first to arise. He didn't need much sleep at his age. Besides he loved the quiet of the early morning, especially Sundays, like today, when most of the rowdies had gone home to sleep off their Saturday night drunks. He slept on a cot in the back room. It was more private and he could watch over the Citadel's winnings. The room was cold and it was still dark when he reached for a match, lit the oil lamp and sat rubbing the stiffness out of his knuckles. When they started to bend a little more nimbly, he pulled on his boots, stirred the fire in the stove, and put the coffee on.

Mountain mornings were chill even in June. During the night, there had been a dusting of wet snow. Now the sun shot its first slanted rays over the peaks to the east and rimmed their black silhouettes with silvery pink. The soggy spring snow enhanced the smells of the earth. McGillicuddy opened the door and breathed in deeply, then squinted at the early shafts of light that bounced off the shimmering snow. It was the most beautiful time of the day. In an hour the snow would melt and disappear. It would leave a slick coat of mud underfoot—he'd need more sawdust to keep the floor of the gaming room dry.

The reddening sky foretold a glorious day. Sometimes Dan McGillicuddy even grumbled his thanks to his Creator. That was the closest he ever came to praying. He pumped a bucketfull of water and carried it back indoors.

The room was warming nicely. Today was like every other Sunday morning, deliciously peaceful. He finished shaving, dressed carefully in one of his spotless black suits, curled his mustache and donned his stovepipe hat. He used a St. Louis tailor who was the only man ever to fit his diminutive frame and he wore the hat everywhere—it made him look taller.

Early morning was when he always counted his earnings: this was when his mind was fresh. It was also the safest time of day. Thieves were not early risers. Carefully, he barred his doors and stuffed a blanket around the door frame to prevent air currents from disturbing his dust. Last night had been a profitable one. The new man, Cameron, had brought him luck. He began to empty the small leather pouches of dust onto the scales when he heard the thump of boots in the main gaming hall. He cursed. His rifle hung over the door. He was reaching for it when a familiar voice reassured him.

"Dan, that you in your den?" It was John Moulton, Sheriff of Varina. He was an big affable, innocuous man on familiar terms with most citizens of Varina.

McGillicuddy let out a grunt, more in anger than in relief. "I'm not a bear, John. I don't live in a den."

"Dan, I gots to speak to you."

"I'm listening, John." McGillicuddy made no move to open the door, hoping John Moulton would go away.

"You could open the door, Dan, be neighborly. I knowd you'd be up. 'Sides it's cold out here."

"Waking a man at 6 A.M. isn't what I call neighborly, John. Just a minute." He took his time pushing the dust back into the pouches and unbarred the door.

A bewildered John Moulton poked his bobbing head around the corner of the door and sidled in. Moulton grabbed a slat back chair and moved over to the stove. He sat straddling the chair and slapping his arms and stamping his feet for warmth. The coffee was beginning to boil.

"Coffee's hot. I have a cup, Dan?" McGillicuddy poured a cup. Moulton sputtered his first sip. The coffee had boiled.

"Spit it out John. What do you have to say so early in the morning?" Dan McGillicuddy pushed his hat back on his head and waited.

Moulton was slow. "It's about the shootin' last night, Dan. Sime Ervin's mighty mad about what happened to 'is kid."

"You speak to Sime?"

"Curly Shaw rode in this mornin'."

"You don't have to believe everyone with red hair and freckles, John. Spud's no kid. It was a fair fight. I saw it. You have my word."

Moulton puckered his lips and blew hard several times at the steam rising from his coffee. "Well Dan, Curly Shaw saw it different from you, an' you know Sime's temper. He's filin' charges an' I have to find this here gunslinger, Cameron...He here?"

"Cameron's no gunslinger. He's a soldier. Sime's prodding Shaw, starting rumors. Spud Ervin was at fault. He should be more careful with a gun and with his old man's gold and have more respect for his elders—he even insulted me! And he needs to earn his own living." McGillicuddy spoke as simply as he knew how—Moulton wouldn't understand any complications.

"Cameron plugged him good, Dan. Tore 'is arm off. If he were your son, you'd be mad too." Moulton's head dangled forward.

"I'd be mad but I wouldn't be accusing a man falsely. Spud Ervin's trouble, John. I didn't sire him. If I did, I might've reined him in a couple of times before I give him his head."

"You're bein' difficult, Dan."

"John, I run a business. You bust in here in the middle of the night wanting to arrest my dealer. Spud Ervin drew first. He was drinking; he was armed; he was betting high and he couldn't control his temper. That's no kid in my book. That's a dangerous man. Cameron was right to defend himself."

"Sime says there's a feud goin' on.... says Cameron was gunnin' for Spud. You see, Spud's been sparkin' Mrs. Emma an' he says Cameron's her old beau, that he an' her were thick before the war, that he fathered her child, an' that he's jealous of Spud.

"Sime told you that!"

"Curly told me that, but the whole town's talkin'...."

"Curly's a prankster, John, it's all political. Sime's a Lincoln Republican sticking the prod to another Georgia Reb, that's all, and Curly's salting his rumors like Sime salts his mines. What would Emma want with a colt like Spud?"

"Gold, respectability. She'd get to walk up the hill."

"She's got that now. I met Emma and Pierre Dubois coming upriver aboard the Molly Jones. Pierre Dubois was the first pilot—no finer side-wheeler ever was—and Dubois was a good pilot too. Dubois held us straight in the channel past all kinds of shoals and driftwood and kept us out of range of Indian arrows too. He took sick out past Fort Union.... stomach cramps. He ailed terrible. There was no doctor on board and there was nothing we, any of us, could do. He died."

"She have a kid, Dan?"

"Yes, she did, later." Now it was McGillicuddy's turn to look aside at the steam blowing from the kettle. It was not a good memory, that first winter in Benton. "Emma was pregnant. The water in the river was low. We had to put off at Cow Island and we came the rest of the way by Mackinaw.... bull boat....You know what that is, John, rough. Can't leave a pregnant lady alone there on the prairie and she knocked around some in the boat." He stopped. Moulton sat patiently, nodding stupidly and McGillicuddy wondered just how well the simple sheriff comprehended the narrative. He continued, "We got where we were going. We stayed a while in Benton—I started a business. She lived off what she had from Dubois. Along about November, Marie was born....one of the first white babies they'd ever seen in Benton and a beauty like her mother. Next spring, Emma sent the child downriver with Father Manno, the missionary, to the sisters in St. Joe."

"Why didn't she go back with the kid?"

"Nothing to go back to. Bought into my business and organized some girls for a dance hall. I needed someone to find girls—they keep marrying off or going back downriver. I would've married her only I'm too old, too ugly and too short. And I make a better father than a husband. Couple of younger fellers would've married her but she didn't want them either. At the news of the gold strike, we both decided we'd do better down here."

"You're a fine lookin' man, Dan! Not a bit too old!" Moulton had missed the point.

McGillicuddy shook his head and the tall hat wobbled. "John, she didn't know Cameron. She was a married woman, and then she kept to herself, didn't encourage suitors."

"She knowd 'im somewheres, Dan."

"John, he just got off the boat."

"Well, I just got to talk to 'im. Ya know where he is."

"Maybe he went to church. It's Sunday."

"Dan, gamblin' men don' go to church. I'm only doin' my job."

"And I voted for you John.... Now listen. Spud Ervin wagered the Cleopatra Mine. He was a foolish, blustering kid trying to march center stage. He tripped, fell, lost it and thought he could bluff his way to getting it back. Cameron called him. That's all... Cameron didn't know whose son he was.

"Where's Cameron, Dan?"

"I don't know. Asleep." McGillicuddy had lost all patience with John Moulton.

Moulton set his cup down carefully on the table and got up to go. He scratched his bare head trying to digest all that McGillicuddy had told him. "Thank you, Dan. I'll see what I can do."

McGillicuddy barred the door again and frowned at the mud Moulton had tracked over his rag rug. He turned to the safe. When he reached for his pouches of dust, his hand fell on Pat Lysaght's nugget and the leathern deed to the Cleopatra mine. Gambling in a gold camp, was good business.

Chapter 8

A sharp ray of sunlight sliced cleanly through a crack in the Citadel wall and stabbed Lee Cameron across the eyes. He lifted his head up from the table, out of the glare and groaned. He had a headache and a nasty kink in his neck. He'd been dreaming again, a frustrating dream about a woman. The woman looked like Emma Dubois and he always woke up when he was about to bed her. He looked around, remembered where he was, still seated in the Citadel Saloon. Gamblers and miners bustled around him. He rubbed the sleep from his eyes and smacked at a buzzing fly—if only he could erase old memories with a smack, as easily as he had squashed that bug. Emma had never left his consciousness all these years and now after seeing her again he could think of nothing else.

In spite of his dreams, he was amazingly well-rested. The air was warming rapidly. He wouldn't need his grey coat today. His gear was at the hotel, and he got up to go and collect it. It was late, about eleven o'clock Sunday morning. Tonight, if he could afford he'd sleep in a real hotel, one that didn't wake you at 7 in the morning because they needed the sheets for tablecloths.

He retrieved his gear and dressed in a new red shirt that he had bought before he left St. Louis. The old coat he folded neatly and tied into his bedroll. The only thing he wore from the old days now was his hat. It was the broad-brimmed grey felt and drooped now at the brim from years of wear. Like his coat, it was still good protection against the burning sun of Varina's high altitude. There was a barber shop across the street. He needed a bath and a good shave with hot water and soap.

The barber, a skinny, balding, little man with thin reddish sidewhiskers, turned as Cameron entered and tossed his bedroll into a corner. A look of recognition crossed his brow briefly, but he snapped his towel briskly toward a large leather chair and Cameron sat down and closed his eyes.

"Shave it all off or just some?" Shave it all an' you'll be a mite cooler this summer."

It was a warm day. "A hot wash and a trim'll be fine, thanks. Is there a bath house nearby?"

The barber slapped his blade loudly across a leather strap and Cameron opened his eyes. "Just around the corner. You want to go to church, we got that to, in the old Masters Saloon...."You're the gunman from Fort Benton, who done the shootin'. I know."

This was not a question but a declaration and it was intrusive. Cameron didn't answer. The puffy little man reminded him of a pigeon, the way he strutted around. And pigeons were nosy, always poking their beaks into holes where they were not wanted, always leaving their droppings to smell and rot in the sun. How had the barber heard of the shooting so soon? Tongues wagged.

The pigeon prattled away, "No offense intended... but you don't have to be humble in front of me. Varina here is a small town, if'n you consider them eastern cities, an' we been livin' with Spud and Sime Ervin for some time. You took him fair. We all know that. But there'll be hell to pay. Yer a Reb. Old Sime's a Kansas abolitionist."

Cameron groaned but the little barber dribbled on like water from a leaky spiggot, "You're Lee Cameron. I'm very pleased to meet you. I heared all about you. An' I don't mind you Rebs. I'm a Democrat. Name's Martin Behnke from Minnesota. Where you from, Fort Benton?" He held out a wet palm.

Cameron took the soggy hand reluctantly. He was annoyed that news travelled so quickly. How many more good folk of Varina would recognize him, Lee Cameron, on sight? "I got off the boat at Benton...I'm from Athens, Georgia, but that was a long time ago."

Behnke had turned around to rinse his razor and babbled on about how he favored most Rebels. "Sime Ervin's Kansan. That ain't real South, but that's bloody fightin' territory an' he hates you Rebs like you was rattlers in a pit." Cameron was fast taking a dislike to Behnke. There was a pretension lurking within the man. If Sime Ervin had sat in his barber's chair, Behnke would've hated Rebs. He'd agree with anyone, shedding his loyalties like the skin off a snake when they didn't suit his current customer.

Cameron interrupted. "Tell you what, shave the beard and cut the hair too." Then maybe people wouldn't recognize him. If the southern boys found out he was handy with a gun, they would expect help every time one of them got drunk and started ranting about Abe Lincoln's mercenaries and Andy Johnson's tyranny.

"Cost you more." Gold seeking was not limited to miners.

Cameron nodded. "I know."

Behnke went to work. The train of chatter continued. "Me, I come west after my wife left me. Never could understand it. Women's peculiar creatures. I had built ourselves a cozy little homestead up until the Indian raids—Santee Sioux. They comes one day an' just burns us out and kidnaps my poor wife. I was in town for supplies or I wouldn't be here.... Some big stud buck carries 'er off. Well, the U.S. Army come in an' rescues 'er an' can you imagine what she told 'em?"

Cameron had no idea.

"She said she wasn't leavin'. That she actually liked that big dusky savage better'n me. Can you believe it?"

Yes, Cameron could believe it.

"So's I just left. Figured I'd try my luck in the gold fields. Get rich. That'd show 'er. Got here in August of '65 and nearly froze to death that winter. Next spring I caught myself a death of cold out pannin', standin' in that icy water up to m'knees all day long. Decided I'd live longer with an indoors occupation. An' you know what?"

Cameron nodded and wished he could plug his ears. Behnke answered his own question. "This here shop is my gold mine. Them miners appreciate a good groomin', livin' like they do out in the brakes, dirty, wet. They'll empty their pokes to wash up and smell sweet an' look good an' I always have good hot water an' soap. They pay me in gold. An' I stock Dr. Munson's de-lousing lotion. It don't smell too good so I sells 'em some Airs de Paree scent to overcome the odor. I even have some lady customers—strictly confidential that is. Ladies ain't supposed to git varmints."

Cameron wondered if anything was confidential the way Behnke's tongue flapped.

"An' Spud Ervin's been in here too. Ain't got no respect—told me I talk too much....You done me a favor puttin' 'im out of my way for a while."

Behnke put a sympathetic hand on Cameron's shoulder. Cameron cringed. "I understand if you don't want people to know you're good with a gun. A handsome man like yourself doesn't need that kind of a reputation. Tell you what—I'm gonna give you a present an' my thanks to you for lacin' Spud Ervin." He shoved the bottle of Airs de Parree into Cameron's hands.

"That'll be two bits. In gold dust. Five in bills."

Cameron realized Behnke was finished. "High price for a shave."

"Oh but I'm the best. An' you got the latest news. Better than the Montana Post. I know everything Tilton's newspaper prints an' more afore he prints it. Comes to me for the news, he does. And them's can't read always come here to hear about it."

Cameron paid Behnke and was glad to leave. He felt cleaner without the beard, but he wouldn't go back to Behnke's and he'd buy the Montana Post for news. Would they really print the story of the shooting? He headed for the bath house but the smell of bacon frying lured him first to a restaurant and a good meal.

He had a bath and left the bottle of Behnke's scent in the bath house. Clean and well-fed, he had time now to look around town. He headed down Missouri Street, passed Meeker and came to the corner of Jefferson. Jefferson headed uphill from north to south. Varina was confusing to Cameron because north had always been up from Georgia. In Varina, north was downhill. The southernmost corner in Varina was the town's highest point. He stood there now, looking north over the rooftops, the few wooden houses of the richer folk, the hovels of Chinatown, the tents, flumes and rockers. Dusty, false-fronted buildings of one or two stories lined the streets like links in a chain rambling down to where Sunshine Creek flowed from the east into Garnet Creek's northward flow. Garnet Creek was a muddied, two-mile trench of mining activity. Sunshine Creek was quiet, meandering, pristine and clear. The gold was in Garnet Creek on the north face of the mountain. Varinans drew their water from Sunshine Creek to the east. That and a few springs high up were all that was left potable from the slopsink of the mines.

Cameron climbed high up Garnet Creek and looked over foothills that rose steeply from these two waterways. Between them sloped the triangle of land where Varina lie, on the cooler north face of Lone Mountain. Her two main avenues followed the contours of the mountain slope parallel to each creek. Jefferson Street ran north-south along the banks of Garnet Creek. Warren ran east-west one block above Sunshine Creek. Missouri Street paralleled Warren upslope. Wealthier people lived here. Jones Street, where Emma Dubois lived, ran east to west, below Warren, along the peaceful banks of Sunshine Creek. This was the lowest and least desirable part of town. Only Chinatown was lower. It huddled in isolation on the opposite side of Garnet Creek on flats that looked to Cameron like they would flood after a mild spring thaw. Jefferson and Warren merged at the western edge of town above Jones and Chinatown, to form the toll roads which veered west toward the Beaverhead and Bannack or north toward the new strike at Last Chance Gulch and Helena.

The same two streets, Jefferson and Warren, enclosed the triangle that was Varina's commercial heart. The Citadel Saloon and Plantation House stood at the west end of town, at the corner of Jefferson and Warren, at the hub of a wedge of settlement. The bank, the assay, telegraph and post offices, The Montana Post print shop, the best hardwares and outfitters, the saddlery and the Masonic Temple lined Warren. The Queen of the Nile Saloon stood at Warren's far east end. Glenby's Mayfair Livery was at the entrance to town just below the Citadel at the point where the two streets converged, with the blacksmith shop next door. It marked the beginning of Jones Street. Jefferson claimed most of the other important establishments—the Sagebrush Saloon, Excelsior Dance Hall, grocery and some prominent residences further up. Mayor Thatcher, Doc Lubbock and the vigilante lawyer, Major Landon, all lived here in freshly painted houses.

Cameron was surprised at the size of these houses and at the bright shutters on their windows. He stopped for a minute to watch the construction of the new Masonic Grand Temple, soon to be the largest stone building in the territory. It dominated the middle of Warren Street. At the far east end of town was the Brewery along with the street and the smell that bore its name. Cameron walked down Missouri to Brewery. Beer-making was good business in a mining town, but Cameron hated the smell—he preferred bourbon like a true southerner and he wondered who in town must make a good mash. Finally, he turned into Jones Street and headed back toward the Livery to see about his horse.

Cameron stopped abruptly. He was standing again, he realized, exactly where he had been yesterday, facing the house with the bright green porch where Emma Dubois lived. She stood on the porch watching a burly man in a brown hat disappear down the street. She wore a pale green gingham dress and no jewelry. Her arms were bare. A chill still lingered in the fresh morning air, and she slapped her hands against her arms for warmth. Her dark hair hung loosely, alluringly, down her back. There was a suppleness about her this morning like the budding innocence of a farm maid. She had not seen him. He gaped. Her caller must have surprised her on a Sunday morning or else he had been there for the night. Cameron felt his hackles rise. He studied the silhouette of the man receding. He was powerfully built, but somehow seemed soft, unthreatening. He shuffled along, head tilted forward, bobbing, brown hat slightly askew. He didn't look much like a suitor but a tinge of jealousy made Cameron bold and he squared his shoulders and advanced. Emma didn't see him approach. When finally she did look, she didn't recognize him.

"Ma'am." He tipped his hat.

She knew his voice. "Mr. Cameron, what do you want now?" She sounded irritated, but then her voice eased. "You certainly look a lot better this morning." Her eyes brightened, her chin lifted, she smiled and his heart surged with confidence.

"Soap and hot water, Ma'am, and a pretty lady's smile, renews a man." He blinked as if he hadn't believed his own words and took a deep breath. "Ride out with me this afternoon. I've only seen the town. You could show me the countryside." It was an impulse. He listened to his own hopeful words, half believing he was dreaming. Was he too eager? Somehow, he sensed a warmer reception than he had received yesterday. He knew she wanted to come. He didn't have a second horse to offer, much less a fancy rig and team, but he resolved to get one on the spot.

She didn't answer immediately, just stood there looking at him with that perplexing smile. With her hair down, dressed in plain calico, standing there hugging her bare arms to herself, she was softer, more welcoming than yesterday. "You are the bold one!"

He laughed at that, took off his hat politely and met her gaze. "I've come a long way." He added. The deep, languorous tones of his voice washed over her. She flashed her dark eyes again. He waited for what seemed an eternity.

"I have an engagement this afternoon. Mr. McGillicuddy and I are going to the races."

Cameron felt a knife twist in his chest.

"But perhaps the three of us... The whole town goes to the races."

"Three." The number rolled haltingly off his tongue. McGillicuddy, a chaperone, the whole town—this was not what he had anticipated. But he would play his hand as dealt. His face broke out in a forced grin.

"Yes, the three of us could go."

"Mr. McGillicuddy has a team and rig. Shall we meet at the Citadel—about two?"

He nodded. "Two o'clock...at the Citadel....Ma'am." He tipped his hat and drawled this last syllable so that the letter "a" trailed away like the end of a nostalgic song.

She watched him as he replaced his hat and turned to go. The wind brushed a sweep of brown hair across the nape of his neck and the sun splashed brilliant stripes on the red flannel shirt pulled tight across the bulge of his shoulders. Her heart jumped like a leapfrog and she swallowed hard. "Lee Cameron, you're a handsome man. It's been a long time." It was only a mumble and he was out of earshot. Emma Dubois remembered very well.

Cameron didn't hurry but neither did he look back. Emma was including him in her afternoon. After the drubbing she had given him yesterday, she had surprised him. He watched the water of Sunshine Creek splash gently against the rocks. The morning sun beat down between his shoulder blades. He threaded his way along the creekbed amid marsh marigolds and daisies to a split rail fence and turned back into Jones Street. Beyond the fence was a corral and the Mayfair Livery where he had stabled his horse. A black horse, a very fine animal, stood in the corral. The sight of good horseflesh always lifted Cameron's spirits, like the sight of a beautiful woman. Today he was a doubly happy man.

Chapter 9

Lee Cameron approached the livery. Two men sat on crates near the door. The older one faced the street and would be a tall man standing. His face bore the deep furrows of premature aging. The blue eyes were clear, the hands, gnarled. He was handsome in a rough sort of way. His shoulders and biceps were built to fight but his mouth opposed the downward curve of mustache and curled indelibly upward at the edges. The younger one, clean shaven and hatless with bright yellow hair, sat facing him and away from Cameron. An old Army blanket spread between them and was covered with a tangle of dirty harness. They each had a bucket, a couple of grain sacks for rags and a can of grease. They were oiling harness. The older one saw Cameron coming.

"Do somethin' for ya, Mister?" The voice was deep and friendly, but clipped and northern.

"My horse, the little grey, I brought him in yesterday?"

"Yessir. You're Cameron. I'm Rob Glenby, and this is my barn." He didn't get up but held out his broad, greasy palm. Cameron shook it.

"How'd'you know my name?"

"Open your mouth, I know you're a Reb. That an' your hat. Word travels." That was all the explanation Glenby was going to give, but he liked to talk, "We sees most of what comes 'n goes, Clem 'n me... settin' here at the city gates, see ever'thing comes in, ever'thing goes out...." He nodded toward the other man. "That's my sister's boy, Clem. My sister died. Clem's wi' me now."

Clem looked around. His head tilted forward and swayed slightly like a heavy ball on the end of a coil. Cameron recognized the wide forehead, flat nose and friendly, wide-eyed stare of a half-wit. "I surely am, Mr. Glenby." Clem's words slurred together and Cameron had to listen hard.

"Hello, Clem." Cameron smiled at the boy and Clem grinned back like a kitten who had just been stroked. Glenby switched to the topic that prefaced so many conversations in the post-war west, "What'd you do in the war?"

Cameron was brief. "Captain, 19th Georgia, Company A. My commanding officer was General Archer."

"I fought for the North, misself...come from Carlisle, Pennsylvania, but you're welcome here. I knowed some Rebs, even admired some. Carlisle was as far north as they come. You boys fought well an' I'm proud to know you." He looked over at Clem. "I don't hold no grudges like some folks here abouts, an' Clem don't know how to grudge, do ya Clem?"

Clem gaped wide-eyed at Cameron and continued rubbing a trace mechanically. "You in the Rebel Cavalry?"

"Yes I was, Clem."

"You go to the Shenandoah?"

"Yessir."

"You see Turner Ashby an' his white horse? He jumps a fifteen foot ditch!" He spoke in the present tense, as if the Shenandoah were right over the hill and Ashby were about to ride out on a raid from Varina.

Cameron remembered Ashby. He answered respectfully. "Ashby's dead, Clem, and the Shenandoah burned to ashes...but I saw Ashby ride and there was no better...but no, I didn't know him."

"Clem don't mean no harm Mista. An' he don't need to be locked up like some folks say he should. He just has his heroes an' them's any man who's handy with horseflesh. North an' south don't mean a donkey's tit to him."

Cameron sensed how Clem's innocent ignorance erased the differences between them. Colonel Ashby was an expert horseman. Clem's admiration was deserved.

Glenby interrupted his thoughts. "You want your saddle cleaned, we don't have the time today, but you can set a piece an' do it yourself, you don't mind gettin' your hands dirty. You be glad for the company, wouldn't you, Clem?" Glenby motioned to another crate behind the door. Clem's head moved in a circle. Cameron guessed it meant he agreed.

"You don't mind, I'll see to my horse first."

"Sure thing. Three stalls down on the right."

Cameron counted down three stalls. The horse was blood bay. He recounted, "Glenby, this isn't my horse."

"I put 'im there misself. Just fed 'im this morning."

"Come see for yourself. Cameron wasn't angry, just annoyed. The horse wasn't worth that much and he saw in Glenby a patient strength and honesty that sustained the retarded boy. He never doubted his horse was there, somewhere.

Glenby heaved himself up and marched down the aisle. He stood an easy six feet in laced lumberjack boots. He took one look in the stall and yelled, "Clem!" It was an officer's voice, used to being obeyed on the instant.

Clem bounded to his feet like a jack rabbit. The bobbing head snapped to attention.

"Clem, where'd you put Mr. Cameron's horse?" Glenby was firm but gentle.

"I let him out yonder for a roll in th' grass."

"Beggin' yer pardon, Cameron. Clem thinks horses is human. Folks don't much talk to Clem, so's he talks to the horses, them's he takes a shine to that is, an' he says the horses talk back to him.... But you can be sure that horse of yours will get good care in this barn. Clem treats 'em like queens at the king's banquet...Come with me. I know where to find your horse."

They walked the length of the aisle and out the back. There spread several acres of green grass that rolled all the way down to the sparkling water of Sunshine Creek. Five horses were turned out, none of them grey.

"There he is." Glenby pointed.

Cameron had to look twice. The little horse was there, but he wasn't grey. He'd rolled, in the wet dew-melt and mud near the Creek. He was covered with it, a dull mouse brown.

Glenby raised his voice again. "Clem, you clean 'im up for Mr. Cameron." Then he turned to Cameron, "'Nother hour, the sun be warmer, Clem'll give 'im a nice bath an' dry 'im out. He'll look just like new and he'll give you a better ride 'cause there won't be no grime 'tween 'im and the saddle. Right Clem?.... Freighters goin' out tomorrow. I could use some help with th'harness. Set yourself a while."

Cameron sat, picked up a rag and a rein and started to rub. Rob Glenby continued, "Don't you dirty them fine clothes. I don't want to pry, but I'll wager you're goin' to the races this afternoon." Glenby was a mind-reader. "An' I'll wager you got a gal goin' with you, handsome feller like yourself, clean shirt, shave, all gussied up. Don't worry, Clem'll do right by ya. You spoke kindly to 'im. I appreciate that." He added with a twinge in his brow, "Lotsa folks don't think Clem's human...."

Cameron had no answer to that but felt an immediate warming toward Rob Glenby. The two men's eyes locked together for an instant in understanding. Glenby slapped a broad hand on Cameron's shoulder and steered him away. "Come with me, I got somethin' to show you that I don't show just anybody."

They walked around the side of the barn. There was a separate corral there and in it the black horse that Cameron had noticed before. He looked again. It was one of the most beautiful horses Lee Cameron had ever seen. "That one don't race this afternoon. She's too good. An' she ain't for sale, 'cept to rich folks I like. Rich cause I'd only sell 'er high. An' I like you. You strike it rich, you lookin' for a good horse, you come see me."

Cameron walked over to the horse. Her coat shone like silk velvet. He ran his hand down her back, then down her legs. The bones, the tendons were lithe and smooth. He picked up a foot. Each hoof was trimmed and carefully shod and firm.

"I do her shoeing myself. Don't trust nobody else."

Now this was a horse! Cameron couldn't resist asking, "How much you want for her?"

"A gold mine." Glenby wasn't fooling. "I been savin' 'er for the right person....She ain't been ridden these last few years but she's had the best care Clem an' me can give. She's no filly anymore, but she's only nine-year-old. Ain't no stallion good enough or I'd breed 'er."

"Where'd you get her?" Horses of this caliber were rare. Most had not survived the war.

"Owner left 'er with me an' went back stateside. She ain't comin' back... Mrs. Slade. You heard of her?"

"A woman owned her!" Cameron was incredulous.

Glenby looked Cameron straight in the eye. "Now there was another filly to behold, beautiful gal, but married, the wife of Captain J.A. Slade. You ain't heard of her maybe you heard of him?" Glenby's favorite subjects were horses and women.

Cameron shook his head.

"Jack Slade, generous to all when sober, wilder than a cornered she-bear when he got drunk. He was no real Captain like you. She came from a respectable family in Clinton County, Illinois, an' she could ride! He gave her this here horse for a weddin' present and she rode astride—shocked a few folks here abouts. Maybe that's why she married him, cause she wanted a good horse. He treated 'er kindly but he came west because he killed a man. You liked him or you hated him. He was good to Clem and I liked 'im. Liked her better, a real looker! There were some wanted to shoot Jack Slade on sight. He an' his cronies would liquor up an ride down Warren shootin' anything that would smash or bleed. Folks barred their doors an' boarded their windows. The Lamb brothers, Ed and Bill, the hardware people, threatened to kill 'im if ever he set foot in their store an' they'd a done it. But he sure had a beautiful wife and she cried rivers the day he died. I could never figure why she loved 'im... They had a ranch 'bout two mile out, nice house, two floors. Raised horses. We could use a good breeder like 'im today." Glenby pinched the bridge of his nose and rubbed his eyes.

"What happened to him?"

"They hung 'im. Oh I'm not saying he wasn't askin' for it. He'd been drinkin' all night. He was savage, shoutin' an' strugglin' an' cussin', flingin' his gun around like 'twere a piece a meat, an' foul talkin' ever'one he met, even the judge. They say six hundred miners came up to Varina swingin' a noose. Set up court on the tail of a buckboard. They hung 'im right there—off the gatepost beam of my corral." He pointed. "Kicked a crate out from under 'is feet... broke 'is neck, first time. Lucky he died quick." Glenby stopped to clear his throat and cough.

"And Mrs. Slade?"

"She went back to Illinois. Pickled 'is corpse and took 'im with 'er. Lotsa men would've married 'er, but she didn't want that. That's how I come by that horse. She left. Never paid the horse's keep so I surmise I own 'er. I ain't heard nothing since."

"Too bad."

"No, it wasn't too bad at all. I got a good horse. Turned out Captain Jack Slade killed a string a folks when he was workin' for the Overland...This town just got too civilized for 'im. Me, I ain't too civilized myself. Guess that's why I liked 'im."

Glenby seemed very civilized to Cameron, the gentle, patient way he handled Clem.

Time had passed. Clem came up with his little grey, bathed, saddled and shining and Cameron mounted.

"You won't like the races. Scruffy stuff mostly. Nothing like my high-brow mare. Breedin' an' bloodline show. Out here the big horses go to the freighters an' the stage line. The Injuns, they steal some of the better ones. What's left, we use here about town. Some of 'em can run but not for too long an' folks won't race anythin' that can't afford to get hurt. Someday, you want to bet on a sure thing, we race that black mare. But you put 'er in front, you stay there. I don' want that mare wired or tripped."

"I just want to ride her.... When?" Cameron was almost afraid to ask.

"Come by tomorrow. I'll be here."

Chapter 10

Lee Cameron rode up Warren promptly at one o'clock. A sparkling new landau, the latest model from a St. Louis carriage-maker stood in front of the saloon with a fine, eager bay in its traces. It was the first landau Cameron had seen since he left Missouri. McGillicuddy was a rich man. Cameron was about to dismount when McGillicuddy appeared from behind the swinging doors. McGillicuddy looked younger, taller. His hair was freshly combed and he wore an immaculate black cut-away coat and grey vest and gold watch chain. He carried a looking glass and wore a new stovepipe that gleamed in the sunlight like patent leather. It perched jauntily over his curled white locks and stiff white collar. How old was he? Cameron could only guess but the costume clearly enhanced the commanding presence of his small frame. He was pure patrician.

Now, he trimmed the end of a cigar, lit it, spotted Cameron, waved and went back inside. Cameron watched and waited.

Suddenly, McGillicuddy burst again through the batwing doors with Emma on his arm. She was only a few inches taller than he but she dwarfed him. She was radiant. Her dark hair swept back in swirls above the nape of her neck. She wore silk brocade of emerald green which pinched at the waist, princess style, with matching pouch bag, peaked hat and veil. She walked out into Warren Street as if she were entering a grand ballroom in a court of Europe. Cameron couldn't take his eyes off of her.

"Good afternoon, Mr. Cameron." Emma's queenly poise was back and she was smiling down on him.

Involuntarily, Cameron sucked in his cheeks to steady his nerves and mask the pounding in his chest. He stretched tall in the saddle and swept his hat from his wavy hair in a wide arc. His fingers tensed on the reins. The little horse dropped his head and backed a step. Cameron bowed his head with the graceful, proud manners of the southland to which he had been bred. "Ma'am, it's a lovely day."

Emma stopped and stared. The ragged look was gone. Clean-shaven, clothed neatly and astride a horse, he looked still the dashing figure she remembered.

McGillicuddy was a keen observer and the moment was not lost on him. He broke the spell by pulling out his watches. He had two of them, his pocket watch and a stopwatch, and he consulted both. McGillicuddy took racing seriously.

Warren Street was noisy and crowded. Everyone was going to the races on a sunny Sunday afternoon. Cameron noticed a tall, very thin man, lounging against the side of the building, immobile, amid the bustling crowd. The man was hatless, with a massive head of red curly hair and was watching Emma closely. Lots of men watched Emma but it was the quantity and color of hair that triggered Cameron's memory— the Ervin bodyguard from last night, Curly.

McGillicuddy led the landau up to the boardwalk so Emma could seat herself without soiling her silks in the dusty street. He climbed in next to her and picked up the reins. "Cameron, you ride alongside. You dress up like a damn Christmas tree, Moulton's sure to find you. He has some questions about the shooting." McGillicuddy released the brake and smacked the reins on the bay's fat rump. The landau lurched forward and they headed up Warren. McGillicuddy added with a wry glance at Cameron, "And Moulton's the sheriff, in case you didn't know."

Cameron was watching Emma and never heard a word.

At the eastern edge of town, the street became a double track that led across Tug's Ravine, up Sunshine Creek almost to its mountain source. Buckboards and hay wagons yielded to the landau. McGillicuddy's bay, a tough muscular little horse, was overtaking most of them. The fluid, rippling motion of the horse as he pulled hard uphill propelled them. McGillicuddy cracked the whip and the landau jostled over the ruts. Cameron watched Emma, her straight yet supple shoulders, the curve of her hips, sway and bounce with the motion. There was just enough room for him to ride alongside and he had to spur the grey to keep up. His maneuvering was not lost on McGillicuddy who worked to hold the bay to the left-most ruts and studied Cameron out of the corner of his eye.

It was a pleasant ride up Sunshine Creek, up a north slope where a fresh breeze always tempered the baking sun. The aspens were green. Their tiny leaves quivered, flicking lively shadows across the trail. Two miles above the town, the trees thinned and the creek disappeared into the folds of mountains. The slopes fell away and flattened in an expanse of high alpine meadow. Here was the race course. It spanned a flatland high above Varina, just below a hogback ridge. Emma, McGillicuddy and Cameron arrived early. Mc Gillicuddy pulled the landau into a choice spot at right angles to the finish line.

The field of horses to be raced was as disappointing as Glenby had predicted, a scrawny looking lot for race horses. They stood calmly with heads down and tails swishing the ubiquitous black flies. Too calmly, Cameron thought. Like his own little grey, they were short-legged, hard-hooved, endurance horses, built for climbing the tough terrain, but without the long legs and distance-eating stride needed for real speed. There wasn't a decent runner among them. They were not yet saddled. The excitement and popularity of the race was more a social outing than an effort to produce a good contest.

Lee Cameron sized up the race horses at a glance. He had little money and even if he had, he would not have bet on any of these. One good thoroughbred could beat the lot of them. All of them were long shots. Any one of them could win. Back home, he would have been in the thick of betting and bickering, but here, he had no prospective winner in mind and the preoccupation of Emma Dubois.

He found himself studying the people and their reactions to her. Most of the women ignored her. All the men stared—she had far better bloodlines and conformation than any of these horses, except maybe McGillicuddy's bay. But she was a finer breed than they and held herself aloof. She used McGillicuddy as a buffer to hold off less desirable advances. Cameron didn't know if this was deliberate or not. And he wasn't sure how he fit in.

McGillicuddy put his glass to his eye, inspected the field of horses, checked his stopwatch and hopped down. "You'll see better from up here... " He beckoned Cameron into the driver's seat. "Picket your horse over there. Let him graze. I have some bets to place." He walked off toward the line of bookies. Cameron waited for a nod from Emma, then did as he was told. From the wagon seat, it was a chaotic sight. Grooms called orders to jockeys, tightened cinches and polished hooves, buckled and brushed. Horses stomped and whinnied. Bookies screamed their odds like hawkers at a street fair. The odds changed constantly as they all tried to outshout each other.

He was very visible in his new red shirt against the emerald sheen of her dress, presiding over the most elegant carriage. Cameron felt himself become the object of scrutiny. It was not a comfortable feeling—women took discreet note of the handsome, brown-eyed stranger—and he wished McGillicuddy would return. Warily, he scanned the faces in the crowd. He saw the curly-haired man again. It took an instant for Cameron to realize why Curly Shaw stood out—he was looking directly at him, Lee Cameron, not at Emma like most other men. Cameron met the gaze and the man smirked brazenly in his face.

Cameron turned to Emma. "How well do you know Curly Shaw?"

The question surprised her. With him sitting next to her in the driver's seat, she still kept a comfortable distance between them. She followed his eyes. "Curly Shaw, works for the Ervins, part of Spud's impertinent contingent." And she changed the subject. "McGillicuddy wouldn't dismiss you. What did you do to make him like you so much?" It was an honest question.

Cameron snickered softly and steered his eyes away from her and away from Curly, toward the horses. He waited before answering, felt the sweat bead in his palms and rubbed them against the soft leather of the reins, "McGillicuddy likes me does he? I saved his whiskey and made him laugh...in Benton." He studied the preparations for the race, trying to control the emotional swirl pounding at his ribs like a caged wildcat trying to get out. While he was struggling to find appropriate words, he blurted back his own question, "Why did you invite me to the races?"

"I'm sorry if I offended you yesterday. I didn't mean to be uncivil. We do share memories." There was a warmth in her soft voice.

Her tone surprised him. Cameron pushed his hat back, squinted at the sun and relished its warm caress on his face, groping always for a proper response.

Suddenly, the bay horse shied nearly upsetting the landau. Cameron reached for the brake handle to steady himself, missed and fell against Emma Dubois. He was about to apologize when he turned and stared into the face of Curly Shaw and a long-necked man in a brown hat. Shaw gripped the reins just behind the bit in an iron fist that held the bridle rings jammed against the horse's jaw. The bay threw his head and Curly jerked hard. Cameron held the reins uselessly. He reached for the buggy whip.

"Let him go, Shaw."

Shaw ignored him and leered lecherously at Emma.

The long-necked man spoke to Emma, "If you don' want this man's attentions, Ma'am, I'll be glad to escort him aside....Mr. Ervin's man, Shaw here, told me to look out for you." The man's head bobbed stupidly like a long-necked fowl, swaying from side to side with the direction of his bulbous eyes.

Emma made introductions. "John Moulton this is Captain Cameron. Mr. Cameron just arrived." She put her hand on the buggy whip over Lee Cameron's. "Mr. Moulton's our sheriff....And this is Curly Shaw...Gentlemen, Mr. Cameron's a friend." She pressed her fingers into the back of Cameron's hand. Cameron eased his grip. "You can tell Curly to release the horse, John..."

Moulton looked like he hung on every word but his next direction didn't relate to anything he had said before, "Mr. Cameron, you come with me."

Emma repeated, "John, tell Curly to release the horse."

John Moulton stared back dumbly.

Curly Shaw jumped into the void, "He come nigh to murderin' Spud....I saw it, Moulton! That's the Reb blew his arm off."

Moulton nodded hard at that. It was as if he only understood after many repetitions. "I know. Behnke came runnin' with the news right after it happened. Sime sent word. I been lookin' for 'im all mornin'.'"

The bay threw his head again more fiercely, jerking Curly's arm. Curly bore down harder.

Emma pulled the buggy whip from Cameron as she spoke. There was anger in her voice. "You mean you want to arrest Captain Cameron for the disagreement in the saloon last night? I saw that, John Moulton. Nobody murdered anyone. Spud Ervin walked out quite alive! Ask McGillicuddy...." She paused and her voice lowered menancingly, "And tell Mr. Shaw to release that horse's mouth before he makes his gums bleed or I'll swipe this whip across the nest of fuzz he calls a beard!"

Curly Shaw purpled in anger.

Finally Moulton reacted, "Let go the horse, Curly." There was a pause. Moulton had to concentrate to regain his train of thought..."I did ask McGillicuddy this mornin'. He don't like Ervin an' he wouldn't help me find Cameron."

The horse threw his head a third time and Curly turned his anger on the animal. He raised his free arm to swipe the animal in the face. Emma swung the whip and it licked out across both of Curly's cheeks. Curly's hand released the horse finally to cover a reddening welt and his freckled face turned ugly.

"Thank you, Mr. Shaw." Emma handed the whip back to Cameron. She had not lost her poise or even raised her voice and she turned her attention back to a stupefied Moulton like a queen accepting tribute. Finally, she held his unadulterated attention, "The whole saloon saw the shooting. Spud Ervin was a poor looser. He drew first. Now if you'll excuse us, John, Mr. Cameron and I would prefer to enjoy the races."

Moulton nodded dumbly at the fury in the eyes of Curly Shaw. "I don't reckon I can arrest 'im, Curly. You heard Emma. A man can defend himself. That's the law." Curly scowled but he didn't have the patience to convince John Moulton to change his mind.

But Moulton's next words were for Cameron and now he launched into a sermon. "We don' tolerate no Dixie renegades lookin' for Yankee scalps, Captain. We took care of their kind coupla years back....with a noose an' a crossbeam. Now you come in here an' on your first day in Varina, you mark that boy for life. Sime may be a mite odd but he ain't crazy—I knowed 'im fer years—an he's steamin' mad..." Moulton's voice was rising in pitch, listening to himself talk, but he only sounded more and more foolish. "An now Curly says you're pushin' yourself on Madame Emma. I don' want you causin' no more trouble. You want gold. You don't have to go very far. There's lotsa gold downriver by Confederate Gulch. You be with your own people. Just so's you put some distance between you an' Varina an' Sime an' me an' that boy." It was a laughable performance. Moulton ended by squawking his words like a parrot, his knobbed head moving up and down with the sound of every syllable, his eye staring sideways, unblinking like a bird, to see what effect his speech was having on Curly Shaw. Curly would remember his speech and repeat it verbatim to Sime and Spud Ervin, who were Moulton's employers-of-the-moment. John Moulton was the perfect parrot. The width of his shoulders and mass of his pectoral muscle were supposed to lend persuasion to his words but it was other people's words that were the width and breadth of John Moulton. This was why he'd been elected sheriff, not for the capacity and independent power of his brain, not for any ability to exercise a threat. He was big enough to be dangerous, greedy enough to be bought, but thoughtless enough to be used.

"Yessir," Lee Cameron snapped a crisp salute to Moulton. It was a deference Moulton expected and he walked away satisfied. The irony of Cameron's gesture was lost on the simple-minded sheriff, but not on Curly whose red face masked low, boiling fury.

Moulton had one more admonition for Emma, "An' you should be more careful who keeps you company, Ma'am." John Moulton bobbed his head all around and replaced his brown hat. He shook an index finger at them all like a first-time school marm whose class misbehaved with impunity behind her back. "Good day, Ma'am."

Curly Shaw lifted his eyebrows and smothered Lee Cameron in a surly stare. "I owe you, Dixieman." He pointed his index finger like a pistol and wiggled his middle finger to pull the trigger.

"John Moulton find you?" McGillicuddy had returned.

Cameron was grinning from ear to ear. "He and Shaw want to run me out." The image of Emma cracking the whip pleased him immensely. He was proud of her.

"You running?"

"From them?" Cameron winked complacently. "Does a coon run from a rat?"

The crow's feet at the corners of McGillicuddy's eyes barely turned up with a suggestion of mirth. "Moulton's fronting the badge. You take notice when Sime Ervin sends Curly Shaw on the prowl. Shaw's sneaky smart an' he's a dead shot."

A gunshot broke the stillness. The race had begun. McGillicuddy leapt up on the running board with his spy glass and all eyes focussed on the track. He was shouting and waving his arms like a ten year old in a candy store. At the finish, he fell quiet, the glass glued to his eye. A roan horse won. An ugly dun placed second by a nose, but his supporters, McGillicuddy included, had run to the winners' circle protesting foul. Cameron wondered how much the dapper old gambler had riding on the race.

Emma sat erect and stared blankly ahead. She was enjoying the race about as much as the early Christians enjoyed lions, but this was her Sunday ritual and her moment of revenge on the respectable matrons who restricted sporting women to Jones Street. She enjoyed making their husbands gawk. Cameron reacted predictably. He was jealous and he wondered how many more races he could endure.

Chapter 11

On impulse, Lee Cameron jumped down, adjusted the bit and cheekstraps and climbed back in. The landau swayed with his weight and startled Emma. "What are you doing?"

"It'll take them an hour to decide who won this race, another hour to settle arguments and pay off bets..." He looked sideways to see if he'd insulted her and plunged ahead, "They tell me the Madison valley over the rim is very beautiful." He picked up the reins, backed the bay away from trackside and turned toward the summit. She did not protest. She even smiled faintly and bounced against his arm when the wheels hit the inevitable rocks. The bay pulled eagerly up over the hogback and down a few hundred yards into the valley. Curly Shaw watched them go.

Cameron stopped on a grassy bench that hovered over the Madison Valley. The vista spanned a hundred miles. Red-brown foothills broke away eastward to the river and rolled steeply up again on the other side to the Spanish Peaks and the Madison Range. They loomed ominously above a deep rust rim of bluffs, their snowcapped peaks like hoary sentinels even now in late June. The quiet blue stripe of the Madison River watered a broad green valley where wild game thrived. The waters snaked past groves of gnarled cottonwoods that leaned gracefully over the banks, and ponded where beavers had dammed the flow and where colorful ducks and herons swam. The human noises of the races receded. The murmur of the wild, the rustlings, gurglings, buzzings and twitterings enveloped them. Emma was silent, wrapped in her own thoughts.

Cameron urged the bay on for another mile down a switchback trail toward the rushing river and pulled up. Silently, they stared out at the stark mountains. One lone peak stood out from the rest. He wondered what primeval fires rumbling within the depths of the earth could have raised such a giant, so cold, so alone. He knew what it was to be so alone and to form walls like granite around the powerful emotions he held within.

Emma stared straight ahead. Tentatively, he reached out and touched her cheek.

She stiffened. He drew his hand away.

"I didn't mean to offend." He apologized.

"You didn't offend." She turned great sad eyes upon him. "You don't understand. It's too quick...too sudden." Whatever that meant, she did not explain.

"Have you been here before?" He tried petty conversation.

"Not here. Not this far.... It's not safe for a woman to come out alone." She made no reference to the majesty of the mountains so plainly confronting her. She was like most Varinans, too busy insuring their own safety and survival, to notice the beauty of their surroundings.

With hunched shoulders, elbows on knees, he studied her, trying to comprehend how such a creature of beauty could not help but admire the powerful splendor of the view, how one who grasped her independence so avidly could not respond to this wild and pristine land. She was so near yet so unreachable, inviolable.

He broke the silence, "I would like to see the child. You'll write and tell them I can visit her?"

"You're going back? You just arrived." She turned a full white face upon him.

"As far as St. Louis. When I have enough money, I'll go back. Saint Louis, New Orleans, maybe Galveston, not Atlanta. There's nothing left for me there...."

"I'll write that you can visit her but they think Dubois is her father. I'll not tell them differently. She bears his name."

Dubois again. The past would not disappear. Had he lost so much? Could he not even acknowledge his own child?

They sat there quietly looking, in the warmth of the afternoon with only the hum of the flies, the swish of the horse's tail and the rush of the river waters below, all the subtle symphonies of nature.

Cameron watched her closely and slowly realized from the crimp of her neck and the way she had tilted her head away, that she was crying. She too had walled in her emotions like the granite mountain for too long. Now they began to seep through cracks.

He grew uncomfortable as many men do with such obvious feminine distress. "We'll go back." He picked up the whip. She put her

66

fingers on his arm. "Not yet...We have our memories too. Why didn't you write?" That question again, the same that she had asked yesterday and that made him feel guilty. The horse stepped forward a few steps and stopped.

The question jolted Lee Cameron and he sputtered an answer. "I did write—when I could find a pen and ink and some paper, and I gave the letters to the Seargeant Major to post." It wasn't very often. He admitted to himself that the Sergeant Major had probably opened them, read them aloud and laughed. He'd done it himself—there was so little to read, so little to smile at—but Cameron had trusted him to reseal and post the letters.

Her tears dried. She continued bravely. "I was so lonely. Dubois helped, but he was never much of a husband except in name. I suffered.... I was so alone." She arched her neck. It was gesture that he remembered well—the stubborn pride would not let go. "Seeing you, brings back what I tried so hard to forget." She stared down at her fingers that twisted awkwardly in the laces of her purse.

"I suffered too." He had to force the words out from his throat. What had happened in the war was to him something too sacred for casual speech. He had never spoken of it before to any but his closest comrades-in-arms, and most of them were dead. But it was his turn to remember. He would not let her go without knowing his story. "Hear me out." He pulled her around gently to face him and lifted her chin so her eyes met his. His words came out haltingly in awkward staccato measures. "I was hit.. at Fredericksburg...in the shoulder...near Marye's Heights—We gave Burnside everything we had when I was hit again....in the head this time and I don't remember much else except that I bled and I screamed and Ezra White carried me away. He didn't have a stretcher.... How he even lifted my weight, I'll never know but I'll be forever grateful... You remember Ezra....from Columbus...." His next words came slowly, softly, from quivering lips and his eyes settled away from her on the granite mass of eternal mountain. "Ezra died at Gettysburg. I'm here and he's dead.... Where is God's justice in that?" He stopped then and shook his head at the incomprehensibility of it all. But then his voice rose in muffled anger. "When I came to, I was in a farmhouse near Warrenton. I'd lost my unit, my horse, my saber....Some scavenger even took my boots....I had a hole in my hip and a crack in my skull." He stopped again, breathed deeply and turned repentant eyes on her. "There was old Mrs. Carter, the farmer's wife, and two old female slaves...Dicey and Kate. They nursed me. After that, no, I didn't write."

A shot rang out from the rocks on the divide and a splinter flew from off the fender of the landau. Cameron cursed, grabbed Emma and pushed her to the floorboards. The horse started and nearly crashed a wheel on the stump of an old bull pine. Cameron reached for his Navy Colt but it was useless at that range. He didn't have a rifle. He grabbed the reins to steady the wobbling rig and looked up. Curly Shaw was standing in full view, rifle cocked for a second shot and Lee Cameron was in his sights. Cameron whipped the horse forward and Shaw's shot missed.

Curly Shaw shouted down at them. "I heard you're a great warrior, Cameron! You scared? Varina's a dangerous place for cowards. Shoot back or get out!" He put up the rifle. "An' tell the pretty lady, I don't appreciate gettin' swung on by a woman...Next time, I might aim at that shiny gold trinket hangin' around 'er neck but then she's Spud Ervin's gal an' I wouldn't want to mess Spud Ervin's gal." Peels of laughter echoed off the rocks. "But you're dispensable, Dixieman. Don't you forget. Mr. Ervin give me the order, I'll shoot you like a fat rooster in a hen house, an' Moulton'll be none the wiser." He turned on his heel and disappeared over the crest.

Blood flooded the veins in Lee Cameron's head. He was burning mad and he couldn't mask his rage. His knuckles were white. There were reddish bruises on Emma's arms, the imprint of his fingers where he'd grabbed and pushed her, "I'm sorry—I've hurt you." He looked away, swearing that he should have come better armed and furious at Shaw's suggestion of cowardice.

His heart pounded as he tried to apologize. He spat his words, "I didn't plan today this way. Like the war, I didn't plan that either." Humiliated and angry, he couldn't face her. With his emotions raging, he jumped impetuously at the easiest solution. "I'll leave tomorrow and Sheriff Moulton will be happy and you can marry Ervin and forget me."

She stared back at him wide-eyed, "Load your rifle, Captain Leland Cameron, and stand and fight for what's yours. I'd no more marry Spud Ervin than a bare-assed grizzly!"

Cameron dropped the reins in shock. Riverboat, bull-whacker language! Where had she learned that?

In a tumult of conflicting emotions he turned on her. The golden locket glimmered on her white neck. "Dammit woman, you do know how to rile a man!" Abruptly, he cupped her face in his hands and kissed her firmly on the mouth. Her lips lingered there. When they came apart, she looked up at him, white-faced. A wind had picked up. She pulled her shawl around her shoulders and held it there. She lifted her hand. He thought he was going to be slapped but she lay it gently against his cheek and kissed him back. She drew back and they stared at each other for a long moment, afraid to lose the ecstasy of the moment and shaking from the cool of the wind.

Lee Cameron finally broke the spell. "It's getting colder. I'll take you home." Nothing more was said. They left the grey horse trackside for McGillicuddy.

Cameron helped Emma out of the landau and onto the green porch. She shook his hand, thanked him formally and but didn't invite him in. Rachel ushered her inside.

He led the bay to the stable in the alley behind the house. His hands trembled as he fumbled with the harness buckles. The touch of her lips, the supple feel of her arms in his grip and the soft pressure of her hand on his haunted him. He took a rag and rubbed down the bay, round and round, the motion of his arm turning and returning like the churning of his brain, like the chapters of his life folding back, circling, repeating and marching on.

A fat rat, attracted by some spilled grain, ran past him out the door. Impulsively, he grabbed a broom to kill it and ran after it. It fled away toward the creek. He should have shot the rat too, like Spud Ervin, like Curly Shaw. He stopped just short of the Creek to regroup. What a fool he must seem, allowing Emma, a woman, to chastise Curly Shaw, and him without his gun, unable to defend himself, rooting around like a tomcat after a scampering mouse, leaving his coat and what little gold that he had with the bay on the cross ties alone in the barn! He replaced the rake and returned to the stable to retrieve his coat and put the horse away, but the activity did not settle his emotions.

When the bay was dry, he led him to his stall, and wiped the sweat from his face with the sleeve of his coat and threw it over his shoulders. His heart wouldn't stop hammering and his mouth ran dry. Activity was what he craved, enough to deflate his emotions through sheer exhaustion. He walked across the street to the creek. A good splash of cold water on his face and a drink always renewed him. Most of the townspeople were still at the races. Even the Citadel was closed. There was nothing to do until people returned.

He continued along Sunshine Creek. It was aptly named and a happy place. He picked up a flat rock and made it skip across the ripples, like he did when he was a small boy. He wished his life was like that stone, touching down for the brief happy moments and sailing swiftly over the long years of anxiety and loss. A magpie pecked a grub while its mate looked down from a nearby willow. Should he dare to hope for a mate like that?

Pink phlox, yellow marsh marigolds, brown-eyed susans, wild roses and cow parsnips, a profusion of color, surrounded him. An occasional cottonwood sprinkled the wild flowers with shade. The flowers massed together; birds paired and flew in flocks. They were never alone like him. The flowers were beautiful, like the woman. He broke off a few flowers. Their graceful faces stared up at him. He realized he couldn't leave Varina, not now, not until he could resolve the burning in his soul, not until he could settle with honor the question of Spud Ervin and Curly Shaw, not until he could marry Emma Dubois, reclaim his daughter, build a home.

Cameron looked up beyond Sunshine Creek to the north, at Outlaw Bar. This was a stark hump in the land, grey and bare, an ugly protrusion of tailings and debris, heaved to the side when the creek roared in flood. It was a graveyard. Cameron had heard of it. Vigilantes had hung five road agents and buried them there. Five wooden markers perched on the hill. They commanded Cameron's line of vision now.

He forded the creek then bent down for another drink. When he stood up again, the five graves stood grimly outlined against the white-tufted clouds of the afternoon sky. Cameron hiked up the hill. Loose gravel skidded out from beneath his boots. He slipped and righted himself and climbed higher to the gruesome markers.

From a distance the graves looked forbidding. Up close, they were dirty and poor. Weeds poked out from beneath their footings and dust blew over the cracked and stony ground. The names and dates were burned crudely into the hardwood—George Ives, Clubfoot George Lane, Buck Stinson and Jack Gallagher. The other name, Cameron didn't recognize. He had heard of Ives in Fort Benton. He was notorious. He was the first man hung by a miners' court in Varina for brutally torturing, murdering and robbing a seventeen-year-old boy. His execution launched the Vigilante war on lawlessness that made Varina livable for decent folk. The barrooms of Fort Benton and Helena were still alive with the stories of Gallagher and Stinson. They had gunned down the deputy sheriff in cold blood and broad daylight. All these had come to Idaho Territory—Montana Territory was established the following year—to escape prison or execution in the States. They saw to it that no man carrying gold could leave Varina with his riches. He would be found dead on the trail, pockets empty. Or he would not be found at all, left for the wolves and the mountain lions to hide the grizzly tale. This was why Sime Ervin had never shipped his gold. He would have lost it to the thieves.

Cameron had seen cemeteries before. He'd visited the graves of soldiers who had fought beside him, of his own savior, Ezra White, of his younger brother, dead of swamp fever at the age of twelve, and of his mother, dead of a broken heart so they told him when she heard he had died. This was different. These men had died hung by the neck. These were the men Sheriff Moulton had described. They had been executed. They slept in barren, lonely graves. Union and Secesh, Democrats and Republicans, the Vigilantes had joined together in condemning them.

Beyond the graves were two empty ditches and signs of digging. Mining activity? In a graveyard? Suddenly Cameron understood. The good folk of Varina had removed the coffins of their loved ones from the company of these criminals and not bothered to fill in the holes. They gaped up at him menancingly like trap doors. He could end up here. Moulton, Ervin and Shaw would laugh at that. Lee Cameron vowed that this would never happen. Varina had schools and churches and men like Glenby and McGillicuddy now who would build up what these men would have torn down—and he could be one of them. And Varina had women like Emma Dubois who should love a man, mother a family and build a home—and he would be part of her life. But doubt still haunted him because justice in this far place was still raw. Moulton could be bought like Clubfoot George and Ervin was rich like Henry Plummer, the bandit sheriff of Bannack. Cameron turned to go. Varina was a better place because these men had died. But there were still thieves and murderers walking the streets. There always would be. He thought of Spud Ervin—the seeds were there. Cameron's handful of flowers were wilting now and his emotions had calmed to rumblings. He left the flowers on Gallagher's grave and the wind whipped up and blew them into the creek where they floated away on the ripples of the water. Cameron sauntered along the crest of the Outlaw Bar back toward the town. Varina lay quiet now. Shafts of pink light darted from the garnet outcroppings of rock. The dull buildings shone rose-colored in their reflected light. The sun was still high. Buildings spilled down the bare mountainside toward Chinatown, the brown ribbon of Garnet Creek and the gold diggings. At its foot, the Helena/Benton road crossed a log bridge into town. Lee Cameron inhaled deeply. Could he call this place home?

He continued on. Road and bridge were deserted this Sunday afternoon and the only traces of humanity were the bizarre scents of pork, rice, onions and ginger root and the clanking, alien noises of the Chinese. Sunday was a work day for them and they bustled about like so many industrious insects. Cameron started up the road and approached the bridge. An animal groan, a sucking sound stopped him in his tracks.

71

Chapter 12

Cameron approached the bridge warily. Chinatown was distant but this sound emanated from nearby. The brush by the bridge was a perfect place for a thief to hide—he shoved his arms into the sleeves of his coat and he ran his hands down the gold sewn between the seams. For the second time this Lord's Day, he reached for his Navy Colt.

Cameron circled out into the brush at the water's edge downstream from the bridge until he had a clear view beneath. He saw no one. He listened. The water babbled. Another groan and a strange voice stammering off to his right—he veered that way, sneaking like a skirmisher, well-hidden in the scrub willow and the rushes that choked the junction of the two creeks. The ground oozed noisily under his boots. He could not be quiet. The voice was clearer now. It was high, excited and foreign and spoke in accented English. Whoever it was did not hear Cameron.

He broke from hiding onto the graveled bank. A terrified Chinese leaped up and fled. He glimpsed the conical hat, the streak of black hair and rounded torso disappearing into the bushes. It was a woman. The men wore pigtails and this one's hair was loose. A few splashes and she was gone.

The dark form of a man lay huddled at the edge of Garnet Creek. Clumps of mud and weeds stuck in the folds of his skin and matted his hair. He looked as if he had been drowned although the creek was not deep enough for that. A black quilted cotton jacket, gift of the frightened Chinese, covered a shivering body. Cameron could hear the teeth chatter. He came closer, stooping to see how badly the man was hurt. He choked and gurgled as if someone had held his head under water and he had struggled to get free like and beaver in a trap, then gasping, had been left in the creek to die.

Cameron wiped back the hair from the face and stiffened in shock. Here was Patrick Lysaght, his sentimental Irish drinking partner of the night before. The old man had suffered drastically from exposure. The icy mountain runoff was frigid. Who would attack an innocent old man and leave him to die? Cameron answered the question himself. The old man was rich. He had displayed his wealth too often and too openly after the card game. Eager thieves still populated Varina. How long had Lysaght been out here?

Suddenly a brown mongrel leaped out from under the bridge. The dog ran up and started frantically licking Lysaght's face.

Cameron spoke, "Rest easy, old man, we'll get you in. Keep your secrets private next time. Your tongue wagged worse than the tail on that dog." Pat Lysaght stared up at him without comprehension. The dog slurped water from the creek.

Cameron took off his coat and lay it over Pat Lysaght for added warmth. He took his bearings. He was about fifty feet below the bridge, about half way between a rotting cottonwood stump and a large red flat rock. He scooped up the old man's mangled body, and started up out of the creekbed.

Glenby's stable was a short walk over the bridge, but Chinatown was much closer and smoke curled from the makeshift chimneys of its tiny hovels. Smoke meant fire and fire meant vital heat. And Chinatown meant anonymity. Sheriff Moulton would leave the Chinese alone. Someone had almost killed Pat Lysaght. Cameron headed for Chinatown and the mongrel dog followed.

He burst with the filthy form of Lysaght through the door of the first smokey hovel. Six startled faces turned to stare. Cauldrons filled with hot water spewed steam and a large stove rimmed all around with triangular racks for heating irons filled the center of the room. This was a laundry and its warmth was welcome but language was a barrier.

"Blankets, get blankets, we need blankets and water, lots of hot water." Cameron shouted an order and repeated his words for fear of not being understood. Blank yellow faces stared back at him but the Chinese proprietor arrived from around a corner and had no trouble with English.

"Yessi, yessi, blankets and water.... Water right here all around. And plenty clean sheets." He indicated a line of copper tubs not yet filled with local laundry and clapped his hands and spouted a string of cacophonous syllables.

A man returned immediately with an old army cot. He placed it in the center of the room near the stove. Cameron laid the old man down gently, lifted his coat from the battered body and started to probe for further injury.

"No, no, let my daughta do." The Chinese pulled him away.

At this a diminutive figure in black—the girl by the creek?—entered. She placed a gentle hand on Lysaght's brow and his eyelids flickered. Bewildered, Cameron stepped back.

"I Fu Ling." He bowed deeply. "My daughta, Mai Ling, very good nurse. She learn medecine in Shanghai."

Cameron stood back while the girl unbuttoned the black quilted jacket and removed it. Lysaght moaned deleriously. The shirt beneath was torn in several places, but it wasn't until she cut it off that Cameron saw the bullet hole. The icy water had washed away the blood and slowed the bleeding. Lysaght was lucky. The hole was on the right side, about an inch below the waist and the bullet had missed the bone and gone right through, not unlike Cameron's old hip wound.

Cameron stood watching the Chinese girl. Images of the smelly, filthy, battlefield hospitals loomed in his mind. There, Lysaght, like too many of his countrymen, would've died. There, he, Lee Cameron, would've died, had Ezra not carried him to a Warrenton farmhouse. Here, in Chinatown, in Varina, Montana Territory, far from the civilization he knew, an alien woman's practiced hands worked diligently, undressing, sponging, wrapping. She was gentle and considerate of the old man's pain. Lysaght was awake now, but in shock. Another Chinese entered with a cup of steaming broth and a water pipe.

"He take this....no pain...he sleep good." Fu Ling lifted Pat Lysaght's head to the liquid and the old man sipped and swallowed. Then the Chinese put the pipestem between his teeth.

"You breathe. You sleep." Cameron watched. Opium, they were giving him opium. But Pat Lysaght had stopped moaning.

"He rest quiet. He need sleep."

Other Chinese chattered and bustled about and took the muddied clothing and put it in a tub to boil. They wrapped the old Irishman in clean white sheets and a woolen blanket. Through it all, Lysaght stared blankly at the activity. The taut muscles of his face had relaxed, but he did not acknowledge Lee Cameron. He said nothing and hours passed. Slowly, his eyes closed and he slept.

There was nothing else for Cameron to do. The finest medical man could not have done more. Cameron thanked Fu Ling and dug deep in his pockets to repay him but all he had was paper. The Chinese shook his head.

"No money. No need. He get well. Then pay."

"Take good care of him....I'll pay you in gold. I'll be at the California Hotel or the Citadel. You come for me there if you need me."

"Yessi, yessi, we know the Citadel. No let Chinee in hotel. When friend betta, we find."

Cameron sensed vaguely that there was another kind of debt to be paid. He was not at all sure what all this meant. Fu Ling ushered him out the door.

Outside again in the crooked, narrow paths of Chinatown, he was lost. Dusk had fallen and the pitiful shanties closed in on him from all sides. Only the vague light from cooking fires and an occasional lantern punctuated the dimness. Cameron was seized by the sudden fear of a flimsy lantern toppling and the whole maze igniting like dry straw. The brown dog moved up beside him like a ghost and rubbed against his leg. Cameron leaned over and scratched its ears.

"Lead me home, boy" He didn't verbalize what else he was thinking—the anguish that gripped him at seeing this innocent old man so abused, the frustration at being Curly Shaw's target, the powerful attraction of a beautiful woman, the lingering anger of a man who had fought his wars and sought only the peace and light of a Sunday afternoon. The attack on Pat Lysaght was worse than war because it was senseless. Glenby, McGillicuddy, Lysaght, even Behnke the gossip, deserved better.

The sun had just set. The dog struck out away from the sunset to the east back toward Varina. He crossed a primitive footbridge, no more than two logs with some planking nailed over them for even footing, and up a narrow footpath. Suddenly, they were at the head of Warren Street. It was only a short walk to the the California Hotel and clean clothes. Cameron went there first, picked up his rifle and checked the chamber. It was empty. He loaded the gun and closed the chamber. He cleaned and reloaded his Navy Colt and shoved it into a hip holster. His short dress cavalry coat hung unbuttoned leaving the gun free to draw. When Cameron finished packing his gear, it was dark. He headed back to the Citadel with all his belongings and the brown dog still trailing at his heels.

The click of the dice, the slap of the cards and the clink of glasses were his only greeting until McGillicuddy spotted him across the room. "I brought in your horse. He took me to Glenby's. That where you want him?"

"Yes. Thanks." Cameron was standing with his back to the wall scrutinizing each member of the crowd. McGillicuddy eyed the dog

75

who clung to Cameron's side. He took out a cigar and placed it unlit between his teeth.

"You're late. Left the races early you two did?" McGillicuddy lifted an eyebrow and gently pried further, "Emma came in without you."

"I took her home." Cameron signalled toward the back room. "Can I leave my gear here and can we talk alone?" McGillicuddy sensed the urgency and followed, reaching behind to close the door. He sat back and began to pour two glasses of brandy.

"Pat Lysaght, the old geezer who lost the nugget last night...I found him in the creek."

"Dead?"

"Just about. Shot through but lucky."

McGillicuddy cursed. "The old fool should've known better, flaunting that nugget like stupid John Moulton flaunts his badge for every greedy mucker to see.... Where is he now?"

"Chinatown.... at a laundry....It was the nearest place with a fire going. He was wet and cold. Chinaman's daughter is some kind of nurse. She cleaned him up and drugged him with something...I think it was opium. He was asleep when I left."

"He say who did it?"

"He didn't even recognize me." Cameron's dark eyes shot sparks. He was angry. "Shouldn't we tell the authorities?"

McGillicuddy struck a match against his desk, held it to a lamp then to his cigar and puffed the first few breaths. He would not be rushed. Before speaking, he laughed, "Authorities—you know who that is." He answered his own question. "John Moulton. Stupid, simple-minded, bigoted—he wants to lock you in jail!"

Cameron acceded. To John Moulton's simple comprehension, he, himself, any outsider, would be suspect.

McGillicuddy spoke again. "Hank Ryder comes back, we tell him. He's the Territorial Marshal. He's nobody's fool and he's honest. But he's not always here. He's got a wide jurisdiction and he travels lots. He took a prisoner up to Helena."

The dog lay down quietly with his nose on McGillicuddy's boot. "Who's this?"

Cameron shrugged. "He followed me from the Creek when I brought Lysaght in. Hasn't left me since. Did Lysaght have a dog?"

"Could have. I didn't notice." McGillicuddy was still puffing on his cigar and staring at the wall. "You can leave him here. I feed him, he'll stay." He lifted an eyebrow and spoke from the side of his mouth. "Lysaght turns up missing, folks'll wonder what you're doing with his dog. We'll go see Lysaght in the morning...You look tired. Get some sleep."

But Cameron didn't move. His dark eyes stared at the steam pumping from the kettle on the stove.

McGillicuddy sensed his uneasiness. "You don't like it here, say so. Don't you up and leave without tellin' me—I'd have to find a replacement. Varina's rough but she's young and she's building and I like you. The job isn't what you expected is it? It's new and takes some piecing together and settling down."

Cameron still didn't speak and sucked in his cheeks as if smothering words and thoughts that he couldn't verbalize.

"What is it?" And then McGillicuddy knew. "Her, it's her, isn't it? You're worried because of her. She tell you to go? She playing an ace to your deuce?" He put a steadying hand on Cameron's shoulder. "You leave her to me. I been watching out for her a long time."

Cameron went out to the gaming tables but he couldn't concentrate on the game. Presently McGillicuddy came out too. He sat himself at a black boxlike piano and began to plunk away unevenly. The melody was "Beautiful Dreamer", too slow for the miners, too sweet for the toughs, pre-war, sentimental stuff. And Dan McGillicuddy sang. His voice was harsh and breathless, punctuated with coughs and interrupted by puffs on the ubiquitous cigar. The piano was out of tune.

But it was a good song for the goldfields. All these men were dreamers. They had visions of gold running inches deep in their pans, like McGillicuddy, like himself, Lee Cameron. He was a dreamer too and he was angry with himself for it. He should know better. He'd been to war. Yet the sight of the woman waylaid the ugly memories and made cruel reality fade. He watched her now and he craved the good life too, not for himself anymore, but for her.

She was seated at the tables. He took a seat at her side. He could smell her perfume and feel the brush of her arm against his and even see the mist as her breath split the smoky air. She dealt and the stakes rose and fell. The closeness of her soothed like spring rain and he felt better but he still wondered about the intentions of Dan McGillicuddy. McGillicuddy favored Cameron, gave him a lucrative job and a future, wanted him to stay in Varina in spite of Sime Ervin, in spite of Curly Shaw, in spite of John Moulton with his threats of banishment. Why? Cameron cashed in his chips and asked Garrity for a drink. He spent the rest of the evening sitting in a corner, head resting in his hands, drinking and dreaming, watching Emma, the way she smiled, the curve of her neck, the soft rise and fall of her breasts as she bent low over the green cloth to rake in her winnings. He fell asleep listening to the deep peels of thunder in his heart. McGillicuddy had reasons Lee Cameron would never suspect.

When the last client left, it was nearly dawn. Emma had walked home with Garrity, the big bartender, and Sanford, the bouncer. McGillicuddy was closing up when the dog bounded into the room. McGillicuddy had turned him loose and he nuzzled the sleeping Lee Cameron.

"He needs a walk. Want to go see Lysaght? You need a witness for what he has to say. Nobody here will believe a bloody Chinaman and a gun-toting gambler fresh off the boat, even if you are their fellow Dixielander!"

"Let's go." Cameron dragged himself to his feet. His muscles ached; his head throbbed.

They headed for the door. "Not that way. Best stay out of sight. Someone wants him dead. We let them go on believing he's dead." They went out the back door, unobserved. The dog ran on ahead and Cameron thought they might have lost him. Suddenly, he dashed out from behind a building like a bloodhound on a scent. He knew where he was going.

Chapter 13

The alleys of Chinatown were dismal even though dawn was breaking but the dog was going to see his master and found his way easily. Cameron and McGillicuddy followed.

Even at this early hour, the Chinese businesses were humming. Cameron marvelled at the energy of the pigtailed foreigners. To him they were oddities. He had never seen them before he arrived in Benton where there were one or two, but here in the gold mines, where gunpowder was needed, there were crowded villages full of diminutive little bodies. They were experts with black powder and they were up before dawn, before the first rooster crowed, hauling water and wood. He could smell food cooking and hear the scrapes of their crude wooden buckets. They carried everything in those buckets and used pack animals only for long hauls. The smell here was spicy and not unpleasant. There was no stench of whiskey like in the saloons. But the noise was deafening. Men were setting out for the gold fields, pans and picks clanking and rattling, animals braying, feet scuffling, voices chattering and yelling their strident syllables in all directions. They kept ducks and chickens, pigs, cats and dogs, all underfoot and conducted much of their mysterious business under flimsy canopies in the street.

Fu Ling was not there when Cameron and McGillicuddy arrived at the laundry, but a man named Sung was. He spotted them immediately—they were the tallest people in Chinatown—and motioned them inside. Mercifully, he spoke a broken English.

"Missa he much betta."

Lysaght was sitting up propped against a pile of silk pillows. He smiled gleefully when he saw the dog.

"Shamy begod! I was worried for ye. Ye run when I told ye? 'Tis a smart bitch, ye are." He toussled the dog's thick ruff. The animal licked his face and thwacked his tail against the floor.

"And who's this ye be bringin'?" It was dark in the laundry. The air was steamy and the walls wet. Cameron and McGillicuddy stepped into the light of a lantern. "Me friends from last night!" Lysaght had skipped Sunday and didn't remember his own rescue. "Come in, come in."

Cameron stooped under the low door jamb. The room was hot and humid and stuffed with ironing tables and piles of clean linens and the tiny Chinese who ironed and folded. Candles shed an eerie flickering light. Lysaght was propped on pillows in the corner of the room. "How you feel, Lysaght?"

"Hotter than Judas roastin' in hellfire. Chokin' on the steam I am, and sweatin' like a workhorse on a treadmill. 'Tis the fresh mountain air I'm cravin' so I can fill me old lungs!" He coughed lightly and winced when he motioned Cameron to come closer but the blush was back in his wrinkled cheeks. "I'll not be walkin' today, but I'll mend...." He cocked an index finger at Cameron and shook it. "Now I don't want to be seemin' ungrateful to me hosts, but 'tis a strange bunch they are... A potion they give me and makes me drink—foul-tasting it is. And rice that's brown like the soil under your feet! And tea that's green as shamrocks! 'Tis uncivilized, savage fare.... But I'm glad to see ye, Lee Cameron. And Mr. McGillicuddy ye've brought. Sit down."

McGillicuddy sat on an old milking stool that stood by the bed. He took off his coat, folded it neatly over his arm and shoved his pipe between his teeth, Cameron remained standing. "Lysaght, you almost died!"

"Aye, almost. But I did not. Like playin' the cards." He winked at Cameron. "I almost won, but I did not." Lysaght was not concerned. He paused and glared at Cameron, a wild light in his old blue eyes. "Ye can doff your coat too, Captain Lee Cameron. Me fever's risin' just watchin' ye sweat....and listen carefully...I need explain before they set me dreamin' again.... I've a job for ye. I want ye to sit my claim before they jump me." He was a true gold digger—His claim and his gold counted as much or more than his life.

But Cameron was new to the goldfields and not sure what the old man was asking. He looked to McGillicuddy for an explanation. Lysaght continued to scratch the dog. "We've a strike, Shamy! We're rich!" His voice was shrill and raucous. He was grinning like a clown.

"Lysaght, do you remember what happened?" McGillicuddy was losing his patience.

Lysaght stared back glassily. "Today,... today, I have to get a man

80

on me claim today, I say. There's gold there, lots of gold!"

"You tell us who did this, and I'll send a man out."

"Not just any man, no!"

The two older men glared at each other. They left Cameron completely out of the conversation.

"Who did this?" McGillicuddy repeated. The old man refocussed. His glaring eyes shrank back into their sockets and he lifted himself on his elbows. "Worms! Vipers! The she-devil Victoria's henchman! The accursed English yoke that saps the fair, green sod of Erin and sends her children naked and starvin' across the farthest seas!...." His voice fell off abruptly, "I did not see who did it. If I knew I'd tell ye true. But I have me suspicions! Liar Ervin says I been sniping his gold!"

Sniping—mining someone else's claim—It was a term Cameron had heard before and a killing offense.

Lysaght continued, "This Liar Ervin is a cardinal sinner. Sends his demon, Shaw, to do his mischief. A disgrace to his good Irish surname, Shaw!" At the mention of Shaw, Cameron started. Lysaght continued. His eyes fairly bulged and his voice pitched high with excitement like a preacher spouting hellfire. He reached up, grabbed Cameron by the lapels, pulled him close and hissed into his ear, "The saints of the Lord shall condemn them to eternal flame...I found the lode—the mother lode, I did. He found out, the Liar Ervin, but it's on my claim and coveteous of his neighbor he is." He lowered his voice almost to a whisper. "Liar Ervin is a wily fiend.... I should never have showed him my deed but I fought fair. Hurt him, swung me pick at his rangy legs. I hit him too and watched his black sinner's blood spurtin' over his boots. He took to bed and is limpin' hereafter, that I know. If I were younger, I'd have licked the brute sure an' he'd be walkin' God's good earth no more." He paused to catch his breath.

McGillicuddy spoke an aside to Cameron. "It's an old standing feud. He calls Sime Ervin 'Liar' to his face...." He indicated Lysaght's bandages. "But Sime didn't do this." And then to Lysaght, "I hear you old man, but Cameron found you below the bridge on the Helena/Fort Benton road. Ervin's camp is up above Highland."

Lysaght ignored McGillicuddy, "So it is, and so is mine. Cunning that Liar Ervin! Wants to kill me, and he almost did." He keened his eyes hard on Lee Cameron. "Young Captain Lee, ye must sit me claim. An abandoned claim is free for the takin'. 'Tis the law. Patrick Lysaght will die a pauper's death before he gives up his claim to a villain and a knave." He hung desperately on Cameron's sleeve. "'Tis bounden I'll be for life to ye, my boy."

Cameron thought the old man was delerious, that the opium had affected his brain.

McGillicuddy cut in. "He's right, Cameron. He's got to get somebody on that claim or he'll lose it."

Cameron felt foolish. Lysaght's flaming oratory unnerved him. He would've laughed but for the gravity of McGillicuddy's tone.

"I'm a gambler. I play the cards. I don't know anything about mining." Cameron had heard of "gold fever" and the obsession it caused but Lysaght's single-minded fanaticism was new to him. It was a deep emotional attachment like close friendship, religious devotion or passionate love.

The old Irishman implored. "Ye don't have to dig, boy. Ye just have to be there. An' ye can shoot. They all know that. Ye have your Colt I see. Possession is the law..." He calmed a little and lifted an eyebrow toward Cameron, "But were I you, I'd dig a bit to pass the hours. Down deep 'tis rich, the ore. It lurks in the cracks like the black peat of Erin, but you wash it down and it gleams golden like the castle spires of Cashel!"

Cameron was tempted to laugh but kept a straight face. The old man was serious.

Lysaght's clear blue eyes narrowed to slits. "Lee Cameron, I've a bargain to strike...'Tis a gambler ye are... Sit on me claim. There's gold there.—I'll tell ye where to look. Ye stay with her 'til me head and me hip heals and I can walk....ye pan...ye sluice...ye blast if ye takes a notion, I've a good rocker hidden. Whatever ye takes, ye keep. Ye've seen me nugget. There be more of the same, enough gold to pave the streets of Dublin! An' ye won't be havin' to split it wi' Mr. McGillicuddy here. Ye be bettin' on a sure thing, lad.... And I've a snug cottage."

The mining life, the wet feet, the cold hands, the flour and water diet, the sleeping under leaky canvas did not appeal to Lee Cameron. He'd had enough of that in the army camps. But the soup-stained and sweaty sheets of the California Hotel were no better. He looked to McGillicuddy for support, but McGillicuddy agreed with Lysaght. "It's a sure stake, Cameron. No wager there. No house percentage. You'll make more than you ever would working for me."

A jumble of thoughts pounded at Cameron's brain. He would be working the claim adjacent to Sime Ervin's, the man whose son he had just shot night before last, the man who had tried to run Lysaght off. Would someone try to run him off too? Had this occurred to McGillicuddy? He wondered.

"I could get killed. Someone tried to kill Pat Lysaght!" Cameron repeated the frightening truth, but neither Lysaght nor McGillicuddy blinked an eye.

"'Twas but a puny scrape! Ye scared, boy?"

Cameron, the soldier, straightened like a ramrod and his eyes flared. He would not give Pat Lysaght's question the satisfaction of a verbal answer.

The old brow furrowed. The old eyes crinkled. "Aye, I challenged ye. Had I a glove, I'd shake it under yer crooked nose and smack it across yer handsome face...I talk too much and I get away with it—comes from livin' alone and outlivin' the rest of ye rascals. I'm old. I be three score and ten this year. But I've never turned me back on a fight and I'm still alive. When it's me time the blessed Lord will take me as I lay in me bed." Then he glared at Lee Cameron with eyes that shot streaks of fire. "Ye don't want to guard my claim. Are ye afraid to die, Captain Leland Cameron?"

All through this speech, Cameron's fury boiled higher. Lysaght had blocked any possible retreat. If Cameron refused now he was a branded coward, like a deserter who fled under fire, disgraced. The Confederate Army executed cowards who deserted their fellows in the heat of battle. They knelt them down, blindfolded them and the sharp-shooters took aim and fired. Death was swift and bloody. How dare this old man besmirch his fighting record! Cameron clenched his teeth and balled his fists. He would have liked to strike out but could prove nothing by attacking an ailing old man.

Lysaght rambled on. "They tried to kill me, but they didna. They killed Liege O'Connor who came with me all the way from Galway. Like me brother he was and always seein' golden rainbows in the heavens beyond the clouds, but he chattered too much like I did last night—'tis a fault we Irish harbor. We be the world's finest orators! An' poor Liege was never a fighter. Had to do the fightin' misself. We Lysaghts were warriors for three hundred years, in all holy Ireland's wars and some that weren't hers. Ye're a soldier, a fightin' man, like us, with a soldier's honor to uphold, Lee Cameron. Ye respect duty and courage and bravery. And ye're honest, like McGillicuddy here. Ye won't steal me bare. I was eyein' ye last night. Ye didna line your pockets with the house's winnings. Ye locked them in the safe....And they'll not try to kill ye—Ye're too good with a gun. But sure as the demons fry in the fires of hell, they'll jump me claim if nary a soul is there."

McGillicuddy was nodding in agreement but Cameron glowered. One day in town and he had already assumed a reputation as a gunman. Another day in town and he was branded a coward. And to clear his good name, on the third day, he was banished to the mountains just when Emma Dubois started to favor his fumbling advances. The last thing he wanted to do was ride shotgun on a gold mine. But they didn't leave him much choice. So much for courting Emma Dubois. So much for riding Glenby's black mare.

McGillicuddy twirled the ends of his mustache and removed his cigar from between his teeth as he did only for his most serious pronouncements. "It's a great favor you'll do for him, Cameron, and you'll earn a good stake. Try it for one week. He won't be bedridden forever. I'll send Stanford out to pace you on Saturday next and I'll put in a good word with Emma."

"You better. And tell Rob Glenby I still want to ride his horse...."

McGillicuddy nodded, but Pat Lysaght couldn't resist having the last word, "Ye sit me claim, God will reward ye, my son, one hundredfold! 'Tis Pat Lysaght's vow."

Cameron somehow sensed God's presence more in the feminine curves of Emma Dubois and the sleek lines of the black horse than in Lysaght's cold, illusive gold.

He muttered to himself. He still had not agreed but he had no way out. If he was to maintain his self-respect, Lee Cameron could not refuse. McGillicuddy slapped him on the shoulder suddenly, shook his hand and was gone out the door back to the Citadel to count last night's winnings. There was no one to notice the scowl on Cameron's face in the dark steamy half-light of the Chinese laundry.

Chapter 14

When he stepped outside, a cold night breeze chilled the dampness on his skin and Lee Cameron pulled on his coat. He checked the load in his Navy Colt, shoved it back into its holster and buttoned the flap. With Shamy at his heels, Cameron trudged wearily back to the California House. The fatigue of the last twenty four hours overtook him. Even a lumpy straw mattress and stained sheets that smelled of other men's sweat along with the noise that leaked through the paper-thin raw plank walls, couldn't keep him awake. He collapsed.

The clerk eyed him when he emerged at noon to pay his bill.

"Sleep well?" He spoke in a voice loud enough to be heard across the street and his tone was intrusive. "Headed for the diggin's like all the rest. Better off here, you know. Earn more money right here in Varina than most of 'em do sloggin' around in the mud." The voice vibrated in Cameron's ears like the squeak of a whetstone. He counted out some bills.

"Cost you two more in paper."

Everything irritated. Cameron nodded solemnly, counted out the money and swore under his breath.

From the hotel, Cameron headed for the Citadel. He'd left his rifle in McGillicuddy's back room. McGillicuddy was there when he entered, slowly scraping gold dust from a pair of hand scales into rawhide pokes. A thin wisp of smoke rose from his cigar which lay in a tray at the side of his desk.

"Just a minute, Cameron. Close the door gently, gently so the draft don't scatter the dust....I have something for you." His words were muffled. He shuffled over to a big mahogony armoire and pulled out a Winchester 66 and a small arsenal of ammunition. It was a new gun, the latest model breech-loader and repeating rifle. It looked huge in McGillicuddy's small hands.

"Your old Enfield's not worth a Confederate sou. Misfires, jams... s'why you Rebels lost the War." He held out the new gun to Lee Cameron. "Take this... And if I were you I'd buy extra cartridges for that Colt on your hip."

Lee Cameron stiffened. He was not accustomed to taking charity. "Thanks, but I don't need another gun."

"Yes, you do. Shaw caught you on the bench yesterday perched out there like a duck in a shootin' gallery. Emma told me. You wanna get her killed? Defend yourself, man! Like you did in the saloon. With that old gun you couldn't have hit 'im if you tried. There are bears and wolves out on that mountain. They'll come after you, or maybe that Ervin kid'll take a better aim than Curly Shaw."

Reluctantly, Cameron accepted the gun. The Winchester was a beautiful piece, with polished walnut stock and oiled, gleaming barrel. What the Confederate Army could have done with weapons like this! But Cameron didn't really intend to use it. The war was over. He had enough memories hammering in his brain.

"And wear these....There's other ways of dying out here besides bullets." McGillicuddy brought out a brand new pair of gum boots. "Leather don't last long when you're standing in ice water all day. Miners die of pneumonia."

"I'm obliged. I'll stay on Lysaght's claim, but I won't work it."

"You'll change your mind. Take the boots and wear them!"

"And take this." He held out a poke full of gold.

"I don't need that."

"Yes you do. I saw what you have—two night's winnings and notes. Paper's worth nothing." McGillicuddy sensed Cameron's surge of southern pride. "It's a loan. You can pay me back with what you pan."

Reluctantly, Cameron took the poke.

McGillicuddy stopped, picked up his cigar and clamped it tightly in his mouth—the important part of the interview was over. There were just a few more details, "You can stop by Tilton's office, at the Montana Post...Tell 'im I sent you. He has some back issues. Read about the vigilantes—that'll teach you about why you need a good shootin' arm... You have a good coat? Be cold nights."

"I'm wearin' it."

"Sime and Spud are Union men, so get yourself a new coat...green, red, blue, brown but not grey. And buy some flour, coffee and bacon or you'll be eating Lysaght's Irish stew—that's leftover gopher meat boiled down to saddle leather. No Irishman can cook."

"I'll do that." Cameron would do what he pleased. McGillicuddy reminded Cameron of his mother.

"And good luck."

Cameron fetched the little grey and a pack saddle from the livery. Glenby wasn't there. Clem nodded blankly and watched him go. He led the grey to Lamb's store and hitched him at the rail. When he ordered the ammunition, Ed Lamb scratched his bald head and muttered objections, "He's raisin' an army bigger'n Tommy Meagher. Buyin' all my black powder." Meagher was the Territorial Governor who mustered a huge force to fight Indians. Lamb only had half enough powder for Cameron.

"Who'd you say is raisin' an army?" Cameron had a soldier's curiosity.

"Old hermit, Sime Ervin, holes himself up like a lord in a fortress and don't never come out. Crazy old coot. Sent near fifty telegrams to old Injun fighters, Meagher's ole recruits. He didn't find no Injuns to kill, now he's sickin' 'em on us and they're buyin' all my cartridges." Lamb shook his bald head and turned a curious stare on Cameron.

"Plan on doin' some shootin' like t'other night?"

"Not me, I had enough of that in the Army."

"Yer a Dixie boy?.. Guess you swallowed yer share a lead....You pack grain fer 'im?" Lamb indicated the horse. "Grass ain't fit fer goats up where yer goin' lest you want 'im to eat rocks."

Cameron went back for some grain. The grey had a heavy load. Lamb was looking over his shoulder. "That yer dog? Thought he belonged to an older feller named Lysaght."

"He does. The old man's a friend of mine." Lamb followed him like a nosy old maid while he assembled the rest of his gear. Like at Behnke's, Cameron was glad to get away.

Finally, Cameron went by the house on Jones Street. He knocked twice before someone came to the door. It was Rachel who explained that Miss Emma had already left for the Citadel. Captain Cameron had just missed her. What else could go wrong? His spirits sank to bedrock. He told Rachel that he wouldn't be calling for a few days and plodded slowly out to the road, engulfed in his thoughts.

Lysaght was crazy. That's how he saw it. He lived up the mountain, a steep climb and good distance from town. The dog knew the way and romped happily ahead poking his nose into every nook and dashing off with each new scent. Cameron had to prod himself and the grey horse to keep up.

They walked up a narrow path beside Garnet Creek that looked down on Outlaw Bar with its gruesome markers. The road paralleled the creek past Central City, Pine Grove and on up to Highland, the highest settlement at the head of the gulch, just under the cliffs of Lone Peak. Claims and mines, The Cleopatra, the Dobbin, rich old Cruperman's, lined the creekbed all the way. Above Highland, Mary's Lake backed up the creek, but only briefly. Beyond the lake, the creek ran faster and tumbled more wildly over boulders and off ledges and through narrow chutes. The incline grew steeper, rockier and more exposed. Cameron marvelled at the tenacity of old Lysaght, carrying all his supplies and climbing this same track back to his claim, weekly, monthly, sometimes in the dark. He concluded that Lysaght must have a place in town, just wasn't telling anybody.

The track switchbacked constantly between dull grey boulders of sharp black lava rock and silvery limestone. Imprints of soft shells and ancient foliage spattered the exposed surfaces. Vegetation grew sparse. Mosses and lichens grew, yet at one time it must have been teeming with another kind of life, crustaceans, fish, amphibians and strange aquatic plants. Cameron wondered at it all. This was sedimentary strata and contained fossils of an ancient sea whose heaving floor had thrust upward.

The little grey picked his way cautiously and followed Shamy who held his nose to the ground. Suddenly, they rounded a sharp bend and Cameron knew they were approaching Ervin's camp.

A high bench hung like a cornice over a cliff and faced north over Garnet Creek toward its juncture with the Stinkingwater. Much of the camp was still hidden from his view but a gunman manned a platform at the forward lip of the cliff. The position dominated the trail which wound up beneath it from below. It was a perfect defensive position. Cobb and his artillery would've loved it. Cameron wondered if Ervin had thought of artillery—it would have made the position impenetrable and certainly ended Patrick Lysaght's easy access. The guard recognized the dog and motioned them by.

Lee Cameron climbed upward around the next switchback and emerged on a level with the camp itself. It was a large maze of sluices and spillways and clung to the massive face of the cliff like a spider on a wall. A dam had diverted the creek where it poured down a narrow chute and men were shovelling mud from the soggy creekbed into a series of boxes and washing them down with hoses. They had harnessed the force of the gushing water to scour out the old creek bank. At the rear of the camp, nestled into another precipice, Cameron spotted a dugout or a mine adit. It backed into the mountain underground—

there was just enough room for the road to snake by. Immediately above, two log houses nestled beneath the only tree in sight, a giant, lightning-blasted, Ponderosa pine.

Cameron could smell bacon frying and coffee boiling. He heard the clank of picks as two men dug lazily nearby in the side of the cliff. Hard-rock mining—Ervin must be looking for the mother lode, where the quartz vein emerged from the mountain's depths. This was no ordinary placer mine. They were digging the granite and drilling out emplacements for black powder. Cameron spotted the kegs, a full dozen of them. He wondered how many men were working for Ervin. Lamb, the storekeeper, had referred to them as Ervin's army. Anxiously Cameron looked for cover. There was no concealment and there was no silencing the sound of the horse's shod hooves. They were heading straight through the camp.

Another guard, a swarthy hunchback dressed in dirty buckskins waved a greeting from a ledge just above the adit. He had an old Enfield rifle like Cameron's old gun, the same old muzzle-loader that the Confederate States of America had issued to her troops, tucked under his arm. It wouldn't do much damage. Cameron smiled with relief.

The hunchback saw Shamy first. His looked out over the trail, a view that spanned the entire gulch for at least a mile. He recognized the dog and leaned forward on his rifle.

"Where's the ole man?"

"Stayed in town."

"Didn't know he left. If I'd known, I'd have jumped 'is claim." He had a deep beastly laugh. "What's he sendin' a shaggy grayback like you to watch his place for?"

Cameron grimaced—he should have bought the new coat. He hated the grayback comparison. It was insulting. He fired back, "He wants to make me a richer swine than you." The man with the rifle laughed louder—Cameron thought he hadn't understood but gradually, the laughter changed to a scowl. The man was slow but not stupid.

"T'ain't funny, mista."

"And neither was the Confederate Army." Cameron tipped his hat politely and rode quickly out of range.

The road climbed further. Shamy clung to the narrowing creek, only a trickle now, that wound down from another alpine lake around the base of the limestone cliff from the north to the eastern face of the mountain. Cameron could sense the rise in temperature as they escaped from the northerly wind and entered the lee of the mountain. Here the creek disappeared altogether into the bowels of the mountain. The trail clung to the side of a cliff that walled it like a fortress on one side and fell off abruptly on the other. In the dark, it would be impassable for the old Irishman, especially now with a bad hip.

Cameron squinted and began to sweat. The hot morning sun glanced off the granite rocks. Streaks of white and red quartz shone brilliantly: the red was the garnet of Garnet Creek; the white looked like fine marble and reflected the summer heat. The horse was puffing with each stride and Cameron felt his own breath come in short gasps. The climb had exhausted him. It was all quite beautiful but it was a fearful effort and he didn't see anything that looked like gold.

Lysaght's claim was about a quarter mile of rock-filled trail past the crevice where the creek had disappeared. It emerged again from the mountain farther on. At this height, Garnet Creek was hardly a few feet across. It struck Cameron then—there was bubbling in the water—springs? At this altitude? The water was clear and warm. Some internal cauldron was its source. Pat Lysaght was not sluicing or panning here nor had he mucked out springs or creekbed. The water was too pure. Lysaght must be hard-rock mining the cliff face, like Sime Ervin, looking for the mother lode. Remembering the size of his nugget, Cameron suddenly realized he might have found it. Others must suspect it too. Lysaght had been trying for almost twenty years, since Placerville, in California, and he was cagey enough to hide his good fortune, except when he'd been drinking.

Lysaght's camp showed signs of workings at the cliff's base and several yards away the granite was chipped away. Cameron bent down and picked up some shards. Soft clay crumbled between his fingers. Nothing here.

He hobbled the grey and walked over to Lysaght's living quarters. A canvas cloth was draped across two poles forming a makeshift canopy in front of what looked at first glance to be a shallow cave. There was no separate shelter for an animal. When Cameron entered, he saw that the interior and part of the roof were natural rock, a cavelike depression in the cliff. The outside wall was primitive mud brick and straw—and the roof, spruce poles overlaid with sod. A supply of dry firewood was piled under a tarp. There was water seepage at the rear of the cave inside the cabin! It bubbled into a little pool that Lysaght had carefully rimmed with flat stones. A bucket and dipper rested upon the stones for household use. The water then spilled out into a small flume under the side wall and on down the mountain.

The furnishings included a bed of pine bows covered with a thick buffalo robe, a stove ventilated cleanly by a tin-pipe chimney extending through the adobe wall, and several crude crates for chairs, all surprisingly swept spotlessly clean, cleaner than the California Hotel. Equipment was stacked neatly in a corner: several pans, two picks and a sturdy shovel, with more paniers of provisions nearby. Lysaght's clothing hung tidily on antler hooks. An old Winchester, hung on nails horizontally over the door and an Enfield was slung on a peg within easy reach. A frying pan, a coffee pot, a cauldron, some tin plates and cups completed the household effects. Cameron was surprised. Pat Lysaght lived better than most miners who wouldn't have given a care to shelter and nourishment until the deep freeze of winter encased their treasure in ice.

Cameron turned to his horse. "No grass, no water, no place to run." He rubbed the horse's nose. The grey would have a week of enforced rest, but he would thrive on the grain. He unstrapped the pack saddle and mopped the sweat from the horse's back. The saddle he placed under the canvas with the dry firewood but the grain, ammunition and food he brought inside where the dampness wouldn't spoil and rodents wouldn't scavenge. He spent another ten minutes drawing a porcupine quill out of Shamy's nose, then built a fire in the stove and set on the coffee pot. Not even a hot cup of fresh coffee was enough to keep him awake. He stretched out on the buffalo robe and fell asleep.

It was late evening when he awoke. He was cold. The fire had dwindled to coals and the coffee had boiled to grit. The sun's rays slanted from the west casting a vast shadow over this, the eastern face of the mountain. The air was cooler. In spite of the cliff's shadow, there was still plenty of light. It caressed the peaks and seemed to linger there, lengthening the high-altitude day for hours. Summer evenings didn't fade until about ten o'clock. In the soothing twilight, Cameron ate supper and went exploring.

Shamy followed. The dog poked his sore nose into every cranny. There wasn't much to see, only granite, gneiss, some limestone, a high talus slope—Cameron didn't know one rock from the other. They were just there, mute testimony to ages past. But as he walked around the south side of the cliff, he saw the sun setting in the west. It sank slowly behind the ridges of the Beaverhead, like a flaming frigate sliding slowly beneath the ocean to a watery grave, retreating, lessening, gracefully and relentlessly, until not a ring was left on the surface of the water and every spark has vanished. He sat on an outcrop and watched.

Cameron saw it then! At another time of day, he wouldn't have noticed. The sun's last rays came directly from the west and fell into a small crevice cut into the mountain long ago by what must have been a channel carved by the snowmelt running off a high glacier. Inside the crevice, the rocks shone not grey, brown, red or black like the face of the cliff, but gold! Cameron got up, walked slowly over and reached inside. He drew out a pebble, weighed it in his hand, rubbed it clean against his sleeve and scratched it with his fingernail. It was softer than most rock. The tiny scratch glittered in the last rays of the sun—like Lysaght's nugget! He scratched again—more glitter. He scrambled quickly back to the dugout to wash it and polish it and he began to understand the frantic drive that consumed Patrick Lysaght's life. It was like watching your horse speed first across the finish line and knowing you held a winning bet. It was like hazing a retreating enemy or raising the victory flag on a hard-fought hill. It was an exuberance, a thrill and a consummate power that he felt. It made a man expand his chest, straighten his spine and hold his chin high.

The next few days sped by. Each day, Cameron scraped more gold from the interior of the crevice, but always quietly, and always just a little bit, no more than he could carry in his pockets comfortably and no more than he could safely hide and carry through the Ervin camp on his way down the mountain. He talked to the dog. He talked to the horse. To these simple brutes he confessed his dreams; the ranch he would settle; the herds he would build; the family he would sire. He told them of his love for Emma and of her kiss that he could still taste. And he told them of his regrets, of the years lost and his aching desire to see his daughter.

He devoured the old newspapers, fed the animals, cooked his meals and poked around with the pick and shovel in the crevice for more gold. Watching the sun set from his perch under the southern cliff became a ritual. The gold was only visible for about twenty minutes just before the sun sank behind the western mountains. If Lysaght meant what he said, and he, Cameron, could keep what he found, he had found the stake that would make all his dreams possible. Except for Emma. Would she have him? Did she still love him? His frustration had turned to optimism in one short week. Finding the gold excited his soul and fired his will. But it was not the gold that fueled his happiest dreams. It was the woman.

Chapter 15

On the fifth day, Cameron had dozed off again when a sharp crack woke him up. Blasting at Ervin's camp? But this was different, softer, more persistent and immediate. And it was raining. Wet powder didn't explode. Cameron sat up and rubbed his eyes and gradually the realization dawned. Not blasting. Pistol shots. He called in the dog, jumped into his boots, grabbed the Winchester and scrambled silently down over the slippery rocks. When he came around to the north face, more shots echoed off the cliffs from somewhere on his left.

Belly to the ground, wet, dirty, he crawled forward into the shadowy rocks. Huge drops of cold rain pounded down and blurred his vision. He slid like a snake to a point behind two boulders where he could peer out to see what was happening. When the rain let up, he looked over the top.

There was Spud Ervin. He looked thinner than he had at the poker table and he had a ragged bandage on the stump of his right arm. But there he was standing in the rain by the edge of the camp, his gun hanging loosely, butt forward on his right hip. He had set up a plank target a few yards off against a rock along the rim and he was practicing a cross draw with his left hand in the rain. The draw was slow but he had a good eye for a target.

What driving ambition had repaired his young body so quickly? Cameron winced. He didn't like Spud. Spud was a bully and a braggart. He was young but not as young as some of the drummers who died on the battlefield. Cameron lifted the Winchester, caught Spud in the sights and stopped. This was a coward's way, from ambush, in cold blood, like Curly Shaw. He lowered the gun. Cameron could take on Spud Ervin one day face to face, gun to gun, but not here. He was a soldier and he lived by a soldier's code and he was not afraid of Spud Ervin. Spud would live and Spud would remember him and Lysaght too, because Pat Lysaght had taken Cameron's side in the fight. Lee Cameron was more horrified at his own deadly impulse.

Spud Ervin looked down to reload. He was hatless. The rain had plastered his blond hair to his skull and the bones protruded at unshapely angles. His wet shirt clung to the youthful frame of his body. When he lifted his head, Cameron saw new lines etched in his face. There was a sharper, straighter angle to the jawbone, as if Spud were grinding his teeth to control chronic pain, but if he was in pain, he ignored it. The veins bulged at the sides of his temples. His eyes narrowed to slits and receded into the recesses of his skull. It was a face of grim determination, cruel and unyielding, no longer youthful. He called to Shaw who was lounging under a blanket in a tent near the camp. Cameron was close enough to hear every word.

"Curly, come see this."

Curly whined, "Not today, Spud. It's rainin.'"

"Five dollars says you want to come see!" The mention of money was like candy to a five-year-old.

Curly jumped up and paraded over. Ervin shifted the gunbelt, licked his lips, drew and fired a bull's eye. He smiled waiting for praise.

"Too slow! You got me out in the rain, you got to do better'n that fer five dollars gold.

Spud threw a poke of gold dust at Curly who caught it in the air and slid the wet pouch beneath the front of his shirt.

"I'll put the next one in the same hole." Spud fired again and hit his mark.

"Not bad fer a stump." Curly pushed his dripping red hair back from his face. He hadn't noticed the cruel lock of the jaw that defined Spud's face at the word "stump". His voice droned—he was getting wetter. "I hear Gus Terry's in town, from Californie. Your pa sent for 'im. Had to leave Californie. Terry drew faster'n Cal Turner, an' Cal Turner was faster than a strikin' rattler....but he's a dead snake today."

Spud lifted the gun for another shot—also a bull's eye.

"Gun's gonna misfire, it gets too wet." Curly turned back to the tent.

"Gonna beat Cal Turner." Spud fired again. "Gonna beat the greyback Dixieman shot my arm off an' plant his stinkin' carcass with Gallagher and Ives!"

"That what you want? Maybe he'll plant you."

Spud Ervin didn't answer. He didn't have to. Curly read it in his eyes that peered out at the target in concentrated slits of fire. There was a fierceness, an evil concentration of hatred that made even Curly Shaw recoil. Curly had seen it before. He could smell the smoke and feel the hatred like the shots that split the air. So complete was Spud's attention that he never blinked. Curly went in but Spud kept shooting until water soaked his ammunition.

The wind picked up from out of the north and the rain intensified. Thunder rolled across the peaks and lightening bounced from rock to rock. Cameron felt the ground sizzle beneath him and fled slinking like a lizard close along the ground back to the dugout.

The little grey horse stood huddled and trembling, rump to the wind. Lightning cracked again and the frightened horse shied nearly snapping his rope. Cameron grabbed a second rope, brought the animal with him into the dugout and rubbed him down. The horse stood trembling at the end of his lead. Shamy was already cowering against the rock wall. Slowly, soothingly, Lee Cameron spoke to both animals. High mountain storms arrive suddenly and flail the naked peaks like executioners. There is very little shelter and lightning bolts seek any tall exposure but they were very safe under the rock overhang.

The storm's fury was shortlived. It was soon over, and the animals calmed, but Lee Cameron didn't sleep well that night. He oiled and cleaned his new gun. He whittled, he read until his eyes squinted in the dim light of the flickering candle, but the thought of Spud Ervin, the vicious revenge he could work with his left-handed draw, haunted him. Cameron had come through a war and survived. But now he was more angry than scared. He'd faced another enemy. Bitterly he cursed himself for not having shot Ervin like any good skirmisher and he cursed Lysaght for living in such a god-forsaken place.

The next evening, as he was starting out to watch the sunset, he heard a call, "Halloo! I'm comin' in." Sanford had arrived. McGillicuddy had kept his word.

"Am I glad to see you!"

"McGillicuddy said I should spell you. Said you'd like your Saturday takin' a turn at the tables and your Sunday courtin' your ladyfriend." Sanford looked around furtively. "Find any gold?"

Cameron ignored the question and grinned like a schoolboy at the end of classes. "Saturday already?"

"I'm a mite late. Did some chinnin' with a humpbacked feller I knew in Lewiston, works for this Sime Ervin now... said you fellers had a nasty storm last night. Didn't even rain in Varina."

"Thought it would wash us clean off the mountain."

"Always worse in the high country. Funny, down Varina, all's we got was a little wind.... I brought some vittles. You better get crackin', you want to be in Varina by dark."

Cameron had his gold and his gear all packed. He loaded the grey horse. "You say you came through Ervin's camp. Was Spud Ervin there?"

"I didn't see 'im."

Cameron started off leading the little horse over the rocks—the gold ore was heavy and the footing rough. Sanford held the dog. As an afterthought, he screamed, "I'll take good care of 'im. What's 'is name?"

Cameron called back. "Shamy. Short for Shamrock." The horse pulled on the lead eager to leave this place of rock, fire and crashing noise. Cameron had to hold him back. He led the horse to the down-side of the trail so the horse would not land on him if he stumbled and fell. Going down was more dangerous than going up and the little grey was edgy. He moved forward in nervous little jumps, like a jackrabbit. He would start to settle then shy at his shadow or swing his haunches sideways in an excited dance as Cameron held back his head. His shod hooves clattered over the rocks. As they neared the Ervin camp, Cameron knew there was no disguising his approach. He had to bluff his way through in his grey coat as he would in any card game and he headed straight down the trail with McGillicuddy's Winchester in his hand.

Ervin's guard tipped his hat and spat a few words at the horse. "Giddap boy, take the Reb fer a good old Yankee sleighride!" He laughed and waved his hat and fired his gun. The grey snorted and lunged forward nearly pulling Cameron off his feet, loosening the load and nearly spilling Cameron's gold all over the mountainside. Cameron held on and righted the pack saddle. His hands were too busy to draw a gun before the guard drew back out of sight. It was a nasty prank. Cameron was resenting the Ervin outfit more and more.

A little farther on, the horse quieted and the footing improved. He reached Highland in late afternoon. From there, it was a long walk to Varina but the road was smooth and wide and there were none of the Ervin crew to work their vicious mischief.

Cameron arrived happily in Varina about seven o'clock and turned the horse out in Glenby's pasture. The animal had a good shake and lazed off sniffing the ground, looking for a good place to roll. As Cameron turned to go, Clem rounded the corner of the barn. "Evening Clem. I have an errand to run. Can I leave my gear with you?"

"Sure thing, Captain Cameron."

It was good to hear the sound of a friendly voice after the isolation on the mountain. Cameron shouldered his gold and marched in the darkness across the bridge and back up Outlaw Bar. In an open grave behind Gallagher's marker, he buried his gold with a covering of tailings and gravel. It looked like a simple pauper's grave. When he returned for his gear, Clem was rubbing down the grey horse. "I take good care of him, Captain Cameron."

"Right Clem." Cameron parrotted Glenby and grinned widely at Clem. He went straight to the Citadel.

"Go clean up and dump yer gear in there. There's shaving things. Pump's out back. Lysaght's better." That was all McGillicuddy had to say. He kept chewing his cigar, pointed toward the back room and blew smoke out of the sides of his mouth.

Cameron looked in the hazy mirror. He was shaggy as a buffalo in a blizzard. A week's growth of stubble, matted hair, streaks of mud and rumpled clothes—he was hardly recognizable. He smelled so bad he avoided Emma and helped himself liberally to the soap at McGillicuddy's washstand. He even splashed on some of Behnke's Airs de Paree.

Ten minutes later, he emerged in black frock coat and string tie, shaved, sweet-smelling and cleaner. Emma, surrounded by a swarm of players, spotted him from across the faro table. He elbowed his way straight to her side. To be near her, to see her, hear her, smell her perfume, to find out all she had done during the week, flooded his mind. It was six days that he'd not seen her, but he'd thought of her constantly. And now he had some wealth to back up his courtship.

"How's Lysaght?" He mumbled the obvious.

Her dark eyes flashed from card to card and she answered distractedly, "You can see for yourself later. He's at my place... ornery... complaining... demanding... much better. Only behaves himself when I give him a nip of his Irish. He asked for you." In fact, Lysaght had talked incessantly about Cameron and what a good lad he was to care for an old man's mine. His stream of chatter had kept Lee Cameron foremost in her own thoughts.

"Can he walk?"

"He thinks he can. Are you betting?"

"Not against a sure thing."

Emma Dubois lost the next hand. Cameron had interrupted the game and broken her concentration. He knew he couldn't say what was on his mind in front of so many people. He moved away.

McGillicuddy himself was behind the bar. He signalled to Cameron. "Sanford get there."

"He was late...Why'd you move Lysaght?"

McGillicuddy tapped the ash of his cigar onto the mahogony surface of the bar. "I didn't. When the pain subsided a little, he threw a tantrum worse than a mother grizzly defendin' 'er cub. Scratched and clawed somethin' awful—the Chinese wouldn't give him his whiskey. They finally had to hold him down and I had to sacrifice three bottles of the house prime to get 'im to calm down. Fu Ling hauled him up to Emma's in one of those hand carts or he would've started bleeding all over again." He crushed out his cigar on the heel of his boot. "Emma's was a good idea. He behaves himself better in front of the ladies and they're taking good care of him. You go on over to see him when you wrap things up here." McGillicuddy lit a new cigar and took a few healthy puffs. He added with a sideways glance and a twinkle in his eye. "You can walk Emma home." Cameron grinned, then broke out laughing as soon as Mc Gillicuddy turned his back. Dan McGillicuddy was a good matchmaker.

Chapter 16

It was two o'clock in the morning when Lee Cameron and Emma Dubois left the Citadel. Warren St. was roaring wild and grizzly. Most of Varina's twenty saloons faced this street and never closed. The light spilled out their doorways into the blackness outside. Laughter and talk sang to the background click of chips and dice. Horses stamped and jammed the hitch rails. Drunks bumped into doorjambs, fired guns, hurled curses at imaginary opponents or fist-fought like prize fighters without rules and without reason. Some fell dazed onto the rough splinters of boardwalk or sank in a stupor into the mud and woke only when the morning sun hit their bloodshot eyes or when a horse kicked dirt in their face.

In front of Frank's Saddle Shop, Emma swore she saw Spud Ervin brooding under the window. She had grabbed Cameron's arm to his immense delight and pressed into his shoulder. Cameron nudged the sleeping form with the toe of his boot. It was not Spud Ervin. Whoever it was had the same blond hair and two arms. At the Queen of the Nile, she saw Curly Shaw peering out over the batwing doors. Cameron saw him too—his unruly red curls hung down to his eyes. When they turned downhill into the steeper and more crooked Brewery St., with its alcoves and deeper shadows, their pace quickened. Brewery was slippery and steep. There were no lamps. The establishments were poorer and most were closed. Brewery was nearly deserted.

Suddenly Emma tripped and rolled. When Cameron stooped to help her up, he too crashed to the ground and slid another 10 feet. A scratchy voice in the darkness of an alley laughed like a banshee. At them? Sarcastic words followed, "Captain Cameron, the greyback,

Dixieman card cheat, you're crawlin' in the dung where you belong!"

Cameron's temper exploded. He knew that rasping voice. It inflamed him like the first clash of battle. Lee Cameron reacted instantly. He balled a fist around a clod of mud, pulled out his Navy Colt and rose up like a demon breathing fire. Wild laughter echoed from the alley and he lurched after it, flailing the air in front of him with the butt of the gun and straining with his eyes to see. He swung hard into the darkness in the direction of the sound. There was only a mere shadow but he struck decisively with all his strength. The gun butt hit home. There was a howl and a scramble and Cameron dragged his limping charge from the alley into the moonlight by a hank of his unruly hair. It was snarled and red and hung over his glassy face like a badge. It was Curly Shaw.

"You broke my ankle." Curly whined. He squealed like trapped piglet.

"You're walkin' on it." Cameron pulled Curly's gun from its holster and pitched it out into the street. Curly threw a mean right that Cameron ducked. He came up fast in a brutal swipe to the side of Curly's head with the gun that he still held in his hand and Curly went down hard. Blood gushed from over Curly's eye. Mud covered the front of his shirt. Cameron felt a cold lust to kill, the overpowering will to strike first and die fighting. It was a sudden snap in his brain that unleashed all his muscles in a frenzy to stab, shoot and maim. He'd been trained for this. He was in combat. He grabbed Curly's head and forced his face down into the muck of the street. Curly gagged.

"You ever jump me again, Shaw, I'll kill you!"

Cameron held Shaw by the collar, his gun raised for a second blow. In the dim background, he heard a scuffle of feet, a rustle of cloth and excited voices—Varina sounds, human sounds. Emma! A knot of spectators was gathering with lanterns. Cameron hesitated for only a moment. He held the gun next to Shaw's temple. "Laugh, Shaw, Laugh. Your jokes aren't funny when you see them up close. I should blow a hole in your granite skull, scalp you with a dull knife, and hang your red baby curls on my belt for Sime Ervin to see...or sell them to the Blackfeet—they're partial to colorful hair."

Shaw cowered. He stuttered, "I was foolin', only foolin'..." His voice rang with fear.

"Yer gun'll misfire mista—barrel's full a mud." It was a new voice, deep and even. A strong arm restrained the next blow and Emma spoke, "Lee, it was prank. Stop it! Let him go!" Slowly, Lee Cameron relaxed his grip. Curly Shaw wrenched free and fled. Emma blocked any pursuit. Lee Cameron holstered his gun. The air tingled with his rage. Emma lay her hand on his arm. At her touch, he drew back and breathed like an excited animal through flared nostrils.

A burly man in a flat-crowned Quaker hat stood beside him. "Settle down man. Curly's had his beatin'. Emma's all right. No harm done. Better go clean yourselves up, oil that gun."

Cameron replaced the Navy Colt and buttoned the flap on his holster, threw a fiery glance at the spectators and looked around for his hat. He studied the square shoulders and flat hat that formed the outline of the man beside him and apologized to the nodding stranger, "I been the butt of his jokes once too often....Lost my head."

"Old soldiers do, but we ain't fightin' a war here... almost, sometimes, the way some a you veterans get yer hackles up." The man in the Quaker hat had a deep bass voice and a body built entirely of right angles like a boxer from the ring. Cameron couldn't see his face in the dim light. The voice was calm and even like a referee in a prize fight. This had not been the first fight this man had broken up.

The spectators chattered passively. They did not approve, but neither did they condemn. All they saw was an uneven match, and a fierce predatory attack. Cameron was about to hit Curly when Curly was down. Now Curly was gone. He had limped away. It was over. The audience dispersed, but the boxy man in the flat hat stayed.

Emma spoke up, "Thank you Marshal."

"Obliged Ma'am." He turned to Cameron, "I'm Territorial Marshal. Hank Ryder's the name." He held out his hand and Cameron shook it. The grip was strong and sure. Ryder hesitated, brushed Emma off, then picked up Cameron's hat, dusted it off and handed it to him. He unsheathed his knife and slashed down in the black air. A taut wire twanged loose. "That's a trip wire Shaw had rigged. His stunts are gettin' meaner. Used to play kid games, like settin' a snake under a lady's skirts. Why'd he pick you?"

Cameron shrugged. "He doesn't like Dixiemen. That's what he calls me."

Ryder lifted an eyebrow at Emma. "That an' women troubles, I'll wager. Be careful, the two a you." He turned on his heel and stopped once to glance back at Cameron.

Cameron stood for a moment, watching the receding figure. So that was Ryder, the lawman McGillicuddy had been waiting for. He dusted off his sleeve and offered Emma his arm. She hesitated a moment stunned by the violence in him, then quietly gripped his arm and they walked on in silence. There was a certain new admiration in her glance.

On the green porch, he spoke, "I was angry. It won't happen again."

"You had reason." She did not condemn him.

"I wouldn't have stopped hitting him but for you and that man Ryder." His hands gripped the door frame in a cold sweat.

"But you did stop and you defended yourself."

She put her hand over his and he felt his tendons go limp and his muscles implode like an ice jam breaking up on a frozen river, when the spring flood finally breaks its grip and pushes a million tiny crystals out to sea. But his heart beat faster and his breath came in short gasps. He reached for her. Her body eased and meshed against him. A full moon cast its inky shadows on the sheen of her hair. He kissed her gently then and again more urgently and she responded. Her fingers pressed firmly in the small of his back. He wished it were not so dark, that he could see her face, somehow read her reactions. Visions of St. Louis and the old desires hammered in his head like drumbeats ever increasing in speed and volume. It was a delerium and an ecstasy like he remembered from years ago. So many years of loneliness, so many years of hard survival and desperate hope made the reality a thousand times more compelling.

She felt it too and took him by the hand. They leaned against the door when the latch gave way.

"I don't want you to leave." Her voice hovered.

He nodded dumbly. They stepped inside. She shut the door quietly and locked it. It was then he reached out hesitantly to pull the combs from her hair and she did not resist. It fell luxuriantly like a waterfall over silvery cliffs and he rubbed it back and forth between his fingers as if to confirm that it was real, and that she was alive and he was really standing beside her. The years peeled away like scales in the immediacy of the present. He pulled her to him. They fell together onto the silky horsehair weaving of the couch, consumed in the intensity of each other. Gently, he unbuttoned her bodice as she slipped her smooth hands under his shirt. The night air was chill and the stove had burned down to embers. They pulled a buffalo robe around them, their bodies warmed to each other and their coupling filled the immense void of so many years apart.

When it was over, Lee Cameron slept deeply like an infant held tightly against his mother's heart and Emma rested soundly in his arms beside him.

They awoke in the early morn. Pat Lysaght hammered the wall demanding his breakfast and the banging resounded like a volley of gunfire. Lee Cameron jumped up with a jerk and reached for his gun. He stood there, disoriented, with the heavy hide draped at his feet until Emma wrapped a blanket around his shoulders.

He was breathing rapidly and his hands were shaking. "The bullets, they rapped against the barn boards just like that. Splinters flew. My men were hit and bled and screamed and died." He sat down on the edge of the couch, elbows on his knees, staring glassily at the wall.

Lysaght pounded more incessantly and they ignored him. She put her arms around him and cradled his head on her breast, rocking him gently back and forth like a mother soothing a sick child. The clink of dishes and muffled complaints of the old man announced Rachel's arrival.

Cameron wiped the sweat from the back of his neck. "I scare you don't I?" He sat up and stared at her. "Sometimes, I scare myself...The visions come when I'm tired and when I feel something very deeply...I hear things...I see things." He rubbed his brow and turned his liquid eyes upon her. "But you make me forget. I must love you very much." Her answer did not come in words. Silently, she clung to him even more tightly.

Finally, she spoke, "You do scare me, but not like Spud Ervin scares me....Rest, sleep. Lysaght's like a puppy. He'll fill his belly and he'll quiet down." She kissed him lightly then, with compassion, on the cheek, and added wistfully, "We need to create good memories, you and me."

He stretched out with his head in her lap. With her touch, with the soft hum of her voice, the tension drained out of him. She stroked his brow and he slept again and so did she.

The sun was high when Cameron awoke the second time. Gradually the room came into focus: the desk, the quill pen and silver-lidded inkwell laid carefully beside the ledger; the gamblers' catalogue; the cupboard on the opposite wall; the onion patterned China: the black iron stove; the doorway to the green-painted porch outside. It was the same room he had entered one week ago when he had first arrived, only now he felt warm and welcome. His right arm encircled the woman he loved. He blessed his good fortune.

Gently he removed his arm and reached over to trace the outline of her cheek. She awakened slowly and smiled.

"Begod, ye clumsy woman, ye nigh to burn a man!" Lysaght's voice shattered the stillness like cold glass on a hot stove.

Rachel answered directly, "Lordy Patrick, I told you to be careful. The tea's hot the way you like it....You'll wake the missus."

"High time she be awake of a Sunday mornin'! All God-fearin' people should be in church."

Rachel fired back, "Missus Emma don't need no fire-eatin' preacher! She's a good woman, an' kind but Church-goin' would sure shake the devil outta you an' maybe shake some manners in!"

"Sass me, will ye! Have ye a soul as black as your hide!"

They heard a crash after this, the teacup breaking against the wall. Lysaght was throwing things.

Rachel was shouting now, "That's the good china! You crazy Irishman! You break it, you'll feed from a wooden trough with the pigs!"

They heard another crash and a loud thump.

The door opened and Rachel backed into the room. "He's wild, Missus Emma, outta his bed an' outta his head." Rachel stared straight at Emma. "I ain't gonna wait him no more." She was so furious, she didn't even notice Cameron. She stomped right through the room and out the door.

Lee Cameron pulled on his shirt and stuck his head through the doorway to Lysaght's room. He couldn't help laughing. Lysaght lay propped up on his elbows on the floor. Bed linens rumpled around him like the nestings of a packrat; his breakfast lay in a soupy puddle on the plank floor; his dishes were reduced to blue and white shards and lined the baseboard of the opposite wall.

The old man smiled brightly at the sight of his friend. "My friend, Captain Cameron, help me up....Tis a manservant I be needin'. The females been beguilin' me like the black flies, always buzzin' an' fussin' around a man!"

He winced when Cameron picked him up bodily and lay him back in bed but he realized Emma was present and blushed. "Begone woman! You should never see a man in his weakness."

Patrick Lysaght had been at Emma's for several days. No matter that the Chinese had given him excellent care. He'd complained constantly of a long list of ills but worst of all was not understanding their language—even their English, what little they knew was accented. He had no one to talk to and this the eloquent little Irishman could not abide.

The exasperated Chinamen packed him in a hand cart, hauled him off to the Citadel and dumped him on McGillicuddy's doorstep. From here it was decided he would stay at Emma's until he was well enough to return to his claim, hopefully very soon. At least at Emma's they understood English and cooked beef and potatoes, not brown rice and green tea.

But Lysaght's disposition did not improve. Women were almost as alien to Pat Lysaght as the Chinese. He'd never had a sister or a wife, living as he had all his life on lonely moors and wild mountainsides. His mother, who had died when he was five, floated in his mind like some romantic vision of the Virgin, enthroned with the saints in heaven. Now for the first time in his life, he had to rely on the female sex and this galled him like a canker.

When Emma was away at the Citadel, Rachel tended to him. A woman was bad enough but a black woman—he had never talked to a black woman in his life! He proceeded to play lord and master to the former slave. Rachel delegated his behavior to that of low class white trash: he bossed her. She sassed him back. She called him "Lordy Patrick", with a sharp edge of mockery in her voice. Nobody had ever called him Patrick in the last sixty years and 'lord' bore intimations of the hated English! He blubbered in shock. Finally the harassed women closed their ears but he knew they ignored him and complained louder. When their indifference continued, he let loose the full torrent of his Gaelic rage.

Now Lysaght in his bed on this Sunday morning suddenly realized that Emma was in her dressing gown and that Cameron was bootless, beltless and had not buttoned his shirt. His voice was damning. "What be your intentions, Captain Cameron, at this early hour of a Sunday morning, may I ask?"

Emma Dubois put her hand to her lips. Her eyes were laughing. Her lips parted but she said nothing. She arched her eyebrows impishly at Cameron, put her arm securely through his and kissed him playfully on the cheek. Lysaght couldn't mistake her meaning. The moralistic Irishman was horrified. "Ye marry the lady before ye bed her, Cameron. I thought you were an honorable man. Ye've brought me into a house of sin!"

Cameron said nothing and Pat Lysaght growled. "I cannae eat properly on me back... I be gettin up...." Lysaght tried again to get out of bed unsuccessfully. Rachel came in to remove his tray. He slapped at her fingers. "I do for misself. I don't need your sooty fingers all over me clean sheets, woman." He fell back against the pillows, breathing heavily.

This time Rachel laughed. "That's my skin, Lordy Patrick. It don' rub off." She always had the last word.

Cameron stepped in before Lysaght exploded once more. "I'll lift you to the chair, ole man?"

"Begod Lee of the crooked nose! Sure'n ye be livin' in mortal sin, I'll plant my fist in yer face an' give ye another crook in your nose if ye don't call that black fiend offn' me! Don't lift me to a chair man! Get me back to me claim and stop callin' me old!

Emma positioned a chair by the window. Cameron put his strong arms under Pat Lysaght and lifted him with ease. He set the old man

105

down gently and sat himself on the bed with Emma beside him.

Lysaght objected, "Have ye no shame, woman, sittin' in bed with a man!"

Emma stood up. "I'll get a dust bin to pick up the pieces."

"Knock before ye return, woman. I would speak to Captain Cameron man to man." After she left, Pat Lysaght spoke to Cameron with the gravity of God in Judgement. "What's this I see so early of a Sunday mornin' wi' me own eyes. Ye playin' Adam to the temptress woman. That be Eve with her forbidden fruit, livin' in mortal sin! An' me gold left all alone, layin' in the accursed dirt for the thievin' scoundrels to line the pockets of Satan!"

For Pat Lysaght, gold had its own personality and Cameron couldn't help laughing at the idea. His laughter infuriated the old man even more.

"Your gold is safe man. Sanford's standing guard. And I love the lady, Pat Lysaght, or is love for a woman alien to your righteous old soul?"

"I'm your elder. You watch your snivelling talk." Lysaght looked away disgusted and changed the subject, "Sanford? Another villainous knave! And me, an honest man, has to lay abed."

"Caleb Sanford works for Dan McGillicuddy and me. He's honest, he's big and he's minding your treasure."

"I don't know Caleb Sanford.... You, I know and trust. A fair judge of mankind is this old brain." He pointed a long fingernail at his head, scratched, then shook it at Lee Cameron. "But ye don't have patience, boy, or ye'd 've stayed and mined your own fortune."

"I did that, Pat Lysaght."

"Good." The blue eyes twinkled from beneath the bushy brows. "At least ye use your brain, Captain Cameron." Lysaght was tiring. His voice gradually faded. "I tell ye, Lee Cameron, she's beautiful, but beauty is best appreciated from a distance. Beautiful women are the curse of brave men. Only the gold will never betray ye. You remember, Pat Lysaght told ye so."

Lysaght still glared disapprovingly. "The tea is cold. Bid the lady warm it a bit and bring some nourishment for yourself." Lysaght called to Emma but would speak to Cameron only after she had gone, "Sit by me boy, I've something more for ye....Me boot, hand me me boot."

Cameron leaned over and picked up a pair of heavy brown leather boots lying in a corner. They were the boots of a lumberman and showed the wear of a man who walked distance. Laces strung the front all the way from the toe to the knee.

"That one there, the left foot... and a knife, ye've a bowie to lend."

Cameron handed him his knife.

Pat Lysaght started by unlacing the boot completely. Carefully, he slid the knife under the top of the toe. There was a slim pocket there. Now Lysaght cut the stitching and pulled out what looked like the leather lining. "I like ye, Lee Cameron and I've no heirs. Take this."

It was an old patch of buckskin that Lysaght handed him. Cameron was dumbfounded. Lysaght babbled on. "This be my testament, Lee Cameron, and I thank ye, that ye found these old bones worth the healing. I can at least pay ye for yer troubles." Cameron was about to refuse but Lysaght very deliberately put his hands on the back of the chair and pushed. He straightened with a grimace of pain. "I feel better. Ye promise an old man, Captain Lee Cameron of the crooked nose, to guard this testament and keep it ever safe, lest the little people throw a curse on ye and tomorrow bid you hook your crooked nose over the edge of a coffin!" He stopped breathlessly but he wasn't finished, "An' leave the lady alone until ye marry her!"

Lee Cameron marvelled at the old man's foolish superstition and stubborn rectitude. They were a strange admixture with the feverish lust after gold, and they seemed to anesthetize Patrick Lysaght to physical pain.

Emma arrived with lunch and Lysaght stopped abruptly. She placed a tray of bread, cheese, chokecherry jam and coffee on the table when they heard a wagon pull up. There was a knock at the door and the sound of boots and the pungent smell of a cigar. It was McGillicuddy.

"Race day, Emma. You coming?"

Emma Dubois had never missed Sunday afternoon at the races but today she had completely forgotten. She hurried now to get ready.

McGillicuddy nodded to Lysaght but addressed Cameron, "You're welcome to come too."

"Thanks, but I'm hungry." The food looked too good to pass up. "I wouldn't want to sully the lady's reputation further. Emma, you'll be safer alone with McGillicuddy..." He smothered a slice of bread with chokecherry jam, sliced a wedge of cheese on top and poured himself a cup of coffee. "If you'll excuse me, I'm going to have a good meal and a look at a good horse." He sat down and offered a plate to Lysaght. He hoped he hadn't offended McGillicuddy, but Emma would understand.

When she emerged again in the dress of emerald green, he decided he would buy himself that new coat, a brown one, to offset the green.

Chapter 17

The cheese and bread were filling and the jam delicious. He hadn't eaten since yesterday at noon. After his fourth cup of coffee and third sandwich, he paid his respects to Lysaght, and elbowed through the race-day traffic, to Glenby's Mayfair Livery.

Glenby sat dozing on a stool propped back on two legs against the barn boards.

"Glenby, you still have that black mare."

Glenby jerked upright. "Cameron! I thought you'd left us fer safer parts. Sime Ervin's in a fury. Even came to see me." He rubbed his eyes and pulled his hat down squarely onto his head. "You want to look at 'er or ride 'er?" Cameron looked like a bloodhound on a scent and Glenby continued, "I shouldn't have asked. I'll go bit an' bridle 'er....Meet you out back." He turned away and called, "Clem, Mr. Cameron's here. You're gonna want to see the show!"

Something in Glenby's tone warned Cameron. Glenby was friendly, but he was a horseman and all horsemen love to shake out the green-horns. The idea was to whittle a newcomer like Cameron down to size, especially an easterner who claimed he could sit a horse. If he could ride, he had nothing to fear. If not, he could be bucked over the moon and into the creek in the next few minutes and end up with anything from a few bruises to a cracked skull. Cameron chuckled to himself. He was ready.

Clem led the black horse prancing out of the stable. The mare was alert, ears pricked, nostrils flared, sniffing the fresh mountain air. She rippled her shoulder to chase a fly and swished her tail. Cameron noticed the sleek sloping shoulder, the deep heart and powerful hind quarters. She reminded him of the jumping horses his fellow officers from Virginia had ridden in the beginning of the war—thoroughbreds.

It was their power in the hind quarters that made them good jumpers. That same power made them mean buckers. More than one huntsman would buy a horse on a buck and more than one huntsman had landed red coat and colors in the mud. But Cameron hadn't seen a hunting horse since before the war. They had suffered the same fate as their masters—most of them were dead. He looked at the bit and checked the cinch. It was tight. Glenby didn't take him for that much of a fool. "What you put in her mouth?"

"Snaffle bit. You oughtta know."

Cameron did know. It was an eastern bit, easy on a horse, not popular in the west.

"That's what she came with. She was a ladies' horse, used to gentle hands."

Cameron nodded. Glenby didn't offer any more clues.

Cameron put his left foot in the stirrup and pulled himself up. The mare started to walk away before his seat touched the saddle and his body moved with her. She was eager, but so was he. He touched his calves to her flank and she moved out across the grass at a long even trot which broke into slow rolling lope. Cameron sat back with the gentle motion.

It happened in an instant. Suddenly, the horse ducked, nose to knees, humped her broad back, reached with the powerful hind legs far under her girth. She heaved herself skyward and threw her tail into a vicious spin. It was a cruel buck, straight up off all four feet. She landed hard on the forehand. Cameron jerked forward, almost landed on her neck, but threw himself desperately backward and righted himself. He came back squarely in the saddle, pulled her head up and dug his heels into her side. She sped forward like an arrow from a bow and levelled out in a flat run. Cameron kept his heels in her side. It was a wild ride. He slowed her gradually circling. Clem whooped and hollered with each turn. Finally, Cameron pulled her up next to Glenby. He and the mare were both pumping for breath.

"She's notional." Glenby grinned and his yellowing front teeth covered the lower half of his face. "You can ride good, Cameron." From Rob Glenby, this was high praise.

"She do that all the time?"

"To most folks, an' I don't warn 'em. Folks think she's a renegade. That way nobody tries to steal 'er cause they know they'd get bumped up a bit." Glenby was a master of understatement.

"When's the last time you rode 'er?"

"I don't ride 'cept to get from here to there an' I don't ride her. She's been turned out this past year. That Spud Ervin tried 'er 'bout a year ago. He wanted a fancy looker an' she's that. She landed 'im like a shot from a sling... Billy Lamb stayed with 'er once."

"Anyone ever jumped 'er?'

Glenby hadn't anticipated that one and twisted his mouth from one side to the other as if trying to chew his cheek. "Jumped?..." His eyes narrowed and he took his time. "You mean like them red coated chasers that gallop over cornfields with their hound dogs yappin' after house cats?"

Cameron only smiled. "Or like your Captain Slade when he jumps the creek with the vigilantes on his tail?"

Glenby pursued his train of thought. "Jack Slade couldn't ride, drank so much he'd roll right off 'er. She was Mrs. Slade's horse...an' Mrs. Slade was quality, rode sidesaddle. As fer jumpin', no sir, only mountain goats jump in these parts."

"Horse that bucks like that ought to be able to jump."

Now Glenby lifted an eyebrow. "It's your neck, you want to try." There was more than one way of landing a cocky southerner on his rump.

Cameron turned to Clem. "Clem, bring a rail from the corral."

Clem stood staring. He only took orders from Rob Glenby.

Glenby repeated, "Bring a rail, Clem, we're goin' to the ball!"

Cameron selected soft, level ground. "Hold the rail against the fence."

Glenby held the rail. Cameron turned the mare and approached trotting straight and even. The mare jumped high the first time but brought her knees up squarely, and loped effortlessly away.

"Damn!" Glenby had no other explanation.

"Raise it Glenby."

The mare jumped with ease and liked it. And Cameron was enjoying himself—he hadn't ridden a horse like this since the Valley Campaign. Back then, the southern cavalry had good jumping horses from all over the Carolinas and Virginia.

They raised the jump to nearly four feet. The mare didn't back off or rush. Glenby was dumbfounded. Clem cheered with each new height. He had found a new hero. Finally, Cameron dropped the reins and let the black horse walk. She was sweating mildly but not puffing. "Enough for now. How much you want for 'er, Glenby."

"Three thousand dollars." He read the shock in Cameron's face. "That ain't high. You southern boys would pay that fer a good house slave." Glenby didn't want to sell.

"What good is she to you, Glenby? You can't ride 'er."

"I kin admire 'er...Maybe I don't have a woman, but I got a damn good horse!... You come ride 'er any time you like. Clem's always here an' he'll cinch an' bridle 'er fer you, right Clem?"

"Shore thing, Mr Cameron..."

"Now you git down an' Clem'll walk 'er out."

So that was that. Three thousand dollars was an exorbitant price for any horse. Cameron dismounted.

Clem led the horse back into the stable. "Thanks, Glenby." He turned on his heel to go, then stopped. "Glenby, do you know a place where a man can stay, quiet and clean, not some fleabag hotel, where Ervin and Moulton won't be about to crash his door down?"

Glenby didn't hesitate this time. "Next door." He pointed to a neat log cabin. "That's my place and Clem's. Any man who kin ride like you do is welcome to bunk in with us... Right Clem?" Clem beamed from ear to ear. "Normally we don't socialize with you southern boys, but if'n you don't mind us risin' at sunup, we don't mind you risin' at dusk.... Your line a work, that's probably about when you be leavin'. You'll have the place to yourself daytimes, but you have to make your own bunk."

"Thanks, I'll get my gear."

"You're welcome."

It was dinner time, when Cameron finally deposited his gear at Glenby's and walked back up to Warren. His gold was safely buried. He stopped at Grandma's Restaurant and devoured three helpings of elk stew. The restaurant was empty. Most people had not yet returned from the races so he took his time. Biscuits, gravy, a slice of Rachel's apple pie, churned butter and clear coffee without the grounds floating on top like dead gnats on a stagnant pond, these were luxuries he hadn't enjoyed since before he'd sailed up the Missouri.

When he came out to the street again, thunderclouds threatened and the wind had picked up. Its force slanted hard from the west. Another storm was coming. He leaned into it and walked across to the Citadel. Wagons and riders were hurrying back to beat the storm. Dust devils swirled in the street. As he entered the swinging doors, McGillicuddy dismounted close to the landing. McGillicuddy cursed loudly because he still had to put the horse away and he was going to get wet. Cameron didn't volunteer. Emma came inside and the heavens opened with hailstones that beat a hard tatoo on the roof, and then turned to a slathering rain.

Customers flocked to the Citadel to avoid the sting of hail and smack of rain. The roar of thunder silenced the usual noise. Conversations stopped. Oil lamps blew out as the pressure fell and gaming stopped. Lightning flashed and split the evening sky in all directions. The storm arrived swiftly and violently and shook the very foundations of the mountain like cannonballs that thumped into a battlefield and dug craters in the earth. It terrified animals and sluiced the dust from the walls and windowpanes and turned the streets to bogs.

Then it was over. The wind died to a whisper and the earth lay cleansed. Riders went out to wipe down horses and remove tarps. Shopkeepers swept puddles from porches and wiped benches dry. Teamsters heaved wheels out of mud holes. McGillicuddy came in cursing, with his new suit soaking wet, and disappeared to change his clothes.

Cameron stepped out to breathe in the moisture. It always smelled good after a hard rain, wet and clean and earthy and fertile. He inhaled and watched the sun set, red and flaming, over the Stinkingwater to the west. Pink light glanced off the surface of the red rocks which sparkled like polished jewels. "Ruby" was what some people called the river valley because the rosy light bounced off its ferrous rocks to color even the hovels of Chinatown which gleamed like jewels or the red hot coals of a fire.

Emma Dubois came out and stood beside him. She had closed the faro bank and wrapped her shawl around her. She leaned against the rough outer logs and closed her eyes. The pink twilight drew rosy shadows into the exquisite lines of her face. Soon McGillicuddy called them both inside. Lee Cameron went to another poker game, but Emma lingered outside and another night of revelry began.

McGillicuddy in a fresh dry suit of clothes and newly starched shirt, started to play the piano. He wasn't very good, but there were so few pianos in the territory that even he was a celebrity. The lonesome miners gathered round as he plunked out the mournful songs leftover from the war, of sweethearts lost and homes left behind. The slow songs were easier for his old fingers and ballads were everyone's favorites anyway. Whiskey oiled the vocal cords and everybody sang. A few were excellent singers with trained voices like Ed Lamb and Dave Thatcher, the city mayor. They sang in church Sunday morning and in the saloons Sunday night and they always prevailed on McGillicuddy to play. They knew all the words and sang loud enough to drown out his mistakes. Emma listened from the porch.

A circle of Masons gathered across the street discussing the construction of their Temple. They were solid men, like their building, honest and hard-working. They looked like any other congregation of miners, shopkeepers and ranchers but these men were feared. A few were rumored to have been vigilantes. Only three years ago, they had imposed the first awakenings of justice on infant Varina. They hung twenty-three men.

Chapter 18

Emma watched the Masons now. They lent an aura of safety to the rowdy street. Daylight lingered, the street was busy after the storm and she was very tired, but still she hesitated to leave alone. She waved to the bartender and stepped into the street. Lee Cameron didn't see her go. She crossed Warren and walked to Brewery uneventfully. A short, stocky bull of a man, one of the group by the new Temple, followed her to the corner. She knew him and his presence made her bold. He was the Territorial Marshal Ryder and he wore the same Quaker hat he'd worn last night. He'd worn it for the last three years, ever since she met him on her way to Varina when he had ridden shotgun on the Helena-Varina stage. He never took it off even when he had flung the hangman's rope over the crossbeam and whipped the horse from beneath the outlaw, George Ives. Now he watched from the corner of Warren as she descended Brewery and turned into Jones.

Rachel came every evening to trim and light the oil lamps but tonight she was outside on the porch and hurried down the steps. The fear in her face shone in the whites of her eyes.

"Missus, he's come back."

"Who's come back, Rachel?"

"Spud Ervin. When I was lightin' the lamps, he knocked. He pushed right past me an' dripped rain water all over the floor an' ordered me around like an almighty overseer with his black snake whip. He's sittin' on the sofa now. That's all wet too."

"What about Patrick?"

"Lordy Patrick left...Says he's through livin' in a house full of women."

"I'll see to Mr. Ervin."

"Missus Emma, one more thing....I gave 'im some coffee, but he been drinkin', Montana lightnin' or I don' know what. He ain't touched the coffee an' he been spittin' tobaccy juice all over the rug. The devil's in 'im, Missus!"

Emma Dubois nodded and steered Rachel toward the alley and home. Emma mounted the steps to the front door.

Spud Ervin heard her step and loomed in the doorway. "Come in, Ma'am. I been waitin'." He was dressed neatly now in a red plaid shirt, black vest and pressed grey pants. The empty right sleeve was pinned carefully to the vest pocket. His lips and cheeks moved continually around a wad of tobacco. Emma could smell his breath six feet away.

He swayed toward her and held his hat politely in his left hand. As she entered he backed away, blocking the path to her desk.

"Sit down, Ma'am. We've a need to talk." He motioned toward the couch. She sat. He put his hat on the desk and walked over to close the door. Then he sat beside her, his knee brushing hard against the folds of her skirt.

The silver coffee service rested on a marble-top table in front of them. Spud lifted the coffee pot, fumbled a minute, poured out two cups, set the pot down hard on the stone top of the table and reached for a flask from his vest pocket. He couldn't hold the flask and unscrew the cap with one hand.

"You'll have to uncap it for me, Ma'am...I keep thinkin' I have two hands." He held out the flask presumptuously.

Emma uncapped the bottle warily and handed it back. He poured the whiskey into his coffee.

"You want some? Light a fire in yer cold blood."

"No thank you, Mr. Ervin...." She waited for him to explain himself.

He took his time. "I'd a come sooner but I was recuperatin'." He patted his stump. "You thought about my proposal?" He glanced at her sideways, calculating.

Emma Dubois had forgotten about his proposition. Now in a flash she remembered. She brought her shoulders erect, lifted her chin and responded softly but firmly, "Mr. Ervin, my answer is 'no'."

"No?" His comprehension dawned slowly. His eyelids fell and his eyeballs shrunk back and he turned their steely glare upon her. "Maybe you didn't understand." He spoke condescendingly. "I told you, I'll pay high. A house on the hill...an' my daddy don't foreclose."

She interrupted him. "Mr. Ervin, no." And she repeated it for emphasis, a final, decisive, "No."

114

Spud's face froze in the cold angular stare of a man without sympathy. His jawbone went rigid; his teeth snapped together. Again he hesitated and the effect was chilling. Then deliberately, he took out a poke, tossed it twice in his hand for effect, laid it on the table, pulled the thong free and emptied the dust in a dazzling torrent onto the white marble top of the table. It was a grandstand gesture. The dust sparkled temptingly against the polished silver of the coffee service and the white marble table top. Emma's eyes widened in disbelief.

Spud's tongue flicked out like a lizard's and licked his upper lip. His lips kept working. "Still no?"

Emma had not tried to ingratiate or to soothe. Now she stared bravely back at him. The palms of her clenched hands dripped with sweat but she straightened indignantly and measured every word. "I don't want your gold, Mr. Ervin. Your foreclosure threats are bluff. The answer was and is still no."

Spud Ervin's eyes narrowed. He drew back his head and swallowed hard. The node at his throat bobbed once; the sinews of his neck bulged. His mouth worked, phrasing words that he could not verbalize. When he finally spoke, the words snapped like whipcracks, "If I had two hands, you wouldn't have said that."

It was a moment before Emma caught the prickly malice in his voice. She struggled to maintain her courage and answered with the appearance of great calm. "Mr. Ervin, a missing arm does not diminish a man. I don't love you and I won't provide the kind of services you seek, not for you or for anyone else whom I do not love. Have I made myself clear? That's all."

His jaw clamped tight. Emma realized the fearful effect of her rejection and tried to soften it. "Surely a handsome man like yourself...."

The cruel lines of Spud Ervin's face moulded into an insidious snarl. It was a wicked smile and his words flicked from his throat as from the tongue of a snake. "Liar! I ain't blind! I seen Cameron leavin' here this mornin'...Where'd he sleep all night? What's he got that I ain't got? A right arm? Two hands?... You service him all night but I ain't good enough, like a stallion without 'is balls, gelded. I ain't whole!" The veins at his temples were throbbing, pumping blood to his reddening face.

Emma saw his eyes roll to the back of his head and his mouth hang open. She waited for a deafening shriek that never emerged. Her eyes widened and her voice trembled as she searched desperately for a way out that would calm his raving and make him leave and assure that he never came back. It came to her instantly, "Captain Cameron is my intended. We are to be married!"

Spud Ervin said nothing. His nostrils dilated but his face froze like granite. The clenched jaw opened slightly and closed again over yellow teeth. Emma couldn't see his eyes, they had shrunken so. She stared back in silence, proud and unattainable. Suddenly, his good hand swept up and hit her squarely across the mouth, hard, splitting her lip and knocking her cruelly against the marble-top of the table. The silver service crashed. Coffee spilled and gold dust blew like fine snow across the floor.

Spud Ervin was standing over her laughing. "Damn you, whore! Damn your Captain! Shoot my arm off! Steal my woman! Where is he? I'll kill him now, tonight!" He stormed out the door. It crashed and careened back off the wall. Rachel rushed in from the back room. Blood gushed from a split in Emma's lip.

"I'll git some ice, Missus, an' a napkin."

Emma wiped her mouth on her sleeve and stared back. "Rachel! You heard? Did you see his face?"

Emma grabbed her gun from the drawer, shoved it into her pocket and ran out the door. Rachel ran out at her heels, caught her when they reached the street and tugged at her arm. "Missus, this way." She pointed. "Past my house, down the alley and through the stores. It's faster."

The two women hurried up the alley past the stable and past the tiny cabin where the black family lived secretively in this town of former slave holders. Rachel grabbed Dad Long's rifle from its rack as they passed. They ran across the storeyard and up the stairs to the Lamb Hardware's back door. Ed Lamb himself opened immediately. One look at the blood on Emma's face and he asked no questions. They rushed down the aisle to the front and out into Warren Street directly across from the Citadel. Mud from the evening rain spattered and tugged at their skirts. Spud Ervin was nowhere in sight.

The street was quiet now. A lumber wagon stood unloading outside the Masonic Temple. The teamsters cursed at the late hour but took no notice of the two women. It was almost dark. Activity had moved inside.

When they burst into the Citadel, men stared open-mouthed and stood back. McGillicuddy's hands crashed on the piano keys as he pushed himself up. The bartender spilled whiskey over the bar and reached for a towel and another bottle. Lee Cameron dropped his cards and started to get up. But Emma reached him first and stood quietly before him. Blood had dripped down her chin and onto her white lace collar. The elegant black curls were mussed and snarled. She held her hand over the gash in her lip. "I've come to warn you, Lee Cameron. Spud Ervin is on his way here. He's been drinking!" Silence. A dog roused and started to scratch, steadily thumping the soft pine planks of the floor.

Cameron reached up and took her hand from her mouth. There was a pause. His face flushed in anger and sudden fire shot from the pupils of his eyes. "Did Spud Ervin do this?" Cameron's deep voice pierced the silence. Everyone waited for the answer and when it came, it was an indictment. Emma had nursed many of these men, as she nursed Patrick Lysaght, fed them when they gambled or drank away their riches, loaned them money for ax and pan or just quietly listened to their complaints of loneliness. These were rough men but they had their own peculiar brand of chivalry. Romantics all, risk-takers, eternal seekers not finders, men of expansive dreams, they loved beauty. They would find their gold and build their castles, and in their dreams they would shower a beautiful woman with all that wealth could obtain. For many, the woman who would live in that castle, looked just like Emma Dubois. Each in his way, loved her. She had been assaulted. Lee Cameron had voiced all their concerns. Now he repeated the question, "Who did this?" They all waited for the answer.

It came in a whisper but the silence was so engulfing that everybody heard. "Spud Ervin."

Cameron sucked in his cheeks and felt a reckless fury race through his blood.

A huge hulk of a man shouted, "I say we hang 'im to the doorpost, coward that he is for strikin' a lady!" His name was Con Garrity and he had fought in the ring. Shouts of approval rang out. The miners reacted as one. Their reddened callused hands, that swung heavy picks all day and poured the whiskey and dealt the cards at night, drew guns.

Rachel lingered by the door, uncertain of the reactions of all these white faces. She looked out and now she spoke. "I see'im. He's struting up the street like a cock preenin' for a fight."

Cameron had anticipated an attack from Spud Ervin, but a sneak attack, not an open assault like this in front of witnesses. He looked at Rachel quizzically. "It's dark. Gunfights don't happen at night?"

"Spud Ervin don't know that. He don't think. He's jealous because Missus Emma loves you. He'd like to make you lick dirt and he wants her to see the color of your tongue." Cameron heard only one word, five short letters, and he didn't quite believe his ears. He looked to McGillicuddy for confirmation, then to Emma. McGillicuddy's smile stretched from ear to ear in spite of the cigar clamped between his teeth.

Fear still filled Emma's face when she spoke up. "Spud wants me for his mistress." She was smiling too, a little brazenly, and looked him straight in the eye, "I refused...I told him I was going to marry you."

It was abrupt. It was direct. Lee Cameron's red face blanched and he stared, stunned and speechless while the seconds ticked away to eternity. Finally, he let out a wild Rebel yell to wake the Yankee dead. He grabbed Emma to him and hugged her like he had long long ago. "You hear that boys! Emma's going to marry me! Drinks all around! To Mr. and Mrs. Cameron, a toast! Spud Ervin, come an' get me! No renegade bull's gonna cut my herd." He held her to him rocking back and forth and smothering his face in her dishevelled hair.

When he let her go, Cameron would have headed for the door but well-wishers crushed against him and he ended up at the bar. Glasses clinked. Toasts were offered and backs were slapped. With a twinkle in his eye, McGillicuddy banged the piano keys. A cheer welled up from the crowd of miners. They were jubilant. Emma had chosen Cameron and no one begrudged him his good fortune. They were all like him, come west to Varina in search of a dream. He'd found it and in the finding, gave them all confidence they would find theirs.

But Rachel had remained near the door, oblivious to the revelry inside. She was a dark black girl, a former slave, and she had entered the free white society with suspicion and fear. Some had treated her humanely; some, like Sime Ervin and his son, had derided and cheated her like a stray hound dog. In the darkness, she'd lost sight of Spud behind the lumber wagon. She watched for him to reappear. Oil lamps were lit and swaths of light splayed out from windows and doorways.

A figure did emerge from around the corner of the lumber wagon. It was only a shadow in the twilight and was partially screened, but it strode relentlessly forward like a darkened spectre. There was a slant to it and a hole on one side, as if a piece of it was missing—Spud Ervin, without his arm. As he came into the light from the Broadway Dance Hall, Rachel recognized him. He carried a shotgun in the crook of his arm and wore a holstered revolver, butt forward on his right hip, two guns for one arm. He marched forward with a defiant swagger. The teamster, sensing trouble, whipped the lumber wagon around the corner. The mules brayed.

Rachel raised her rifle, sighted, squeezed the trigger and the rifle cracked. The circle of miners standing nearby heard the report and jumped around.

Rachel whispered softly "Damn! Missed!"

118

She set down the rifle—it was an old muzzle loader. "Like pickin' a pidgeon off a fence."

Con Garrity, put his huge palm over her gun barrel and forced it down. "Killin's a hangin' offense or worse for a pretty black girl. An' shootin' ain't women's work...Lemme do it."

When the shot went off, a group of miners turned at the report like the hardened veterans that many were. Glasses slammed down. A crowd swarmed out the swinging doors and fanned out onto the board-walk. They stood like a skirmish line at the front, waiting for the order to charge.

Spud Ervin stopped in his tracks. "Get outta my way, just gimme Cameron."

Garrity's huge form was outlined starkly in the doorway with the light of the saloon behind him when he spoke up. "What you want 'im fer, kid?"

"Cheatin' at the tables, and stealin' my claim."

Garrity interrupted, "You mean hackin' yer stump an' courtin' yer ladyfriend?" He laughed out loud and stood his ground.

Spud Ervin puffed out his chest like a rooster ruffling his feathers to make himself look bigger. He'd been so angry, he hadn't anticipated meeting anyone but Cameron. He was caught off guard. Worse was the mockery in Garrity's voice.

Now Spud shouted brazenly, "Just send Cameron out here to fight his own battles."

Garrity didn't move. "Jealous, ain't ya, boy?"

"It ain't your fight." The dark form lifted the rifle and took a step forward.

Garrity didn't move. "Stop right there, boy! We're all good southern men here! We got a good range of fire... Vision ain't good from up here on the walk but we got twenty shots to yer one-arm rifle. That's killin' odds. We can pick you off like we picked off Meagher and his fightin' 69'th at Marye's Heights—That's history you should remember boy? Or maybe you was still peein' in yer pants? Like mowin' down blades of grass, an' watchin' 'em blow away, but they was flesh an' bone, some of 'em not any older than yourself boy. We ain't got cannon but it's dark an' we can't see too good...maybe we just start you bleedin' stead a killin' you dead, like you done to Miss Emma."

Spud Ervin gaped. He'd never been challenged, not like this, in front of so many. His momentum was shattered. He stalled, uncertain. The attack on Emma had happened not more than ten minutes ago. How could Garrity know? He questioned, "You accusin' me of beatin' on a woman?"

119

"Damn right boy, an' from the looks of her, you done it right well, stump an' all."

"Who told you?"

"Miss Emma told me ...." Emma Dubois marched out beside Garrity into the light.

Spud backed up a step. "She hit her head on a table." He had left her in such a fury, he didn't remember.

"That ain't what she says."

Ervin hesitated again, uncertain.

Garrity hassled, like a drover with a prod, "Truth is, she says you attacked 'er and she's goin' to marry a good Georgia man here, our friend, Cameron. They're settin' the date right now, an' Cameron just bought us drinks all around.... Ain't that right boys?" The miners nodded agreement. Garrity waited for a reply but Spud was silent. Garrity continued condescendingly. "Now you wouldn't want to spoil the taste of good bourbon for all these good men of the south."

Ervin squirmed. The futility of his impulsive assault began to dawn. "I'm just claimin' what's mine...Cameron's got my deed...the Cleopatra Mine. It ain't his!" He started forward.

Garrity drew his gun and fired into the dirt. Mud spattered across Spud's boots. Ervin stopped in his tracks. He looked around for friends. Ed Lamb stood quietly in the dim light at the door of his store, rifle propped against the jamb. Ed Lamb was a friend of McGillicuddy's. Ervin could be caught in a crossfire. Garrity spoke again, filling precious time, robbing Spud of his last shred of momentum. His voice droned monotonously, "I studied my history when I was a boy. Cleopatra, she was queen of Egypt and she was a queen worth dyin' fer. You wanna be Marc Antony or don't you know who he is?" Garrity fired again into the dirt and never moved an inch from his position silhouetted in the lamplight. Horses shied and one galloped down the street. Ed Lamb looked on stone-faced.

Spud Ervin stood stock still and boiling mad. He raised his fist and shook it but left his gun in his holster. His voice croaked like an angry monster from out of the black night.

"I'll come back, Garrity, in broad daylight, an' I'll bring friends, a whole passel a Kansas Redlegs,.... bloody damn killers!" Spud Ervin fumed. He was outgunned and outmanned. He pivotted on his heel and walked importantly back up the street. "You do that, boy, but remember we got honest folk in this town and vigilantes." Garrity watched Spud's shadowy figure recede. He dismissed Spud with a cursory wave of his big hand and a chuckle, "You do that but watch that they don't turn on you... an' give a thought to the time a day. I like to sleep mornin's."

Chapter 19

Spud felt the eyes of all Varina like so many gnats on the back of his neck. He brushed them off, dismissing them as most people had dismissed him and turned back to their occupations. But his own conscience condemned him. He was retreating, backing away from a fight, breaking the strict ethical code of soldier and frontiersman. Still, he swaggered up the street with the haughty confidence of a toreador in a bull ring but a little hammer at the back of his mind tapped out one word—coward.

He wiped the saliva from his lips with the back of his hand and tried to reach down to wipe it off. He had a sensation of holding a rag in the fingers of his missing hand, of feeling the weave of cloth, the welting of its pleats and the dampness of his own spit. He rubbed his hand on the front of his shirt, swelled his chest, threw back his head, stuck out his chin in the cruel line that defined his jaw and shouted abusively at the backs of the spectators that were left. "What's the matter? You ain't never seen a one-armed man before?"

The onlookers shrugged their indifference and Spud's anger increased. Garrity had called him "boy" and "stump". Only niggers and coolies were called "boy". But "stump"—it was a goad aimed especially at him, at his own peculiar deformity, at him who was not whole. He was the freak in the side show, the ugly beast on display for all to laugh at. His stump was his humiliation and his weakness. He was only half a man without a right arm, half a fist fighter, half a gunman. His firepower was cut in half. He couldn't take on a crowd like the one in front of the Citadel. He would have to seek out Cameron when he was alone and unsuspecting and his devious mind set to conspiring how.

His mouth was pasty dry. He squared his shoulders and anchored his surly eyes on a crudely painted wooden bust of a woman at the other end of the street. It marked the Queen of the Nile Saloon, better known as "the Queen", at the end of Warren, and reminded him further of another inadequacy in his life, that of the woman. The Queen was lit up like a torch, and attracted him like a candle lures a moth.

There was a shuffle of boots on the boardwalk as people moved back inside, and gradually the noise was replaced by competing sounds, from Varina's sixteen other saloons and especially from the Queen, at the other end of Warren. Someone was singing and a banjo was playing but Spud didn't notice. The urge for revenge welled up biliously from his chest into his throat, choking off his air. It colored his face a pasty grey, furrowed his brow and shrunk the pupils of his eyes so that very little besides white showed from within the deep-set sockets. His good hand tensed and unconsciously sought the butt of his revolver. He pulled out the gun, aimed and shot the tits off the sign, stopped and looked to his right and left. No one applauded his accuracy or paid him any attention—gunfire meant little unless someone got hurt. He kept strutting straight down Warren Street like a bloated tom turkey, toward the woman's bare wooden breast hanging over the saloon and he felt the grains of thirst in his mouth and the swell of lust in his groin.

His paint horse was tied around on Brewery and he unhitched him and tied him under the sign, in front of the Queen. He looked back and stood staring long and hard over the cantle at the Citadel and muttering a litany of curses.

"Damn Rebel bastards! Damn yer snooty principles, yer whores and yer whiskey, yer cards an' yer gold!" The words came under his breath but there was no longer anyone nearby to hear. Rejection wetted his appetite. His lust swelled even larger now that its fulfilling had become more difficult. His tongue licked wetness across his lips and hung out like a panting dog's. The wooden bust of the woman hung temptingly over his head. He wanted a woman badly and he fished in his pocket for the gold to pay for a good one. But he really wanted the respect that strong manhood could command. And he wanted his arm back.

He slipped his rifle into its boot, took up the reins to mount and then changed his mind. The banjo music and laughter from the Queen filled the night. It was the noise of inebriation and dissipation, but it was human noise. He had friends here—men who would lick his wounds like a slobbering dog when he paid for a round of drinks, women who would pet him like a puppy until his softness hardened and spilled over. A bargirl would dull his stabbing lust and make him forget his

122

itching stump. A drink would settle him. Spud slipped the reins back over the hitch rail and climbed out of the muddy street up the steps to the saloon.

At the Queen, there were women for hire—guns too. The Queen was the meeting place for a breed of Union outcast, the enemies of McGillicuddy, Garrity and Cameron. They were the dregs of the northern slums, dockyards and rivertowns, tough Irish immigrants, southern deserters, Kansas abolitionists, opportunists all. They had not returned from whence they came when they mustered out after the war, not because they had lost the battle and had no more homes, but because they never had had homes and didn't want them. They were uncivilized, barbaric—war had a use for their kind. They only knew how to fight and kill. Like the gold-seekers who lived for the search, these men lived for the fight. These were the men still fighting the war or creating their own petty wars to consume their need for violence. And these men had their women, tough, toothless and easy.

Yellow light from the oil lamps filtered obliquely through the smoke filled air. No one noticed Spud come in until he dangled his poke in front of a blowsy whore. She smiled a gold-toothed grin at him, pulled the combs from greasy black hair, grabbed his arm like a vise and headed him down the back hall. She was big and busty and had the laces of her corset unfastened before they reached her couch at the back of the hall. She could not compare to Emma Dubois, but tonight Spud Ervin was beyond caring.

When he emerged about twenty minutes later, he ordered whiskey straight. He smelled of sex and sweat. The bar was crowded but people moved aside and gave him space. The bartender, a big, red-bearded man with a bushy handlebar mustache, placed a bottle in front of him and left him alone. Spud Ervin drank thirstily and felt better. He knew the bartender. Sherman was his name. It was a good Union name. Sherman, the other one, the General, knew how to kill Rebs.

Now Spud shouted down the length of the bar. "You any relation to William Tecumseh Sherman?"

The bartender shrugged. "You askin' me? Sure, I'm 'is cousin, but I been out in the territories goin' on ten years."

It was a bald-faced lie but Spud nodded and sloshed his mouth out with whiskey. He never saw the wry smile that lit Sherman's face or heard the snicker that crossed his lips. He'd already turned toward the other drinkers and raised his voice almost to a shout. The whiskey loosened his tongue. "I'm gonna kill me a Rebel an' I hear a prime specimen just came to town! Any a you see 'im, you wanna kill him, I'll pay you high fer it. A hunnerd dollars to anyone who'll kill me that damn greyback, Captain Lee Cameron." But men sensed he was unstable and left him alone.

As Spud drank more, he quieted. His face darkened and his eyes clouded over. He began to mumble morosely to himself—how he'd been a fool to go for Cameron alone. The Citadel was a hotbed of Dixie boys, a regular field of weevils. They swarmed together and stood up for their own. But they'd be easy pickings if you could surround them with armed men—because they didn't run scared—it was against their code. Like buffalo in a stand they'd cling to a defensive position, and Spud could just shoot down one after another. He hadn't heard of the Marye's Heights that Garrity had mentioned or the patient, detailed tactics of successful defense. He gloated on his self-proclaimed daring and the glories of dramatic and swift offense. A self-satisfied grin broke the cruel contours of his face.

His thoughts rambled morosely—he needed a gun, a fast gun. By shooting twice as fast he could make up for the lack of an arm. Tomorrow he'd double his practice time. And he needed gold. He could command other men if he was very good with a gun and very fast and if he paid them very well. He remembered the gunfighter that his man, Barney, had mentioned. The California man, what was the name? Gus Terry. And Barney said that this man, the bartender, Clive Sherman, used to ride with Terry. He'd find Gus Terry and maybe a few more like him, hire them, watch them and learn from them. He was going to shoot better than they could, command his own army. Old Sime had sent for some toughs to guard a shipment. Terry was one. Barney and Curly Shaw had told him that. He, Spud, would hire more. They could take on Lee Cameron, and the crowd at the Citadel, and this whole accursed town and the Army of Northern Virginia what was left of them! That would earn him the fear in the whites of men's eyes that he thought was respect.

He glanced toward the men at the other end of the bar and raised his glass with the rash confidence of callow youth unaware that he was shouting again, "Terry, Gus Terry, he ever come in here?" His words were slurred. The men shook their heads. His thoughts ran incoherently on and salted his lusty words now with morbid hallucinations. Spud Ervin took a deep breath and puffed out his chest, then let his shoulders collapse again as he slumped against the bar rail, drunk.

Sherman took his arm from the waist of a bargirl and approached reluctantly. Spud's gun was still loose in its holster. Sherman pointed to a chair. "You set yourself down, I'll bring the bottle over. Missy'll make you comfortable."

Spud Ervin looked up and blinked. The lamplight reflected in small points from a large mirror behind a row of bottles on the bar. They stabbed his eyes like tiny barbs. His head ached and lolled from side to side. At Sherman's suggestion, he took offense. "I already had a whore an' I carry my own liquor."

"You won't be able to hang yer head on a coup stick, you keep drinkin'."

Spud didn't react. Sherman stepped back docilely and gestured for him to go ahead. Spud reached for the bottle and swiped it sideways, spilling a torrent of whiskey over the bar. He felt himself reaching with his severed hand to right the bottle before it rolled off onto the floor and crashed. His brain was teasing him again, assuming he had two hands, especially for two-handed actions like pouring a drink, mounting a horse or fanning a gun.

Sherman threw his towel acoss the dripping liquid and sopped it up. "That'll be five bits."

Spud threw another poke down and Sherman reached behind him, and uncorked another bottle. But he held it away, out of Spud's reach.

"Here or over there?" Sherman waved the bottle at a table. It was only a question, not a threat. Sherman was a big but a peaceable man and he led the way to the table like a man leading a hungry dog with a piece of raw meat. Spud swore and fell into a chair and Sherman set a glass in front of him and poured.

"If yer lookin' fer Gus Terry, he'll be along 'bout midnight... You lay off the sauce, you might make it 'til then."

Spud Ervin set about finishing the bottle. The smooth liquid scorched as it snaked down his throat. He could feel his muscles wilt, his vision blur and his brain dry up. He knew he'd drunk too much and stayed too long. His good arm lay draped across the table and his legs stretched out long and limp underneath. The crowd had thinned. There was some commotion at the other end of the street. Probably some political rally—they held such things to promote Varina as capital of the territory. The city of Helena was vying for the honor. Feelings ran high and sometimes erupted into fights. His foggy brain didn't care.

Spud Ervin slopped out one last drink for the trail. His thoughts rambled.— "Helena, it was another gold strike named for a woman...No woman was worth that much gold, buy a slave fer five hundred dollars, a Chinese fer less. Good horse or a new gun costs more." He was mumbling again. He ran the palm of his hand across the whiskey that had spilled onto the table and licked his wet fingers. When he tossed a poke of gold dust toward the wavering shadows that his mind told him was the bar, it hit the rail and fell to the floor. Sherman stooped over and picked it up. Spud had forgotten his arm. It didn't feel at all and his head swam in a sea of light and motion. His eyes were closing. When he blinked, the room swayed like the pitch and roll of a ship on a stormy sea.

He pulled himself up on the back of a chair and barked an order. "Tell Terry to come up to the camp... Get me to my horse."

Clive Sherman did as he was told. He grabbed Spud under the armpits, walked him outside, hoisted him onto the paint and looped his belt around the saddle horn so he wouldn't fall off. Then he knotted the reins over the horse's neck, turned him up the creek and slapped his rump. The horse trotted forward. Spud Ervin bounced unceremoniously up the street.

Clive Sherman stood for a moment watching him go and looking at a noisy crowd dancing in the street. Someone said there'd been a wedding. Happy times, weddings, good for business. The dancers were up the street in front of the Citadel. Maybe some of them would drift down toward the Queen. There'd never been a wedding at the Queen. The Queen's customers didn't get married. He was half tempted to join the fun but he came back in and walked to the far end of the bar.

An ugly bear of a man stood chuckling to himself. He wore brown overalls over a buckskin shirt and a brown slouch hat, but his boots were high-heeled with rowled spurs four inches across. Two guns hung at his hips. He looked like a cross between a miner, a pig farmer and an outlaw or maybe bushwhacking irregular left over from the war. The costume either belonged to an avowed eccentric or someone who just did not care what he looked like. He was laughing now. His head shook when he laughed and lice fell from his beard down into the bib of his overalls. He itched and scratched his armpits and he smelled of rancid bear grease. No one wanted to get near him or catch his body lice. They'd had enough of that in the Army and left him alone. He spoke to Sherman from across the bar.

"You lost that one, Sherm, coulda rolled a rich one. An' I ain't heard you take orders like that since you was a barefoot private with Georgie McClellan. We was right to quit that army afore we got killed." He picked up the poke Spud Ervin had left and spilled its contents onto the bar. "Good quality dust here."

"He'll be back an' there's more where that came from."

"Whaddid he want me fer?"

"You were here? I should have known. A hundred sweaty boozers couldn't outperfume you!" He pinched his nose. "That's Sime Ervin's kid an' from what I hear, he's on the prod... Women, them's the troublemakers. An' he lost a gold mine in a card game up the Citadel. Wants it back."

126

"A payin' mine?" Gus was serious.

Sherman nodded. "Good payin'. His pa's likely to claw 'is eyes out when he finds out."

Gus slammed his fat palms down. The whole bar shook. "An you let 'im go on up to the Citadel to do 'is gamin'! I thought you was a businessman!"

"I missed this un."

"He come down the hall with Easy El. She don't look like his problem?" Gus Terry belched.

"Naw, high-brow dame named Emma Dubois, owns part of the Citadel and runs a dance hall."

"I seen 'er. She's pretty....The kid got a good eye."

"Gus, he's just a rich kid who can't pay fer better than ole toothless El. He thinks he's a fast draw, but 'e ain't as fast as you or me, afore I grew this gut an' my fingers stopped workin'." He rubbed his fingers and patted his swollen stomach. "Serves me right fer thinkin' I could get rich pannin' gold.. Ate too much tryin' to stay warm...Can't deal a fast deck like I used to. I can still shoot straight, but I need time to aim. Fingers is all pins and needles." He opened and closed his fists.

Terry wasn't listening. "The kid's only one-handed."

"Mind yourself, Gus. That's raw meat on the end of that stump, but it ain't healin' if you catch my meanin', like the screwflies layin' eggs, tunnelin' right down 'is arm to 'is trigger finger an' itchin' 'im. An' he's got women troubles, worse 'n the itchin', squeezin' 'im somewheres in the balls."

Gus Terry laughed again but the sound was muffled in his matted beard. Sherman smacked a louse running over the polished surface of the bar. "Sounds like you, Sherm, that night on the Platte. Now if you smelled and scratched like me, the women and the black flies won't come within a mile. My Caroline's all the woman I want." Caroline was Gus Terry's mule.

"I like company, Gus, female company, an' they likes me. No laughin', Gus, I heard young Ervin's been target practicin'. Sheriff Plummer, he learned to shoot with his left hand. I didn't think the kid had it in 'im—but looks to me like he's nursin' a grudge an' he's a determined bastard when it comes to gettin' what he wants. I treat him right there's a wage in it." He pointed to the pile of dust on the bar. "Plenty more where that came from an' ain't nobody gonna hang me fer it."

Gus Terry slobbered whiskey in his beard, still chuckling. "Plummer's dead... An' the kid drinks too much." He sputtered, thought a moment and looked up seriously, "He's got more gold? How much more?"

"His ole man owns half Varina. Mines mostly, a few parcels in town... Sime Ervin was one of the four who found the place." Sherman continued, "An' the kid struts around like a preenin' peacock, expectin' ever'one to jump when he fluffs his tail."

Gus Terry was laughing loudly now. "You jumped, Sherm, like a nigger seen a ghost! I'd never believed you'd jump thataway in Californie."

"I use my head now I'm old an' fat an' my hands don' work so good, and that kid drops a poke in here ever' other day. That's steady money, Gus, no one time roll."

Gus Terry stopped laughing for a moment. "That's the trouble with you, Sherm, you get busted up, you itch, an' you quit. The easy life's got to you, too many women, too much money. That kid ain't quittin'... You see 'is eyes? Them's hatin' eyes in that kid's head, ice blue and cold, like Shark Jones. Remember 'im? That kid just might learn to shoot true an' fast with the other hand. An' he'll be a cold killer." Gus Terry laughed more.

"Shark Jones is dead, Gus."

"But that kid's alive an' he's raw an' he's game. What's 'is ole man like?"

Sherman knew everyone there was to know in the gold fields. "Spud's pa? Sime Ervin."

"Heard a him. One of the original strikers, you say? No one ever jumped 'im, run off with his gold?"

"He's a cagey old hermit. Sits on 'is gold with a double barrelled shotgun, like a hen settin' eggs. Hires guards an' pays 'em good. Ain't never shipped anything out. No one ever had a chance to git their hands on any of his gold. But he always has plenty to spread around town, at least the kid an' Curly Shaw do. Don't see much a the ole man. He don't drink an' he don't gamble."

Gus Terry eyed Clive Sherman directly. He lowered his voice and his face turned serious. "You mean it's still all there, in his camp, on the mountain?"

"Yep. Folks say it is. They say he's stacked a real pile in a secret stope. Been minin' since the start, some four years. They say he's gonna ship now the vigilantes have cleaned things up a bit. Leastaways that's what Curly Shaw tells me an' he works fer Sime."

"Shaw...Heard a him too. He from Californie'?"

"Oregon. He don't do much but trail after the kid, play pranks with Spud on them's they can laugh at, an' highgrade a plump share of the old man's gold fer himself. The kid ain't got enough to do."

"I'm tellin' you Sherm... You don't call 'im kid no more."

Clive Sherman grunted and shrugged. Terry chuckled.

Terry put a hand on Sherman's shoulder. Sherman shrugged it off. "Me, I'm gonna pay a visit to this here Spud Ervin an' his pa, seein' as he's invitin' me up to his camp...You with me, Sherm? You have someone to look after this place fer a few days, you come along, point the way. We find out about that gold shipment."

Sherman looked back and wrinkled his nose. "Old times is gone Gus...I tell you what I know, but I got a saloon to run." Terry pulled his slouch hat down over his eyes. Sherman reached past the Red-eye to his best bottle and poured out two glasses. The two men clinked the glasses and downed the contents. Drops of whiskey anchored in Gus Terry's beard. The whiskey smelled like roses compared to Gus Terry. Clive Sherman picked a louse off his sleeve and crunched it with his fingernail on the bar.

He'd go with Terry as far as Highland, the farthest settlement up the gulch, but that was probably all he could stand. He bellowed, "Damn, Gus, ain't you ever gonna git rid of yer bugs!"

"They's faithful company, Sherm." Terry put his hands under the bib of his overalls and grinned.

Chapter 20

Spud Ervin didn't get home that night. At Highland, his horse stopped at a watering trough in front of the Dugout Saloon. Digger Bob Lockwood was a fellow Union man. It was Spud's habit to stop here on his way home. Here he tried to dismount, fell to his knees, crawled under the trough and passed out. The horse drank, and fell to cropping the weeds that grew in clumps along the side wall of the saloon. Digger Bob dragged Spud out of the way and picketed the horse. Spud Ervin spent the rest of the night in the smelly shed outside the Dugout, awoke about noon and started drinking before he left for home.

He rode in about eleven o'clock, drunk, humiliated and angry. Sime Ervin was waiting for him. Now he confronted his son.

"You gamblin' again, boy? What'd you lose today? Another mine or mebbe yer other arm?" The amputation of Spud's arm didn't phase Sime but his son's unpredictable and violent temper did. This was the son he intended to put in charge of his gold shipment, the heir apparent to all his wealth. Would Spud Ervin be meticulous and responsible? Or would he flit from diversion to selfish diversion and squander what his father had worked so slavishly to earn and to keep? So far, that's all Spud had done. Could Sime count on his son to avoid the wiles of thieves in Fort Benton, to control the seasoned gunman he was hiring as guards, to outwit Indians in the passes, and gamblers and con-men in the rough river towns, to strike a favorable deal with freighters, toll-collectors, stamp mill operators and bankers, Salt Lake bankers above all—the Mormons were a smart bunch. He looked at his son and looked away. He didn't like what he saw.

Spud stumbled into the dugout, threw his hat onto his bunk and missed. It landed on the dirt floor and he almost landed with it. His blond hair was matted and wet and stuck against his brow where the hat brim had pressed it down in a tight circle as if a band had been twisted around his head and tightened, squeezing the brain into a round bulbous sphere separate from the lower half of his head. His face was red with exertion and the jarring trot home and the cool wind had sobered him. It had not killed his rage. His father's cruel dismissal triggered an explosion like gunpowder thrown in a furnace. The outburst was more violent because it was contained.

In the dark windowless den, an oil lamp threw flickering shadows on the hard clamp of Spud's jaws. Sime Ervin had seen those jaws clamp before like talons on their prey. As a boy, Spud had tied two coons together until they tore each other apart, and once he had whipped a recalcitrant horse to its knees. Only one week ago, Spud struck out at May, the Chinese girl, because she rearranged his bunk without his approval. Sime had been there to stop it and she escaped with a broken tooth. He could be cruel, this boy. The whiskey made him savage. Now Spud's bandaged arm was sweaty and dirty and his left hand rested on the gun butt at his hip. He lashed out.

"I ain't a boy no more an' I don't have to answer to you!"

Sime Ervin waited. A fire crackled on the hearth. He never lifted his eyes from last week's edition of the Montana Post that he held before him or righted his chair. He raised bushy eyebrows and answered dryly, "You're drunk's what you are. You been pullin' more circus antics for Tilton to write up in his newspaper." He slapped the paper with the back of his hand, righted his chair and raised his voice. "Did you read it? Folks is laughin' at you boy! Callin' you a yellow belly whelp!"

The word "boy" echoed like a marble in a tin can in Spud Ervin's brain. McGillicuddy, Cameron, Garrity and now his own father! "Stop callin' me 'boy'!" His voice screeched.

May, the sleeping Chinese cook, came in and cowered in a corner. Sime Ervin waited. He set down his newspaper. Water dripped slowly, steadily, from a stone ledge in the rear wall. "I'm yer father....I'll call you anything I damn please. How about Aloysius? That's yer name!" Finally, he stopped and his look was more of disgust than of interest.

Spud was shouting, "Name me after some damned saint you did! You think because you named me, that's what you'd get! Some pansy saint! Well I ain't any a that! I drink with men, play with 'em and chase whores with 'em an' I beat 'em all to a draw. Call me a man!"

Sime Ervin's reply was cold and hard. He leaned forward with palms on spread knees. "You owe me, boy! You owe me a mine, the Cleopatra! Pay your debts like a man an' I'll call you a man."

"I'm your son, goddammit! I don't owe you nothin'! You sittin' on more damn gold you know what to do with!"

Sime Ervin didn't raise his voice. He balled a page of the newspaper and threw it into the fire and watched it flare. "You're no son a mine. You're growed, you pay or get out. I'm collectin', boy, callin' in Cleopatra, the rich lady. You're so tight with the whores, you go get 'er." Sime Ervin didn't blink an eye. He laid his palm casually on an Army Colt laying on the table. Spud's good hand tightened on his own gun butt.

"Don't try it, boy. You ain't gonna beat me left-handed."

That word "boy" again. Spud Ervin's brain snapped. His own father was challenging him. His own father was disinheriting him. He, Spud Ervin, should own everything, be respected as a man of means, hire guns to kill Cameron, bed Emma Dubois when and if he pleased, or burn her out if she refused. Seconds ticked by. His gun, the raw, cold power he craved, rested smooth beneath his palm. So would Sime's gold. He stared intently at the man who sired him, a man he never knew and no longer wanted to know, an icy stranger and a vicious threat. His tongue protruded from between his lips like a hungry dog waiting.

The older man's vigilance diminished ever so slightly with the ticking of the seconds. His eyes turned back to the newspaper, and he muttered, "Now go to bed an' sleep it off!"

It was a typical parent's remark and it was uttered routinely as a careless finale. Sime waved his Colt toward the bunk and Spud Ervin sprung.

In a wild leap and with no thought of pain, he flung himself onto his raw arm and drew his revolver with his left hand. It was not a fast draw but true. Spud's practice on the mountainside had not been in vain. His bullet caught Sime in the throat. He fell coughing his own blood and gasping for air. A bloody bubble appeared over the bullet hole as he tried to voice his last but he could only moan and gurgle. Struggling for breath, his eyes bulged out from their sockets, like a toad, and locked on the face of his son, glaring accusingly at the life he had spawned. He dropped his gun, slumped and died beneath his son's frozen stare, without solace, without a last wish, without ever pulling the trigger.

Spud Ervin stood immobile and impassive, like a lizard sunning on a rock. Comprehension slowly dawned and hestared down at the gun smoking in his hand. With his foot, he kicked Sime's shoulder so the body turned on its stomach, and blood dripped into the dirt. The bulbous eyes no longer glared up at him.

May, the Chinese girl, stared at him wide-eyed.

"Who you lookin' at, girl? You're mine now. Go back to work." Terrified, she pulled her bedding over her head.

Spud walked over to the door. Hump, Sime's hired man, was crossing the yard, attracted by the sound of the shot. Spud Ervin let him come. Hump was unarmed.

He sauntered through the open door and stopped short. He was a large, stupid man, physically powerful, but slow. A mental runt, he'd survived thus far by siding with smart men. He looked from the body of his former employer to the young man standing over it, reached up and scratched his head. "So's I guess I'm workin' fer you now?"

Spud Ervin smiled. "Hump, you read sign like a red injun. Tell you what, I give you a raise, another five dollars a week, in gold. Just you see that nobody you don't know comes near my gold."

"I know my job, Mr. Ervin....Yer Mr. Ervin now?"

"That I am, Hump." Spud Ervin squared his shoulders and ran his tongue over his lips.

The hunchback turned to go, then stopped and looked back. "Oh, an' what do you want me to do with him?" He pointed to Sime Ervin's corpse.

"Bury him."

"Where?"

"Some place deep...Stuff 'im down a tunnel alongside 'is gold."

Hump nodded again. "I'll put him in the old south stope. Ain't no gold worth the takin' in there. Nobody need ever bother 'im again."

"Good for you, Hump!"

The hunchback still hesitated to leave. "An' what you want me to tell Mr. Shaw when he rides in?"

"Just tell 'im old Sime met with an accident an' that I'm in charge now."

"Yessir, Mr. Ervin." Hump heaved the body over his shoulder and shambled out.

Spud Ervin let the fire die and threw the ashes over the blood stains, laid down on his bunk and went to sleep.

Curly Shaw rode in an hour later and went to the bunkhouse none the wiser.

Chapter 21

Tuesday morning, Clive Sherman and Gus Terry rode up the gulch from Varina. They passed Central City and Pine Grove and came into Highland, just a few shacks, some tents and the Dugout Saloon. They were two big men on a tough little horse and a rangy mule. The animals were winded from carrying the big men up the steep climb and this was the last saloon on their trek up the mountain. They stopped to rest the animals and have a drink. The saloon was a real dugout, dirty, without windows, and smelled rank of sweat, beer, smoke and horse manure—it had been used as a stable the night of the storm. Water leaked through the sod roof and dripped into your drink if you left it uncovered on the bar. Sherman and Terry entered, ordered whiskey and sat at a table near the flap of skins that served as a door.

Terry wiped his mouth on his slimy sleeve. "Much farther?"

"Around the edge of the cliff. Steep ride gettin' there. Maybe that's why no one ever robbed 'im. Keeps 'imself all forted up like a laird in 'is castle. Can't get in and can't get the gold out."

Terry eyed the yellow liquid and turned it slowly so it coated the glass. A small drop spilled onto his fingers. He licked it off and smacked his lips. "Ole Jersey Lightnin', tabaccy, peppered water an' a pinch a piss to poison yer maw...." He pinched a louse and drowned it in his drink and laughed, exposing the black spaces between his teeth. "We don't ask the ole man, Clive. We work on the youngun, what's 'is name, Spud? He have a real name?"

Clive Sherman sloshed his whiskey around the inside of his mouth, coughed and spat it in a stream onto the dirt floor. "He's been Spud as

long as I knowed 'im....We get home I owe you a decent drink, Gus."
Then he added. "An' we get to Ervin's camp, you let me talk...Sime
don't like strangers, livin' on the mountain like he does, specially
stinkin', swearin' strangers. An' he don't like folks that laughs at what
he says. You got to mind yerself, Gus."

Terry nodded, laughed some more and the bugs crawled.

"He buy any good whiskey with all that gold?"

"Sime don't drink, Gus, just counts 'is money."

"I'll behave this once, Sherm. You just figgur how we can make us
a good profit." He grinned from ear to ear.

Twenty minutes later they started outside. Their mounts were
quiet and cooled. The day was warm and a slight breeze blew away the
smell of Gus Terry. Clive Sherman stayed upwind of his friend and
breathed in deeply. A rider approached on a paint horse.

"Damn, Gus, here he comes, the youngun."

Spud Ervin rode up to the hitch rail.

"Mornin' Spud." Clive Sherman eyed young Ervin. He looked somehow different, larger. His stub-arm was still bandaged and tied against
him but it was cleaner. He was riding taller, standing straighter. His
blue shirt was ironed, his blond hair combed, and he had shaved and
brushed the dust off his hat.

Spud Ervin raised his head at the greeting. His eyes fell first on the
brutish stranger with the shaggy black mane in the baggy overalls.
Spud Ervin wrinkled his nose and then recognized Clive Sherman.
"Mornin' Sherm. Who's your friend?"

"Spud Ervin. Gus Terry."

Young Ervin took in the two guns tied down and smiled like a jack
o' lantern, a big sinister grin, so wide you could see the wad of chewed
tobacco stuffed in his cheek. Terry's reputation preceded him. "Terry!
Sherm here tell you I was askin' for you."

"He did that."

"What brings you to Highland?

Terry spoke ignoring Sherman's advice. "We was comin' up to see
yer pa. Heard he's hirin' gunmen an' I'm the best you can git."

Spud narrowed his eyes, still grinning and punched his first syllable emphatically, "I'm hirin' now." He looked from Sherman to Terry.
They waited for an explanation. "Sime, my pa,...the late Mr. Ervin...
met with an accident." He paused again to assess the effect of his
words. "Horse kicked 'im in the side of the head. He never woke up.
Now I'm in charge." Spud Ervin licked his lips and spat, "An' I need a
good gun. But I need more 'n one."

"I can get more. What you payin'?"

135

"Thirty dollars."....He rolled his wad in his cheek and added without blinking, "A week."

Gus Terry didn't show his surprise. Thirty dollars was more than most hired men made in a month. "How many you want? Them's princely wages—you can hire away the whole Army of the Potomac fer that."

"I could. You get me fightin' men, men who can kill, an' men who can hit their mark first time, better 'n Lincoln's bluebellies, like Quantrill's sharpshooters—I hear every man his boys killed was shot through the head."

Sherman interrupted, "I can git you twenty men. They'll shoot the apples off a tree, cuttin' stems without hittin' apples. An' they'll kill Rebs like pigeons on a fence, keep the Injuns off yer horses an' guard yer gold while they're doin' it... But they'll need repeatin' rifles."

"I got rifles an' cartridges. How soon can they be here?"

"Two weeks, some little more, some little less, dependin' on how fast you start payin' me an' how fast I get to a telegraph office."

Spud held out his left hand. Gus Terry took it with his right hand palm upward. It was an awkward position. But Spud's handshake was strong and his voice firm and if he noticed the lice he never said. "You can call me Ervin or Mr. Ervin." There was a challenge in his voice.

Clive Sherman nodded dutifully and looked at his horse. Gus Terry smirked and raised a greasy eyebrow and shook the hand harder. "The two of you come on up with me now." Spud was eager.

Sherman backed off, "I ain't comin'. You don' need me. I ain't no shooter." The ends of Sherman's mouth broadened into a near-smile but his hands were shaking. He continued, "Spud" and he caught himself, "Mr. Ervin, I'm a businessman. I got me a bar to tend. You hire yer outfit. You send 'em on down to the Queen fer a drink an' a roll in the hay. I treat 'em like prime studs, an' good luck to ye."

Spud turned back to Terry, "Terry, go up to camp. Speak to Shaw, red curly-haired feller. Tell 'im you're workin' fer me. An' Terry, take a bath!"

Gus Terry was not offended. He laughed and rode on up the gulch alone.

Spud Ervin and Clive Sherman rode together down to Varina. Spud stopped at a crudely lettered sign, "Attorney at Law." It was painted in black letters and hung from a porch in front of a neat white house, high up on Jefferson St., overlooking the town. This was the home of Judge Burnwell, the county recorder, circuit judge and lawyer. Ervin knocked and the Judge himself answered. The Judge knew old Sime from vigilante days.

Judge Burnwell removed a pipe from his lips. "Spud Ervin! What can I do for you?"

Spud took off his hat. His words oozed like honey off his tongue. "My pa died yesterday, Judge. You're signed witness to his testament. I brought some papers here, deeds an' such, for you to write over in my name....Keep ever'thing legal."

"I'm sorry. We'll miss 'im. Come in, Spud." Judge Burnwell opened the door wide and led Spud Ervin into a small parlor. A bookcase stood on the right wall next to a roll-top desk and swivel chair. Bright sunshine filtered through white lace curtains onto the desktop. Two slatback chairs lined the opposite wall and a bookcase held the Territorial papers and city documents stacked neatly in rawhide binders. The judge was an important man.

"Pull up a chair, Spud." The judge was solicitous and pulled up the chair himself. Spud sat down. The judge stationed himself at his desk and leaned forward on his elbows. "Now, Spud, first things first. Have you made the arrangements?"

Spud Ervin stared blankly and recovered quickly as the judge continued. "The funeral, the eulogy and the burial. I can help you with the preacher and the undertaker if you need."

Spud Ervin stammered a reply. "Thank you Judge, but we Ervins ain't religious folk. We already buried 'im on the mountain where he lived. That's home. That's how he'd want it."

Burnwell didn't question. No fee here for the undertaker or contribution to the church building fund. Sime died like he lived, hoarding it all.

"You have a copy of the will?"

"I do." Spud stood up and placed a wide roll of buckskin on the desk. "It's all in there." He untied the lacing and unfolded a sheaf of papers. "These'll be all the properties my pa ever owned in Varina, them's he still owns and them's he sold. I figure there's twelve mines he owns and seven he sold. Then there's the claims he never mined and the parcels here in town, nine claims, ten parcels."

Judge Burnwell nodded. "I'll have to go through them all make sure they tally with the county records....You have business in town. I'll need a few hours. And I'll need the death certificate."

"Death certificate?" Spud stalled but he could think fast when he hadn't been drinking. "We buried 'im right off in the mine shaft, just like he'd wanted it."

"I understand, Spud, but we have to have a certificate...Tell you what. I can ask Doc Fielding to write one up. What was the cause of death?

137

"Horse kicked 'im in the head. Brained 'im good. He stopped breathing, that's all."

The judge waited puffing on his pipe. "Too bad...Fifty years he was on this earth. Same age as me. Too young to die."

Spud paused, calculating the moment to change the subject. "I have a question, Judge." He fingered through the first few papers to a yellowed piece written in elegant script.

"This one here....is the original deed to Lot 22 of the original city map, and signed by his honor Mr. Edgerton." His eyes narrowed and he ran a fingernail across the surface of the paper. "It's a claim Sime had when they first struck gold, in the Alder Mining District, Sergeant Lode, City of Varina like it says here. They still thought there was gold this side of the mountain." "Lot 22 is on Jones. Houses sit on that piece now, Madame Dubois and that nigger family, but it rightfully belongs to me."

Judge Burnwell took two slow puffs on his pipe, tilted his chair back, lifted his feet onto the desk, removed his pipe from between his teeth and stared hard at Spud Ervin. "It's registered to three other men besides your father, Spud and you may be evicting folks from their homes, Spud, if you push this claim."

"They're squattin' on my land!... Bunch a slaves an' whores! That's Jones Street! Scum's all that lives on Jones Street!" He was close to shouting. He shoved out his chin like a shovel. Veins pumped at his temples but his face was white.

"I'll look it all over, Spud. Might take mor'n a few hours. Can you come back tomorrow?" The judge shoved the sheaf of papers together, averted his eyes, and let his feet fall from the desk with a loud thud. "The claim may no longer be valid, you understand."

"You do your job, Judge. I just want what's rightfully mine." Spud Ervin had lowered his pitch but his tone had grown spiteful and ugly. He held out his hand. The Judge switched his pipe from left hand to right, stood up and shook young Ervin's hand. Spud wrapped his fingers around the Judge's palm like a constrictor snake that squeezes the breath from its victim. When he let go, Judge Burnwell cupped his hand around the bowl of his pipe in order to restore some warmth and circulation.

Chapter 22

No threat lingered Sunday night at the Citadel after Spud Ervin had retreated. Laughter and song filled the night air. Lee Cameron summoned drinks for all and McGillicuddy followed suit. Even Emma stood her round. McGillicuddy sat down at the piano and the miners broke into the wild havoc they called dance. It was an incongruous ballet. They danced with any girl available, and if none were available, they danced with themselves. A kerchief tied around a biceps marked a female partner. Whiskey loosened their joints and lightened their step. Hobnailed boots cut grooves into the soft pine floorboards and resounded like picks striking bedrock. They stomped and jumped, clapped their hands and twirled their drunken partners into dizziness. The walls shook. The heat in the room rose. Shirts dripped with sweat. Faces flushed from exertion. The air smelled of sweat, tobacco, beer and whiskey and the party went on all night.

The noise acted like a magnet and pleasure-seekers flocked to the Citadel. Mayor Thatcher and Doc Lubbock, who lived up the hill, came to see what was going on and stayed. Hank Ryder, Territorial Marshal with his bull shoulders and short neck, came to ward off any brawling that developed. Ryder never left. He rarely smiled but tonight he laughed and danced and tipped his black hat to the ladies and his glass to everyone else. Behnke, the garrulous barber, stuffy Mr. Lott, the stiff British newspaperman, Tilton, and the lanky Norwegian carpenter, Andy Holter, came along. Holter was a newly-wed: he had just brought a lovely young wife, Paulina, west from Chicago. She came too, this night, even though proper ladies did not frequent gambling establishments. But the Holters who lived down the gulch near their sawmill, had come up for the races and decided to stay in Varina overnight because of the rain. They were staying at the Lubbocks up the hill on Jefferson. Both Mrs. Holter and Mrs. Lubbock couldn't resist a good song and neither worried about "appearances" when they could dance. They worked and played alongside their men and they both had pluck enough to snub conventions. No one condemned them. No one could easily sit in judgement of a neighbor whose materials and skills they may desperately need come winter.

McGillicuddy stopped playing long enough to rest his arthritic fingers, light a new cigar and open a bottle of champagne. Where it had come from nobody knew, but stranger things had survived the bumps and rattles of transportation over the muddy trails and steep mountain passes. The cork popped like a shotgun blast and hit the ceiling like a bullet. Golden bubbles spilled out into tin cups, like the glittering flakes of gold in the waters of Garnet Creek. Only Rachel had held herself apart. This was a white-man's celebration and she had been a slave. Freedom did not mean acceptance. White folk and black folk didn't mix. Uncertain and afraid, Rachel looked behind her out the door at the darkening street. She wanted to go home but she didn't want to walk home alone. For her, the streets were especially dangerous. She was a black woman. Miners and outlaws had their code of conduct which protected white women, even prostitutes, because they were so few. But any black or Indian woman was free for the taking like the gold in the creek, a commodity—As a slave she had been safer because she was worth a sum of money but now the miners valued their gold more highly.

Cameron saw her, walked over and offered her a glass. She stared at him wide-eyed, unbelieving, clinging to her Henry rifle like a beggar to his last coin and shaking her kerchiefed head. Golden bubbles rose shimmering from the bottom of the glass—Rachel had never seen the like.

Cameron sensed her hesitancy and spoke softly. "Taste it. You'll like it....You've earned it. And thank you." He was a southern man but he had addressed her humanly, politely, like her old master.

She leaned the rifle against the door frame, took the glass, sipped hesitantly but still stared suspiciously.

Gently he motioned toward the rifle. "I can keep this for you in the back room. Spud's not coming back tonight."

She grabbed the gun with both hands and her glass shattered on the floor. "My gun stays wi' me, massa Captain." She was not sure how to address him.

"Even dancing?

"Yes massa Captain, even dancing."

"I'm not a master and I'm not a Captain anymore."

A brown-haired youth asked her to dance. Cameron prodded Rachel a little and she went. He didn't see what became of the rifle—Emma had come up beside him.

Emma's cheeks flushed red like garnets against the black sheen of her hair. Spud Ervin was gone and gradually, she inhaled the exhilaration of the night and started to relax. This was her town, her home, her place of business. She had worked hard for this place, like the miners and the shopkeepers around her. McGillicuddy had given her confidence. Now Lee Cameron gave her security.

All this Lee Cameron was beginning to perceive. Life in Montana Territory was different. Necessity ignored convention. Emma earned her living because she had to. There was no alternative. She was a businesswoman. It was a position for a woman that his plantation upbringing had never before encountered. He was intrigued and uncertain—and he was still jealous that she had married Dubois. She'd admitted she had never loved Dubois. In the end, she had been happier by herself, and with McGillicuddy's help, she had survived and prospered. The rough miners understood what she was. It was just Lee Cameron who still shrank from it and from the revelation of a daughter who bore another man's name. Cameron felt the uncertainty, the lack and the pain. In his mind, he drew the child's picture. It was a smaller version of the image of Emma that he had kept alive all these years.

Emma pressed her shoulder into his. Together they drank champagne, danced and sang. All he knew were bawdy old camp songs, but he sang because she sang and the intoxication of the music cloaked their deepest doubts.

Neither he nor Emma could sing like Mayor Thatcher. Thatch had obviously had some training and sang with a lilting richness that carried the rest of the singers. Cameron had heard that Thatch was a good speaker too. That was why he had been elected mayor.

McGillicuddy had been drinking more than usual. He and Mayor Thatcher huddled over the piano like two old generals rehashing scenes of battle. Suddenly McGillicuddy banged the keys. He wasn't drunk. It was deliberate. A few heads jerked up and turned back again to their play. Only the top rim of his stovepipe was visible over the heads of the crowd—he was too short. But Dan McGillicuddy was not to be silenced. He climbed up on the piano stool and clapped his hands. With the added height, he was a striking orator. Now he removed his cigar, "Gentlemen, I'd like to propose a toast."

The circle of men nearest McGillicuddy turned around. Thatcher let out a bellow like a stag in rut and the dancers slowed and stopped. McGillicuddy commanded their attention.

"My good friends", he began. "I thank you for your forbearance. I have important news I want you all to hear." He waited for silence. "Madame Emma is my pride and joy." His voice rolled sonorously over the syllables more masterfully than Daniel Webster. "A more beautiful, more savy and honest girl, I've never met. A toast to Emma! Here! Here!"

Applause and shouts, even gunfire erupted. Clods of dirt came showering down from the roof. "No gunfire boys, that's sod over those rafters. We can't have the roof fall in on this fine party!" McGillicuddy extended his hands again and all went quiet. He looked benevolently at Lee Cameron. "And Captain Cameron, you're new to town but I've come to admire and respect you these last few weeks. To you, Captain Lee, may the South restore her health and prosperity and her conquerors forgive her! Here! Here!" Another cheer went up. Lee Cameron blushed purple. Public displays made him uncomfortable but he sipped his drink with the rest.

McGillicuddy forged ahead like a mule on a treadmill. He mesmerized his drunken listeners with more toasts to friendship and love and family and home. It was a nostalgic speech filled with the maudlin sentiments of too much whiskey. Cameron's head was groggy from so many toasts and he didn't pay much attention—nobody did—until he heard Emma's girlish voice.

"Dan McGillicuddy, stop, he hasn't asked me yet!"

Cameron turned sharply and McGillicuddy's face beamed down on him like a guardian angel. Then it dawned. McGillicuddy must be matchmaking again. Cameron had never officially asked Emma to marry him. And she had not accepted or refused. Their courtship had only just begun. But McGillicuddy was airing their union like yesterday's laundry and there was no stopping him. Cameron moved to get up but Con Garrity's huge hands clamped him to his chair.

Perched upon his stool and swaying happily like a branch in a breeze, McGillicuddy clung to the piano for support, "All you, my friends and theirs, want to come to the wedding! I'm inviting you all....Now there's no church in Varina big enough for all you kind people and as most of you aren't comfortable in the lord's house anyway, I volunteer the Citadel for the nuptial celebration of these two fine young people! Here! Here!" More drinking. Rebel yells, gunshots, more chunks of clay roof showering down, cheers enough for three Sundays of horse races. They were all invited and McGillicuddy was paying!

Lee Cameron gawked, appalled and incredulous. Beads of sweat welled up under his collar. His face turned bright crimson, not with embarrassment but with anger. McGillicuddy had no right. It was a question of pride, of his private intentions and his and Emma's future! It was a theft of his masculine initiative. It was a sacrilegeous parade of emotions that he reserved only for the most intimate moments with the woman he loved. He was horrified and he was powerless. In front of all these people, the die was cast; the hand was dealt.

Cameron seethed. He tried to get up but Garrity's fingers dug furrows in his shoulders, anchoring him to his seat like a galley slave to his oar.

Mayor Thatcher jumped up. It wasn't over. A momentum was building like a storm wave on a high tide. And Thatcher rode its crest. He held up both hands for silence. "Gentlemen and fair ladies of Varina!..." He bowed chivalrously toward Emma who was laughing lightly and enjoying the show. "It's a fine gift Dan McGillicuddy is providing this young couple—the gift of times well-spent, with good friends and neighbors, but more than this, a happy memory that no thief can steal away nor passing year diminish. Good memories are treasures greater than the riches in this creek. And Dan, all of us here are grateful to you for good drink, good song and many happy memories....Now we elders", he looked at McGillicuddy, Doc Lubbock and a few of the other patriarchs present, "know the value of good memories when a man's life turns sour and trails into the wastelands. That's when the memories revive us, for memories bring with them the hope, that the trail will lead to greener pastures." Thatch looked around, knowing he was ranting on too long, but he loved an audience and they cheered him on. "Men of Varina! I have a gift to offer and I'm assuming you all have tokens you will give the happy couple as a sign of the good wishes of this, your fair city." Heads nodded approval and Thatch continued. "My gift is this." He paused for effect and looked at the handsome, brooding face of Lee Cameron. "Leland Cameron, I take it you love this lady?...You surely forded rivers and climbed mountains to find her." He waited for an answer. Cameron's eyes shot darts of flame. He shook loose from Garrity's powerful grip and started to get up, when Garrity shoved a gun in his ribs. Cameron snapped his head back and Thatcher took the motion for a nod of approval. He turned to Emma, "And Emma Dubois, I take it you love Cameron too? At least I've seen the look in your eyes when you're with him. We all did."

Emma flushed but she was not embarrassed. This was the frontier. Things were direct, basic. She knew Thatcher and McGillicuddy better than Cameron and she'd suspected their intentions from the start. She flashed a brilliant smile in Cameron's direction and nodded. Her lips parted but if she spoke, Cameron couldn't hear her over the steady hum of voices in the background. He sat there like a ramrod with the cold metal of Garrity's gun digging into his spine.

Thatcher forged ahead, "Now, being that I am a duly elected official of this fair city, and being that I know a good match when I see one"...

Another cheer. "By the power vested in me, witnessed this Sunday, the thirtieth day of June, by all you good citizens of Varina here present, I pronounce you, Emma Dubois and Lee Cameron, man and wife. You may kiss the new Mrs. Cameron."

Lee Cameron was outraged. On whose authority could Thatcher do this? Cameron stood there gawking like a farmboy with stage fright. Was it a real wedding or a sham? The words were all wrong. Kiss the bride? His old high church upbringing reserved such displays of emotion for private moments. No! He'd kiss her when he damn well pleased, not when McGillicuddy called the cue and Con Garrity held a gun to his back.

But Emma didn't hesitate. She put her arms brazenly around his neck and kissed him squarely on the mouth. The taste of her lips, the crush of her arms on the back of his neck crashed on his heart like heavy artillery. He threw his hat in McGillicuddy's teeth and kissed her with an animal passion that shocked even McGillicuddy. Garrity had to pry them apart.

McGillicuddy poured brandy from his own private stock. He poured one for Cameron who left it sitting on the table. McGillicuddy tried to console. "Drink it Cameron, or is your new state of husbandhood cramping your thirst?..."

Cameron scowled, "This can't be legitimate."

McGillicuddy replied indignantly, "You call sleepin' with her out of wedlock, legitimate?... How do I know? Patrick Lysaght told me. You call the little daughter legitimate?...Think again what's legitimate, my Captain. Yes, I made arrangements but I'll not apologize...She's like my own daughter and I want only for her to be happy. You can do that for me, for yourself and for your own flesh and blood, Captain Cameron. Besides, it's what you came for, isn't it? It's very legitimate."

Cameron felt like punching McGillicuddy in his fancy white mustache but Emma's presence held back the full force of his fury. He held his glass high to McGillicuddy and shouted sarcastically, "You ever been married, McGillicuddy? How would you know?" He picked up the glass and drank to the dregs and flung it against the wall. McGillicuddy brought him another.

Everyone except the groom was drinking joyfully. The Citadel had cause to celebrate. Amid shouts and cheers, hats flew and pistols discharged. More bullets thudded into the rafters. Someone passed a hat, a gift for the happy couple. McGillicuddy thumped the piano. A banjo twanged. A throng of well-wishers engulfed Lee Cameron and his new bride and Cameron fended them off angrily. Finally, he gave up. There were too many.

Chapter 23

About midnight, when Lee Cameron's fury had subsided to manageable levels and Emma Dubois was numb with exhaustion, a weatherbeaten buggy pulled up in front of the Citadel. A swaybacked white nag pulled it and Rob Glenby was the driver. Someone had found wild flowers at this late hour and tied them with colored ribbons over the yoke and down the traces. What bells and tin pans could be had on short notice were tied to the boot and clanked as the poor horse stamped anxiously. A placard hastily nailed to the rear read "TWO FOR ONE! JUST MARRIED!"

As the couple was hustled out of the saloon, someone showered them with dollar bills—rice was too expensive. Lee Cameron scooped up Emma and lurched forward as he lifted her onto the seat. But for Glenby's strong arm, the two of them would have toppled headlong into the mud. Glenby somehow had stayed sober. Cameron hoisted himself up onto the seat, the wagon jerked forward and he fell sideways into his bride. The noisy crowd howled for more.

Two men with shotguns fired simultaneous blasts. The old horse bolted and the wagon nearly crashed into the bystanders. Glenby hauled back on the reins and settled him into a slow trot. Someone threw a carpetbag into the boot. The one-block drive to the Plantation House was a din of clanks, rings, pistol shots, whoops, cat-calls and licentious yells. For Lee Cameron, speech was impossible. He turned a black look at Emma who leaned gently against his shoulder, shivering. She pulled her shawl tightly around her and smiled. He leaned back and let the night tide flow and amid all the excitement, a drunken peace finally seeped into his veins. She was so calm, even happy. He wondered had she planned it too?

It was a short ride to the Plantation House. There was a nip in the night air. The tingle of coldness on his face made Cameron's thoughts begin to clear. He questioned Glenby. "What's going on?"

Glenby answered with his usual frankness. "You just got married. You should be grinning like you struck the mother lode, that's what."

At the Plantation House, Glenby pushed Cameron out of the buggy and helped Emma down. Cameron tightened his arm around her as the crowd crushed in on them. They marched into the lobby.

The Plantation House was no escape from the mob but it was the best hotel in town. It had wooden walls partitioning the rooms, doors with locks, sheets laundered fresh from Fu Ling every day, separate table linens, room service, the only bridal suite in all Varina, and a tough old manager named Stewart who knew what privacy meant. He kept a Sharps buffalo gun behind the reception desk.

"You can beat me at the tables, Glenby, or you can make a pauper of me payin' for this." It was a spiteful remark on Cameron's part.

Glenby maintained his perennial calm. "Dan McGillicuddy's payin'."

Glenby had already signed the register and handed the carpetbag to Cameron. "A rush job, this wedding, but you got yer lady, an' McGillicuddy's gettin' everything he paid for." He giggled an' hid his face.

What was Glenby trying to say? Open-mouthed, Cameron picked up the bag and nodded stupidly. He'd had too much to drink. At least he could sleep it off.

But Rob Glenby was an honest and open man. He held Cameron back now. "I want you to know it wasn't my idea."

At this outburst, Cameron mustered his thoughts. He gave Glenby one of those piercing looks that made Rob Glenby look away. "Lee, I owe you. You're a good man to Clem."

"Owe me what Rob?"

Glenby furrowed his brow and pulled in his powerful neck like a tortoise, as if he regretted what he was about to say. "I told 'em you wouldn't like it...that you'd be madder 'n a hornet. McGillicuddy and Lysaght and Thatcher connived it." Once Glenby started, he couldn't stop and the plot poured forth. "Miss Emma, she's like a daughter to Dan McGillicuddy. He wanted 'er outta the saloon an' livin' like a proper, honest lady, ...an' he wanted to make sure she got a good man... He admires you, Lee, or he wouldn't a done it."

"He likes me so he herds me to the altar like his pet goat?"

"Nossir. Not like herdin' goats. More like spurrin' an already gallopin' horse. You love 'er Lee, admit it, an' she loves you an' it was one hell of a party!" Glenby elbowed Cameron in the ribs and winked. "Get to 'er man!"

Full comprehension hit Lee Cameron like a splash of ice water on a sleeping babe. His wedding day! Staged! An excuse for a good time! He stared open-mouthed at Glenby and vowed to punch Dan McGillicuddy clear over the divide! But Emma was his and he hugged her tighter than ever beside him.

Stewart, the inn-keeper, handed Cameron the key and motioned the Camerons down the hall. The rowdy miners would have surged in behind but Stewart stood solidly in their path. He held the shiny old buffalo gun, cocked, with his index finger on the trigger.

"Let the gentleman and his lady pass." Stewart was British and oozed decorum. "The party's back down the street at the Citadel."

Stewart backed the drunken throng as far as the street where some drifted back to the saloons and some set up an all-night vigil under the window. No one went home.

Cameron felt the tension mount as he walked Emma up the stairs and down the narrow hall. Hoots still echoed from the street below. Slowly, he unlocked the door.

It was a luxurious room by frontier standards. About fifteen feet square, it had a big four-poster feather bed in the center with a marble-topped dresser against the far wall, a small square stove in the outer corner with a wash stand beside it, an upholstered armchair and a rich mahogany gate-leg table with six beautifully turned legs. An oil lamp showered its soft yellow glow over the rich patina of the table. A glass-paned window looked out on Warren Street. Its lace curtains were drawn and a small fire flickered in the stove. It was the best Varina had to offer but the thickest walls could not silence the stream of lewd remarks that jumped like sparks from the street below.

Cameron slouched morosely on the bed. He spoke in tones of veiled resentment. "It's over. We're safe."

Emma looked on apprehensively, with a touch of nostalgia in her voice, "This wasn't my doing if that's what you're thinking...I would've wanted a church wedding."

It was all McGillicuddy's doing, Cameron knew. The last few hours were incomprehensible. "Are we really married?"

Emma was taken back. "Thatcher is mayor. We only have about eighty witnesses." She sat beside him.

Lee Cameron did love Emma. There was no other he would have chosen for a wife, but this outrageous joining left him with a whole collection of doubts. Did she feel the same as he felt? What did she think? She had been married before. She hadn't said much all evening, just smiled sweetly. He still felt a sudden jealousy toward Dubois who had married her properly in church. He was bitterly angry at McGillicuddy who must have invented such a hair-brained scheme and at Pat Lysaght whose Gaelic prudishness had inspired Dan McGillicuddy. He was in no mood for sex. He cursed and glared at the floor. His eyes bored right through it to some faroff hell that condensed his passions and blood rushed to his temples like a gully-washer in a canyon.

Emma moved closer to him but he still brooded. Her hand on his knee did not interrupt his hard stare. When she spoke, it was with doubt, "Should I have said 'I don't'? What would you have me do?"

He turned his dark eyes on her at that and she continued. "It is legal. Thatch marries people all the time. Varina has no church, not yet."

He reached over then and put his arm gently around her shoulder. "It's just that it's not the way it should have been." His anger was melting slowly, one drop at a time.

"I shouldn't have married Dubois. We shouldn't be here. Whatever there should have been, will never be..."

He knew, but the words wouldn't come. There should have been a ceremony, a romantic setting, a columned manor, a pebbled drive between a corridor of elms, a fine carriage with a pair of high stepping hackneys to pull it, a lawn party with the scent of magnolias in the air. There should have been a butler and a footman and servants to serve sweetmeats. She should have worn a gown of white satin with a lace veil in her hair. There should have been a white-steepled church, lilies, a pipe organ, a choir. There should have been....He bowed his head. His thoughts trailed off. There should never have been a war! Why was it so hard to break with the past?

The look on his face had changed to anguish. The old soldier in him wanted to cry.

Emma Dubois gently touched his sleeve, as if he were brittle and about to break. "I do love you." It was the simple truth. "You do love me?" It was a question.

He breathed deeply and squeezed out the words. "Of course I love you." But he only put his hand over hers.

"McGillicuddy meant no harm."

"Don't mention his name to me." For a long time they sat on the edge of the bed sunk deep into the feather matress. The cut on her cheek still oozed a tiny drop of blood. The mud was still caked on the hem of her skirt and his heavy boots had sloshed it from the rain-soaked street across the floor. Her skirt hung raggedly where it was

148

torn and her dark curls were unruly and damp with the exertion of the dance.

"I am Mrs. Cameron now. No more Dubois." She was very beautiful in distress. "I'm tired."

Finally, he spoke, "We'll do it again, get married, in church, the right way."

She cupped his cheek in her hand and turned his head. "Lee Cameron, I've been married before in church with the flowers and the candles and the priest in his satin robes. It's a memory I'd as soon forget. Today, I'll always remember with joy."

She kissed him gently then and he kissed her back. It was not a passionate kiss—his emotions had drained him—but he felt better. He was her husband; she was his wife. They would build their home together. It would not be a columned mansion but it would be solid, built of good lodgepoles cut from the steep mountainside and hewn at the Holter Mill here in the cold dry heights that slowed irrevocable decay, and the home would endure through the years. They would plant trees, not elms but tough pine and juniper. And their garden would not grow cotton but root potatoes and corn and cabbage and the window boxes would be filled with the sturdy alpine bloosoms that carpet the high meadows in July. It was a new reality, a harsher one, a real one.

She walked to the table, pulled out the gate-leg and lifted up the carpetbag. Quietly she opened it—bedclothes, a hairbrush, a clean shirt for Cameron. But there was more, something heavy packed deeply under a linen cloth—leathern pokes of gold dust, twenty, thirty, over fifty of them.

"There's a fortune here!" The remark was unexpected and he answered sharply. "Don't talk of gold, not now, not on our wedding night."

"Look at this!"

He came up behind her and stared down at the riches with incredulity. "We can't accept this.... give it back."

She turned to him and their eyes locked together. He felt her eyes on his face, on his shoulders, on his breast, boring into the depths of his soul as if comprehending for the first time a new dimension of the man she had married. She spoke very softly, "I do love you, Lee Cameron. You're a just and generous man."

A passionate rush of anger and desire consumed him now like a tempest unleashed by an ancient god. He crushed her against him. They stood for a moment, then she pulled away and put her hand over his mouth.

"Don't think I'm cold, Lee Cameron. I will love you in passion and ecstasy. I will love you to my death. But I'm frightened and you're still angry. Wait 'til morning, Lee. It was to be tolerated with Dubois but you and I, we will love with abandon and joy. And Lee, we must keep the gold. It was given in good faith. I fear for you, that Spud Ervin will kill you. The gold may buy your life."

He took her hand and moved her fingers from his lips. His eyes narrowed and he looked away from her into another far reality. "Spud Ervin will never kill me." He sounded so confident, so determined, but he knew she was right. Suddenly, he realized how dreadfully she feared his loss, that her fear was so great, but for McGillicuddy's ruse, she may never have married him. Spud Ervin could kill him. Or he, Cameron, could kill Spud Ervin first.

Emma Dubois watched him as he undressed. She saw something she had not seen before—a raw, muscular power and commitment in the man. It was buried deep as the richest veins of ore in the gravels of the creek. It was simply there, a basic and sturdy core supporting every movement. He had survived a war. He would survive his wedding day and he would survive the struggle that was to come. She prayed that this time, he would win.

The noise still echoed in the street below. He got up to stir the fire. When he turned again to face her, laughter was back in his eyes. They were married now. It was abrupt. It was crude. But sometimes life called for quick decisions and men with the confidence to act upon them. They were Mr. and Mrs Leland James Cameron.

She was shaking and it wasn't cold. She sat squarely on the bed, pillows propping her against the hard wooden headboard. Her voice stuttered with deep emotion. "It's different with you." He waited for her to continue. "With Dubois, I did what was required...for Marie, for propriety, for some kind of life for us beyond a needle and thread and a copper laundry kettle....or worse the cribs and saloons."

He could find no words. His heart seemed to swell to fill the capacity of his chest, stifling any speech he could have made. He suddenly realized that she had fought her own war against rejection, poverty and scorn, the war of an unmarried woman with child in a society that ostracized them.

There were tears in her eyes. "I blamed you. I was so angry...and all the while I loved you...I couldn't forget you." Now she closed her eyes and twisted her knuckles around the edge of the blanket. "I wanted you dead....Nothing else made sense... after what we had promised...."

He stretched out beside her. It was his turn to be quiet.

"I'm trying to apologize, Lee Cameron, and my tongue is dry and hard. How can I tell you? I want you alive, living, breathing, standing beside me, fathering my children! Spud Ervin wants to strike you down! He must not, Lee Cameron, not now!"

A grim ruthlessness clouded his handsome face and he stared like a hawk over his hooked Saxon nose. He was still angry but the direction of his anger had changed. It no longer railed against the guileless conspiracies of McGillicuddy and Lysaght, but against the deep, insidious evil of the Ervins. "I'm a soldier. I know how to fight."

She rambled on as if she hadn't heard. "You're very dashing when you're angry..." Her voice trailed off. The look on his face scared her.

But he was struggling with a new emotion—the fear that the forces of Spud Ervin might harm her, might cause him to lose what he had so recently won. He stroked the crevices of her neck and held her close against him, trying to convey a calm and hope to her that he knew he did not have. Gradually, she relaxed. She slept. But like a prairie fire, his thoughts raged on. The mist lifted from his brain and he saw clearly what he must do. He must get her away from the Citadel, away from the whiskey and gold. McGillicuddy wanted a home for her. He had forced the issue but he was right.

In the grey cool hours of the dawn she awoke and reached for him. It was quiet then. Last night's passion had condensed to a stubborn white-hot flame. They were alone. A wildfire swept over them, welding them together, licking up all the dry undergrowth of summers past and leaving the ground cleansed and bare for new sprouts of life to come. When it was done, the first rosy light of day streamed through the curtains as if the War and last night's violence had never happened. They slept late into the day.

Chapter 24

The bright days of June spun busily into a warm July and a cooler, rainier August. Cameron made peace with Dan McGillicuddy and went back to the tables at the Citadel. His old southern pride surfaced—he objected to his wife working in a gaming house. Ladies did not frequent the tables—there was a private parlor for their exclusive use next door. Emma acquiesed but the inactivity bored her. She didn't return to the house on Jones St. except to pack her belongings. She remained at the Plantation House and let the rooms to Midge and Gertie and Pat Lysaght whose hip still pained him.

Boredom fed her anxieties. She read old newspapers and whatever books she could find. She daydreamed—they were bad dreams. Fear of Spud Ervin would not diminish. She imagined Lee thrown from his horse, injured or gutshot and Spud Ervin in the shadows blowing the smoke from the barrel of his gun. She would wrench her thoughts from such lurid scenes, but the images always returned.

Spud Ervin surfaced from time to time like a dead fish laying flat on the oily surface of the water, with a bejeweled bawdy girl on his arm, breasts overflowing her whalebones, walking lustily by the hotel, one hip at a time, loud and lewd, or like a rabid wolf, shouting, ranting, shooting off his gun in the middle of Warren Street in a drunken fit, until he collapsed and someone dared get close enough to take the gun away and send him home.

And Curly Shaw continued his pranks, once spattering McGillicuddy's gleaming black suit with mud and once shooting the sign loose from over the Citadel. Rumor spread that he commanded a growing gang of thugs who monopolized the east end of Varina and ruled sleepy little Highland. But they were hatching future schemes and left the Camerons alone.

Lee Cameron worked steadily at the Citadel. If trouble materialized he would melt quietly into the dark of McGillicuddy's back room. But he looked for permanent quarters in vain. Clean, safe living space was scarce in Varina, and it grew more scarce the higher you climbed up Jefferson Street. Fortune hunters, like swarms of grasshoppers, descended upon Varina regularly. Some struck new riches, and like Emma, craved respectability—a house on Jefferson Street, in the respectable part of town. That was how Spud Ervin had phrased it. The houses at the top of Jefferson dominated the top of the hill like deities on their thrones and they cost dearly. They were small by plantation standards but each was porched, painted and gingerbreaded after the latest vogue and had bedrooms, not lofts, upstairs. But none were for sale. Not even an empty lot was to be had.

In the end, Lee and Emma Cameron stayed at the Plantation House and watched summer wane. Flowers wilted. Grass turned yellow. The house on Jones St. suffered mildly from neglect. The porch grew a slippery icing of mud and the paint began to bubble from the dampness of the August rains. Spud Ervin hadn't even filed for eviction. Emma was no longer there and he was strangely absent this last month.

But Lee Cameron had not forgotten him and went everywhere armed. Each flutter of window curtain and glint of light in a doorway held his attention. The smallest creak of floorboard, scuff of boot or squeak of saddle leather made his muscles tense. Above all, he feared for Emma. He feared the cramp in his heart and shrinking in his throat when he thought of losing her. He feared the blinding rage that pounded at his temples when he thought of Spud Ervin violating her. It was far more intense than any resentment he still harbored toward McGillicuddy. It rose like a bile in his throat and took all his will to choke back down. He feared one day it would rise and consume him, that one day all Varina would condemn him for it. He was a gambler with a gunman's reputation that he could not dispel. He had married a dance hall girl and saloon dealer. Would the families, the shopkeepers, lawyers and craftsmen who were moving into Varina, accept him or her as equals? Would he ever build a house on the hill? Would Ervin allow him to build his home in peace?

He hadn't slept well in weeks. His thoughts rattled his brain deep into the night. Night was the worst time. Cameron was never a dreamer but it was at night when he lay awake with Emma breathing softly beside him that old anxieties came to haunt him. The shrieking shells, his dying and moaning comrades-in-arms, the burned out houses of his homeland, the sweet putrid smell of decaying flesh, and over all, the wasted, livid face of Spud Ervin—he shrank from the horror. So much was destroyed and for what reason? He had put down his arms. He had tried so hard not to antagonize Spud Ervin. But the old animosities reappeared without warning and new evils reinforced his old hatreds. Cameron could not think of Spud Ervin and Curly Shaw without resentment at their audacity and senselessness. Could he contain his rage if one of Curly's shots hit flesh and bone, if Spud Ervin attacked his wife? Who could predict? He doubted himself, because deep in his heart he harbored a primitive impulse, the urge to eliminate an enemy.

Lee Cameron's worries intensified now that he was a married man. He wanted a home. To shed the wandering life, to rest in his own bed, and sleep with the confidence of a man who owned his own piece of God's earth, a ranch, a family, his daughter, good friends, permanence, roots, these were what war had cost him and what he deeply craved. In the night, he clung to the languid, sleeping form of the woman he loved as if her presence were fleeting illusion. He would clutch her desperately and she would awake and they would talk into the darkest hours. But the dreadful fear that his ecstasy was not for a lifetime but only for a moment, fueled his doubts. She had the same doubts and they hammered at her soul. The walls were so thin, they would hear Spud Ervin reeling and shouting his angry threats in the street below. Lee Cameron repressed the urge to run downstairs and silence him.

Meanwhile Cameron worked and saved. He and Emma had posted a telegram for little Marie and their need for a permanent home became more urgent. He turned then to the only other thing he knew besides war and cards—horses. He could raise and train horses. They could run a ranch.

Time was pressing. The autumn of the year arrived early. Marie was coming west soon with Father Manno and the good father would continue on to his mission with the Flatheads at Mary's Lake. He and Marie probably had already started—the Camerons had not received word. The good father should choose the Mormon trail which was much longer but safer for the child. They could not risk her to Indian attacks up and down the Bozeman cut-off where the hordes of Red Cloud raged. Riverboat would be faster and safer but the Missouri waters were already falling and the last boats had embarked. A trip by boat would have to wait another year. Already, the waters were freezing in the highest altitudes. The priest and child would pass through Corinne, in Utah, and the Mormon settlements and the highest point at the Pleasant Valley Divide where snow could fly even in August. Winter came fast in the high country and they still had six weeks to two months travel before them. Lee Cameron agonized about the child he had never met.

Financially, Emma and Lee Cameron were secure. McGillicuddy had bought Emma's share of the Citadel—his clientele was steady, even without Emma. The girls drifted in from the dance hall next door. Cameron had earned good pay gambling and had banked his gold. With Emma's proceeds from the sale of the Citadel, they laid plans. Cameron's treasure on Outlaw Bar, what he had dug up at old Lysaght's mine, was still his secret, not even revealed to Emma.

On land, somewhere east of Varina—they would build a ranch, raise horses. Glenby's black mare would make a fine dam. If Glenby would agree to sell her, Cameron would find a suitable sire. In the Gallatin Valley, near the new Bozeman City, there was good grazing land. Fearful settlers were leaving like curs from a kill when a larger predator challenges. The Montana Post had just reported an Indian raid at Bozeman City, 40 head of horses and 10 mules lost. The Crows blamed the Flatheads; the Flatheads blamed the Crows. The settlers blamed all Indians. The whites panicked. They rushed to get out before the winter's freeze and snows closed the high passes. The snows arrived later on the Bozeman cut-off east of the divide but that didn't help: nobody was going by John Bozeman's trail who wanted to keep his scalp. Bozeman himself had died there last April. The Sioux had even attacked and defeated the United States Army. The fleeing settlers chose the Corinne road to the railhead but like Father Manno and Marie, their time was short. Snow on the Pleasant Valley Divide threatened. Many settlers simply abandoned all in their frenzy to leave, accepted whatever pittance was offered and turned tail and ran. It was a crazed exodus of a volatile population. There was always more land, more gold farther west in Idaho or Oregon. And news of more Indian raids arrived every day. Only a few brave people stayed.

Lee Cameron was brave. He feared Indians less than the Yankee rabble and less than Spud Ervin. He left Varina now in the second week of September and Rob Glenby went with him. They rode toward a different life, more solid, without the glamour and gaiety and the broad human acquaintance of Varina, but without her prejudice and brutality. Cameron wanted more for his family than a gambling hall and a house on Jones Street with peeling paint. He wanted an identity with the land, his land. He'd grown up on the red clay Georgia soil, ground it daily into the soles of his shoes and wiped its dust from his boots, lived with it and parted with it like so many of his southern compatriots. It was a deep, basic craving. Would Emma admit or deny his need? She had lived in a city all her life. Could she stand the isolation and emptiness of these open grasslands? Could she muster the courage to live away from community under the wide sweep of sky and mountain that was the Territory of Montana, separated from friends by broad mountain ranges and wide rivers? When finally he did speak to her, he poured out his feelings in a torrential flood over coffee in McGillicuddy's back room.

Her reaction was immediate. She stood opposite him, hands on her hips. "I came upriver didn't I...with paunchy Dubois!"

He had never heard her describe Dubois that way and it filled him with a hesitant relief.

Then she added with a smirk. "I love you much more!" It was stated harshly as a practical matter of fact. He hadn't realized how much she, too, yearned for permanence and respectability. He chased her then around the table and she teased and jumped away until McGillicuddy interrupted their playful exuberance. Their love-making that night reached new ecstasy.

The next day, Cameron asked Glenby to be his partner. Glenby was delighted with the idea. "A ranch. Clem would like that—but I have my contract with the Overland."

"Keep it...I supply fresh stock and rest the jaded ones. I'll do it cheaper on free grass than you can paying for feed here in town."

"Might work. Might work right well, even with a Dixieman partner."

Cameron and Glenby outfitted themselves with a pack horse and the best rifles available and set out east over the rim and down into the Madison Valley. They were looking for good grazing land and they carried payment, a thousand dollars in clean gold dust. Downstream where the junction of rivers nourished a lush plain, the grass was waist-high, watered by creeks and rivulets and the plain teemed with game. The ponds were thick with fowl. Lewis and Clark had passed that way and named the rivers. That was 1805. Jim Bridger outran his Blackfoot captors there at the headwaters of the great Missouri. It was a wide flat plain that stretched like a languorous woman between the reaches of snowy peaks, verdant and fertile. The air was fresh and clean; the waters clear and icy. Homesteaders had come into the valley to farm where John Bozeman had established his village. They brought seeds of potatoes and wheat, corn and cabbage and sheep, chickens and pigs. Their cattle grew fat on the broad reaches of waist-high grasses. Now many of those same homesteaders were leaving.

Constant vigilance was necessary. This was Crow country. Cameron was new to the country and rode relaxed—he had always been in the company of a wagon train. But Glenby's eyes scoured the landscape for the movement of each blade of grass. Nothing escaped him, a chickadee in a cottonwood, a rock chuck in a burrow, the buzz of a lowly bee.

Thefts, especially of horses, were common and he knew it. Road agents still lurked, even after the vigilantes had cleared them from Varina. They moved farther out and masked their depradations in the guise of Indian raids. Blackfeet, Crow, Bannack, Snake and Flathead raided the settlements and raided each other. Acting Governor Meagher had waged a hapless campaign against the tribes. Hatreds grew and violence persisted: Sioux vs. Crow; Crow vs. Blackfoot; and white man vs. white man if gold or profit were to be had. With his new repeating rifles, the white man was most murderous of all.

Into all this, Lee Cameron carried the new gun McGillicuddy had given him with his hopes, his fears, his southern pride and a persistent optimism. Rob Glenby rode in front. He knew the way. Cameron came behind. The trail wound down the western wall of the Madison valley in tight switchbacks which widened as the slope levelled. The Spanish Peaks stood like black daggers, slicing a fiery sunrise into three triangles of flames. Cameron squinted into the morning light. He and Glenby must cross the river and follow the base of those black peaks northward.

Cameron rode Glenby's black mare who stepped gingerly between the rocks. Glenby's bay was wider boned and clumsier and stumbled from time to time. Heads down, the horses crimped their rumps under them as their weight shifted hard to the fore. The men carried new Winchester 66's and 200 rounds of ammunition. They rode in silence. The only sound was the strike of hoof on stone, the lap of water on sand and the faint whisper of air churning through the trees. Aspen and cottonwood were still green where they sucked moisture from the river but the grassy slopes had parched.

As they neared the river, they saw elk grazing and a bear interrupted his berry-picking and wandered off into the brush. A fish jumped and splashed, then another. A bald eagle circled higher, higher until he was barely a dot on the highest updrafts. Glenby stopped suddenly, on a bench overlooking the river. "We can rest 'ere a piece. Good water an' open space. We'll have a fair view of anyone wants to come join us. Horses can use a blow."

Cameron dismounted.

Again Glenby spoke, "Stay by them horses. Water 'em good. I'll go pick some berries for dessert." He took his Winchester with him.

Lee Cameron, except for the ride from Benton to Varina, was a novice in the wilderness. He relied on Glenby. Cameron led the three horses to the river. The shore was flat and hard with a thin coating of gravel, and the horses tugged him along eagerly. While they stretched their necks to drink, he leaned his gun against a boulder, took a long swallow from his own canteen, then reached into his saddlebags for some biscuit.

Out of nowhere, behind him, he heard a horse stamp and blow. Two Indians, sat staring down on him from behind a cover of saplings about 20 yards away. Cameron sensed their presence before he saw them so well were they camouflaged behind the stripes of trees. He turned warily. Each held an old muzzle loader. They were tall muscular men. Where was Glenby?

With hand signals the Indians made their intentions very plain. They rode scruffy, tired ponies. They wanted the black horse in particular and the new rifle. One brave motioned toward the horse, walked boldly up to Cameron, held his right palm upward and pointed with the left to the horse. The other brave edged his horse around Cameron to where the rifle stood uselessly, reached down and picked it up. Cameron held firmly to the reins of the three horses. He shook his head no and the brave held up two fingers and pointed to himself, one finger and pointed to Cameron. Two Indians. One unarmed white man. Cameron understood very well. Suddenly, the first Indian lurched and snatched at the reins. Cameron slapped back at the horses who shied free and trotted down the riverbank. The other Indian loped after them when Glenby appeared. He fired once and winged the mounted Indian, knocking him from his horse. The Indian rolled off into the brush. At the sound of the shot, the second Indian charged Cameron, knocking him sideways, grabbing the rifle and running into the brush after his companion. Glenby ran for the horses, mounted, and came back to Cameron who was flat on the ground, red in the face and light in the head.

"Surprised? They don't fight in no regular army, no formations an' rifle pits, generals an' tactics. They never heard of Napoleon an' they got your gun...half of what they come for...Mount up! We ride out fast before their friends arrive. Them Crows travel with company." Glenby clutched his rifle like a miser hoards his gold, and added. "Didn't they teach you Rebs to hang on to your weapons?" Lee Cameron blanched almost to the point of striking out but Glenby didn't mean to insult. He was right. Cameron should have been more careful. But Glenby wasn't finished, "And you take the pack horse, now you have a free hand." Humiliated, Cameron obeyed.

They galloped down the valley, north toward the Three Forks of the Missouri and the white settlements, slowing the pace only when Glenby felt they had outrun the two Crows. Glenby led Cameron across rock ledges and stony bars. They splashed through water—anywhere that would leave no trace of their passage. Cameron felt the big horse tiring beneath him. She was blowing hard and beginning to stumble.

Finally, after two hours of grueling riding, they entered a narrow spruce glen about a half-mile back from the river. "Lucky they wasn't Blackfeet—we'd be dead. We'll rest here, cross the river after dark." Glenby glanced grimly at Cameron. "I ain't gonna let redskins steal that mare..." It was another reproach. Cameron bit his tongue hard. Now Glenby pointed to a flat bench above a ten foot boulder. "I'm goin' up there. You catch a few winks, feed the horses... And don't build a fire!" It was a terrible dismissal for a military man and officer—Cameron had been reduced to the level of groom.

Cameron picketed the horses close, sat down and laid his head against the rough bark of a spruce tree. He held his pistol tightly in his lap. Sleep wouldn't come. His every muscle tensed. He could hear the brush of leaf against leaf, the steady breathing of the animals, the fall of a spruce needle like the caress of virgin snow on frozen sod, just above the threshold of his perception. He watched smokelike clouds unfold across the evening sky. He smelled the wetness of oncoming rain in the air. It was quiet. A magpie hooted. The wind picked up and hissed venomously through the spruces, a cold damp, bone-chilling wind. The temperature fell. Cameron pulled his old greatcoat from his blanket roll and slipped it on. He had no gloves. He tucked his hands into his sleeves and turned up his collar. Still, sleep wouldn't come. The humiliation had been too great.

Finally, Lee Cameron climbed up to join Glenby. "I can't sleep. You catch a nod."

Glenby grunted and stifled a cough. He looked haggard with strain. His chest rattled when he spoke, "You sure?"

"It won't happen again."

"Again and we're dead men. We'll ride at night, stay out of sight. It'll be cold and maybe wet. Lay low now and don't move around. Indians have eyes that can see through rocks." Grudgingly, he added, "Thanks, I need the sleep...And treat this rifle like it was yer own newborn babe!" He handed the rifle to Cameron, found a level spot in the grass and lay down.

Cameron had never been so alert, not even on the night of the flank march when General Jackson ordered the 19th Georgia to march unseen around three divisions of Yanks. From the bench atop the boulder, he had a good view of the river. It wound peacefully down a wide valley covered with yellowing grasses, red willow sprouts, tall shaggy cottonwoods, and rimmed with great hulks of purple mountains. Snow already dusted their peaks and dark green spruce and fir dotted the higher slopes as they did the spot where he and Glenby hid. Cameron revelled in the wild silence and in the singular sounds that invaded it. A pine cone fell through the needled branches, thumped gently against the earth and rolled away down the slope. A marmot scurried over the rocks to his den. An insect twittered. Gradually, a gray-green mist swallowed the Spanish Peaks.

Blackening clouds swept down like ghosts on the wind and blanketed the light. It grew colder still. Cameron looked out from beneath the brim of his hat. The metal of the rifle barrel clung cold against his side. He stroked the wooden stock to keep his hands warm. He could see only what was immediately before him—the great grey boulders, monstrous toeholds of the giant mountains. Indian trails wound through them. Fear struck him then. What menace did the rocks conceal? Bears, mountain lions and wolves lurked amomg the crags. He thought of Emma. How could she live out here in the wild? Was he a fool to think he could make her happy here? Glenby slept on. Cameron's worked his icy fingers and stamped his feet to restore warmth. When it was completely dark, he woke Glenby. They could barely see to saddle up.

"We go by Pinon Ford. We're goin' to have to expose ourselves for about a mile 'til we hit the trees but it's faster. There's a cabin near the ford. Old man named Burton lives there, traps some, runs a still. If he's home, he'll stave off trouble. Stay close. Don't lag 'n hold on to your pistol. They'll shoot first now they got a good rifle and they want that horse!"

They rode more slowly now. Shades of blackness, the purples and blues, enveloped them like smoke that rises from wet wood. Cameron felt the black mare ease her pace. She tensed, arched her neck and Cameron could feel her bend away from the shadows. He cocked his gun. He could hear the river now and could just pick out the narrow ribbon of trail.

Suddenly, he smelled pine logs burning. Warmth, hot food, companionship was near. Glenby pointed, "Burton's cabin is over there." They followed the smell, through the cottonwoods. About twenty feet short of the cabin, Cameron halted abruptly. Four horses were tied at the hitchrail outside. Raucous laughter and loud conversation sounded from inside. Cameron couldn't make out the words, but he recognized the voice and knew the horses. The nearest one was paint.

The mist had camouflaged their approach and for now, Cameron and Glenby were hidden behind the thick trunks of the trees. But they had not been quiet and the laughter and sound of the river only partly muffled their arrival. As they watched, a man came out, looked left and right, bit off a chew of tobacco and stood for a minute listening. Cameron and Glenby didn't move. Finally, the man clapped his hands together, unhitched the horses and led them to a stockade behind the cabin. Had he heard them or had the sounds of his own four horses disguised the sound of their coming?

Cameron signaled Glenby and wove his way backward and downstream through the trees. The ground was soft and dry. The horses hooves scuffed quietly as the cottonwoods began to give way to clumps of willow and sage.

"We gonna have to swim, we don't use that ford." Glenby's voice rasped.

"Then swim we will. That's young Ervin back there and Shaw must be with him. They don't like me an' I've no cause to stir the hive."

"You took on Ervin before an' you're still here."

"I'm a married man now." Glenby understood. Cameron didn't need to explain.

They rode on hugging the riverbank. The land began to rise in relation to the river which cut down between steep embankments thick with brush.

Glenby called to Cameron. "We got to cross before the bank gets too steep or we'll be cuttin' rapids." He stopped to dismount and handed Cameron the reins. "Hold my horse. Wish I could see better. I'm gonna find us a ford."

Cameron saw him slide down the embankment and heard faint ripplings in the water, like a large fish slapping its tail or a small animal testing its depth before it drank.

Glenby scrambled back out and up the bank. He was wet to the waist and muddy. "Right there, the way I figure it." He pointed to a spot a few yards away where some faint reflection of moonlight seemed to linger. When he mounted again, he pressed his heels to his horse and plunged down the bank and into the cold river. Cameron followed, tugging the pack horse behind. The startled mare swam in leaps, pulling the lesser animal. He grabbed mane and held on. With a rush, the current pulled them both downstream and Cameron felt the mare's powerful muscles struggle hard. He lost sight of Glenby and he could not pick out the opposite bank. He heard a splash and a curse. Then he felt the mare scramble for footing and they were coming out of the water up onto a wide bar. The mare stopped and shook off the water until every bone in Cameron's body rattled like a coin in a can. But they were across and the shaking animal warmed him.

He strained his eyes for some sign of Rob Glenby. He heard a scraping on gravel farther downstream and headed toward the sound. Glenby lay stretched on a near vertical bank clinging to the reins. The frightened horse stood trembling looking down at him from atop the bank. Its knees and hocks were bloodied, its muzzle muddied. It had lost its footing in the torrent, lurched forward and pitched Rob Glenby into the icy malestrom. He had held tightly to the reins and the frightened horse had pulled him by its jaw, scraping and kicking its way through the scrub up the steep embankment. Once on dry ground, the animal forgot its fear, felt the tug on its jaw and stopped, leaving Glenby bruised, half-drowned and on the brink of tumbling back into the icy water. The two thin leather reins and Glenby's own iron grip were his only salvation.

When Cameron spotted his friend, he dared not move too quickly for fear of spooking the horse again and upsetting the tenuous balance that kept Glenby above the sweeping current. He reached over the embankment, grabbed Glenby by the wrist and pulled. With the slackening of pressure, the horse reared backward, heaving Glenby and Cameron into a huddle up on the bank. Cameron rolled free then rushed to Glenby.

Glenby was already sitting up, cursing. "Damn! My gun's wet! Pack's gone!" Then, he choked up a stream of water and rasped. "Mount up! Can't be stoppin'." His breath came in gasps like a horse with broken wind and his teeth chattered like hammers, but he stood up without help.

Lee Cameron balked. "You need a fire, man. Dry out and get warm!" Cameron took off his coat and wrapped it around Glenby's shoulders.

Glenby shrugged it off. "No fire. Git that Rebel rag off a me! I never wear grey!"

Cameron caught the forceful rejection and drew back. Glenby barked an order. "Mount up. We ride or git caught on the trail at night. Horses are just as cold as me. The exercise'll get my blood movin' an' I ain't lettin' those Injuns catch me with a wet rifle that don't shoot." He looked angrily at Cameron, slapped down the hand that would help him stand, pulled himself up on the horse and led off. The soggy saddle leather squeaked with every movement of the horse. Cameron followed the sound into the trees. The rifle he held was useless and he slid it into its scabbard and kept his hand free for his pistol. Miraculously they found the pack horse about a mile downstream. The packs had slipped and now hung beneath the frightened horse's belly like wet shredded rags. Their contents were gone.

They rode fast all night, Glenby leading most of the way. Lee Cameron followed by sound and sense. He could not see. He gave the mare her head and let her pick her own way.

From Varina, just east of the Jefferson in the Ruby drainage, they had ridden farther east, crossed the Madison River and now they travelled north down the Madison valley until the mountains flattened into high, rolling plains. From here, they paralleled the Gallatin River to where the valley rolled away easily in a wide park toward a small settlement nestled at the hot springs.

Dawn broke slowly. The vast sky greyed ominously with sweeping ironclad clouds that moved with the wind out from the Gallatin Range across the foothills and on to the pinnacles of the Bridger mountains to the northeast. The mist was lifting. Gradually, out of the greyness, the larger park revealed itself. They could see beyond the junction of rivers at Three Forks where they formed the great Missouri. Cameron rubbed his eyes. It was very beautiful. The Gallatin River spewed over granite boulders out of mountain canyons in a wild exuberance, onto the rolling plain and its marriage with the Jefferson and Madison. Dark green spruces littered the sloping canyons at the edge of the park and accented the pale silver bark and yellow leaves of the aspen. Waves of golden prairie grasses, waist-high, rippled in the wind. Giant cottonwoods, still green, clung to the riverbanks and reddening stalks of willow poked out of crevices. Here were buffalo jumps and fumaroles. Here Indians hunted. Buffalo, elk and antelope grazed. Bozeman City was still miles to the east. It hovered on the fertile plain, like an insect on a pond, in the distance below Jim Bridger's massive peaks and John Bozeman's rocky pass. In shear expanse, the park dwarfed the Allegheny valleys where Cameron had lived and fought. Now Cameron looked upon the land with amazement. It was a majestic land. Southerners lived and died and ached in their hearts when they lost land like this. This was the land Lee Cameron craved for his home.

A blast of cold off the mountaintops reminded him that he was in a new place, where the growing season was shorter, where snow blanketed the earth early and where you could sometimes see the Arctic lights that streaked the midnight sky. This was not Georgia. It was more primitive and fierce. As he rode on, it occurred to him that he would have to fight, to struggle and to persevere for the possession of this land. And Emma would have to fight alongside him. He vowed to die before he would lose this war. He had gained too much.

The going was smoother now that they had reached the grasslands and the horses hooves thudded dully on the softer turf. The sun rose in a blue sky, but it was still cold. Glenby had lagged far behind. Cameron pulled up, then swung the mare round to look back for his friend. He was appalled at what he saw. Glenby sat huddled in his saddle, shivering from cold and exposure. Icicles had formed overnight on his hat and beard and with the warming of day, had started to drip. He was wet and shivering, and the cruel wind was robbing his body of whatever warmth it could generate. But Rob Glenby never complained.

Lee Cameron halted abruptly. "We stop here. I'm building a fire." This time, Glenby did not object even when Cameron released the rifle to gather wood and strike a fire. His pistol was tucked in his belt and the rifle was still wet and there was no hiding a fire if Indians lurked nearby.

Glenby had swallowed a good portion of icy mountain snow melt. It had chilled his insides and the effort of keeping warm had robbed his body of strength. His breath came in a forced staccato of gasps and gurgles. When he coughed, his face went white. Cameron helped him down from his horse, stripped his damp clothing, covered him with a dry blanket and propped him against a log near the fire. Then he set branches in the ground to form a windbreak and boiled some coffee. "Where's the nearest settlement?"

"Bozeman City. That's where we're goin'."

"Isn't Three Forks or the hot springs closer?"

"Nobody there. A few homesteaders, but that's out of our...." A spasm of coughing seized Rob Glenby and shook him like a snowflake in a gale.

"We go to Three Forks." Cameron had taken charge because Glenby was too weak to resist.

"There's a man I know, Dawson, has a place near the hot springs. It's closer." Glenby could barely whisper.

Chapter 25

All summer long, Spud Ervin practiced shooting every day at his targets on the mountain. Rumor spread that he was improving fast. For the past month, he had lived like a recluse, like his father, Sime, in the mine. Spud perfected his shooting and guarded his gold with the same single-mindedness as his sire, but unlike his sire, it was a woman he wanted and the power to make her want him.

He'd thought it all out. He had first to erase the looks of pity that the town matrons grudgingly bestowed. How he hated them! Dexterity with a gun would overshadow his deformity and earn their fear. Gold would buy the instruments of power. But would fear and power secure the woman he desired or had he confused fear with simple human respect? He wanted Emma to come to him begging, on her knees and he could be patient. Spud Ervin concentrated all his efforts now on this desire with the crazed insistence of an obsession. He practiced his shooting, organized the shipment of his gold and lusted in his heart.

He was reported occasionally to have been in Varina, but he avoided the Citadel and conducted most of his business at Clive Sherman's Queen of the Nile, at Judge Burnwell's home up on Jefferson or up the gulch in Highland. There he hired wheelwrights, carpenters and teamsters and organized the building of wagons and the purchase of oxen. Highland buzzed with activity. Spud Ervin's men constructed heavy freight wagons with boxes ten feet in length and wheels five feet in diameter. The planking came from Holter's new mill which hadn't stopped sawing logs since it opened only a few months before. Two smiths clanked out nails, clamps and chains. He had employed all the cartwrights within a ten mile radius.

Garrity had spied Ervin and his paint horse at the hitch rail at Judge Burnwell's house about a month ago. Spud had held a sheaf of papers under his arm and had spoken heatedly with a tall stranger in black. He had looked haggard and angry like he had been frustrated in his business. His face had greyed over and hardened like a slab of granite, with a sharp angle at the jawline that clamped his mouth into a tight line, recessed his cheeks and forced his eyes back into darkened sockets. Garrity voiced the description to McGillicuddy softly with knitted, worried brows.

McGillicuddy, too, reported seeing Spud glaring intently at the Plantation House from the edge of Garnet Creek. He had scared Rachel who had come running to Emma because her husband, Jimmy Long, was away working at the sawmill. Spud was there, standing grimly. Emma wondered what subtle revenge he could devise and sat stiffly on the hotel porch with a gun in her pocket. But Spud did not accost her.

Emma was not out of his reach even though she was married and lived at the hotel. She knew Spud's wounds were raw. They refused to heal like the cancerous hatred in his soul. Through the years she had known bad men. Spud Ervin was one and very young: his age only punctuated the erosion of his youth and enhanced his reckless and merciless depravity. Emma shivered and withdrew at the sight of Spud Ervin, behind a curtain or doorway or into the anonymity of a crowd and turned her thoughts to Lee Cameron.

Two days later, a man in black stood with Spud and Judge Burnwell on the steps of the Judge's house. It was Clem who pointed Spud out to Garrity this time. Spud had spurred his horse until it bled and this angered Clem who wanted to rescue the horse from the hitchrail immediately. Garrity held him back.

Spud was about to leave the Judge and his long sinuous fingers stroked a watch fob sensuously as if it were the soft breast of a woman. But the action was cold. He could have stroked a trigger or the barbs of a whip exactly the same way. The other man was a hired gun or that's what Con Garrity said he looked like. Garrity had seen him before, but he couldn't place the man. He made Clem stay away.

The stranger was an enigma and Emma and McGillicuddy went to check the hotel register that afternoon. Stewart opened it and read the name aloud. "Charles Slade."

A flicker of recognition lit Stewart's face. "Slade. Only other Slade I knew was the Captain J.A. That'd be Joseph Albert." Stewart glared into Emma's anxious face. McGillicuddy was nodding. All three knew of Captain Joseph Albert Slade. His wife had owned the black horse

166

Lee Cameron was riding. His body lay with Boone Helm and Georges Ives under the tailings on Outlaw bar. The vigilantes had hung him. Could this be a brother of the notorious Captain Joseph Albert Slade? McGillicuddy raised an eyebrow. And why was Slade talking with Spud Ervin?

It was Charles Slade. Slade had checked into the Plantation House on July fourth, in the midst of Varina's first salute to the stars and stripes. Before the celebration, the Southern cross or the Texas Lone Star had flown over Varina. The flag-raisers, who had stitched the pieces of the Unionjack together and hidden it between the quilts of their bed, feared Varina's population of former Confederates, some of whom had threatened to shoot the organizers of the Independence Day celebration and tear down the offending flag. Amid the commotion, Charles Slade had arrived in Varina unobserved.

Stewart approached Slade the next time he appeared in the lobby. Emma stood nearby.

"Knowed a man once named Slade." Stewart spoke as he read the signature. "Captain Joseph Albert Slade. Same last name as you." Stewart glanced poker-faced over the rims of his spectacles.

"My big brother." answered the stranger. "You hung him." His voice sliced like a sharp blade through soft hide. Stewart blanched but Charles Slade smiled and tipped his hat to Emma Cameron.

The brother, Captain J.A. Slade had been a tall, handsome man and a fine dresser, poised and mannerly. He was a town legend. When he was sober, the town adored him. He was generous and personable to all and patient with the half-wit, Clem Glenby. When he was drunk, the whole town barred its doors against the reincarnation of Satan himself.

Charles Slade had the height and dark good looks of his brother, Joseph Albert, but he was restrained and polite, almost to the point of snobbish imperiousness. And he was eminently self-assured. He went quietly about town, tipped his hat to the ladies, spoke courteously and paid his bills. After a few days, curiosity waned and the town accepted him. He was surely a cut above the rest of the toughs arriving in Varina and a cut above his notorious brother. And Charles Slade stayed quietly to himself.

This summer, numbers of hardened men, like Gus Terry and Charles Slade, arrived and stayed. They were not prospectors whose nature was to be transient, always to seek and even when they found, to sell out quickly to the highest bidder and continue the search. The new arrivals were too well-dressed and well-horsed to pan for gold. They paid for the best lodging. They didn't freight goods or storekeep or cut timber or shoe horses. They did not work to earn money and still they had money for whiskey and women, cards and horse races. They loafed and drank and gamed and whored. Sporadic fights increased, yet there were no murders or thefts. They spent money freely, not paper but gold. McGillicuddy and Emma saw some of them nightly in the Citadel but most went to the Clive Sherman's Queen. They were fighters, dismissed from the ranks of General Meagher's short-lived army and newly hired to guard Spud Ervin's gold. And Spud Ervin swaggered like a prince among them but not at the Citadel, the scene of his defeat, where his prestige lacked lustre. He went to the Queen. Gus Terry snickered when he saw him and lifted his glass in salute.

Tonight, Gus Terry's musings with Clive Sherman drifted to another man. "Trust Charlie to smell easy money, Gus."

"Charlie who?"

"Slade, ain't you seen 'im?" Sherman wondered how anybody could smell anything over the stench of Gus Terry. "I'll wager he's collectin' wages from Ervin, just like you."

"Slade don't collect wages, Sherm. He pays 'em. He's not here to root around after someone else's gold." He ran his fingers through his beard and Sherman stepped back. "Charlie Slade is here fer brother J.A....He don't bow to no Ervin." Gus Terry nodded as if to confirm his statement and laughed loudly. The buckles on his overalls bounced up and down on his massive chest.

Sherman wiped the bugs off the bar with a wet rag and let Terry ramble on. But Gus Terry had stopped calling Spud Ervin a kid. He continued. "Spud's got salt. I been teachin' 'im how to hate. He's drawin' with 'is left now an' he's gettin' faster all the time. Gonna go after that Reb dandy who stole 'is girl, feller named Cameron. He's fast an' gittin' faster, I tell ya."

"Not faster 'n you I hope." Sherman was simply extending the conversation but the remark irritated Terry.

Gus Terry frowned. "You callin' me stupid! No pansy brat gonna outshoot Gus Terry!"

Clive Sherman backed off. "I won't tell 'im you said that."

Terry continued, "If he is workin' fer Ervin, Charlie Slade's expensive. You thought a that, Sherm."

"Ervin'll pay him off and he'll leave."

"Ervin'll pay him off with a chunk of the gold shipment that could've been yers and mine." Terry rubbed his big knuckles in his beard and spat a stream of tobacco juice into a brass spitoon. He missed and the brown juice etched a neat puddle on the barroom floor.

"Sometimes, Gus, Spud Ervin aims better 'n you!" Sherman wrinkled his nose and turned his face away.

Gus continued, "We'd have to count in Charlie Slade, Sherm,... unless we can eliminate him first."

"I ain't gonna draw a gun on Slade, Gus, and neither are you if you want yer hide."

Gus hiked up the straps of his overalls and rubbed his greasy fingers in his black mat of beard. "Spud Ervin would. You git 'im mad enough."

"You mean young Ervin go gunnin' fer Slade. Get smart, Gus. He don't have to. He may be young but he's boss of the whole outfit. He don't do those jobs himself."

"How about woman troubles. Slade's a handsome man. Plummer plugged his best friend 'cause he wanted his gal."

"You let me think on it, Gus. I'll fix us a plan'll git us the gold and nobody ever suspect. I'll do the thinkin' but you do the actin'. I got me a business to run. An' you just leave Charlie Slade out of it. He's one of us."

"Fair enough." Gus Terry straightened and headed for the door. He didn't like the way Sherm wrinkled his nose whenever he came near. Sherm had gone soft, gotten fat. The old times when Sherm was tough and fearless were gone. Sherm had always been the cautious meticulous one, always cleaning his gun, counting his bullets, checking his cinch or filling his canteen. But Sherm's nerve had cracked and dried like old harness that somebody forgot to oil. He had acquired property. He had friends and owned a saloon. There was a new factor in the equation—Sherm's position in Varina.

Gus did his own thinking now and he thought hard. He ambled out to Caroline, his mule, standing at the hitch rail, and while he stroked the animal's soft muzzle, he mumbled in her ear, "Caroline, you an' me, we go needle Mr. Ervin, eat 'is brain little by little, give it a good chew an' spit it back out, see if we can gull 'im to lettin' us pocket some of 'is precious gold. The mule licked the salt from his fat palm and he pet her like a long lost love. Passers-by thought he was drunk or head sick.

Chapter 26

Rob Glenby was sick. His cough had deepened when he and Lee Cameron rode out of the high valley onto the rolling plain. Here the wind blew unimpeded. Prairie grasses bowed to its force like slaves to the lash. The north wind robbed man and beast of warmth even now in summer. Glenby's whole body shook. His face had flushed red, his eyes had glazed, he had dropped the reins and he was swaying sideways in the saddle. Cameron stopped once to tie him to the saddle and felt his brow. It was wet and burning hot but Glenby shivered. Pulling Glenby's horse behind him with the pack horse, Cameron's shoulders ached and he wanted desperately to sleep but he rode as fast as he could for Dawson's at the hot springs... Who was Dawson? Was his a real homestead or a flimsy shack? Or was it only a filthy hole in the ground where the lonely traveller paid for white lightning, ate yesterday's rancid beans and slept on the bare cold ground?

Over the next roll of prairie, in a hollow by a bend in the river, steam rose ghostlike from quiet pools. It obscured the smoke that rose steadily from behind three tall cottonwoods. Lee Cameron could smell it before he saw it, the damp heavy aroma of wood burning—a homestead and people, Dawson's at the hot springs. The house was well situated, facing south with a broad roll of grassy hill at its back. Cameron spurred the black down the gentle slope. Three mongrels leaped up barking and raced nipping at the horses' hocks. The mare kicked out violently and one dog ran away yelping. A gruff voice called them off.

The house was large by frontier standards and well built with a chimney at each end. Dawson was well off. Still Cameron could see no one. A voice called sharply and the dogs backed away snarling.

"State yer business and yer name."

Cameron spied a gun barrel poking through a hole in the chinking. The house had been built like a fortress with gun ports in case of attack.

He shouted, "Lee Cameron from Varina City. I've a sick man here—Rob Glenby. Says you know 'im!"

"An' yer business!" Dawson was taking no chances.

"Looking for land, a homestead. Want to raise some horses."

"All the land in these parts is filed fer."

"There's some for sale. I'll pay...Glenby's ailing badly, getting weaker while you're talkin'."

The gun barrel disappeared. "Ride on in."

With his gun cocked, the settler stepped outside and waited. He was a tall man whose ragged clothing did little to hide huge, bony shoulders and long spidery arms and legs. Only when Cameron stepped down and hitched his horse to a stump, did he put up the gun. The clear grey eyes were hard but friendly. "Name's Dawson. What's the matter with Glenby?" He jerked his head toward Glenby but held his gaze on Cameron.

"He was caught in the current crossing the river. Soaked through. Some Indians were shadowing us and he didn't want to stop."

"Thought you was going to say he was shot. Too many get shot, them's that do the shootin' and them's they shoot at. Then they come by here bleedin' an' expectin' me to plug the leaks like I'm runnin' a goddamn hospital. But I owe Glenby—bring him in. I'll tell the wife to set the kettle on. Glenby 'n me's old war buddies." He eyed Cameron's grey coat skeptically. Lee Cameron unlaced Glenby, eased him down and helped him inside.

They entered a wide room with a hearth at one end and an iron cook stove at the other. A boy about ten and a girl of five or six poked sticks at a fire that was blazing on the hearth. The room was snug. They eased Rob Glenby into a slat-back rocker near the fire. Mrs. Dawson, a large, puffy woman in a yellowed apron, bustled in with a bucket of water and poured it into a pot, then swung it over the fire. Dawson found a blanket for Glenby.

"You could've dressed him in something dry!"

"He wouldn't wear a Rebel coat—that was all I had."

"Can't blame him. Rob Glenby don't acquaint with many Rebs...No lover of Rebs misself... Gen'ral Gibbon's Division, Winfield Hancock's 2nd Corps....sergeant." There was a lull. Dawson's sharp grey eyes scrutinized Lee Cameron like a savy horse trader appraising a colt.

Cameron stiffened under the scrutiny. "Nineteenth Georgia, General Archer."

Dawson noticed three dirty gold bars stitched to the stand-up collar of Cameron's coat, "Cavalry! And Captain you was!"

Cameron answered straightforwardly, "I fought as hard as you but we lost."

171

Dawson's grey eyes narrowed and he puffed his pipe before continuing. "John Gibbon was from North Carolina....Good General and fine man, fought agin' his own people, fer his principles so he said." He wrinkled his brow and added without blinking. "Terrible thing, war. You was proud opponents, damn good fighters..." He knit his brows together in a quizzical glance, "You fought for states rights but you held men in bondage. I never understood that."

Cameron had never thought of it that way before. It was such an obvious contradiction, the way Dawson said it. Cameron had no answer. His lips quivered as if he wanted to speak and couldn't.

Dawson smiled and his voice resumed its easy tone, "You hold no grudge, neither will I."

Cameron breathed with relief. "Thanks Dawson." and he offered the settler his hand. Dawson took it in his massive palm and squeezed hard.

The two men headed toward the door. "You can leave Glenby with Mother. Jed and I'll help you with the horses." The boy jumped up. "Boy's Jed; girl's Jenny."

Together they walked out. Cameron unlaced the paniers from the pack horse and started to loosen the cinch on Glenby's bay. Except for scratched knees and a little swelling of the ankles, the horse bore no ill effects from the near drowning. Dawson unsaddled the black.

"She's a nice black." Dawson was direct. "She yours?"

"Glenby's."

"Thought so. Seen a lady ride that horse a few years back. Couldn't miss her—Mrs. Slade, right pretty lass. She went back east.... Jed'll finish up. Let's go eat." They led the horses to the barn in silence and went back inside.

Mrs. Dawson's black eyes fastened on her husband. She confronted him now. "He's burning up. Looks like Sedgewick's ailment an' I don't want that here..." She noted Cameron's grey coat with obvious distaste.

Dawson's temper flared. "I'll not have my family denying an honest man help when an' where he needs, so long 's we got it to give. It could be one of your own out there, Mother! I know Rob Glenby an' he put his life in this man's hands. Now set to." Sergeant Dawson was not used to being questioned. His wife turned grudgingly. Cameron couldn't help but witness this testy exchange and escaped to the fireside.

Glenby had heard it too. "I owe you, Dawson." His voice was thin like hot water.

"Glad to have you an' your friend with you. Mother's just a mite overwrought. Neighbors was ailin' an' they died. She's scared that'll happen here."

Glenby lay immobile, his face, a dull grey purple, the skin pulled taught over his temples. With every breath, he wheezed. Worst of all was the look of fear in his eyes. Cameron had seen that look before and Dawson had too. It was the face of the wounded in the rifle pits, watching in silent agony for the stretcher-bearer and dreading the ordeal that was the field hospital. Glenby was a strong, active man. People depended on him. Clem depended on him. Now he was helpless. He gasped for air and Cameron put a steadying hand on his shoulder.

Glenby rolled his head back at the touch. "Chest hurts. I got bad lungs. You go on without me."

Cameron hesitated. He tightened the grip on Glenby's shoulder. He could feel the great effort of the man, the tension of every muscle that sucked for air.

Mrs. Dawson came forward with a cup of broth and Glenby drank. She handed Cameron a cup of coffee. He sipped the hot liquid and felt the fatigue of the night and day wash over him. He unrolled his bed on the floor next to his friend, collapsed and fell asleep by the warmth of the fire.

The next day, Glenby's cough deepened to a heaving choke, like the scrape of rock on rock when black powder in the crevices explodes and sends them crashing down, but his fever had broken in the night and he looked better. Lee Cameron sat by his friend, fed him, then ate sparingly himself and pushed his plate aside. His eyes were red in spite of a good night's sleep and he hadn't shaved. Now, he clutched his coffee and sat anchored, staring at the Dawson children playing with the dogs. It was a happy scene but his thoughts of Glenby unnerved him. He had brought Rob Glenby into this. He had lost a good rifle through his carelessness. He had insisted on not crossing at the ford and Glenby had nearly drowned. He, Lee Cameron, was at fault. Conflicting desires tormented him: he wanted to wait for his friend's recovery but he wanted desperately to go home. Where was home? Certainly, not in Varina where Spud Ervin lurked after his wife. Coming here was part of finding a home and a safe haven for her and now he felt he'd abandonned her. He couldn't turn back. He couldn't go forward. He forced a smile for the sake of the children but his brown eyes spoke only anguish.

Suddenly, Jenny Dawson plopped a ragdoll in his lap. "Jenny! Leave Mr. Cameron alone!" Mrs. Dawson remonstrated.

But Jenny wasn't listening and prattled away at Cameron. "She has curls, an' eyebrows an' that's 'er mouth." Her tiny finger outlined some crude stitching on the doll's face. "You rock her an' sing and she goes to sleep..." and she hummed a simple child's tune.

Lee Cameron's response was immediate. He thought of his own

daughter. He could have cried, but he forced the tears back into liquid eyes and encouraged the innocent child with a smile. Her child's prattle, warmed his heart and peopled his loneliness. Even Rob Glenby perked up at the child's simple pleasures. Only Mrs. Dawson did not approve.

Dawson called her off. "Mother, leave Jenny be. She'll nurse his soul." Then, turning to Cameron, he wrapped his long fingers around the bowl of his pipe and pointed it at Glenby. "We'll take care of him while you tend to your business won't we, Mother?" His next question was unexpected, "You married?"

Cameron nodded and filled the silence, motioning toward Glenby. "He takes care of that light-headed kid, Clem."

"I know. But you're no help to him here... Mother will nurse him. He'll mend ....Tend your business and come back and pick him up when he has his strength back. You said you was lookin' for land." He took a stick from the fire to light the pipe.

"I don't even know where to look."

"You have kids?"

"One." Lee Cameron looked away. His thoughts ran wild. He held his eyes on the red-hot coals and didn't even blink at the glare. When he turned back squarely to Dawson, he had himself in control, "My wife has one by her first marriage." It was only half a lie.

"You should have a passel of kids. From what I can see, you like them an' they likes you." He looked at Jenny. "Where are they, your wife an' kid?"

"Emma, my wife's in Varina. The little girl will arrive soon—from St. Louis, with a priest friend of my wife's from the Flathead Mission."

Dawson nodded. Then he lifted an eyebrow, studied Cameron for a second and offered, "No place for a kid, Varina, wide open rough town...especially a girl..." He stared at the plank floor and traced the grain of the wood with the toe of his boot, "You might begin by ridin' over next door. Place needs a family. Sedgewicks just pulled out last week. House is empty. Right pretty place. Curtains is still hangin' in the windows—Mother don't even have curtains. I told her to walk in and help herself, but she's a righteous lady, says that's stealin'. All you'd have to do is move in.... an' settle with Hauser's bank in Helena...Now that Hauser's a canny one. Knows a good investment, he does. But he'll sell this time of year an' be glad of it....You ride up to Helena; take the road leads to Elkhorn. It's a straight ride, no mountains, up Canyon Creek, west of the Belts, that's the mountains over to the east. A friend a Rob Glenby's 'll make us a good neighbor." Then he added with a wry smile and a sideways glance from under his shaggy brows, "Even a Georgia, Rebel friend."

Chapter 27

he next day, the weather warmed. The sun shone in the great cavern of blue sky. Rob Glenby felt better and Lee Cameron rode over to the Sedgewick place. It was all Dawson said it would be. There was a solid two-room house built of logs, daubed and chinked securely against the storms, roofed with sod, and a connecting barn and shed. The house was set on a little knoll, really only a big heave in the earth. The two rooms spread across the width of the knoll from east to west. The door and two windows faced south to welcome the warmth and light and another window opened east at the side of a stone chimney. A larger hearth and chimney covered most of the western wall while a lean-to shed spanned the entire length of the rear to create a double wall, storage space and extra protection against winter's blasts. The shed projected from the house at the eastern edge for a few yards to create a covered access to the barn and corral in case of storm or attack. Cameron saw gun ports at intervals beneath the eaves in house and barn. The whole was built like a small fortress and dominated the land surrounding. Cameron could imagine a family holding out indefinitely against Indians here. A major general could not have chosen better.

A creek had carved out its rocky channel to the west and north of the knoll. It gurgled cheerfully. Cameron noticed it was only half full. Yet there was ample water for stock even now in the dry season. He noted the high water mark, about twenty feet down from the house. Someone had erected a small breakwater out into the stream. It channeled water to a ditch which carried the water to a vegetable patch on the east side of the house. The water flowed there now and the patch had yielded a recent harvest. Dry cornstalks stooped in the wind. The potato plants and a few cabbages were green. Sedgewick had planned wisely and built to last.

175

Beyond the creek, was a wide pasture, blanketed with waist-high grass and rimmed with sturdy jack-leg fencing. But the land here was not flat. It rolled away in folds of prairie, cut here by a crag, there by an outcrop, a creek with its line of shaggy cottonwoods, all the way to the base of the Bridger mountains to the north and the Belts to the east. White clouds brushed their grey peaks like silk ribbons in a child's fair hair. Cameron's heart stopped. He could be happy here. Emma could be happy here. Care and effort had built this place, the kind of care and effort that doesn't melt away at the first thaw. Then why had Sedgewick left? Dawson had not told him why.

Cameron rode slowly around the buildings. Then he dismounted, removed saddle and bridle from the mare and turned her into the corral. He gazed hard at the house. It was weather-beaten and solid and strong like the granite peaks, but it had a welcoming quality, like the shade of the cottonwoods on the sunny plain. It was lonely now, but Cameron imagined he saw smoke curling quietly from the chimneys, a cow grazing in the pasture, dogs scampering in the yard and heard the voices of children. Lee Cameron would have been hard put to leave a place like this. Only war and catastrophe had made him leave Georgia, and bitter firey memories.

He tried not to think of them but they peeked out of the cracks in his soul when he least expected it. His mother and sister had survived but General Sherman's raiders had stacked hay against the walls of his family's home, poured on the turpentine and lit the torches. All that was left of his childhood memories went up like a druid's fire in the darkest solstice of winter. Only the row of tall elms was left and even they were scorched. His mother and sister moved to Savannah and lived for a year in a rented upper room on what small income they had left. There, his mother had died. He had heard his sister had a Yankee suitor, had married and gone north. He had not approved the match and she did not write. That was the last he saw of her.

Now he saw the quiet markers. They brought him back to the present and to another's tragedy. Newly cut, unweathered and still yellow, they stuck up rigidly beyond the waving stalks of corn. Cameron hadn't noticed them at first. They were just simple stakes dug into the ground, no roots, no growth, no life.

Cameron walked over. A loving hand had carved each name into the soft wood. He removed his hat and read aloud. "Mary, Edwin, Jasper, Hettie." Four Sedgewicks. One grave was fresh and large; the other three small—children.

"So that's why you left." Lee Cameron voiced his thoughts despondently. Indians? Illness? How did they die? The last mound was tiny—a baby. It was not like the battlefield or any other death in his experience. This one had hardly lived at all to be reduced to a puff of dust, some dry grass and a stick of wood that would probably rot and blow over in the next storm. Cameron reached out to touch the rough lettering. This was Hettie, a little girl. She had died this year, "June 9, 1867", the marker read, just about the time he had arrived in Varina. So young, so fragile, like he imagined his own daughter to be. Like Jenny Dawson. The mother, Mary, had died a few weeks later, in early July.

With a heavy heart he strode around to the front of the house. A black snake slithered into a row of sunflowers that drooped in front of the window. Some of their seeds had dried and dropped to the earth. Sedgewick had left shortly after his wife had died. Was the work of tending a homestead alone to much for him to bear? Was the pain of loss too great? Lee Cameron knew something about loss. You had to fight the loneliness not just for one battle but for an entire war. You had to people your life, try not to remember too much, think ahead and cling to every shred of hope. There was a future in store for those who could wait for its coming, even for the sunflowers, old and brown and dry, whose fallen seed harbored new life and lay dormant until the warming of the soil.

Cameron removed the peg that held the door closed and pushed. He stepped into the house. It was rich by frontier standards. Three bunks were built into the rear wall, Dutch style. A cupboard and dry sink, home to a nest of brown spiders and their egg sacks, stood by the stove and a crude table and seven chairs filled the center of the room. The space by the big fireplace was empty except for a gun rack over the mantle. The mantle was bare, swept clean of family heirlooms. A fire was laid in the hearth and dry logs stood nearby. The plain muslin curtains Dawson had spoken so admirably about, puffed gently in a draught from the open door and a plank floor covered the damp ground underneath.

Cameron pushed open the door to the second room. Except for two large crude cupboards and more spiders, it too, was empty. But Cameron could see the square outline of dust on the floor where a large bed had stood. Sedgewick had never swept underneath the bed.

His heart was heavy when he went outside again and found a bucket to water his horse. She drank deeply and he walked to the creek for more. Then he turned to the barn. It was not large. Rock and daub formed the walls to within a foot of the eaves. The sod roof spilled over the beams, nearly overlapping the stonework. Wooden planking filled most of the space in between roof and wall with openings along the south side for windows. A haystack stood in the yard like a sentinel. Corn half-filled a crib. The heavy door opened inward so it could not be frozen shut in heavy snow. The barn was stronger than the house. Like the house, it had been built to endure. Sedgewick had built wisely and well.

Cameron entered carefully. The interior was dark, except for bright streaks of sunlight that pierced the south windows and streaked the earthern floor. Cameron let his eyes adjust to the dimness. Mouse droppings littered the floor. There were six tie stalls for horses and a larger space opposite the door for a wagon. Cameron could see the wheel ruts in the dim light. A horse collar and pieces of dusty harness hung from nails like funeral drapery. There was even an anvil too heavy to carry away, at the rear of the carriage stall. The whole could be converted to a ten stall barn. He would have to add some larger boxes for the mares with foals.

He'd heard a scampering overhead—mice? He looked up. Mice usually stayed nearer the ground where grain had spilled carelessly. Cameron climbed the ladder to the loft. No light entered here. As he poked his head over the sill, four sets of green eyes reflected the dim light from below. This was why there had been no mice. The kittens were half grown and not used to human hands. He reached out to the mother. She leaned into his palm and purred and the kittens' fear subsided. In spite of everything, she and her young had survived in this lonely place.

Before Cameron left for Dawson's, he found an old flour sack and packed mother and kittens inside. Cats were valuable rodent killers. The Dawson children could add these to their own menagerie and maybe the Camerons could adopt one or two after they moved in.

He rode into Dawson's yard late. The dogs barked as before. Cameron had forgotten the dogs. They smelled the kittens. Dawson, ever on the lookout, waved him in.

The family was at dinner when Cameron stomped in. Glenby was sitting up and looked at least warm and rested, but his breathing was still uneven.

Cameron set the flour sack on the table. He looked at Mrs. Dawson apprehensively.

"What you have there?"

Cameron pulled the kittens from the sack. "I couldn't just leave them."

The two Dawson children squealed in delight and jumped from the table. They hadn't finished eating but their mother let them go, got up to clear the plates and called after them, "You keep them away from them hounds an' they'll live to be good mousers." And she finally

178

smiled at Cameron. "Set yourself. Food's still warm."

Dawson pointed at a chair with the end of his fork. "Mother's partial to cats. They kill rodents an' they warm a cold bed come winter." He forked a chunk of meat into his mouth. "Elk stew, Mother's best."

Mrs. Dawson brought a clean plate for Cameron who sat and helped himself. The aroma alone was enough to make him hungry. He hadn't eaten all day.

Dawson pushed his chair back from the table. "Well, what did you think?"

"Sedgewick's got a nice place there."

"He don't have it no more; Hauser's bank does."

"Sedgewicks left their pets. They leave in a hurry?"

"Yep, Sedgewick was a hard worker but he was notional. Said he'd seen his wife's spirit—that she was callin' to him every night. Mebbe the sickness did somethin' to his head."

"How did they die?"

Dawson lifted an eyebrow. "Sorry tale that." He forked a mouthful of meat into his mouth and pointed the fork at Cameron. "They was all powerful sick. Folks around says it was mountain fever 'cause that's what the horse doctor said. But the fever spreads like grasshoppers in a cornfield and we here the closest neighbors, we never got sick....Me, I think it was bad meat, somethin' they ate. Ma Sedgewick was a high-brow lady, used to servants waitin' on her, from New York. She didn't keep too clean a kitchen, didn't know how, didn't belong in Montana." He put down the fork deliberately.

Cameron chewed his food slowly and nodded. He'd seen epidemics in the army: dysentery; typhus; and the fearsome cholera. And he'd seen the filth of the army encampments, dirty water and rotted, wormy food. Men died before they ever fired a shot. In no way would he expose his wife and daughter to that. "You're sure?"

"No, I ain't sure. Never know for sure an' neither will you....I was you, I'd take the place. Let her set for the winter. Couple a good northers'll freeze out the foulness. Water's good, fresh off the mountain, same water from out our own creek. Come spring, dust her out, clean her up an' you got yerself a first-rate spread."

Cameron mopped his plate with a chunk of bread. "What about Indians? They've been raidin' around. Empty house, they'll burn her down."

"You believe everything Governor Thomas Francis Meagher an' them eastern newspaper people have been shoutin' about? Got everyone riled like hornets at a picnic. You don't fret Injuns with them fresh

179

graves in yer front yard. Injuns won't touch it. They've had their share of white man's diseases an' they believe in ghosts. They'll steal that horse a yours, right out from under your snooty southern nose, but if'n you corral her near dead folks, they'll leave her be like she was to burn their fingers right off their hands. Besides, they lay low when it snows."

"John Bozeman's dead.... Died not too far from here. Indians got him just this spring." Cameron still wasn't convinced.

Dawson pushed his chair away from the table and puffed his pipe. Mrs. Dawson bustled about clearing the dishes and cleaning up. "Don't believe me do you, Cameron? I'm here three year an' they ain't ever even shot an arrow into the yard....Bozeman died because he riled them deliberate. Took wagons right through their huntin' grounds, Sioux huntin' grounds, east of the Big Horns, an' they were promised their huntin' grounds forever. Wagons come, they chase the game, muddy the water, cut down the trees. An that's not the end of it. Bozeman brought soldiers in. They built forts. Injuns hate bluecoats even more 'n gold diggers. Bluecoats is a challenge, like slapping their face with your glove. Bluecoats come for war an' the Injuns give it to them." It was so simple the way Dawson told it.

"And the massacres? Lieutenant Fetterman, the wagon box fight?"

Dawson picked up his pipe, pointed the end of it at Cameron and leaned forward on his elbows. His sharp blue eyes glared at Cameron. His shaggy brows knitted together over his nose. "You want my opinion, I'll tell you straight 'cause you're a friend to Rob....Lieutenant Fetterman was a primpin' peacock, all tail fluff, no substance. Injuns is smart. They called his bluff... And they was Sioux. Sioux ain't never come west of the divide. Crows live here. They'll steal a good horse but they're friendly. We get some Flathead, Snake, an' a few Blackfeet time to time. You look out for the Blackfeet—they'll kill you if you ain't English from Canada—but the Crows'll fight along with us if they can kill some Sioux or Blackfeet."

Cameron's plate was empty and Dawson's long arms reached out and pushed the pot across the table. "More stew?"

Cameron ladled himself a second portion and continued to eat. His dark eyes fastened on the homesteader who fell silent and puffed steadily on his pipe.

"You watch the place for me over the winter?"

Dawson nodded. "No need."

"You say I can ride to Helena from here."

"Direct route, no mountains, an easy climb all the way. Tell Hauser at the bank I sent you."

Chapter 28

Emma Cameron slept fitfully and woke abruptly to pandemonium in the street. Bawling animals and shrill, air-splitting curses shattered the morning quiet. Emma pulled her robe around her and ran to the window. It was raining. The window dripped with a year's dust and grime. Impatiently she pulled back the curtain and threw up the sash. The damp cool air gushed in. She had a good view of the street except for the light rain and grey mountain fog which drifted in from the mountain.

A scruffy, pigeon-toed, white horse paddled calmly down the street. The cowbell strapped around the horse's neck clanged rhythmically to the motion of it peculiar flicking gait. This was a bell mare. Behind her trotted the docile mules, a whole train of them, like a pack of eager hounds behind a bitch in heat. Emma had not seen a mule train since last spring. Freighting was usually by ox and wagon but mules were faster and more efficient than wagons in snow and mud, when the wagons wheels bogged, axles broke and harness snapped and stranded cargo and passengers in the narrow passes. This was a long train. Emma counted 60 mules.

The bell mare passed, an ungainly animal easily spotted for the toe-in motion of its front legs and the dingy patches of yellow on its white coat. The mules were heavily laden. Their packs swayed forward and back on their rangy backs like boats in a windy surf. New white tarps covered each pack but fresh mud was quickly splattering their white sheen. It settled in sticky globs on every exposed surface and the rain washed it in dirty streams back down the animals' legs into the mire. Mud was everywhere. It colored animals, packs, people and buildings the same slick brown. The packers eased the pace lest packs slide too far forward and overwhelm the mules as the slope descended more steeply down into the gulch at the west end of Warren, near the Citadel. The mules veered and swayed and kicked and scrambled. Some were newly trained, nearly wild animals, unused to the discipline of the trail. The skinners shouted and cracked their whips and the whips licked out like vipers' tongues in an effort to prod or restrain. Some animals skidded in the slick mud, bumping hitch rails, knocking holes in flimsy buildings, catching a hoof in wagon spokes, ripping the whiffle tree from a spring wagon and toppling a load of plank lumber into the street. It was a chaotic advance and the mules intimidated anything in their path. Three huge Murphy wagons, eight-horse hitches, brought up the rear. These held the camp supplies and several heavy barrels of whiskey.

Along the length of the train, outriders trotted ominously, armed and dangerous. They looked like the tough mountain soldiers they were, Indian fighters, recruited as a Territorial Army and now disbanded. With hats pulled down and beards covering grim concave features, they carried new repeating rifles and wore bandoliers Mexican style. They rode shaggy mountain horses who dodged the awkward mules and whose short shuffling strides splashed even more mud on horses and riders and wagons. They guarded the whiskey and the gold and each held his own convictions as to which was more valuable. They worked for Spud Ervin now—he promised to pay them more than the U.S. government.

Behind the wagons, distant enough not to be muddied, a big pinto marched nervously. Emma recognized it immediately. The horse arched its neck, bobbed its head and pranced sideways in an effort to escape the bit. This was Spud Ervin. He rode ramrod straight with his long legs pushed staight forward like an ancient warlord in his armour. Dressed for the trail, he was a flamboyant figure in a new black Stetson, black duster and two guns for his one hand. The black sheen of his new clothes contrasted sharply with the white and sorrel colors of his paint horse. A defiant smile defined the lower half of his face, no longer the playful grin of the prankster or the leer of the braggart. It pulled grotesquely upward against the harder frown-lines, mature, cruel, sadistic, etched as if in stone. Spud Ervin was different since his father died, more determined. No one noticed his missing arm. It had healed now and the only remaining sign of his injury was a slight sag of the right shoulder and cavity of the right breast. People noticed the look on his face. If ever they doubted that Spud Ervin could command this rabble, they stopped doubting now. Spud nodded condescendingly to sleepy onlookers. Everyone knew why Spud Ervin hailed them so heartily this morning. Everyone knew what the huge, heavy packs, the rumbling wagons with their cargo of barrels, meant. Everyone knew why the outriders carried such fearful arms. Spud Ervin wanted to inspire fear. He was shipping his gold! Road agents would not dare attack and rob such a large company and he would be rich, the richest man in all Varina. It was his justification, the restitution he craved for the loss of his arm and his father's mine. It was a confirmation of his manhood, his ultimate recognition.

The people of Varina watched the parade with interest, some in fear and some in disgust. They peered through doorways and looked out from behind pillars. Ed Lamb, who had just painted his storefront, raised a fist and swore as a clod of mud hit the doorjamb broadside. But the Ervins were good customers—Ed Lamb himself had filled an order for fifty new pack saddles and five kegs of whiskey and quantities of flour and bacon. The price of a good mule had doubled—Spud Ervin was hiring not just Indian fighters, but wheelrights and harness makers and mule skinners and he was paying good wages.

Business in Varina was booming. Clive Sherman at the Queen was enlarging his saloon. Besides the houses of pleasure, real businesses were thriving, the barber shops, bath houses, restaurants, liveries and grocers and outfitters. Andy Holter was cutting and milling more lumber every day. Bill Crittenden, the butcher, sold out all his beef and had to recruit hunters to fill his shop. The Brewery was even running short of hops. But everyone knew who was buying—they were tough, saturnine men who carried their guns handy and worked for Spud Ervin.

McGillicuddy, ever the early riser, clean-shaven and fully dressed strutted out to the corner of Jefferson and Warren. He observed Spud with the disdain of an old patriarch for a young upstart and commented to Marshal Ryder who interrupted his inquiries in the assay office. "Thinks he's Napoleon come home from the wars, paradin' his wealth like a struttin' cock. Makes men greedy. Five to one says Spud comes home poorer if he comes home alive."

Ryder answered stone-faced, "Napoleon had two hands an' a corps of generals... Spud gets to Utah alive, he ain't my problem. He comes back alive, we may need to learn him some prudence."

Tilton from the Montana Post stood casually jotting notes for next week's edition. He had a comment too, "Damned bloody impudent young lout!" and he would print it. Tilton was British and never feared speaking out blatantly because he was dying from consumption anyway.

Some cursed Spud more violently as they pulled on boots and suspenders and ran to remove animals from the train's path or chase the ones that had broken loose and ran with the pack. But it was a show for all Varina to see—better even than an opera, a match race or a prize fight. Spud Ervin was lord of it all.

Emma watched, engrossed, from the safety of her second-story window. She had heard of the frantic surge of activity in Highland but she had seen Spud Ervin only twice. He had leered and muttered suggestively each time but she had always been accompanied by McGillicuddy or Garrity and he had no opportunity for closer contact. But Judge Burnwell and John Moulton had visited Midge at the house on Jones. They had finally served an eviction notice.

Now Spud Ervin rode up close under Emma's window and reined the paint around cruelly. The horse jerked at the reins in his iron grip, jolting him up and down in stiff little leaps. Vainly, he tried to muscle the big animal. Emma froze. He shouted up at her brazenly, "Ho, pretty woman!" The self-important bluster boomed like the blast of a shotgun. The black hat shaded his eyes but the hard set of lines around the mouth were ominous. Emma drew back behind the curtain.

Spud Ervin would not be so easily rejected. He bellowed loudly like a hawker in a freak show, "Emma! Emma Dubois! Come on out pretty woman! Lemme see the blood on yer claws." It was a gruesome command, beastial in its implication that made Emma feel depersonalized like a slave or a cow upon the auction block. Spud continued, "Where's that Reb you married? ... Hidin' like a bullsnake under a rock? He whip you like a good husband, make a respectable woman of you, or is he too pansy soft?"

Emma answered him disdainfully, wondering why she answered at all. "You may call me Mrs. Cameron."

Spud laughed and the sharp peels reverberated off the wet buildings. "Mrs. Cameron,.... I heard about that wedding. You ain't married! You're a filthy breedin' whore! Your Rebel stud comes back, I'll slice off his balls, serve 'im up to you on a plate!"

Emma wanted to recoil in horror and disgust at the brutish vulgarity of the man but she didn't move and stared him down.

"Respect, Mr. Ervin, doesn't tolerate vulgarity or threats."

Not sure he understood, Spud laughed anyway but his face purpled when he turned self-importantly to the crowd of shocked onlookers. "You all watch!....I'm comin' back a rich man! Gonna buy whiskey and women for ever' one of you, ever' man in this whole damn town....ceptin' Cameron an' his bitch!" He shreiked this last and wrenched the reins around. Men stared dumbfounded. Women covered their ears. Spud's horse reared to escape the tearing bit in his mouth as he laid his spurs into the terrified animal's flanks. They galloped recklessly to the head of the column.

Emma pulled the curtain closed so hard it ripped away from its rod. Her hands shook and her lips quivered, but her words, uttered in the privacy of her room, were deliberate, "If you hurt Lee Cameron, Spud Ervin, by the good God on high, I shall kill you!" She looked out again at the receding figure and repeated her threat but her words washed away in the steady splash of the rain. They were hateful words and they shocked her. Fear, anger, insult and abuse had meshed in a tight web of emotion. She had never before hated any man, but she hated Spud Ervin.

McGillicuddy, stood on the boardwalk below Emma's window at Jefferson and Warren. He had heard Spud's challenge especially the denial of her marriage and he had seen Emma withdraw. McGillicuddy looked up at Emma's window wanting to tell her why he had arranged her marriage to Cameron but she had closed the window and pulled the curtain taut. He felt old and tired. Hopefully, Mormons or road agents would take care of Spud Ervin. He crossed the street to the Citadel.

In the quiet of her room, Emma shuddered. Spud Ervin repelled and frightened her. She lifted her hand to the scar on her cheek. It was healed now but a nasty red ridge remained. Why had she listened to Spud Ervin? She should have simply retreated into the darkness of her room at her first sight of him. It was as if he'd known where she was all along. Was she safe here at the hotel? Could mild-mannered Stewart protect her? Or Garrity? Or McGillicuddy? McGillicuddy was getting old. She looked out once more from between the curtains at the backs of the mules fading into the rain on the Salt Lake road.

"Damn you, Spud Ervin! Damn your black heart to the deepest trenches of hell! May devils pick your bones!" Her voice cracked. Never in her life had she condemned a man so mercilessly. She glared dumbly at the stark walls of her room. Walls, they were the only backgrounds to her life. No human contact, no laughter and song, no accounts to add, no beckoning mountains, no gurgling creek. The confinement of four walls compressed all her fears and anger, magnifying, intensifying, refining them into a compact hatred. It made her shudder at the violence in her own soul.

If only Lee would come back. The four-poster loomed large. It thrust its emptiness into her consciousness with every living hour. He was a week overdue. This morning the bedding was hardly rumpled. In the corner, Lee Cameron's trunk stood unopened. No mud on the carpet, no boots behind the door or boot-pulls flung across the bed, no man smell in the bed sheets. The image of him riding off to war still loomed in her memory and she kept reminding herself that this was a new place, with new people, that the war was over. She was older now and more resourceful. She could take care of herself and attend to her own safety. Even when Cameron was here, she handled her own affairs.

Waiting, like a lady in a castle tower, privileged, prim, posing and useless, while her champion went out to fight her battles, this was was not her way. On an impulse, she flung open her trunk, lifted out the tray and scratched like a pack rat down to the bottom. When she stood up again, she held an ivory-handled pocket revolver. She dressed, put the gun in her pocket and walked downstairs. She seated herself at a table near the window, alone. When the waiter arrived, she ordered breakfast and sent for McGillicuddy. He arrived while she was still sipping her coffee.

"Dan, sit down. Have you eaten?"

McGillicuddy ordered eggs and coffee.

He started to slump into a chair. His shoulders were wet from the rain and he flicked off the drops with his napkin.

Emma did not wait for him to be seated. "Dan, I want to come back to the Citadel."

McGillicuddy's chair scraped the floor. He remained standing. He dropped the napkin and stooped to pick it up. His white brows knit together. He looked down on Emma like God the Father, if God the Father ever spoke with a cigar between his teeth. "You're a married woman now and a respectable lady. You don't have to soil your hands in a gambling house." He remained standing, as if his stance added to his stature and to the impact of his words. Carefully, he removed his cigar and added, "You're worried about what Ervin said this morning?"

"I hate that man, Dan McGillicuddy. I'm lonely and bored and the hatred grows larger with every empty minute. But Spud Ervin isn't the question. Nor is Lee Cameron as much as I love him and intend to be a good wife. They are not here and I am. I need an occupation. I cannot sit respectfully by and tat my way through life. As for soiling my hands, my hands are cleaner dealing cards than Rachel's are baking her pies and weeding her precious garden. I'm not happy playing the lady you want me to be." She stopped abruptly.

McGillicuddy's frown deepened. He said nothing. He sat down slowly and stared grimly at the sun's reflection in his cut-glass goblet.

Emma prattled on, "I want to go back to my own house on Jones Street.... Midge is threatened with eviction. I own the house."

McGillicuddy took off his top hat. His white hair lay close against his head. Suddenly he looked small and sad. "Spud Ervin threatened you."

"He threatened me and he rode away with his mules and gold and whiskey and his wolf pack. I hope they kill him for his gold before he reaches Point of Rocks."

McGillicuddy lifted his cup as if to drink but then noticed it was empty. He was deep in thought. Finally, he answered, "They might...they might not. It's his gold. He's got whiskey enough to make sure they sleep good every night an' I hear he's payin' 'em a hundred a month and he's mounted every one on a good mountain horse that they can keep. He's rich, he's single-minded ..." He paused for effect, "and he's a vengeful man.... You ever think of that."

Emma flashed a firey look that made McGillicuddy wish he were young again, "I'm going back to my house, Dan, no matter what you say. It's home."

McGillicuddy glowered his disapproval from across the table.

Emma never flinched. "Spud Ervin, Lee Cameron and you, Dan McGillicuddy, and your peculiar prejudices can't change me." Her words spat out to match the fire in her eyes. "I'll not play the proper Mrs. Cameron and deny what I am... And I'm coming back to the Citadel." She was telling him, not asking him. McGillicuddy twirled his waxed moustaches and dusted the non-existent lint from his lapel, searching for a rebuttal. He had none and Emma gave him no quarter. He lit a cigar, puffed and poured himself a cup of coffee.

Her next sentence flowed more smoothly, "Lee will understand...and you will have to understand." She poured sugar into the coffee and watched the steam rise from the cup.

McGillicuddy nodded grudgingly and laid the cigar on the edge of his saucer. His eyes focused on a flicker of sunlight shining in the window. He held his head very still. He worked his lips and rubbed his mouth with the back of his hand, as if waiting, expecting her to change her mind. Finally, he changed the subject, "It stopped raining." He sipped his coffee and coughed when he scalded his mouth. Emma offered him her napkin.

There was a lull. Breakfast arrived. Finally, McGillicuddy steeled himself enough to meet Emma's stare. "I don't feel good about this. I'm not going to explain this to Cameron." He looked away again. "And you'd better pray Spud Ervin doesn't come back." He picked up his cigar and pushed his chair back.

"Aren't you going to eat any breakfast?"

He stood up, hands in his pockets, cigar between his teeth. "You ruined my appetite, Mrs. Cameron. What I need's a good stiff drink."

Chapter 29

Emma was at the Citadel when the Salt Lake—Varina stage rolled in the next day. It was a six-horse coach and delivered eleven passengers and the mail. The driver threw down the canvas mail bag. The horses stamped and blew. The eleven passengers stretched their aching muscles and chattered noisily as they sorted carpetbags and trunks. Emma waited eagerly every morning for the arrival of the stage and a letter from Lee. Today there were two, posted from Helena. She ripped them open immediately and devoured each one. He was negotiating for a homestead—good news—but he was delayed another week. She missed him dreadfully and walked despondently back to the gaming tables.

They were busy and the activity banished her worries. She was laughing at a grim mustachioed miner as she lay out her faro spread. He'd lost his stake and won half of it back again when a commotion outside the Citadel's swinging doors interrupted them. The miner suddenly cashed in his chips. She should have noticed and reacted but Con Garrity had to walk over and tap her shoulder. When she finally looked, she froze. There stood a short, stout, priest. The roundness of his body in his black flowing cassock gave the appearance of a small tent. His belly stuck out over the rope belt that held his cassock in place and his jowls hung down over his stalk of neck. He was clean-shaven, with full, jolly lips, laughing blue eyes and red cheeks like some black-robed St. Nicholas bearing gifts but without the beard. He would have been a comical figure except that his voice was deep and sonorous like the quick spread of oil over the surface of murky water. It silenced all laughter at a man wearing skirts. When he spoke, no one dared even laugh, much less ridicule or interrupt.

He held a little girl by the hand and spoke directly to Emma. "Emma, you look well. They didn't want me to bring Marie to the Citadel, but I knew you'd be here. We came immediately.... Mr. Story was very kind to allow us to accompany him. It was a fast wagon train. We came by John Bozeman's cutoff. I have to get to my mission at Mary's Lake before the first snows... I apologize for the hurry but there was so little time."

The child stood white-faced and serious, quietly staring at the menagerie of scruffy gamblers in the smoke-filled room. They stared back. Conversations halted in mid-sentence—children, particularly girl children, did not frequent saloons. Nor did priests. And this child was beautiful, even dressed in the staid navy blue flannel and stiff white collar of a convent uniform, her hair pulled stiffly into a single braid that hung primly down her back. She was lithe and straight-limbed with the pale complexion, and black hair of her mother. But there was a cast to her brown eyes and oval face that was unmistakably Lee Cameron—Emma noticed it at once. The brisk ride in the open stage had left her cheeks a rosy pink. Now the child withdrew from the curious stares behind the black, voluminous skirts of the priest.

Emma's silver dealing box clattered to the floor. The cards scattered. Her hand reached up to cover her mouth. That this holy man and her daughter should find her here, in a gaming house, she had not imagined. Why had they not sent word?

The priest did not cast blame. He wrinkled his nose at the stale barroom smell and he could not bring himself to say "saloon" or "dance hall" but he held an ethereal smile on his lips and the liquid brown of his eyes was kind. There was no sign of rebuke of even disapproval, only calm acceptance of a situation as it was.

He defined his speech with the simple gestures and words that convey meaning to the very young as he smiled gently at the child. "Marie, this is your mother. She works in this place. And that," he pointed at McGillicuddy, "is Grandpa McGillicuddy." McGillicuddy's whole body jerked erect and sprayed the whiskey he was sipping across the front of his coat and sleeves. But he did not take offense. He brushed himself off, swelled his chest and seemed to grow just a little taller.

The priest continued. "It's a different life than you've had with the nuns—You'll have to get used to being around men. They don't smell as good and they talk much more loudly and drink beer and smoke." He swept his arm in a wide arc and laughed. "They come here to dance and sing and play games because they work very hard. When they finish working, they play very hard...They want to be happy just like you. And they want you to be happy." He drew the little girl out from behind the skirts of his cassock. The rough faces stared, dumbly, almost intrusively.

Emma did not hesitate. Years of separation melted into the immediacy of the present. She stepped forward. Her arms reached out. Marie hovered uncertainly still clinging to the folds of the priest's cassock.

Emma stooped low to the child and whispered, "You remember me?" Her heart pounded at the three little words. It was an awful question for a mother to ask her own daughter. She looked to the priest. "Father Manno, I'm so grateful." The child still hung back.

"She was too young to remember much. Have patience." The priest nudged and the child stepped forward to greet her mother.

He made simple excuses. "She's tired, Emma. We had the center seats on the stage, leather straps for back rests. All our bones are aching." Emma put out her hand. The little girl looked back at the priest, who took her tiny hand, slipped it into her mother's and they stared at each other without saying a word.

Father Manno broke the silence. "Do you have a place for her to stay?"

McGillicuddy spoke up then. "The house on Jones Street. She'll be welcome there." There was a lull and McGillicuddy strained for something to fill the silence, "Father, you say you came the short way? The Bozeman cutoff? Red Cloud has been raiding all up and down the trail. You should be dead." To McGillilcuddy, and to the rest of the miners present who had read the newspaper accounts, travelling by the "bloody Bozeman" was suicidal. And to take a child that way, to endanger a young and innocent life, was criminal!

But the priest stood in stoic tranquility, his lips curled vaguely upward as he told a story that stunned the tough gold-seekers. They listened in awe. McGillicuddy decided that he was either a very foolish man or really did believe that God protected him with some miraculous shield. That this Father Manno was a true saint, McGillicuddy firmly believed.

Father Manno's words confirmed it. "The Lord protects his own." This was his only explanation and he went on to the his next concern. "A school? Does Varina have a school?" He looked around at the whiskered faces and stated proudly, "Marie knows her letters and numbers. She'll be ready to read soon."

Now Emma recovered. "Mr. Tilton has started a school."

The priest nodded. "Here is her bag. She'll need more and warmer clothing for the winter...I hope Mr. Lamb has her size. If not, I'm sure you can find a good seamstress." He stopped. No one in the gambling hall had anything else to say. His world was so distant from theirs. He smiled again, "I'll be going then." He bowed his head reverently and turned toward the door.

"Father, one thing more!" Emma's voice was urgent and the holy man turned back immediately. She continued, "I was recently married... by a magistrate. Would you marry us again according to the church?"

"Of course, I'm honored, Emma. Who is the favored gentleman?"

"His name is Lee Cameron. He's new in town but he's away seeking out a homestead...Could you come back in maybe a month...six weeks when he is here?"

The priest ruffled the child's hair. "So you see, Marie, you're to have a proper father." And then to Emma, "I'll be back before the snows close the passes." He waddled out through the doors on his stubby little legs, as suddenly and soundlessly as he had come.

But the play at the Citadel did not resume when the priest left. A reverent hush fell over the noisy miners. They drew back from the place where the priest had stood as if it were too holy on which to tread.

McGillicuddy broke the silence. "Garrity, pour the drinks. One for every man! A toast to welcome the little lady!" But the toast died away like the sweet chime of a clock. The reunion of mother and daughter was too sacred to these lonely men.

McGillicuddy looked at Emma and issued a command. "I'll see the two of you home." He picked up Marie's carpetbag. Emma took his arm on one side and Marie's hand on the other and walked out of the Citadel without looking back.

The child brightened with the sights and sounds of the town. Gone was the pounding lurch, the bruising bumps and cramped quarters of the stagecoach. Gone were the strict regimens and starched uniforms of the convent. Marie ran ahead freely on the boardwalk and Emma let her go. It was like watching a foal buck and run when it steps out to pasture for the first time or a chick flap its wings in first flight. Marie's flannel tunic billowed in the mountain breeze and the skinny plaid knot on the end of her pigtail bounced gaily between her shoulders. She was exultant. She poked her face into doorways and plastered her nose to the grimy windows of shops. She jumped down into the dust and petted the sleepy nags at the hitchrails.

McGillicuddy called to her when they rounded the corner from Brewery to Jones. "That's your house—the one with the green porch."

The child ran up the steps. The sweet smell of bread baking pervaded the air.

McGillicuddy held Emma back momentarily. "You can't raise a young one in a saloon."

"Not in a saloon, but not in a hotel either." For a brief moment, she stopped with her hand on the doornob. There were other responsibilities to face with a husband and child. They needed home, roots, belonging. McGillicuddy understood. It was something he'd never had and he stood now, at the edge of the porch, so small, with his stovepipe in his hands, worshipful. But Emma knew from the gleam in his eye, that he had helped create this match, like a conniving, but very discreet, old Irish biddie.

The warm scents of the fresh bread filled her nostrils. "Are you hungry?" The child nodded eagerly and Emma smiled as much for joy at her newfound happiness as for loss of the life she was leaving behind. She turned the knob and they entered. She would miss the saloon. She would miss dapper, pontificating McGillicuddy. She would miss the rough, dirty miners, their loneliness and laughter, their profanity when they lost and their exuberance when they won. She turned once to watch McGillicuddy turn on his heel and walk away, hat still in hand, shoulders hunched and heaving like those of an old man sobbing. She closed the door.

The front parlor was occupied. Shamy lay on the rug and thwacked his tail against the floorboards. Pat Lysaght slumped on the couch with his feet on the marble-topped table, snoring and sputtering like a steam engine. Marie reached out to touch him and he jerked and mumbled a Gaelic curse. She jumped back. Lysaght blinked awake. The old man and the small girl stood apart and stared at each other.

He spoke first. "I be dreamin'! What's this? A bairn and a beauty like her mother!" The likeness was unmistakeable. "Come here my pet, sit by me, bring the June sunshine into an old man's autumn." Marie sat hesitantly at the opposite end of the couch. Pat Lysaght lifted his feet off the table and grimaced. "Tis the hip, painin' again now that the winter's comin' on."

Rachel called from the back room, "He says he's come to see Doc Lubbock, though he don't ever abide what Doc Lubbock says." She came in with her dark hands white and sticky with flour brushing bits of dough from her apron. "He's really here 'cause 'is nose tells 'im I got pies in the oven." She stopped abruptly when she saw the child.

Emma spoke quietly to the child, "That's Mr. Lysaght, and that's Rachel. Midge and Gertie will be here mornings. You'll sleep in my room, so take your bag in there."

Ornery old Pat Lysaght was smitten on sight like a young swain. The old owl eyes swivelled in his head and followed Marie's every move. He wouldn't go home, even to guard his claim. He went out to Warren Street and hired the Tyson boy to guard it. He would sit by the hour with Marie on his knee, filling her head with stories of lords, leprachauns, treasures and rainbows. Leprachauns live in the great cottonwoods, he swore to her, and buried their treasure beneath them. Someday they would dig up a great cottonwood near Sunshine Creek and find a golden hoard to prove it. What the miners thought was gold was really treasure laid down by the little people one thousand years ago. Emma had to scold him when he started giving Marie real nuggets as proof. Marie believed every word.

The women paid their attentions to Marie too. Rachel added honey to the baking bread and took Marie berry-picking. The luxury of dessert suddenly became a part of every meal. And Rachel would sing Marie to sleep, the soft, sad melodies of her shackled people. Midge and Gertie bought her a new yellow sunbonnet and high button shoes and stockings. The little household crowded into the four small rooms, Midge and Gertie in the loft upstairs, Emma and Marie in the bedroom and Lysaght more and more often in residence, sleeping on the couch in the front room. In good weather, they spilled onto the porch.

Emma did not return to the Citadel. Her house was no longer a boarding house. It was Mrs. Cameron's home. It housed a family and Judge Burnwell would not press eviction while Spud Ervin stayed away. Only Lee Cameron was still absent.

September came and still Lee Cameron did not return. Emma bought Marie woolen clothing and enrolled her with a handful of other regular students, in school. The three Manning girls looked out for Marie who was the youngest one. Only righteous abolitionist Mrs. Baird complained that her Johnny and little Abigail should have to sit in the same room with that bastard rebel child from Jones Street, and said so to Emma for everyone to hear. Emma chose not to remind Mrs. Baird that she was a widow and that Marie did have a proper father and had learned far better manners in her five years with the nuns than Mrs. Baird had in her forty and some. Mrs. Baird protested that she had not passed thirty.

With Marie in school and Lee Cameron still away, Emma languished in the lonely hours of midday. Midge and Gertie still worked the saloons and Rachel cooked and delivered pies to Grandma's eatery. Emma looked forward to conversations with Lysaght and to his overblown Irish chatter, but he usually went out mornings and did not return until late afternoon when he walked Marie home from school. To fill the lonely hours, Emma kept a diary, knitted and tended her garden, but the mountain air in September had already begun to cool and the garden was browning. Soon she would be restricted to the indoors. She began to pot some of her favorite flowers to bring inside. And one bright September afternoon, when Emma was elbow deep in garden soil, trowel and pots, Lee Cameron arrived.

He did not see her at the side of the house and jumped from his horse, leaped the steps two at a time and flung open the door. Emma felt her heart leap into her throat, followed him quietly and watched from the doorway.

He stopped just inside the door. He drew himself up. He knew. Marie stood behind the desk, the same raven curls that escaped the effort to braid them and curled haphazardly at the nape of the neck, the same pale skin and arch to her neck. She conversed with a floppy rag doll.

"Marie?" Emma heard a shyness in his voice as he reached out a hand impulsively. This was the daughter he had never seen. His words tumbled out, "I'm your father."

Marie turned her small head defiantly and stated, "No you're not. My father's dead." She turned back to conversation with her ragdoll. "Hettie, you know he's not my father!" She held up the doll and shook it as if expecting it to agree.

Emma ran to him then. It was as if a dagger, worse than anything he had ever experienced on the battlefield, ripped through him. Could she ever make up for the terrible loss? He was still a stranger to his own daughter. What to say? How to make Marie come to him, accept him, love him? Emma had no idea. The child had created her own imaginary world and he was the intruder. Here was his own flesh and blood, the bonding of the deep love they shared, so distant and unreachable.

She saw at once the white shock on his face where he stood frozen to the floor. She touched his arm and he trembled to her touch, turned and wrapped her gently in his arms. He held her there revelling in the warmth of her flesh and she in the security of his embrace.

For a moment, Marie was forgotten and the child fidgeted nervously. Tucked away behind the convent's walls, Marie had not witnessed physical closeness of a man and a woman. The only touch she knew was the rough pull of the matron who plaited her hair and the hard bump of human cargo in the stagecoach. Gently, Emma pulled away, stooped down and addressed the child. "This is your new father."

Marie still held back. "He's too old." She looked askance at Cameron, clearly uncomfortable with the display of affection.

Cameron understood the simple child's logic and the awful spell was broken. He didn't like the sound of "new father" either but it was better than a denial. He held out his hand again patiently and waited. "I'm your mother's second husband, and I've never been a father before, so I'm new. Is that better?"

Marie remained on the other side of the desk.

Emma motioned the child forward, "He has lots to tell us. He was gone to find us a home."

"I like this house and Mr. Lysaght and Shamy."

Lee Cameron had won the mother. Now he would have to win the daughter. He began by taking Emma and Marie out to see the beautiful black horse and lifting her playfully into the saddle. The three of them walked from there down to the creek where he poured out the story of his wanderings. "I've bought us a property, near the hot springs on the Gallatin." His own anxieties of the past month spewed forth: the delay because of Glenby's illness; the helpful Dawson whose neighbors had died; the negotiations and purchase in Helena, the trip back to Varina. He described the Sedgewick place, Sam Hauser's new bank, how Helena too was a city building, how it was already vying with Varina for territorial dominance. His enthusiasm for the future of the territory and their own future was infectious. Spring would see them in a good place. Spring would see them put down their first roots. Emma Cameron rejoiced. There was not one mention of Spud Ervin.

Chapter 30

pud Ervin was exultant too. Gold had bought him an army.
He was in command of his troops and he'd only killed one man.
It had happened the second day out at the Old Cottonwoods
Campground. Grumps Smith, a tough ex-infantry sergeant, reached
into his pouch of tobacco while he was unloading packs of Ervin gold.
Spud thought he was stealing and shot Grumps in the back three
times, rolled him over and shot him twice in front. Grumps choked on
his own blood and died with his hand on his gun. Spud laughed,
picked up the pouch, emptied it and threw it in the fire.

Spud had picked the moment carefully. When the shifty old codger
got up from his meal and started to pull his bedroll from the wagon, he
always checked the load in his gun. That was when Spud fired. Spud
could say the old man was going for his gun, that he, Spud, shot in self
defense.

Wes Mumford, his head drover and second in command, saw it,
shoved a huge chaw of tobacco into his cheek, narrowed his eyes and
spat a hard stream into the smouldering fire. It sizzled like fat in a hot
pan. When Ervin approached him looking for approval, he turned his
back and walked away.

Curly Shaw saw it too and recited his prescribed lines like a parrot, because that's what old man Ervin had paid him to do. The other
men believed him—it was hard not to trust his unruly red hair and
freckled face. But Curly was beginning to have his own doubts. Spud's
nerves unravelled too easily and the only thing that could tie their
frayed ends back together was whiskey, and Curly knew it.

Curly was developing the same annoying habit of drinking too
much himself. He knew he'd concealed the truth about the killing of

Grumps Smith. He was straddling a fence, walking a tightrope and Curly Shaw sensed his own vulnerability. He had to be very careful now to maintain Spud's good will. Any little imagined slur could send Spud Ervin into a drunken tantrum or worse provoke him to violence. Unconsciously, Curly would suck in his lip between his teeth when he couldn't have a drink. Spud Ervin did the same thing but with both his cheeks—that was what made the his jaw look so cruel and hard.

Curly weighed his options and decided to call it quits with the Ervins, collect his pay in Salt Lake, wait out the winter there and join the first spring wagon train for California or maybe Nevada. There were better opportunities there. This job just wasn't any fun any more.

Wes Mumford wasn't as careful as Curly Shaw and broached the subject of Grumps death openly to Curly and the other men. Grumps had been one of his best drovers.

"You lied, Shaw, you know that."

"Smith was stealin'. I know that too."

"Your friend Mr. Ervin, is a cold blooded murderer. Never gave Grumps no warnin'." Wes Mumford pronounced his employer's name with a slow soft slur of defiance. He held a long black snake whip and curled it calmly across his callused palm as he spoke. But he was a careful man and never confronted Spud Ervin.

Curly sensed a threat in Mumford and tried awkwardly to placate him. "Mr. Ervin is not my friend!... I'll help you bury Grumps so's the wolves won't get 'im."

Mumford lifted a surly eyebrow and drawled back, "You do that an' see if you can breathe back life into 'is cold veins, an' I'll help you bury Mis..ter..high an' mighty Ervin if he tries it again with one of my men....You tell 'im that for me. An' you tell 'im I want double my pay if he wants me to keep a clamp on it."

Shaw nodded. Mumford's icy calm scared him. Shaw wasn't quite alert enough to decode Mumford's veiled threat but the antagonism in the man's voice was undeniable. "I'll tell 'im." Curly Shaw started to walk away.

But Mumford wasn't finished and walked after him, "An' were I you, I'd ask for triple pay."

"He'd kill me first." Curly Shaw admitted the blatant truth.

"I believe he would." Mumford pushed a wad into one cheek, then the other, "You ain't worth the price of a bullet to 'im." Wes Mumford paused again. He was in no hurry and repeated, "I'll keep the men in line. Double pay. You tell 'im, or are you feared? An' my men'll want their wages paid in full, pronto, within the hour, we git to Salt Lake.... You see to it or we takes our just due an' Mr. Spud Ervin be damned!"

Curly Shaw just stood there. He didn't even nod and Mumford turned and walked away.

They buried Grumps beneath the tall cottonwoods, no questions asked. It was hard digging. The roots were thick and gnarled so the grave was only four feet deep and the wolves would probably dig him up before the ground froze for the winter.

Curly Shaw was very careful from then on. He watched Wes Mumford and he watched Spud Ervin. The sore in his lip where he sucked it, abcessed and grew like a cancer every day. He wiped the red hairs away from his face and they kinked from the sweat that dripped beneath the band of his hat. His nerves tingled; his head ached. Wes Mumford bossed his men with a surly frown and would receive his double pay but Curly Shaw never asked for a raise.

As for Spud, Mumford's request surprised him, but he acquiesed. He had no choice. The movement of the gold had already begun and he could not dismiss the men without leaving his gold unguarded. But he brooded. Huge black circles developed around the sockets of his eyes. He lost weight. His missing arm itched. His mind had still not erased his absent limb and anxiety made the deception worse. He would scratch the stump, slap it, wrap it in rags soaked in cold mountain water, pour whiskey on it, anything to dull the maddening itch. He couldn't sleep even if he had wanted to. In daylight, he occupied himself taking pot shots at luckless animals, birds, rabbits, snakes, anything that moved. He was a dead shot. Men, even Mumford, feared him. They went about their business in a silent pall. At night, Spud lay awake and tossed. Like a cat, he watched, his eyes rotating in his head, all night long, listening, anticipating threat, theft, delay, whatever other disaster his imagination could conjure. When it didn't come, he grew even more watchful until he trembled convulsively with every movement, trying to stay awake. When his exhausted body would finally drift off to sleep against his will, the slightest noise would rouse him. At these times he would jump up frantically, gun in hand.

Only whiskey, in quantities ever greater and greater, could calm him. He drank more each day. He and the men consumed all the good barrels during the first week and turned then to the Red-eye of the Indian trade. His stomach churned on this witches' brew of water, tobacco, camphor and a pinch of strychnine to give it tang. There were times when he sickened so badly Curly had to tie him on his horse like Clive Sherman used to do after an all night spree. But the train made slow and steady progress. The men did fear Spud—a drunken man was unpredictable and this one had proved himself impulsive and violent. Spud Ervin had killed Grumps and the memory lingered.

They passed Point of Rocks without event, Lovells, Beaverhead, Red Rock and the dreaded canyon on the divide that was so ironically named Pleasant Valley. The valley was really a high mountain pass where fierce blizzards had stranded many wagon trains and where outlaws had waylaid many a traveller. Rain slowed them here and Spud doubled the guard. The train marched through unharmed.

They trekked across the parched plains of eastern Idaho, down the valley of the Snake River, past Camas Creek, Eagle Rock, old Fort Hall. It rained again and left the trail a bog of gumbo mud. The men thought Spud would stop if only to save his investment in his animals who were loosing flesh and weakening. The mud sucked them down with every step but they were nearing Salt Lake and Spud drove relentlessly on. If an animal lamed or bogged, he shot it unmercifully and doubled the load on the next mule. And he had room now in the whiskey wagons whose provisions they had used freely. He was lucky. The train moved steadily southward across Idaho Territory. At Rocky Ford, a few miles north of the bridge, they crossed the Malade or Sickly River, tributary of the Big Snake, named because some trappers sickened after eating the flesh of decaying beaver that had fed on some poisonous parsnip that grew along its banks. At the Honeyville ford of the Bear, and at the Ogden River, the water was too high and they had to cross on bridges and pay the heavy Mormon tolls. Through all this, Spud Ervin's good luck held. Except for the Mormon tolls, he held on to his gold.

Three nights out from Salt Lake, between Square Town and Corinne, Utah Territory, he called Curly in for orders. He'd been drinking and his mood was maudlin and his words slurred, but his thoughts were clear.

"Coupla more days, Curly, and I'm a rich man..." It was a crude boast. Spud hesitated and questioned with a skeptical sidelong glance. "You still with me?"

Curly nodded warily and padded his speech with compliments. "You brought 'em through, Mr. Ervin. Sime'd be proud."

Spud coughed green bile out of his throat while he rubbed his red eyes. "If Mumford's gonna make his play, now's when he'll do it." Spud Ervin was not stupid. "Curly, we got to ramrod this outfit for a few more days...You take a fast horse, and a second relay if you need and ride ahead. You tell them Saints that we've had some thievin' an' we need guards. Tell 'em we had Injun trouble... tell 'em anything but get some a Porter Rockwell's boys, Avenging Angels or whatever they call 'em, to help keep Mumford an' company in line."

Curly was incredulous. "Mormons? You want Brigham and his people to help you?"

"You don't have to go all the way to Salt Lake. Probably find enough of 'em in Brigham City. They sniff out gold like bloodhounds...Tell 'em I'll pay 'em."

"You an' me can handle Mumford." They could if Spud Ervin could stop drinking. "We don't need no greedy saints."

Spud's surliness turned violent and he snapped back, "I say we need 'em. You tell 'em I'm a new saint waitin' at their gates....that they'll collect their ten percent or whatever they call it from me like all th' others....You do what I say an' you bring me back some bootleg, you hear."

So that was the reason! They'd run out of whiskey. Mumford was an excuse. The freighters they met going north weren't selling any, not in Utah. The Mormons disapproved. Bands of angry Mormons would stop a train at the bridges or the fords if they caught them selling. The toll collectors would seize the whiskey for themselves and resell it, diluted, at a healthy profit in Idaho. The Mormons didn't drink, not even coffee, but they knew how to run a good business. In Utah, if you wanted good whiskey, you had to deal with Mormons and they only dealt high.

Spud Ervin was so crazy for booze, he was going to pay. He craved whiskey even more than wealth. Curly had seen his shakey hand and red face and heard the violent outbursts—the signs were all there. He stifled a laugh.

"I'll leave right pronto, Mr. Ervin." Curly had no love for Mormons but he was glad to get out from under Ervin control. He had no idea of where to find bootleg in Utah. He rode out of camp with an idea never to come back.

For the first time, Spud Ervin was alone with his hired men. Spud could see the blatant scorn in their surly looks. He cursed their impudent stares and what he imagined were their thieving schemes, but they were former soldiers and followed orders even if they disagreed. And he cursed the absent Curly Shaw who hid his fits and trembles from the suspicious men. He cursed Utah and he even cursed the name of Ervin. A few more nights and he could drink his fill. A few more nights and he would bank his fortune. Just two more days ride and he would pay off these grizzly drovers. And then they'd show some respect. He liked the mules better than the drovers. At least their big brown liquid eyes looked at him without judgement. They were a stinking, biting, bucking collection of stubborn animals but they weren't trying to steal his gold. Two more nights and he'd be rid of them too. Two more nights and he could buy out the richest bootlegger and drink himself into oblivion.

Spud Ervin chewed a piece of raw bacon to relieve his constant thirst. He couldn't swallow because it would make his stomach heave. His lips were dry and cracked to bleeding. He wore his Stetson pulled down tightly over his bony brow to hide the bloodlines in his eyes and the direction of his glance which darted constantly from person to person. He had no friends. Everyone was suspect—even Shaw, his father's old retainer, and he'd entrusted Shaw with an important errand. Shaw would come back because he wanted his pay.

The fire blazed brightly amid the tall cottonwoods at the Twin Fords Campground near Corinne and drew Spud Ervin's hypnotic stare. It was four in the morning, September 20th. Curly Shaw had left hours ago. Spud willed himself awake. A north wind blew and chilled his wracked body. The company of Mormons would arrive in just a few more hours to accompany the gold train to the Mormon Bank. Then he could relax. A wry smile creased the constant tension in his jaw.

The Mormons would welcome his gold shipment. They'd charge a healthy interest rate on all deposits in Salt Lake banks. They were getting rich. But so was he. He would pay the Mormon bankers their percentage and the wages to this wolfpack of mule skinners and watch them take off for the whorehouses like yapping, starving dogs. The men would find their pleasures even here in the straight-laced Mormon settlements. They'd waste every cent they'd earned. He chuckled hard at that and hatched his own vengeful plans.

He was heading for the nearest saloon for a bottle, then to a good hotel to sleep it off. Then he was riding straight back to Varina. He would enforce his claim to all his property as it appeared on the original city grid. Burnwell should have figured it all out by now. Varina owed him that—what rightfully belonged to him. He would buy back the Cleopatra Mine or take it if it wasn't for sale. No late-comer saloon bully could keep it from him, now he was a rich man. Varina would have to call him "Mr. Ervin". His bloated imagination fed on his own importance. He would be powerful and respected, dominant in the eyes of men.

Dominant, he liked the ponderous sound of the word. The whiskey drew pictures in front of his eyes. He saw himself in black cut-away and top hat in a huge, stone mansion, bigger even than the new Grand Temple of the Masons that was rising so majesticly in Varina. He would erect iron gates to keep out the rabble and build stables filled with bloodstock like Glenby's black horse. No filthy, biting mules. He pictured the town, the county, the whole territory, his own private playground to pillage and whore. His desires had never been thwarted; his every want had always been met. He had no scruples, no standards or morals. Weaker men were inferior. The infirm, the poor, the Chinese were to be scorned. Blacks, former slaves were to be whipped. Woman were to be possessed. Like animals and like Emma Dubois, when they balked, you beat them.

Thoughts of women tormented him especially now, alone without his whiskey. For sex, he had always paid the price, in gold dust and his attempts at gratuitous seduction had always met with failure. The women who had refused him became the subject of perverted obsessions. Emma Dubois was foremost of these. He could feel his organ harden when he thought of her. If he was riding a horse, he would have to dismount because of the discomfort and he raged secretly at Emma for intimidating him.

Now in the early dawn, huddled in his blankets, he dreamed of sex but he was shrunken and soft from exhaustion. Shadows of craggy cottonwoods danced overhead like gremlins across the fragments of his vision. His blanket prickled his absent arm. His body trembled and oozed sweat. He dreamed, half awake, half asleep, and he hallucinated. He saw Emma's face, in the coals of the fire, blushing and beautiful and laughing like a banshee. He saw the slumbering hulks of the men, grunting and rolling unconsciously by the orange light of the fire like bodies piled in a death cart. Even the mules grazing on the perimeter of the camp, and the wagons behind them loomed like monster shapes. Everything threatened.

He sat up, suddenly shouting uncontrolablly, "My deed, my woman, my house, mine, mine..." Whether it was the possessive or the possession he meant, no one cared. The long vowel trailed away on the wind. He howled it like a demon predator into the cavern of the wilderness, woke the men and started the animals braying.

Mumford ran up and seized him by the shoulders. Spud struck out, gun in hand, but Mumford ducked and wrenched the gun away. "You crazy Ervin?...or are you dreamin'?"

Spud stared blankly back and whined like a spoiled child who can't have his way. "She don't want me. She sent me away."

"You woke this whole goddamn camp on account of some whore!" Mumford pulled his arm back and balled his fist but Spud Ervin pulled up his tarp and rolled away. He couldn't sleep. He lay awake in a cold sweat and Wes Mumford went back to his blankets.

Chapter 31

Gus Terry keened his ears to the whole performance. He could hardly hold back his laughter. He enjoyed watching Ervin drive himself to distraction then drink himself into a stupor and lay awake anticipating a challenge to his authority and waiting for a theft that never came. Spud was so intent that he couldn't see what was going on under his very nose. Gus had tricked him easily. To Gus, it had been one hilarious prank. He grinned beneath his beard every time he set eyes on Spud Ervin.

Next morning, at the camp between Square Town and Corinne, Gus Terry was the first to awaken and stirred the fire. He trudged to the river with the coffee pot, rinsed it once, filled it and threw in a handful of grounds. He waited a few minutes for the coffee to boil and approached Spud Ervin. Gus was solicitous, even humble like a faithful dog.

"Coffee, Mr. Ervin?" Gus held out the coffee pot.

Spud jumped. He was not asleep. He sat bolt upright with empty gun in hand, pale, haggard and shivering.

Terry didn't flinch, "It's only me, Mr. Ervin. You kin take your finger off the trigger." Spud focused, frowned at Terry and lowered the gun. "What you want, Terry?"

"You want some coffee, Mr. Ervin?" He shook the pot and the liquid sloshed like whiskey in a bottle. "Pour you a cup, Mr. Ervin?" Spud Ervin eyed Terry suspiciously, and shrank back from his rank odor and lousy beard. "You could shoot me now, Terry, if you wanted to."

Gus Terry played the simpleton. "An' I could poison yer coffee, Mr. Ervin...but if I did, I wouldn't get paid."

Spud Ervin laid his gun in his lap and picked up the tin cup. Terry didn't usually come this close. There had to be a reason. He waited.

"Mr. Ervin, I was wonderin' when you gonna pay us?"

Spud Ervin cast a black glance at the big oaf of a man. "I pay when the job's done. We ain't in Salt Lake yet."

Terry prodded gently, "Will be soon." He rolled his eyes in his head. "I figgur we worked mighty hard pushin' this train through pronto." Terry shoved his hands into the front of his overalls. "You're a hard man to work fer, Mr. Ervin." He smiled blankly and loomed bald-faced over Spud Ervin. The nits fell into Spud's blankets. "You gonna pay up soon as we git there?"

Spud rolled quickly out of his blankets away from Gus Terry and sat up. He evaded the question, "You in a big hurry, Gus? You goin' drinkin' or maybe sparkin' a sportin' woman?" Spud's sacarsm would've stung another man but Terry never blinked.

He unbuttoned the front of his shirt, stuck his hand in, scratched between the pokes of gold he had stolen from Spud Ervin and stared back innocuously. When he spoke it was with mock sincerity. "Don't need no women. Need a drink o' real lightnin' though like you, get the smell a muleshit outta my beard and warm the blood in my gut. An' I figgur to get me a bath and a shave." Spud Ervin cackled with laughter, "For that, Gus Terry, I'll give you a bonus. We git to Salt Lake, you be first in line."

Terry emptied his cup and stalked over to the woods to relieve himself. When he got out of hearing, he unhooked his overalls, pulled out the three chunky pokes of gold, and burst out laughing so hard his belly shook. The gold he placed in the crotch of an old spruce and went back to tending his needs.

Gus was actually having fun on this trip playing up to Spud Ervin. For him, it was like a theatrical performance or a child's game of make-believe. He could have been a great actor if he'd liked people more. But the applause of his fellows meant little to Gus Terry. He was orphaned very young and simply lived by what suited him and what tickled his fancy at the moment. He'd never really been close to anyone, not even Clive Sherman. Clive had simply been there when Gus needed an accomplice, like the sapling growing near the road when the wheel broke, there for the taking and flexible enough to bend to the purpose.

Over the years, Gus had learned to use people and things expertly to his own advantage. Gus used his smell. He enhanced it a bit with a smudge of bear grease—he'd learned that from the Indians. Even the thick smell of bacon frying and coffee boiling couldn't overcome his stink. Smelling bad kept the black flies and mosquitoes away, but not the lice. The greybacks kept the people away. Men gave him wide berth and this allowed him more room for his own designs. He was a true loner. When other men got too close, he grabbed a louse from the back of his neck and crushed it between his fingernails. Folks would back away like horses from a bonfire. Even reckless men like Spud Ervin, took care never to touch him.

There was an order of importance for positions around the camp-fire, a hierarchy of the trail, which Gus Terry knew well. He used this too, to his advantage. First night out, Gus started to unroll his bed next to the fire. He picked the most comfortable, most intrusive bedground, upwind, out of the smoke, on dry, soft, even sod.

A lean, narrow-faced tough challenged him, "That's my place, Terry. Move over."

The tough's name was Granger. Granger was newly arrived from the bloody Kansas troubles and he had never heard of Gus Terry. He had his hand on his gun with the flap off and he had two friends standing behind. Outgunned and outnumbered, Gus Terry moved meekly to the other side of the fire where the wind blew the smoke in his face and the ground was rockier. He started to make his bed again and deliberately chose the most attractive spot and again they made him move.

A drover named Andy laid out his black snake whip in an arc around the best bed locations, "You stink, Terry. Cross it and you're a dead man." And Gus Terry moved meekly off alone, downwind of everyone, to the far edge of camp, away from the fire and the circle of sleepers.

He was exactly where he wanted to be. He voiced a protest for the sake of convention. "You call yourselves men and you can't stand the smell of a little sweat and a few friendly bugs." But when he was out of earshot, he laughed. The others ignored him.

September nights were colder on the perimeter of the camp, and darker. The darkness shrouded Gus' movements. The cold kept night prowlers tucked snugly in their blankets. Watching Gus Terry was an uncomfortable, unappetizing job. Spud Ervin tried but even he gave up. Gus repeated the same actions at the same hour, day in and day out. Watching him took dogged patience that Spud Ervin did not have. Finally, Spud Ervin and his guards forgot about Gus Terry. Gus was free to do as he pleased and Gus pleased to steal Spud Ervin's gold.

It wasn't your everyday, stand-off, hold-up theft. It was an insidi-ous draining, bit by bit. Every morning, when Gus Terry walked to the woods to relieve himself, he picked up a small pouch of dirt. Minutes

205

later, when Gus went to saddle his mule, Caroline, and load the pack mules, he removed a few pokes of gold and filled the sacks with the dirt. He stashed the gold beneath his ample beard, in the big bulge in the bib of his overalls where he kept his wad of tobacco. When he would stick his hands beneath the bib to warm them or to check his pouch of tobacco, he patted his gold. He loved the feel of it!

Gus' supply of tobacco never dwindled but grew steadily larger. Every night, before Gus crawled into his blankets, outside the ring of firelight, he emptied his stash into the hollow of a tree, the crack of a rock or the lea of a deadfall. No one noticed because no one came near him. And it was very dark and very cold in the mountains in September. On the divide, it snowed. Even the night of the full moon was chilled by clouds locked tight in the valleys against the back drop of the jagged peaks. But in the full moonlight, Gus stashed an ample chunk of Spud Ervin's gold.

Each day's success made Gus bolder, until he woke at night to check Caroline, and make several trips to the woods and back, replacing ever larger portions of the gold. He marked each cache carefully in a tally book as a herder keeps count of his cattle and this he carried with his pouch and his gold under his bib, attached to a leather thong around his neck. He never took off his shirt. The ruse worked smoothly for the duration of the trip and he indulged in fits of midnight laughter. Those who heard him thought he was crazier than Spud Ervin.

Gus Terry acquired a good stake, nearly one-third of all Spud Ervin's shipment. Still it wasn't the prospect of riches that exhilarated Gus. It was walking past the guards undisturbed—they even turned and looked away. It was passing unnoticed amid the packs of treasure and sauntering into the forest any time he wished. It was acting a role so convincingly that no one ever imagined his true intent. Most of all, it was outwitting presumptuous, greedy, young Spud Ervin.

Gus Terry didn't care about getting rich. When he had money, he didn't always spend it. He just wanted an easy life for himself and his mule, Caroline. He might not even return for all his caches right away— they were too heavy for Caroline and he was very careful with Caroline. After the pace set by young Ervin, Caroline would be tired. When he got to Salt Lake, he'd find a nice green meadow and let her graze for a few days while he'd sleep and eat and laugh and dream of how to spend his riches. He might even buy a new shirt. It didn't occur to him that he could wash the old one.

Gus Terry would retreive his gold bit by bit as he needed it, or leave it lay. If he missed a cache or two on his return trip, he'd still walk away rich at Spud Ervin's expense. Gus Terry in all his odorous, nit-ridden splendor, on the edge of the woods, in the cold and dark, cackled to himself long and loud, until the drovers threatened to blast him out of his blankets if he didn't shut up and let them sleep.

Gus was working now to trick Spud Ervin to pay off his skinners before discovering the theft. Gus manoeuvred the pilfered packs to the rear of the line to delay detection of the theft. He checked each pack to make sure a layer of gold covered the pokes of dirt beneath. He misplaced personal items, fumbled with equipment and worked to reinforce his image of innocent ignorance. He'd pretend incompetence and shoot at some jack rabbits way wide of the mark. He'd deliberately loose a bet. Even if the missing gold were discovered early, no one would suspect dumb Gus. Not even Spud Ervin sensed that Gus Terry had any intelligence, certainly not cunning enough to concoct a clever ruse.

Gus had let a bond develop between him and Spud, something a little bit human, like a hawk and a crow. The crow preys on other birds, drives them from their nests, steals and sucks out their eggs. The hawk sits immobile and watches, then swoops down and murders the crow. Gus always liked to watch the hawks when he was a shaver. He learned patience from them. He liked Spud Ervin as much as he had ever liked any man but he had patience that Ervin didn't have and he would wait to snap Spud Ervin's spine with a crack of his beak for the fun of the chase, for a good meal or a healthy portion of gold.

Two days later, in Salt Lake, Gus headed the line to collect his pay—$200.--. The drovers actually pushed him to the front and cheered when they heard he was going to take a bath and buy a new shirt.

It was a good wage for three weeks of work. Gus left Spud Ervin believing he would come back to work at the mines as a guard, not a digger. No one could possibly work beside smelly Gus within the close confines of a mine, even a placer mine. Then Gus and Caroline sauntered off for a grassy pasture in Idaho, with a jug of whiskey, a belly of laughs and enough gold stashed along the trail to pay for a daily bath for the rest of Gus Terry's life.

Chapter 32

T he Mormon escort arrived with Curly and two barrels of whiskey. Spud Ervin started drinking immediately and never com
plained about the high price. The Mormons snickered behind
their bushy beards.

Spud and Curly unloaded the packs at the Mormon Bank with
four bank guards and Crawford, the bank's manager. Spud opened
the first pack and immediately paid his drovers. They took their pay in
gold and not one shook his hand. Each one weighed his earnings with
care. Mumford, as arranged, collected double. Crawford handed Spud
a bank draft and he headed for the nearest saloon and whorehouse.

The bank guards finished the job of weighing and assaying the
gold. Curly took his own bedroll and Spud's and headed for the hotel.
He threw his belongings in a corner and collapsed, boots, spurs and
all. In seconds, he was snoring evenly.

Spud came in hours later, shaking and nervous. His eyes darted
toward the door, toward the window. He heard voices through the thin
sheeting of the walls. His missing arm twitched, his legs wobbled and
his hand shook but he was smiling. He had done it. He had brought
the Ervin gold safely to bank. He was rich; he was a man to reckon
with. Other men would recognize his riches.

For the first time since he left Varina, he was hungry. He stumbled
downstairs for a meal and ordered the most expensive plate on the
menu. Oysters, he'd never tasted an oyster, but he nibbled a little and
revelled in the satisfaction he felt when he complained and sent the
oysters and his hapless waiter back to the kitchen. He wanted his
oysters cooked like a well-done steak.

It was late when he came up to bed. The hotel was full and he had to share a room with Curly. The door creaked when he entered. Curly grunted in his sleep, a crude animal grunt, and rolled over on his side with his back facing Spud. Spud looked upon the expanse between the shoulder blades, covered now with blue flannel shirt pulled taught and smooth. A bullet there and he would teach Curly to follow orders! A silent knife slipped there between the protruding blades of the shoulders and Curly would never reveal the murder of Grumps Smith! Curly grunted again and rolled back around.

Spud heard scuffing in the hall, another guest, and suddenly the door to the room opened. The lock had not held. The newcomer excused himself when he realized he had entered the wrong room. But the interruption was enough to save Curly Shaw's life. Fatigue finally took hold of Spud Ervin. He placed his gun with his money belt and his knife under his pillow, lay down fully dressed and slept like a dead man.

At nine the next morning, there was a knock at the door. Spud Ervin awoke, grey-faced and surly with hammers pounding his head like an anvil. He grabbed his gun and leapt for the door. As it flung open, the astonished visitor, a thin man in a brown business suit, backed away. Spud Ervin stood, gun cocked and aimed like an arrow straight at the heart. In shock, the visitor stammered.

"Mist' Rervin?" The newcomer stood wide-eyed. "Clarence Pratt from Mormon Bank." He held out his card and stopped, afraid to continue. Spud motioned with his gun toward a slat-back chair in the corner. Curly awoke but didn't move.

Pratt perched himself on the edge of the chair, still holding his card, his eyes glued to the gun which Spud fingered carelessly. "Mist' Rervin, I'm unarmed." Pratt's face was pale.

Spud Ervin holstered the gun and took Pratt's card. "What's this mean?" Ervin snapped at the banker as he buckled his gunbelt. Pratt was intimidated and afraid. His tongue kept getting in the way of his teeth. He reached into his coat pocket and pulled out a sealed envelope. "Mist' Rervin, I've brought your receipt." He held out a clean white envelope.

Spud grabbed the envelope. Pratt was already backing out the door. In the time it took Spud to unseal and open the envelope, read and comprehend the contents, Pratt was gone.

Spud unfolded the paper and looked down at his receipt. He skipped immediately to the total sum, $458,400.---. His eyes narrowed. He'd never learned his numbers well and now frantically, he tried to figure the sum on his fingers. He ran downstairs to the desk clerk for a paper and pen. He started scratching numbers and the desk clerk helped him. He'd shipped close to 2 tons of gold at an average assay of 960 fine. One ton equalled 24,000 troy ounces at $20.--per ounce for a total of $480,000.-- minus impurities and brassage. The bank owed him $960,000.-- for 2 tons. $458,000.-- was far below that figure. Why? He reworked his arithmetic with the same result. Where was payment for the other ton? His jaw snapped together so hard it cracked. He crumpled the receipt and threw it on the floor, cursed the "thievin' Mormons" and crashed the door against the wall in his rush to leave.

The clerk was just opening the bank door when Spud stuck a gun barrel in his spine. Ervin's face was purple with rage and his tongue licked back and forth across his open mouth. "Open the safe! I want to see my gold."

The frightened clerk straightened and turned the key slowly in the lock, too slowly for Spud Ervin, who pushed his weight against the heavy door flinging it wide and tumbling the clerk to the floor. Behind him, the clerk scrambled to his feet and raced for the alarm bell under the teller's window. Spud wheeled and fired—hitting the man in the calf of the leg. He dragged the man like a bleeding carcass to a desk where they fumbled for keys and Spud unlocked an iron door to what looked more like an arsenal than a safe. His bags of gold were stacked neatly at the rear. Spud threw down his gun, took out his knife and cut the first sack. No glittering golden specks, just fine grey Idaho sand spilled out onto the floor. Wild-eyed, with his bare hand, Spud Ervin dug like a maddened starving wolf, one-handed, down into the sack. When finally he looked up, two guards stood over him, guns levelled at his head. Another man came running, the Crawford who had helped Spud unload yesterday. Crawford took charge. He spoke slowly and calmly, while the burly guards pinned Spud to the wall and removed his gun and knife.

"We always verify deposits, Mr. Ervin, before issuing receipts. You've brought us fifty bags, at 40 pounds each, but only 23 were filled with gold. We are very thorough. Did you think you could cheat us? And now you've shot Caterwall."

Caterwall was groaning, holding tightly to his leg.

Spud heard the accusation and reached for his empty holster. His beady eyes rolled back in his head. The guards slammed him into a chair and held him there. He kicked out with his feet and shouted back, "Bankers, you call yourselves! Thievin' leeches is what you are!"

Crawford spoke again with restraint, "Someone replaced the gold in those sacks, Mr. Ervin. It wasn't one of our employees. You should be more careful of the men you hire. You may at least be grateful that they didn't take all. You have a good stake left. Your draft issued yesterday is still good. You are a rich man." The even monotone of Crawford's words enraged Spud Ervin. He flung himself at Crawford, kicking and flailing, and fell forward. Crawford spoke again, "You may take this if you'll go peacefully and promptly so we can take Caterwall here to a doctor. No bones broken, a flesh wound—he'll survive." One of the guards handed him Spud's gun. He emtied it and handed it back to Spud. The guards pulled Spud to his feet and escorted him out the door.

Spud heard glass tinkle as the heavy door slammed behind him. He drew his empty gun and stared at it dumbly. Bright sunlight hit him in the face and he blinked. A crowd of onlookers surrounded him. A stout man with a small black bag pushed his way through—the doctor. Spud stepped backward out of his way. His gaze darted from one to the other of the astonished onlookers and he shouted at them rudely. "What you lookin' at? Go on home! I'm finished shootin' an' I'm finished lettin' you thievin' saints steal me bare as a baby's backside."

But this crowd was no tolerant miner's court. They closed ranks quickly when one of their own was threatened, a congregation of surly and xenophobic believers. A bullwhip cracked just behind Spud's heels. A demonic voice bellowed, "Sin against the Lord, ye'll forfeit your other arm!" They hooted a chorus of judgement and invective. One six-footer fingered his knife, "Hickman'll skin you alive, use your bones for pig swill!" One man swung a noose.

Spud Ervin heard the crack when guns were cocked and he ran in panic. He didn't stop until he reached the livery where he had stabled his horse. They let him go. Breathless, dripping sweat, in the dim light of the stable he laid his gun on an anvil and reloaded. His good hand trembled saddling his horse. The animal threw his head in fright when he fumbled with the bridle and but for a helpful stabler, he would have galloped off on a halter and shank.

When finally, he slowed the paint, about three miles outside the city, his thoughts reverted to Varina, to the last of his public humiliations. These Mormons were worse than McGillicuddy, Garrity, Cameron and that woman, Emma, their mockery more cruel, their rebuffs more pointed and their religious zeal, fearsome. They resurrected visions of his father sitting judgement always condemning, never praising. His own father's rejection was the worst injury Spud Ervin had ever endured. But the memory of his father was obscured now by all these other conflicting emotions, the frustration, the anger and the bitter, destructive realities that crashed in on his consciousness like so many waves upon a rocky shore. Revenge and an obsessive, relentless justification of self, became his driving force.

In one case, Spud had already exacted his due. Sime was dead. The rest of them would pay in kind. Spud would take them on, one at a time with gun, with knife, with bare hand—except for the woman. She had challenged his manhood and he imagined himself dragging her by the hair through the mud in the streets, in front of all Varina. He could taste the pleasure like a sweetmeat on the back of his tongue.

Spud Ervin rode past Brigham City, north to Montana, on the Corrinne to Varina road. He drove spurs into the exhausted horse and lashed out with the ends of the reins. The animal lunged forward to escape his raking heels but began to stumble and tire. Its nostrils flared; its flanks dripped blood and white foam fell in balls from its neck and shoulders. It lungs heaved in and out with desperate gasps for oxygen. Finally, the horse slowed in spite of all urging, then stopped, and dripping in sweat, quivering in every muscle, staggered and fell. No amount of urging could raise it to its feet again. Spud lashed and kicked and pulled and dug his rifle into the hapless animal's barrel. Finally, he grabbed his rifle, put the muzzle to the animal's head and fired. The poor beast's brains spattered the trail. Spud shouldered his saddle and started desperately out on foot.

He wandered trembling and delerious into Cherry Creek. A Gentile family fed him and bedded him in their cabin for the night, but he awoke before midnight and left for the nearest saloon and the whiskey he craved. He needed a horse too, and stole one from the hitch rail in front of the Top Hat Saloon. He chose the tallest and longest legged animal and raced ahead to Fort Hall. This animal survived because it stumbled hard into a dry creekbed and threw Spud into the water. When Spud came up splashing and wet, the animal shied and headed for home. Some freighters picked Spud up, let him fill himself with rot gut and sleep in the back of their wagon. At Yampatch, he stole another horse.

Chapter 33

Lee Cameron heard the shot but in the absence of Spud Ervin, he was not a worrisome man. Word had come up the trail that Spud had been run out of Salt Lake, and hopefully would not come back to Varina. The shot was loud—a rifle. It came from the direction of the Citadel.

Cameron was at the hotel having breakfast with Emma and Marie and paid no attention. Guns were fired regularly in Varina where everyone went armed and this Tuesday was like any other day of the week. Shots could mean a dead rattler, a merciful end to a colicky horse, some harmless target practice or even a game of pool with guns for cues. Cameron dismissed the noise and sat back smiling at his happy family. Without Spud Ervin and his contingent, Varina was almost a civilized place.

Marie was pouring molasses over a stack of flapjacks when Marshal Ryder and John Moulton tromped into the room. Ryder was the square-built man who had broken up Cameron's fight with Curly Shaw. He was a former shotgun rider on the Varina-Fort Benton road, respected and tough. Moulton, with his glazed blue eyes and bobbing head, was clearly the inferior. In Varina, Sheriff John Moulton collected the salary—it was his jurisdiction—but Marshal Ryder enforced the law. They clomped heavily up to the Cameron family now.

"Emma...Lee, you'd better come. Leave the girl with Stewart." One look at Ryder's sharp eyes and pencil-lined mouth and Emma paled. Moulton stood nodding dumbly, eyes bagged and sad. Stewart arrived directly behind them. "I'll see Marie eats her breakfast and gets to school."

They walked outside where Ryder turned to speak. "I didn't want to say it in front of the kid...It's McGillicuddy." Emma paled. Ryder turned on his heel without saying more and walked down Warren toward the Citadel.

Emma rushed past him and confronted him, "Is he sick? What happened?"

Ryder was a man of few words, "Dead, Ma'am. I'm sorry."

Emma straightened in shock. Her eyes widened; her jaw dropped; she took a hand and brushed a curl back over her ear. "No." The denial was fruitless. Cameron took her by the arm and they walked woodenly forward.

Moulton talked more freely, "I knew Dan well. Used to count 'is money ever' mornin'. Drank 'is coffee with me sometimes when he done." He shook his wobbly head grimly. "Always right hospitable an' neighborly ...Shot in the back, by some yeller thievin' scum." At the Citadel, Ryder and Moulton led the way through the bat-wing doors and the empty gaming room to McGillicuddy's quarters. McGillicuddy sat as he always sat at this hour of the morning, in his shirtsleeves, at his big roll-top desk, over his scales, weighing the gold dust and counting the take from the night before. He had drawn his water from the well, lit the stove, dressed in his immaculate fashion and put on the coffee which had boiled down to inky mush. But he had not barred the door as was his habit. It was wide open. The desk top was rolled back.

His head rested on his left arm which lay upon the desk. Blood oozed from a grizzly hole between his shoulder blades, dripped down his spine and soaked the lower half of his white shirt. It was red and still wet. His head had fallen forward into the scales knocking the weights from the one tray, the gold dust from the other. A stack of bills weighted under a rock lay untouched on the desk shelf next to four unemptied pokes. The draft from the open back door had blown a film of gold dust over his face and into the snow white strands of his hair so that he glittered like some sainted angel from a paradise beyond. But no spirit breathed life into his soul. He was quite dead.

The sight shocked and angered Lee Cameron. He struggled to control the thirst for vengeance that welled up in his chest, clamped his teeth together and bit down on his tongue.

Moulton spoke first. "Damn robbers."

He would have rambled on but Cameron interrupted, "Who did this? It wasn't robbery. They left the gold." He spoke softly and directed the question at Ryder.

Hank Ryder shook his head and shrugged. "I wish I knew... I don't even think he saw who shot him. You're right it was no robbery. They didn't take gold or bills. From the looks of things, they didn't even

214

care....the safe's closed, just wanted him dead. Did he owe any debts, have any enemies?"

Emma had held back and now walked forward silently and stroked the old man's hair. Her wide eyes and bloodless face looked tragically back at Lee. She spoke to Hank Ryder. "People owed him. He didn't owe people. He was always staking this one, feeding that one, generous to everybody and good to me ...like a father." Valiantly, she blinked back the liquid welling up in her eyes.

Her voice was so quiet Cameron knew she was struggling for control and put a steadying arm around her shoulders. He too answered Ryder's question. "Only one enemy that I know of—Spud Ervin, because the Citadel won title to the Cleopatra Mine."

Now Moulton interrupted, "Spud's just a boy! I knowed 'is pa! Besides, he ain't here in town."

Ryder nodded at Cameron, "I thought of him too, but he captained his shipment to Utah. You seen 'im since?"

"No." Cameron shoved his hands deep into his pockets and hunched his shoulders. He was uncomfortable, anxious to be gone from the ugly scene, to sort out his own feelings and suspicions, to take Emma away. She would cry long and bitter tears over Dan McGillicuddy later, in the privacy of their room.

John Moulton was still mumbling to himself, proclaiming Spud Ervin's innocence. For the first time, Ryder addressed Moulton, "Find the undertaker and get Garrity to clean up here." He turned to Emma. "You want to make the funeral arrangements?"

Emma rallied at this. "Yes. Of course. He must be buried with respect, the way he lived." She had stroked most of the gold dust from McGillicuddy's snowy hair and now placed her hand over the old rheumatic fingers. They were still warm. "And we must open the Citadel as usual... He would want that."

Cameron nodded agreement. He walked Emma out to the main saloon. She took one look at McGillicuddy's old piano and her tears came in convulsive sobs. He pulled her against him then and held her there, in the empty beerhall with the smell of smoke and sweat and whiskey in the air, stroking her hair, swaying, soothing, quelling the emotions which welled up in his own soldier's breast with death in the next room. It was always the death of a comrade that ignited a man's will to fight, and fired the will to repay in kind.

Lee Cameron broke the trancelike spell. Vengeance overcame him, "I swear to you I'll kill the man who did this." He only whispered, but his face was white and his eyes, cold as ice. They struck fear, not comfort in Emma's heart.

"Don't risk your life. McGillicuddy wouldn't have wanted that." But her words struck Cameron like playful beanshots that bounce off an empty can. They had no meaning. He walked her in dreaded silence back to the hotel.

Cameron returned to the Citadel about noon. The bar was wide open and crowded in poignant contrast to a few hours earlier. A fiddle played, glasses clinked and heavy boots stomped the floor in a wild mountaineer's dance. McGillicuddy's body was laid out in a pine plank coffin across the bar, with bunches of wild flowers at the foot and an unopened bottle of Irish Whiskey at the head. He seemed merely to be sleeping except that he wore his best black cutaway and green brocade vest. It was his Sunday race-day costume and he would never have fallen asleep in it.

Con Garrity dispensed drinks right over his dead body and mourners paid their homage to Dan McGillicuddy and promptly drowned their grief with drink and song. At first, Lee Cameron was shocked, but Garrity explained. Garrity, like McGillicuddy, was Irish. The only church in town was Anglican, and that not fully constructed, and no respectable Irishman could be buried from an English church. Only a Catholic ceremony would do and Father Manno was five days ride away at Mary's Lake. They had no choice but to improvise the wake and funeral themselves.

Cameron listened impatiently while Garrity explained the Irish wake. McGillicuddy was friend in adversity, fair to his last cent, a fine man who would reap a glorious reward in heaven. Was not this cause for celebration? Burial would be tomorrow morning at the cemetery east of town. Doc Lubbock would read the scripture and Mayor Thatcher, and he, Con Garrity, would sing, and did Cameron want to be a pallbearer? Cameron refused but said he would join Emma and Marie in the procession. Emma's wishes were forgotten, the arrangements were made. The mourners paid their tearful respects and then happily consumed most of McGillicuddy's best whiskey and danced around his coffin.

Cameron paid his respects too and went back to the hotel. Marie was at school. Emma had gone to break the news of McGillicuddy's death to Midge and Gertie. Cameron had time on his hands, time to think back on one of Ryder's questions that had been tugging at his brain all afternoon. Ervin, where was Spud Ervin? Ervin was spiteful enough to attack a woman. Was he spiteful enough to kill an unarmed man? Had Ervin returned for the deed to the Cleopatra mine? Cameron thought back to McGillicuddy's room. The door and the desk were open but the safe had not been touched. The deed was there, inside. Or was it?

Lee Cameron jumped up suddenly, hurried back to the Citadel, shoved the revellers aside and marched to McGillicuddy's back room. McGillicuddy's desk had been cleaned, the gold dust swept and weighed. A coffee pot steamed on the stove and Garrity and Moulton sat by the oil lamp at the table rumaging through some documents. They looked up when Cameron entered.

"Lee, he left this for you." Garrity held out a bright green linen cylinder about two feet long and three inches in diameter. A green silk ribbon was tied neatly around the middle. He handed it to Cameron.

"What's this?"

"It has Emma's name on it, and yours."

Cameron took the package and slowly started to unfold it while Garrity kept talking. "Must've set great store by it. He kept it all the way to the back of the safe. I seen one other. It's like a bible to us Irish families who can't afford better. I think they call it a genealogy."

Cameron had other things on his mind and interrupted, "Later...." He looked around and his eyes stopped at the open safe.

"Who opened it?" He looked from Garrity to Moulton.

Moulton answered blandly. "It wasn't locked. Thief must've surprised 'im after he opened it himself."

"Did you find the Cleopatra deed?"

Again it was Moulton, the simple-minded lawman, who explained, "Not yet. We're havin' a look-see. But it's all here." He pointed to three separate piles, gold, some old bills, Confederate and Federal, and legal papers, neatly stacked on the desk. Slowly and methodically, he sifted the papers one by one. Cameron watched his every move. "Three deeds. Let's see." Moulton placed a pair of glasses on the end of his bulbous nose. "I don't read too good.... This 'ere is the Dobbin out by Gold Creek." He set aside the first page. "An' Cruperman's...found ole Cruperman's body down in the ravine year ago Christmas...And says 'ere this last one is the Camp Bummer Mine. Dan McGillicuddy's a rich man." He slapped the deeds loudly down on the desktop. "No Cleopatra."

Cameron wasted no time. He jumped up. "Ten to one, Spud Ervin's in Varina!" He turned wild eyes upon Garrity. "Find Emma and Marie and guard them with your life!" Before Moulton or Garrity could answer, he had dashed out the door.

Cameron ran for the black horse. He was slipping the bridle hastily over her ears when Glenby and Ryder walked up. "Can't have 'er today, Lee. Ryder here tells me she belongs to Mr. Slade now."

"Slade? You told me they hung him years ago?"

"His brother, Mrs. Slade sent him to get her horse. I ain't gonna cross Charlie Slade."

Cameron protested, buckled the throatlatch and tightened the cinch. "He pay you the back feed and board? You can't just give her away. Slade owes you."

Glenby looked blankly to Ryder. "He's right, but Charlie Slade might not think so."

Cameron had his foot in the stirrup and the reins in hand. "I need a fast horse and I need it now. Tell Slade I'll bank him. Spud Ervin's back!"

"Hold on, Cap'n, I'm comin' with you!" Ryder ran fast as his stubby legs could travel to saddle his own horse.

But Lee Cameron didn't wait. The black jumped forward as his seat hit the saddle. The mare bucked lightly once but Cameron sat back and drove his heels into her flanks. They charged up the gulch toward Highland and the Ervin camp with Marshal Ryder choking on his dust, about five minutes behind.

Chapter 34

Spud Ervin was in Varina. He sat like a young prince, in Judge Burnwell's best armchair, sipping the judge's favorite brandy. He had not been home, up the mountain in the Ervin Camp above Highland, and had come to the judge straight off the trail. His face was haggard and angry, his blond hair hanging in wads over his grimy brow. His clothes hung like sackcloth on his bony frame. He needed a good wash and a meal but he was drinking the Judge's brandy and hardly nibbling a plate of bread and cheese that stood on a table at his elbow.

The judge had felt sorry for this hapless son of old Sime. Now he was having his doubts—Spud had tramped in uninvited, although the Burnwells would never have denied him a meal and a bath. He was abrasive and imperious.

The judge tried to explain why, although the Ervin titles to his properties were probably valid and legal, so too were the subsequent titles of the present tenants. It all had to do with the peculiar rampant development of a boom town, with strikers and speculators, multiple ownership, jumped claims and squatters rights. Varina was a town that sprouted like a weed, opportunistically, and one did not now go about evicting people from their shelters in the face of the oncoming winter. Housing was too scarce.

Spud did not understand most of what the judge said. He stared at the floor and drummed his fingers on the table. He refused to admit that the judge could not advise exercising any of his claims at present. The judge spoke condescendingly, like a teacher to a child, "Folks are living in those houses, Spud."

"Scour the scum out now! They're squattin' on my land, claim-jumpin', snipin' my gold!" Ervin's voice snapped back like a whip, sharp and menacing. He emptied his glass and sunk back into his chair, sulking and angry. The cruel angular jaw set hard. The eyes receded to tiny black dots.

Judge Burnwell read the menace in his stare. "I could issue an order to evict but I won't do that, Spud, not now. You got to consider people, Spud. They'll fight you and you may well lose....if you go to a trial. Now if we wait 'til spring..." The judge placed a consoling hand on Spud's armless shoulder and poured out another brandy with the other. Spud swatted the hand away and gulped his brandy. It burned his mouth and scorched his stomach. He smacked his lips, got up and reached for more before it was offered. When he poured, his hand shook.

His brusque action shocked the old judge who stalled in alarm. "You come back tommorrow. We'll talk further when you're settled and when you've had a good night's sleep." He placed the brandy bottle in Spud's empty hand and eased him toward the door—Judge Burnwell was an prudent man. With bottle in hand, Spud couldn't reach for a gun or a knife or strike out. The judge had bought one more day.

Spud stumbled out the door and down the road. He stopped suddenly, threw back his head, guzzled what brandy was left and flung the bottle violently into Garnet Creek. The glass shattered against the rocks with a clatter that echoed raucously in his swirling brain. He wiped his mouth with the back of his hand and licked his lips. Burnwell had conned him, liquored him up like a worthless tramp and cheated him out of his own property—like Cameron in the poker game, like McGillicuddy and his damn scales, like the hellbound saintly Mormons in Salt Lake and like haughty Emma Dubois who refused a lay!

Blind rage took hold of Spud Ervin. His whole body shook. He threw back his head and let out a deafening howl. He started to weave crazily down Jefferson along the muddy banks of Garnet Creek, circling, stumbling, falling and righting himself. He passed the Citadel on the corner and arrived at the Mayfair Livery. It was quiet and deserted except for a few horses that stamped at flies and munched hay. Opposite the livery, he slipped and rolled into the reeds that lined the creek. They were dry and brittle in the autumn of the year, like a mattress of straw. He lay there on his side staring up at the clouds and the tall false front of the Citadel Saloon and the low long weathered planks of the stable.

No one saw Spud Ervin heave himself up from out of the creekbed, cross the street and enter the saloon. McGillicuddy heard the door swing open but he was accustomed by now to Moulton's routine visit for his cup of coffee and didn't stop what he was doing, didn't even turn around. Spud Ervin entered, took one look at the old man counting his winnings, drew and fired. He rifled quickly through the open safe but could not find the Cleopatra deed and fled back across the street into the willows. He lay hidden in the willows watching, as Ryder and Moulton came running and discovered the body.

That was when his tortured brain realized his advantage: no one knew he was in town. He could do what he pleased. He could act out his vengeance without retribution.

He smiled at that, pulled himself to his knees, snorting like a hungry goat and began to uproot the dry willow stalks from the creekbed. They tore away easily from the loose damp mud. When he had gathered an ample pile, he swept as many as he could under his good arm and headed for the back wall of the livery.

A north wind was blowing hard. Two haystacks stood like monuments abutting the stable. Spud looked over his shoulder. No one was near. Horses grazed peacefully in the corral. He piled the stalks against the livery wall, high enough to reach above the stone foundation to the dry boards above. Spud Ervin fumbled in his pocket, struck a match on the sole of his boot and held it to the dry grasses. It started slowly, without smoke, until the north wind cradled it. Nourished and fed, it licked up the dry boards quickly to the hayloft beneath the roof and to the haystacks near the walls.

When the flames lapped the side of the stable and the smoke thickened, the horses panicked. The first man to sense the danger and smell the smoke was Clem, who did not comprehend the danger, and walked inside calmly to unbolt the stalls and turn the frightened horses loose. They dashed in a stampede out into the street except for Cameron's little grey. His stall was at the very rear where the haystacks ignited in a blow-up of flame and blinding grey smoke. A plank crashed in the horse's path, blocking escape. The animal turned back into the flames and Clem, true to the last to his favorite friend, followed. Charlie Slade saw him go in and ran after and Rob Glenby followed, but both stumbled back out of the smothering smoke red-faced, coughing and gasping great gulps of air. They fell heaving into the arms of Con Garrity, who had come running at the first sound of alarm. Slade had to drag Glenby back by force. In minutes, Glenby recovered and struggled to go back into the flames. In an iron grip, Slade held him down. Clem did not come out.

The fire moved quickly from the stable to outlying buildings south and east. Varina was a town built of wood, on the sidehill of Garnet Gulch. Glenby's livery, at her northwest corner, was her lowest point.

From there, she rose in elevation in a broad triangle of buildings to the south and east. Wind and sun had baked her to dry tinder. The north wind whipped the flames which ranged steadily uphill from the burning livery and sucked in oxygen. Hot gases at the fire's center reached out like tentacles to the buildings at the lower end of Jones Street. The north wind fanned the fire and Varina burned like a martyr on the pyre.

Spud Ervin ran back to the creekbed and lay on his back listening to its crack and sizzle and watching the the eery orange shapes of the burning building dance above him. He heard the screams of animals and the human cries for help, shrieks from out of a hellish dream, until the fire began to spread and even the creekbed heated and became choked with heavy smoke. Then he started up the gulch.

People ran in all directions collecting buckets, rousting the sick from their beds, yanking terrified animals back and away, forming human chains from the creek to the perimeter of flame, wetting down buildings and hauling matresses, furniture and anything that would burn out of the fire's way. But the flames leaped relentlessly from one building to the next. They would not be contained. They burned up the south bank of Sunshine Creek and ignited the house with the green porch. Rachel and Gertie grabbed what they could and piled it on McGillicuddy's terrified bay horse. They fled the stable in the alley just in time before it too came crashing down.

To the east, the Brewery was next, and to the south, Lamb's store and all of the north side of Warren Street. There was no barrier, no fire break. Only the barren tailings of Outlaw Bar and the slim line of firefighters with their pitiful buckets could block the tongues of flame and keep them from igniting the whole east side of the gulch. In vain, every able-bodied Varinan fought until the heat choked their lungs and their muscles ached. Finally, they threw down their buckets and fled.

The wind calmed mysteriously as in the eye of a hurricane. The town breathed sudden relief. The Brewery and the new Masonic Temple could be saved and the townspeople actually made progress battling the blaze. But the respite was brief. The dance hall caught in a giant vortex of flame that generated its own wind, swirling in its own powerful updraft. It was a devil wind and churned in a deafening roar, throwing bits of flame like confetti, high into a column of smoke. The safest refuge was east up Sunshine Creek, in the lea of the wind, across Tug's Ravine, up the road toward the racetrack. But most fled with the school children south up the wider Garnet Creek on the road to Highland or north down the Helena-Fort Benton Road.

Spud Ervin had climbed above the blaze to the bridge above Varina on the Highland Road. Sparks flew around him and danced like so many snowflakes and he reached out to catch them. He was gleeful. The fire was clean and beautiful. Like a child studying ants upon a hill, Spud cocked his head and watched the human herd scrambling over the bridge with their pitiful belongings, driving wagons with fire-panicked teams, hauling wheelbarrows and hand carts, whipping their swine and fowl before them and choking the narrow road.

The north wind shifted and the air around him started to heat once more. Sweat poured over his shoulders and onto his stub. It itched and he scratched. It itched more and he scratched until it bled. His blood seemed to congeal and pump and pound in his head. The smoke made him cough. His lungs ached and he started to pant. When a lull in the wind arrived and the fire calmed, he started to pick his way further up Garnet Creek, higher and higher, but the rising heat and the air around him did not cool.

He slogged through muddy trenches and clawed his way over piles of tailings. He tore apart fifteen-foot sluice sections and kicked over flumes and rockers, all with an approving, admiring eye on the blaze. It died down briefly. But the dry hay at Glenby's livery and a few of the cribs on Jones Street were still burning and spewing clouds of smoke and flame into the darkening afternoon sky. He couldn't see past the perimeter of the fire. He couldn't see the house with the green porch, but he knew it had ignited with the rest of the alley. Lot twenty-two would be cleared and he could mine the Sergeant Lode. Burnwell be damned—he was not needed. Spud breathed deeply and wiped his hand on his shirt, satisfied.

He continued climbing, flinging aside anything that lay in his path. The air was hot and starved for oxygen. His face reddened, his nostrils flared and his mouth hung open in an effort to inhale more deeply. His arm was slimy with mud and his clothing hung in tatters from his sooty shoulders. Finally, he reached an outcropping above the city where the air was cooler, where he paused to rest and catch his breath.

Suddenly the hot wind on his back cooled and struck him in the face. The wind had turned. It was sweeping downgulch now from south to north, when only a few minutes ago, it had blown hard in the opposite direction. The fire's core had generated a heated column of air which rose like a mushroom over the town and began to suck in cooler air from off the peaks. Spud's flight had led him into the lee of this new wind. He was safe. The fire would blow away from him. But when this new wind hit the hot air column and opposing upgulch northerly, they collided in a firestorm of flame that whirled and rained a tempest of fire down on Chinatown.

Spud Ervin had no concern for the Chinese. They were worse than dogs, wallowing in their hovels, built with scrap timber, sticks and reeds. The hovels popped like firecrackers and crumbled in the heat.

The Chinese had no defense, no buckets, no hoses, no organized resistance. What little water was available, was used in the laundries. The rest of the creek that should have flowed briskly, had been dammed and diverted for sale to the miners' flumes. Water had value and was reserved for white enterprise or whatever yellow enterprise serviced the white, like laundries. It unearthed the gold. And gold was more valuable than people. The Chinese who lingered to fight the flames, even for a moment, fell from exhaustion, coughing and choking in the blackening smoke. The inferno immersed them and their screams could be heard in their strange tongue, above the fire's deadly roar.

The rest streamed now, in an advancing line of black tunics, conical hats and pigtails, down the crooked alleys that served them for streets. They carried the crippled and aged on their backs. They fled in droves like frightened sheep before a wolfpack, They fled up the gulch toward Highland and safety, on the heels of Spud Ervin. He watched them come, laughed at their panic, cursed and derided them and ordered the filthy rodent eaters back away from his haven. They kept coming. He resumed his climb. They gained on him. He climbed faster, slamming through the wooden flumes and kicking apart the crude wooden sluices ever more violently. Finally, he reached a bare rock. The fire would not reach here. There was no fuel. But he was at the end of his strength and the frightened rabble still charged upon him, like the dreadful demons of his own peculiar delusions. He drew his gun and shouted for them to get back but the frantic Chinese didn't understand. Implacably, they pressed on and Spud Ervin fired. He was a good shot. A young man in front dropped and crumpled to the earth. The crowd ran over him. Spud fired again. Another fell. He fired three more times at the onrushing horde but still they thundered relentlessly forward like a blind suicidal army. He shook an empty gun like a signal flag in their faces and turned to escape when he looked up.

He was not alone. A contingent of horrified white citizens from Pine Grove, Central City and Highland, had arrived to watch the holocaust and had witnessed the shootings. Grim-faced and rigid, they reminded him of the sanctimonious Mormons. Spud's eyes bulged with disbelief and he shouted crazily, "Vermin! Pick 'em out yer hair, crush 'em with yer fingernail." And he yelled louder, "Shoot the critters! Burn the hive!" He held the gun between his thumb and fourth finger with his third finger on the trigger. With his index finger he pointed. The gun went off and misfired. Now he pointed his index finger haphazardly like a child in play. But it was no child who shrieked a song of death, "Ashes, ashes, all fall down!"

He quieted suddenly and stood for a moment shaking his shaggy head, knowing somewhere in his deep subconscious that he had committed a heinous wrong. He shivered under the accusing eyes that probed like a thousand tiny needles. He looked up and recited what sounded like a ryhme, "Took what's mine, just like Sime..." and seemed to calm. But the Chinese who had stopped to pick up their wounded, began again, and he yelled, "Fools! Cowards! You wouldn't stop! You wouldn't obey!" He shoved his gun in his belt, sat down and fumbled one-handed trying to reload.

The reaction of the Highland citizens was immediate. They thought he was mad and moved to restrain him. Three men approached him from upgulch with Judge Burnwell, who tried to reason with him, at their head.

"Spud, come here to me. Your father was an old friend. I've helped him and now I can help you. Spud, give us the gun. It's a terrible thing you've seen this afternoon and it's shaken you and all of us. Wash up. Eat a good meal....Get some sleep." He held out his hand and as a master would to his pet dog, He pleaded, "Come here, boy."

The word "boy" was like throwing meat to a starving wolf. Spud finished reloading. He lifted the gun and fired again. A horse was hit and whined in pain. The three men dove for the ground as another bullet ricocheted wildly off the rocks. The Judge stood his ground, miraculously unhurt. The horse was not dead and floundered aimlessly on three legs. Spud Ervin suddenly realized that he had maimed a defenseless animal and his whole body started to shake. His emotions condensed into a terrible fear. He shoved his gun back into his belt and pivoted toward the only flight still open to him, up the bank, toward the east rim of the gulch. He ran. This way took him to the flank of the Highland/Varina road. Another crowd was moving here, from off Missouri Street, with belongings and livestock, away from the fire, high on a side hill, parallel to the stream of Chinese. Spud moved with superhuman speed over the rocks, a darkened spectral form now, blackened from the smoke and soot. He shouldered his way against the crowd cringing at their every touch. Instinctively, people drew back and Spud Ervin ran on heedless that he was running against the flow, toward Varina, back into the fire.

Chapter 35

When Lee Cameron charged into the Ervin Camp, only Hump was there sitting on a log by the campfire, chewing tobacco and whittling. He looked up casually. One glance at the grim lines of Cameron's face, his new rifle and the Navy Colt unflapped and ready, and Hump retreated.

"Mr. Ervin ain't here. Ain't been here fer weeks." The protruding shoulders and sunken neck diminished Hump's face in a way that made people dismiss him as unintelligent and unimportant. Cameron sensed that this was not the case, that here was a man who led a secretive life.

Cameron dismounted to reconnoiter. He remembered the hunchback from his sojourn at Lysaght's. His words were brusque. "You in charge here? When's Ervin due back?"

"Didn't say. Water's in the barrel, you want some fer yer horse." Hump indicated the barrel but glued his eyes to the new Winchester in its scabbard on Cameron's saddle.

"Thanks." Cameron led the horse to the barrel.

"What you want Mr. Ervin fer?" The hunchback stared so hard at the rifle he didn't notice the coffee boiling over.

Cameron didn't answer directly. "I have a cup of coffee?"

"Help yerself." Cameron poured out the coffee and took careful measure of this man. He had seen other Humps in the Army. They seemed reticent and stupid, but they were introverted, calculating men. Hump probably hadn't been paid in weeks and his loyalty was unwinding. Hump's next question confirmed it.

"That's a fancy gun you got. That why you lookin' fer Ervin, to shoot 'im?"

Again Cameron let the question pass. He flicked a black look over the camp like a hawk on a limb, watching for movement in the grass. "Dan McGillicuddy was shot. I think Ervin did it."

Hump made no move. "The saloon keeper?"

Cameron nodded. There was no need to explain. Hump had understood. At the first sign of trouble, Hump would leave. Cameron's vicious stare cut off further conversation.

His horse was watered. Ervin wasn't here. Lee Cameron mounted and was riding away when Hump finally drew up the courage to address his back. "I get my pay, I gonna buy me a gun like that." Cameron didn't stop.

Cameron walked the black horse back to Highland slowly. She was tired after the climb and the going was more treacherous downhill. In Highland he stopped.

The black horse needed rest so he loosened the cinch and tied her with a feedbag at the edge of the settlement near a tiny shack. The smell of fresh baking wafted from the shack and Cameron went in. It was a tiny restaurant, with no indication that it was anything more than a miner's shack, except for the delicious smell. Harry, the proprietor and baker, was an arthritic old man with laughing eyes and a wooden leg who wore a white apron over a barrel belly. He served a hearty stew and delicious donuts rolled in real cinnamon sugar. They were so fresh, they were still warm. Cameron stuffed himself and bought a bagful to take to Marie.

The sky was dark when he walked outside but it was early afternoon. A storm was coming and iron grey clouds were massing from the Beaverhead in the west and converging on Varina and there was a peculiar smell on the air, like wood smoke. He couldn't see Varina—she lay around a bend in the gulch. He tightened the cinch and was unhitching the black horse when a lone rider galloped up and halted his horse so abruptly he pitched forward into the dust. Cameron reached down to help him up.

"You stop short, mister, better sit back in the saddle, tuck your aft end down just like your horse." He recognized the pidgeonlike face of the barber, Behnke, and stiffled a laugh. Behnke wasn't hurt but his face was ghostly white and his beady eyes glared in unblinking fright. The horse was lathered and heaving. Behnke moved his lips uncontrollably.

"It's gone! All gone. Warren Street! That's my shop, my scissors, my razors, my lathers, my scents! All Varina's, ruined, destroyed!" Behnke's words sputtered in spasms like water from a broken hose and his eyes stood out like a frog's from a bloodless face. He shook convulsively. Cameron knew Behnke had a bent for hyperbole but he couldn't dismiss the real terror in the little man's eyes.

Two other men rode up and Cameron recognized the hotel keeper, Stewart and Ed Lamb, the storekeeper. Stewart confirmed Behnke's ravings. Varina was on fire! It had started at the Mayfair Livery in the haystacks and now threatened the whole city. Stewart and Lamb shouted the details loudly for all to hear and begged for volunteers. All able-bodied men were needed to fight the flames! Stewart wrenched the reins around and spurred his frightened horse back down gulch. Lamb followed close at his heels.

Lee Cameron's face blanched at Stewart's report. His wife and child were in Varina! He jumped into the saddle and laid his heels in the black mare's ribs. Visions of horrors, of Atlanta, Charleston, leaped up before him. He'd seen cities burn, squinted until his eyes stung at the hungry flames, coughed on the smoke and tasted the dry ash. And he'd smelled the horrible sweet smell of burned flesh in the ashes, the same he smelled now wafting up from Varina! His whole being rebelled at the images! In desperation, he whipped the black mercilessly. His hands shook uncontrollably. The mare sensed the urgency and clambered bravely skidding and scrambling down the rocky trail. She stumbled once, nose to the ground, scratched her knees but came up proudly and forged ahead. The air grew hotter. Cameron was close to panic.

He caught up with Stewart. Cameron's sweaty hands slipped on the reins; his knees gripped the horse painfully. The mare collected her strength, feeling the tension within him, giving her all. But Lee Cameron had only one thought that pursued him like a bloodhound.

"Emma! Have you seen Emma?" He screamed like a wild man at Stewart.

The hotel keeper turned and waved his hat. "No! Nor the girl!"

Cameron's eyes began to smart. More memories flooded back. Explosions, gunsmoke, the heat that singed a man's eyelids and made him sweat until he bled and the smoke that filled a man's lungs with phlegm until he choked. He tried to shake the images loose, to clear the horror from his brain.

The mare was tiring. He could feel her stride shorten and her lungs pump, like his own. A white lather covered the black sheen of her neck. He had to slow down. He must conserve her strength—she could carry Emma and the child to safety. He reined back.

About half way down, the road began to fill with the curious, foolish humans who make sport of tragedy—like a battle fought for society to watch, like Bull Run—as if a holocaust could be casual entertainment for a Sunday outing and an army clambering in retreat, a colorful race to the finish. Just such an irreverent crowd followed Cameron now past Pine Grove and Central City where more bystanders joined them. Heedless of danger, they filled the places and blocked the path of those who would honestly help. Water wagons slowed and rescuers detoured onto the rocky shoulder. Cameron spied Doc Lubbock reins in one hand, satchel in the other, desperately trying to urge his horse forward amid the thickening crowd.

Finally the Chinatown blow-up forced the spectators back. Frantic refugees met them head-on. Livestock and people mingled in a wild melee of terrified voices and animal shrieks until fear rushed in like a tidal bore and they all ran.

A few stalwart souls persisted in a heroic or foolhardy march toward Varina, Cameron, Doc Lubbock, Stewart, Lamb and a pitiful few who had relatives and friends unaccounted for. These truly wanted to help.

The Doctor's horse put his head down and refused to go further. Doc Lubbock, a poor rider, couldn't control the animal. He kicked hard, too hard. The horse whirled and bolted, carrying the doctor thirty yards back up the gulch before he could bring the beast under rein. The horse stood quivering. Doc dismounted. He would continue on foot. Cameron's mare and Stewart's mount stopped too. They were herd animals who wanted to flee with their brother at the smell of one of their worst enemies, fire. Cameron could feel the mare's muscles contract. He held her steady wondering how much farther she would go.

He saw the children then. Tilton and Grandma Mason were driving them in a tight circle like a herd of sheep. There were ten in all and they held each other tightly by the hand. Marie was not with them.

Tilton called to him above the din. "She's with Emma.... Highland, we'll be in Highland. Tell the parents."

Suddenly, Cameron had visions of the children grovelling in the dirt of the Dugout Saloon. He shouted, "Take them to Harry's! Donuts, you can smell the donuts!"

Cameron turned his horse toward the ugly red glare below. Where were Emma and Marie? Tears filled his smarting eyes. The horse was panting hard. Lubbock and Stewart were dismounting, handing the reins to Tilton and the children. Cameron knew it was time he dismount too. The alternative was to kill the mare. He picked up a scrawny boy and plopped him in the saddle.

He tried to speak with confidence for the sake of the child. "Take good care of her, she'll take good care of you! There's donuts in the saddle bag." He smacked the mare on the rump and she trotted away with the bouncing child. As an afterthought, Cameron screamed one last counsel, "Hold on tight: she bucks! And look for Patrick Lysaght!" This he shouted at Tilton, but Tilton had turned and he didn't think he heard.

On foot, he continued down. It was then he spotted a scrawny, dark figure that ran crazily over the rocks toward Missouri Street. Its clothes hung from bony shoulders in shreds without any substance to fill them. It ran as if pursued, desperately, back toward the fire. Instinctively, Cameron knew exactly who it was. And Spud Ervin saw him and ran faster.

Cameron saw the angry mob then and realized why Spud was running toward, not away from the fire. He was escaping from something worse. Suddenly Spud veered away down a narrow street two blocks above Warren. Cameron pushed futilely through the crowd on foot in an effort to overtake Spud but he could not make his way fast enough. Stewart and Lamb had turned off somewhere ahead of him; Doc Lubbock, somewhere behind. And Lee Cameron realized he had lost sight of Spud Ervin.

Lee Cameron was now within dangerous reach of the crackling flames and the road was almost completely blocked. Water wagons and bucket brigades crowded the narrow street. He crept forward, down Missouri which was wider and less congested. The fire had not yet spread there and people here were slavishly at work to save what they could. Men and women rushed to clear fire breaks, haul wagons, animals, building materials, from the fire's path, to wet down anything that they couldn't move. Water sloshed in the flume hoses that had been brought up to battle fire. Water wagons creaked and groaned. Cameron did not see Spud Ervin.

"Lee Cameron, we can use you!" It was Rob Glenby and with him was Charlie Slade. Glenby was so dishevelled Cameron almost didn't recognize him. His shirt was torn, his face streaked with soot, but he hadn't given up. He swung bucket after bucket and never halted for a moment even when he saw Cameron. Slade moved with the same steady rythmn and looked no better than Glenby.

Slade was first to scream above the din. "Where's my horse?"

Cameron shouted back, "Safe, in Highland." Cameron could only hope the boy had stayed with the horse and that mare was too tired to buck him off. "Emma! I'm looking for my wife and daughter!...Have you seen them?" He turned then to Glenby, "Where's Clem?" As soon as the words were out, Cameron knew he shouldn't have asked.

Rob Glenby's shoulders sank. The look in his eyes was of utter tragedy. He dropped his bucket. "I couldn't get to him...him an' yer

230

grey horse. Never hurt nobody, neither one." Glenby turned away. Cameron picked up his bucket and he and Slade resumed the grueling work. They watched silently as the big, powerful Rob Glenby sank down in the mud and buried his face in his callused hands. Rob Glenby cried like a baby. Finally, he straightened, braced his thick shoulders and went back to his bucket.

Lee Cameron struggled with his own dread that Emma and Marie could also be dead. "Has anyone seen Emma?"

Glenby shook his shaggy head but it was Slade who spoke. "No." He stopped for only a second to put a hand on Cameron's arm. "I'll stay by Glenby. You do what you have to do. Go look for them."

For this small human sympathy, Lee Cameron was grateful.

He lifted his face then to look up at the road when the squish of an insect hit him on the cheek. He reached up to brush it away. His hand came away wet. He felt it again. Puzzled, he looked down. Little puffs of dust rose from the hard-packed dirt, sparsely, one here, one there. Charlie Slade slapped at a tickle on his neck and looked up from his own bucket. Rob Glenby was bare-headed and his forehead and chin were streaked and wet, not only from tears. In his grief, he was slower to recognize the sensation. Spontaneously, one by one each man in the chain stopped what they were doing and together, looked up at the sky and back at each other. Drops of water spattered their faces and carved rivulets in the layers of soot. Water spit back at the flames while a thick smoke started to rise from the heat.

Cameron remembered the thunderhead he had seen from Highland. It had not been smoke. The clouds were real. It was raining! The drops fell harder and beat like drumsticks upon the flames, that sizzled and vaporized into little spouts of steam. Cameron took off his hat and bared his head and the cold rain streamed down his face and over his shoulders. Charlie Slade let out a whoop that shook the foundation of the mountain. Rob Glenby collapsed in the mud, smiling in spite of it all, like a child playing in a mud puddle.

Lee Cameron was silent, thinking back to Richmond in the early days of the War, and what it was like to win and how easy it was to lose and how, win or lose, men died, and hoping he could win again this time and find his wife and child. Worry lines scoured out trenches in his face and the fire filled them with soot. The grey coat, his shirt, his vest were soot-covered and soaked to the skin. His eyes were hollowed and glazed. His shoulders sagged. When the first wash of relief passed, Slade motioned to Cameron, "Let's go find them." He took Cameron's arm and turned him with the quiet assurance in his voice that renewed the hope of Lee Cameron.

They walked off with Glenby behind, down Missouri where relief had burst forth into celebration. Men women and children dropped their tools and rejoiced. Today water was more precious than gold! Guns fired. Hats flew in the air. Thunder rolled from off the peaks and sheets of water slammed against the flames. There was a hissing like a pit of vipers amid hoots and yells as billows of hot steam enveloped what was left of Varina. But the merriment rolled like the rainwater off the shoulders of Lee Cameron.

They led a haggard Glenby to the steps of the new church and sat him down. He hauled himself to his weary feet but hadn't the strength to go with them. Then they started at one end and rooted through the town, poking into alleys, under fallen beams, two dirty men questioning everyone they passed. Where was Emma Cameron? The dark-haired lady, the former Emma Dubois, and a small girl with a single pigtail plaited down her back? Finally, a bedraggled stranger, fresh from the fire line, Union or Reb no man could know by the black soot that covered his coat, answered. "You mean Emma Dubois?...Didn't know she was married... I seen 'er up by the Queen and 'er girl is with 'er." Cameron could have hugged the man. Tears came to his eyes and he had not the will power to fight them back.

Charlie Slade respectfully looked away. "I'll go find my horse."

Lee Cameron spoke to his back. "Slade, thanks." He was so tired, he almost fell down.

Chapter 36

Emma Cameron had been at home when the fire started. Standing on the green porch, she had seen the white smoke rise above the livery. She did not hesitate. She drew on her heavy wool cape and stuffed blankets, bread, cheese, a bottle of whiskey and canteens of clean water into a carpetbag. She hid her pocket revolver in the pocket of her dress under her cape. The night would be cold and dangerous. Dreadful thoughts coursed through her mind like devils touching briefly down and sweeping up her reserves of strength and determination. She must first find Marie and then see to the animals, McGillicuddy's bay horse, her cat. Rachel had already loaded two paniers and was leading the bay like a common pack animal out into the street. She stumbled over the whining cat, scooped up the terrified animal by the scruff of its neck and tumbled him into a panier.

She shouted to Rachel, "Marie, I'll get Marie!"

"Come up to the track, Missus, we'll be at the racetrack."

Emma waved her on and ran frantically for the school. This was a one-room log building, the home of a deceased miner, constructed of raw pine logs and hand-hewn planks. It set high up the slope above Varina, a safe position if the fire could be contained. But its logs had dried and peeled. It had been rechinked and daubed for use as a school, but the daubing clay had shrunk and now left wide cracks in the walls, where puffs of winds converged, like a bellows mouth to a fire. There was no escape from its one room except through the small opening that served for a door. But it stood above Missouri, where the respectable families lived, where men would fight hard to save their valued possessions.

Emma prayed they had held back the fire but she knew that gulch fires tended to burn faster uphill with the rising heat and a gripping fear propelled her. Tilton had already herded the children out onto the street when Emma arrived. They were massed tightly together, faces pale and solemn. Even these small ones sensed the danger. Emma grabbed Marie as Tilton prodded his charges ever higher toward the road to Highland. Then from habit, she started for the Citadel. She had always gone to Dan McGillicuddy in an emergency and she hoped Lee Cameron would be there. But it was Garrity she met half way.

Big Garrity and Sanford were struggling to save McGillicuddy's piano. Garrity's face was bloodless and his voice, high-pitched. "When he saw Emma and Marie, he dropped the piano. "You and the girl runnin' to an awful death, Ma'am. We go this way, parallel to the fire—she'll burn uphill before she runs wide."

He was right. The fire licked upward but not outward. Garrity picked up Marie and ran so fast, Emma almost fell behind. They clambered down Warren toward the Queen of the Nile and the Sunshine Creek road. Girls from Clive Sherman's saloon were loading a spring wagon when Garrity came up. As they whipped the horse ahead, Garrity dove for the wagon. He missed and fell to his knees, dropping the child. Emma grabbed Marie.

"Not fast enough to catch the wagon, Ma'am, an' flames lickin' at our heels."   Streams of sweat coursed down his face and his mouth worked even after he had nothing more to say. Big, tough Garrity, who could face gunmen without flinching, cowered in the face of a fire. He stared at the flames now, transfixed.

Emma pulled Marie back. "Con Garrity," she pushed him hard around face to her face, slapped him hard to break the trancelike fear. "Con Garrity," She repeated the name. "Where is Lee Cameron?" Orange flickers danced in the pupils of Garrity's eyes. He had not heard. He didn't answer. Garrity would be no use now except to save himself.

Emma pushed the hapless giant along a few more steps, "Go to the racetrack. You'll find Rachel there and shelter. If the fire burns that way, go over the rim to the Madison. Don't stop 'til you get to the river."   Garrity ran blindly as if he hadn't heard. Alone, she looked down at the shaking child and spoke with forced eveness more for her own self-control than to soothe the child. "You and I, Marie, we must stay together and pray your father is safe."

They followed the tide of humanity inching their way up Warren, to the Sunshine Creek road. How many happier times had she travelled that road, with confidence, with dapper old McGillicuddy! She saw Rachel stumbling along about a hundred yards ahead with Midge and Gertie. McGillicuddy's overloaded bay was stumbling too. Quickly Emma knotted her skirts up to her knees, grasped the child more firmly and ran for Rachel and the horse. As she neared the road, a brutal jerk hauled her back and spun her around. She dropped her sack, almost let go the child and stood for a moment in shock.

Spud Ervin stood in rags before them. His blond hair had grown long and was layered in dirty mats over his ears and anchored there by what was left of his sooty hat. His jaw worked round and round as if chewing, like a wind-up toy, separate from the rest of his immobile face. He spit without opening his teeth and an brakish spray spattered the air. His chest seemed to have shrunken and his shoulders to have hunched inward where he held his flap of arm. But it was the absence of eyes that made Emma tremble. His eyes had diminished and sunk far back in their sockets. Only black slits remained. He stood arrogantly in Emma's path. Finally, he snarled, "You forgot my favors!"

Emma stopped, drew back and released Marie. Cold fear coursed like glacier-melt through the marrow of her bones but she threw her shoulders back bravely, arched to her full height and answered with a forced civility and superiority she did not feel, "You're back in Varina, Mr. Ervin."

"Yes, I came back." He looked behind him and to either side as if he thought he were being watched. For a moment, his mind seemed to wander. But he drew his lips together and spit again. The slime hit the front of her skirt and leaked eerily down. He stepped closer and ran his tongue over his lips, snapping his jaw shut. When he spoke again, the jaw moved separately from the rest of his face, "I can fork a bronc— even when she rears an' hops." His voice thudded dully like a hammer on wet wood. The comment seemed incoherent, irrational.

Emma stood like a sculpture and met his glassy stare. She did not at first perceive the direction of his thought. Icily, she answered only his literal meaning, "You're a fine horseman, Mr. Ervin, I'm sure you can...."

He fumbled with a pleat in his shirt that caught under his stub of arm, turned his head and looked back at the fire. But Marie stood in his line of sight and his glance stopped there. The child shied back.

"Pretty filly, prettier than her dam!" Marie, sensing danger, retreated behind her mother's skirts. Emma's every sense strained alert.

"Forkin' a horse is like mountin' a woman." This time his meaning was clear.

Delay! Stall! Space out the seconds. She questioned more, "Do you break and train horses, Mr. Ervin?"

He broke into hideous laughter, and advanced on her and the

child. His next three words made her blood freeze. "Today, the filly; tomorrow the dam." He extended his arm toward Marie and smiled maliciously. "I throw a leg on you, filly, you go squealin' an' buckin' all the way to the finish line!"

Emma stepped squarely between him and the child and locked her hand around the revolver in her pocket, "You'll kill me first, Spud Ervin, before you touch my child."

Spud stopped for a second and sniffed the smoky air, nose to the wind, like a wolf sensing the direction of his prey.

Emma spun around to Marie. "Run girl!" Marie obeyed instantly. Her little legs spun under her. Spud pulled his gun and aimed it squarely at her retreating back.

Frantic, Emma slammed her full weight into him, "Favors, you've come back for your favors! You'll not get them from a child!" He wrenched himself around and turned his gun on her. She threw off her cape, aimed her pistol and backed a step. Spud Ervin gaped stupidly into the barrel of the little gun as if it were a toy. He advanced on her like a reptile, slowly and steadily, one coil at a time until the final deadly thrust. His jaw worked continuously, his tongue pushing between his teeth and his writhing lips, drops of saliva oozing into his stubble of beard. He held so tightly to his gun that you could see the white of his knuckles and the blue of the throbbing veins in the back of his hand.

"Shoot me, you won't get your favors." Emma concentrated all her attention on his hand.

"Don' want no more favors, whore, and I ain't afraid of yer tommy-popper...I take a quirt when I ride a ornery horse an' I git all the favors I want." Oblivious to her gun, he walked forward, "Might need somethin' bigger like a bull whip fer you."

Emma stepped back farther, white with fear. She had never killed a man but now she pointed her gun and squeezed the trigger. The little gun went off and the bullet ripped through Spud Ervin's thigh. A tiny black hole pierced his clothing and began to seep red.

He looked away from her down at his leg, oblivious to the pain, as if his leg was a piece of carrion and he, meat for the raptor. He lifted his own gun but his hand shook when he fired. Emma felt flames lick down the right side of her face. A hundred stinging powder grains pricked her right cheek, the side of her neck. Like burning splinters they lodged just beneath the skin, but the deadly ball had spun inches wide between the crook of her neck and collarbone. Emma yelled in pain but held her eyes on her attacker.

Spud didn't react to his own wound until he moved to advance on her again and tripped. He put out his arm to block the fall and let go the gun. In mute amazement, he sat and stuck his finger in the wound, raised it to his nose and sniffed. The smell and feel of his own blood on his hand rekindled his fury. "You murderin' bitch!" His lips drew tight in a mask of anger. He seized another gun from his arsenal, raised it and squeezed the trigger back. The gun shuddered with a dull click of metal on metal. He had not reloaded carefully. Ervin cocked his head stupidly at the offending gun and shook it unbelieving. For a moment, the misfire consumed his complete attention.

Emma Cameron didn't wait. She turned and fled. She looked back once and Spud Ervin had replaced the guns in his belt and was sitting in the mud, fumbling frantically, one-handed, trying to reload.

Chapter 37

Emma fled through the dusty street elbowing people aside. She held a handkerchief to her cheek and it came away black and bloodied. The side of her face began to swell and she could feel her right eye seal closed. Ahead she barely spied the bay horse. His proud head rose high above the mob like a beacon, but she could not see tiny Marie. She came up on the off side of the horse behind Rachel, almost staggered and grabbed the harness. The horse stopped suddenly, jerking Rachel around.

The handkerchief fell from her face and Rachel reacted in shock. "Missus, who did this?" But Rachel knew.

Ugly red welts were forming like warts around each black grain and drops of blood seeped from a dozen tiny holes in Emma's pale skin. Speech sent fresh needles through the side of her face. "Only powder burns... They'll heal. Where's Marie?"

"She's not with you?" The question punctuated the reality with such force that Emma lay her head against the horse's scratchy mane and cried.

"We go up by the racetrack Ma'am. There's a lean-to and some fresh-cut hay. Jimmy Long, he fetch Doc Lubbock an' he see to it we have a roof an' a blanket.... The Doc, he'll fix your face. We'll take care of you and I'll go find your baby."

Dizzy with pain and exhausted, Emma followed. The black woman prodded her stolidly ahead when she slackened from the pain and they advanced, weary links in a human chain.

They reached the racetrack just as it started to rain. Jimmy Long was already there and unloaded the bay horse. They sat on bales of wet hay. Rachel tore off a piece of her petticoat, held it out to the rain and swabbed it over Emma's face, but her words fell short of comfort. "Schoolhouse sits high up, Missus. The good lord'll take care of 'is little ones. You have to believe that Missus."

Emma shook her head forlornly, The salt of her tears stung the cuts on her face.

Rachel addressed the immediate need. "Faith, Missus. Lord sent us 'is rain. He'll find your baby. I'll get Captain Lee an' Jimmy Long an' Doc an' Mr. Lamb. We'll all look."   She reached out and hugged the white woman to her ample bosom like a sister.

Emma rallied, "You, me, Jimmy Long, we go now. I can't stay here not knowing where she is."

The black woman recognized her urgency and retrieved a hunk of cheese from the packs. "If you have to choke it down, you better eat Missus. If we gonna go look, we need strength."

Emma and Rachel struck out blindly back through the crowd calling the child's name until their voices croaked from the hot parched air. The hallowed water poured over them. It streamed over their shoulders and soaked their hair and the heavy wool of their capes. Mud spattered their skirts and oozed into the soles of their shoes. Wet and shivering, they reached the steps of the Queen of the Nile and collapsed on the lowest step. They had not found the child.

Emma heaved dry hollow sobs. Ghosts of past emotions raised their gorgon heads. It wasn't Dubois. She'd shed few tears for Dubois. He was a good man and he didn't deserve to die in such pain without notice on a riverboat in the wild lands that banked the Missouri, dumped in the river without a decent burial. Mercifully, he had not lingered long. She'd shed many more tears when Lee Cameron went off to war and still more tears when she realized he wasn't coming back. She had faced down the blame that society had hoisted upon her like a dead weight, a mother without a husband, and she had survived, even thrived, until the anger and loneliness surfaced again when Lee Cameron had arrived in Varina. She drew her shoulders back now and turned her face to the rain. It would disguise the tears and only Rachel would know she had been crying, but nothing could disguise the black powder burns in the side of her face.

Lee Cameron found them there. Rachel saw him approach and drew away, but there was no privacy. Dark circles enveloped his bloodshot eyes, his broad shoulders drooped with exhaustion and everything he wore, sagged with its full weight of water. Emma looked up at him and he gasped in shock.

239

The anguish in her eyes and the droop of her proud neck, the black pocks in her face were never worse than the horrible news she uttered. "Marie's gone! I've lost Marie!"

He didn't speak. He didn't react. His movements were almost ghostlike. He pulled the tarp from the rail and spread it over her to keep off the rain and spoke with definition and assurance that he didn't at all feel. "Who shot you?"

"The bullet missed."

"Who shot you?" His voice was hushed like a mourner at a wake and smothered the scream in his heart. It was a simple question— three little words like 'I love you' that hold the meaning of ages. Who would maim one so beautiful, one so loving and the mother of a child, his child? He knew the answer before she answered.

"Spud Ervin."

He stood stock still and when he finally spoke, his words were wooden and puppetlike and masked the deep rage within. It hammered somewhere inside his ribs and pounded at his temples and his exhaustion congealed into a condensed energy, violent and explosive.

He didn't mention Marie and held his voice low and first tended to the requirements of the moment. "Come inside. Dry off. Rest. Rachel is here."

Emma sensed something wrong. He was too calm. She stood up and leaned her head against the soggy wool of his coat, and he stroked her frazzled hair back from the bloody holes in her cheek. She drew from him a quiet determination that exuded a deep hope and dispelled her tears. But with her near him, disfigured, touching him, leaning on him, wincing in pain, his rage sparked higher in a combustion of revenge that consumed his soul like the fires in Chinatown and there was no rain to put it out.

They went inside. Clive Sherman brought whiskey and made a place for Emma in a chair beside the stove. Darkness was coming on and the rain had not diminished. The saloon filled with wet steamy bodies shoulder to shoulder, crammed together like sheep in a pen around the center stove.

Lee Cameron's silence was frightening. He moved mechanically. He wiped his face on his sleeve, smoothed his wet brown hair and warmed his hands by clapping them against his sides. His lips narrowed into a thin bloodless line beneath his crooked nose. His eyes looked past Emma at a vague spot on the wall. He spoke with the clipped, impassive accents of a commanding officer to a subordinate. "You could lose an eye. I'll find Marie and I'll send Lubbock...." He added with a deathly calm, "As for Spud Ervin, I shall allow no quarter; he shall die slowly and painfully....Stay here."

"No!" She was defiant.

"That's an order!" He stared her down brutally and barked at Sherman. "Sit on her if you have to. Send for Lubbock. Do what you can to get the powder out." Finally, he met her eyes. "I do love you, no matter what happens." He turned on his heel and left without her.

It was a dramatic exit but there was an emptiness like a sinkhole in his chest. It was continually widening and deepening. Where was he going? To find a lost child in a burned-out town, to gun down a criminal or to put an end to the outbursts of a madman? He didn't know. He only knew that he was going to relive all the horrors he had put behind him.

The mud sucked at his boots as he trudged doggedly from place to place, person to person, ashes to ashes, teeth chattering, with the cold of evening coming on, in the dark, in the rain, futilely. It was like searching the battlefield for the buddy who had been blown to bits by a direct hit, never finding, constantly seeking, never knowing. He was back on one of those sleepless marches and his whole body slumped like a tired soldier, so tired he slept to the steady motion of his horse. He used to pray during those marches, before the battles and after the battles. The soldiers all prayed especially when outnumbered and outgunned.

But now his prayer was a bold, presumptuous petition, demanding the Almighty to care for him and for Emma and to shepherd their child and preserve her whole and healthy and happy wherever she was amid the ashes. He cursed Spud Ervin like he cursed the enemy in war and the human agency on both sides that sanctioned the horror. And if his curse annulled the effectiveness of his prayer, he damned himself. But he willed Spud Ervin in the deepest chasm of hell.

He walked down Missouri. His throat rasped from calling her name. He found little Johnny Manning and his mongrel dog lurking under a bench to keep dry and took them both to the Queen. The boy had come back for his pet and got caught in the rain. His parents had been looking too and blessed Cameron for finding their son. But there was no Marie.

Missouri began to fill with people returning. These were the lucky ones who had something to return to. The acrid smell of charred, wet wood and burned flesh pervaded the air, but here homes and businesses were intact. Cameron strode straight ahead. Daylight was waning.

At the corner of Jefferson, he stopped. He looked down on the

241

devastation, toward Warren. The Mayfair Livery was a pile of rubble. Only the south wall of the Citadel was standing and loomed like a scraggly tree over a canyon. A chunk of collapsed roof stuck up like a sentinel. The print shop, Glenby's cabin, the assay office, the Lambs' store, Behnke's barber shop, all reduced to cinders.

He walked farther. Few people had returned to Warren Street. Here red coals still glowed and steam twisted skyward from hot spots under crossbeams and porches. There was nothing here to salvage, no stick of furniture or shred of fabric. Even the iron stoves had melted. It was getting dark and still raining. He should find shelter.

Two men stood at the corner in front of what had been the Citadel. One hunched his shoulders like Glenby when he coughed and held a sputtering lantern. Impulsively, Cameron walked toward the light like an insect to a candle. It wasn't Glenby, but Billy Lamb, Ed's hot-headed kid brother. He was with Stewart and mad as a weasel in a trap—he said the fire had been set. The news inflamed mild-mannered Stewart who now stood armed with his notorious Sharps to catch the man who did it. Cameron listened, his face stony. Stewart led him to the Plantation House in hope that Marie had gone there. The hotel was still standing but an oily soot had coated everything, even the flatware inside the kitchen drawers. Marie was not there.

He left by the kitchen door into the alley and nearly bumped into the black horse. The rain hadn't stopped. The mare stood head down, rump to the wind, wet, still saddled, with a battered tarp thrown over her back. How had she arrived here? She needed shelter, dry hay and a good mash of bran. Blood seeped from a gash in her right knee which buckled slightly and bore no weight. Cameron reached down placed his palm against the cannon bone. He could feel the heat. Cameron stroked the horse's nose affectionately.

"You better talk to 'er sweet. Damn near rode 'er to death!" Charlie Slade shot him a black look from out of the shadows.

Cameron turned abruptly and contested. "She did her share and so did I, but I didn't do this."

There was a sharp edge to Slade's voice. "I found her running loose on the mountain. She buck you off before you run her into the ground?"

Cameron's tense nerves exploded. He balled his fist, drew his arm back and launched it straight at the shadow of Slade's protruding chin. He missed.

Slade ducked, blocked another with a left and signalled no more. "I can hardly see you—I don't want to fight you."

"I don't buck off! I was cavalry or don't you remember?" Cameron breathed in deeply embarrassed by his loss of control. "I gave her to a kid to ride up to Highland, tried to save him and her." His eyes burned holes in the blackness, "I don't know what more happened. I'm sorry." But he stood hunched with his hands shoved deep into his pockets.

"I take it you really are...You ever find your kid?"

Slade's mention of the child called a truce. "No." They stared gravely at one another as seconds slipped by and tempers cooled. Charlie Slade sauntered up on the off side of the horse. "Come with me. I'll give you something to storm about."

"What about the horse?"

"She comes with me." He unhitched the horse and led a ruluctant Cameron and the limping horse up Warren. In front of the Lamb's burned-out store, there was an oil lamp on a post and a huddle of men in the circle of light, Glenby, Stewart, the two Lambs, Territorial Marshall Ryder and the ever-compromising Judge Burnwell. All were tattered, dirty and fresh off the fire line and did not see Cameron and Slade come up.

Slade interrupted their murmurings, "Glenby, you have a fresh horse you'll trade for this one. She's played out, needs a few months rest. I leave for Lewiston in the morning." Glenby just shook his wet head.

All eye's turned to Charlie Slade. Even in the jaundiced rain-streaked light of the lamp, after an afternoon on the fire line, he stood confident and handsome. Cameron stood just as tall but the contrast stopped there.

"Cameron? That you?" It was Glenby speaking, "You look like a ganted bull." His eyes focussed on the bloody leg of the horse and he bent over to feel the swelling.

Cameron looked sharply from Slade to Ryder to the Judge but he spoke directly to Thatcher. "Spud Ervin attacked my wife. She shot him, but in the fracas, our girl is missing."

Immediately, Glenby jumped to a terrifying conclusion. "That cute lil' brat of yours? My God, Lee, you think Ervin's got 'er?"

"I don't know. He's in town. I saw 'im."

"I saw 'im too." The quiet testimony of Charlie Slade carried weight.

"Kidnapping's a serious charge!" Burnwell protested immediately but the other faces stared him down like stolid executioners and the huddle broke open to admit Slade and Cameron.

Cameron's words didn't exceed the fact. "I've looked everywhere."

Charlie Slade's narrow glance swerved from the horse to Glenby, to Ryder, to Cameron, to the grim faces around him. "What's she look like? Where'd you see her last?"

Stewart, the excited hotel keeper, blurted an answer, "Girl, five

243

year old, brown hair, prettier than your black horse. I fed her breakfast just this morning."

Cameron was more precise, "She ran off when Ervin attacked my wife top end of Missouri. Blue checked dress and tan canvas jacket, pigtail down the crease of her back and yellow ribbon."

A tense silence intervened before Slade spoke again. "I didn't see your kid but I saw Ervin. I wouldn't trust him any more than a fox in a hen house.... He's the one lit the match."

Burnwell's teeth snapped shut. Stewart's arm shook and his big gun rattled. Thatcher and Marshal Ryder stood still as a headstones. The Marshal looked out at Slade from beneath knitted brows and the dark wide brim of his Quaker hat and his lips barely moved when he spoke. "Any other witnesses?"

"You saw 'im, Glenby."

Glenby rubbed his eyes with the back of his hand, "I don't know what I saw." Images of Clem still tortured his mind. "But I heard plenty, coming from round back...." Glenby lowered his head and shook it back and forth.

Slade continued, "It was broad daylight, about two o'clock this afternoon. Spud Ervin piled dry straw, between two haystacks, against the livery an' lit it like he was lighting some kindling in the belly of a stove. I was standin' right there, watchin' for Cameron to come back with my horse." Now even Charlie Slade's voice cracked and he stopped and closed his eyes stoically before he could continue. "Glenby and me, we unlatched the stall doors and started the horses runnin' out. I heard Glenby's ward screamin' an' had to stop Glenby going back in... The boy died. Glenby, here would've died too."

The finality of the words and the funereal tone of Charlie Slade held the group anchored. It was the laconic Marshal who finally filled the prickly silence. "We're holdin' a meetin'. You all should come in get out of the rain."

Marshal Ryder led the five of them and the limping horse to the only building still standing on Warren Street, the great stone Grand Temple of the Masons. Its interior was not yet complete, it had no roof but its granite walls had shrugged off the fire. A canvas tarp was strung up over the interior to keep out the rain and oil lamps flickered eerily under its sagging folds. Drops of rainwater seeped through the cracks. Another knot of men milled inside. They carried more lanterns and made way when they recognized the Territorial Marshal. They were all heavily armed. Their hats were all pulled down as if to mask their faces.

Cameron squinted at the dark silhouettes filling the room. He recognized very few and most of those by their voices. There was the tall form of Andy Holter, the bobbing head of John Moulton. Three Chinese were in the group—discernable by their short stature and conical hats. One diminutive form looked like a woman and one spoke English like Fu Ling. The men looked like scraggly human forms filtering out of the stormy blackness, an arm here, a head there, connected somehow like ants from a plundered nest. Close to thirty men, awesome in their ghastly silence, crowded into the congestion of the Temple.

Charlie Slade remained just outside the door and still held the horse whose blackness blended into the night outside. He stood in the doorway, immobile and alert.

Mayor Thatcher mounted a chair in the center of the room where a small stove exuded minimal warmth. Thatcher assumed his running-for-office pose with coattails pushed back, thumbs in his vest pockets, but his curling frown and hammering voice nullified all thoughts of partisanship. "Men of Varina," he began, "I'm callin' you together because one of our own young men has gone bad." He stopped and quietly surveyed the full circle of shadowy faces. His was the strategy of a master politician who senses pockets of opposition and instinctively reacts to control them. Cameron had to admire his poise. Thatcher continued, "I'm not a happy man, standin' here, discoursin', like a preacher spittin' brimstone from a pulpit. It's not a happy duty I have to discharge." He stopped again, his only movement a deep demonic sigh. "Ed Lamb and Nat over there saw young Spud Ervin shootin' down the Chinese and yellin' like a wild man. Fu Ling here says Spud Ervin killed three of his countrymen who were tryin' to flee the fire and two more have bullets in 'em and are fightin' for their lives." He paused for a breath and wiped the cold sweat that dripped from his eyebrows. "Turner here lost a good horse, but there's worse....This young lady Fu Ling brought with him," he indicated a cowering Chinese girl, "says she saw Spud shoot his own dad, Sime Ervin...."

Silence. Forty armed men stood like pillars of stone. The horse stamped and blew. A voice from the rear yelled, "Ain't gonna listen to no yellow pigtail!"

"Quiet!" Thatcher's voice cracked like a descending gavel. Cameron had to admire the even calm with which Thatcher commanded attention while groping for what to say and how to say it in a way that would dispel the mounting tension. Thatcher questioned more, "We all saw Spud Ervin leave. Who, besides Ed and Nat and Fu Ling, has seen him here in Varina?"

"I seen 'im shootin' into the Injun camp!" It was Vince Benson who was married to a Flathead squaw.

"We all know you got stones in yer maw, Vince. That was a year ago, Vince. I said today!....This lady, Miss Ling, has made a serious charge."

"We gonna accept the word of a female?" It was a harsh, screechy voice, Bill Lamb's, from the back of the room.

"She's got eyes just like yours, Billy."

"I saw the shootin'—Looked like Spud Ervin to me, all grimy and black." That was Stewart. His voice came in a short, breathless chop and a knot of men murmured in agreement.

Thatcher held up his hands again. "One at a time. Which shootin' you see, Stewart?"

"I saw 'im shoot the Chinamen!"

"How you know it was Spud?" Thatcher was thorough.

"I know. We all know. He only has one arm."

The next voice raised was deep and penetrating. It had a rumbling quality like an avalanche shaking loose from a mountain. "I saw Spud Ervin light the fire." It was Charlie Slade's at his most dramatic.

"What was that Mr. Slade?"

Slade paused until every face had turned toward his place in the dark doorway. The light shone obliquely only on the bridge of his nose and the ridges of his cheekbones. When he repeated the accusation, his voice was oiled but distinct, with the cold impersonality of a gunfighter. And he added, "How do I know Spud Ervin?... He tried to hire me."

"You know what you're sayin', Slade?"

Slade barely tilted his head in agreement. The shadow of his hat barely moved in the dim light. He stood straight and still. "Yes, sir, I do."

A menancing hum broke out in the confines of the room.

Judge Burnwell interjected as if the sound of a human voice could plug angry eruptions, "Spud came to see me this morning. He wasn't himself but I've watched him grow these last years, he's headstrong and impetuous but..." He was threading words together meaninglessly and he was plainly nervous, aware he was in the minority. Everyone knew that he often minimized blame. Now he attacked Slade, "...this man making the accusations is a killer." No one was listening to him.

Ed Lamb whose store lay in ashes, had no patience for the indulgent Judge. "Shut up, Burnwell, murder and arson, that's what we're discussing, not yer soupy legal slop."

Slade looked at Thatcher but he addressed the whole assemblage. "I've killed men, Thatcher, an' I've taken their bullets in my own hide an' I stood up to trial for what I've done. I've seen men burn and I've seen men die. Every man in this room who fought the war knows what that is—hell. We put our lives on the line an' shot at men who could shoot back. Never picked off people like apples on a tree, like Spud Ervin did. Never fired a building like it was a grisly stump in a cornfield...for no reason at all...like Spud Ervin did." He couldn't resist adding, "...I didn't see Atlanta and Charleston but even Bill Sherman had his reasons..." The antagonisms of North and South had paled in the immediacy of the present catastrophe. "My word's good. That Ervin kid is a menace to this city. He burned your homes, turned you out in the street, slaughtered your animals an' murdered Rob Glenby's boy. I saw him do it."

Slade's was an eloquent speech. Thatcher almost lost his listeners. They were nodding assent with Charlie Slade, grumbling and gesticulating. Thatcher grasped at threads to try to hold his audience, "What's this about Sime? You signed the death certificate, Judge."

"Not me, old Treadwell." Treadwell was doctor and coroner when he wasn't drunk. "I never saw the body. Had no reason not to believe Spud." Burnwell's thoughtless statement fueled emotions further. Hoots and grumbles welled up and talk of vigilante justice.

A high, shrill voice suddenly shouted above the crowd—Fu Ling. "Mai Ling show you Simon Ervin's bones."

Thatcher threw up his hands and stepped down beside the Judge. The charge was murder but the testimony was that of a known gunfighter and a Chinese, doubtful witnesses.

Now Lee Cameron raised his vouce. "I think Spud killed Dan McGillicuddy!"

Charlie Slade added gravely, "An' Cameron here won't say, but he believes Ervin has his kid."

A general outrage broke out in noisy protest. Tempers boiled. Thatcher had given up and Burnwell had been swept aside.

A hot-headed miner shouted, "For stealin' children, we should hang 'im just like we did the killers in '63!"—Everyone of these hard men had heard of 1863. Some of them had been there. In 1863 and the cold first months of 1864, a vigilance committee had gathered in the night, just next door to the shadowy room where they congregated now, and swore a solemn oath to wipe out the murderers and cutthroats who preyed like vultures on their homes and businesses and they rode out from Varina in snow and bitter cold and hung twenty outlaws in two months.

There were men here, now who remembered the words of that oath and began faithfully to repeat it. It began as a whisper and grew in volume. As one man lost his breath, another picked up the refrain. The dreadful words sprouted full-blown from their memories and spilled out relentlessly into the cold night air. Billy Lamb produced a length of rope and began to twist a hangman's noose.

Thatcher shouted above the noise. "This isn't '63! We have justice and law! There are no gangs of outlaws now! The Marshall and Moulton are right here! They'll arrest Spud and bring him in for trial." But the whispered litany of the oath pervaded the room like some funereal accompaniment to a tragic opera. Emotions were running like water through a broken dam and would not be stopped again until they had emptied completely and been satisfied.

Bill Lamb shouted over the hum, "Dig 'im outta 'is hole an' roast 'im on a spit like he done to my horse!"

"We go along make sure you get 'im, Bill, Ed!" Thatcher eyed Ryder and Burnwell. It was the best he could do. The rule of law was disintegrating.

Forty men pushed toward the door. The Lambs, Garrity, Benson, Fu Ling and three dozen more, all were gesticulating and shouting. The lust for revenge curdled their blood and the sacred words of the vigilante oath sanctified what they were about to do. What worked in '63, would do as well today! Thatcher was silenced and lost every vestige of control! Outrage, retaliation and pure wrath concentrated the fury of thirty men.

Lee Cameron cringed. Charlie Slade picked up the reins and backed away. He turned once to speak to Cameron. "If I find your kid where should I take her?"

The calm rationality of the question surprised Cameron. "To the Queen. My wife is there...You're not coming with us?" His resentment of Slade had diminished.

"No. The vigilantes hung my brother. This crowd won't save your kid or heal my horse." Slade's efforts stopped where his own interests left off.

The comment sobered Lee Cameron. As the crowd condensed around him and pushed him ahead at its crest, he watched the horse and Slade hobble off. They vanished quietly, fading like a fox into the woods. Cameron hardly saw them go. And silently he agreed with Charlie Slade—this mob would only infuriate Spud Ervin and entice him to greater cruelties. Lee Cameron asked himself if it could endanger the life of his daughter.

He stayed with the mob. They marched as a unit out into the dripping, darkening night, torches blazing, like Brigham's Avenging Angels, self-righteous in their convictions and single-minded in their wrath. They marched down Warren past the burned out ruins of the Citadel and the Livery. They marched up the steep incline of the Highland Road toward Central City and Pine Grove. Some rode wet, shaggy mountain horses; some slipped and stumbled over wet rocks in the dark; some boarded one of Holter's lumber wagons and whipped the oxen unmercifully.

Cameron's mind raced as he walked. What if Spud Ervin held his daughter hostage? What if he threatened to harm her? What if he already had? Cameron could feel the air bristle as if, in this concentration of bodies and heat, indignation and anger bounced from man to man, gaining intensity with every step forward. Slowly, his tension gave way to resolve. He must soothe. He must cajole. He must tempt. He must recruit the diplomacy of Thatcher, the sympathy of Burnwell. He must help Ryder enforce the precise letter of the law if that was still possible. Above all he must get to Marie first. He whispered another prayer.

Chapter 38

Rumor preceded the marchers. News of Spud Ervin's return blew like the fire wind over the city and up the gulch. Along the roadside, people who had fled for their lives cheered the wet mob onward. Some joined the throng, fired by their own griefs and losses. They abandonned their claims and flocked to the marchers like swarming insects. In Highland, they stopped at the Dugout. Digger Bob Lockwood had seen Spud and offered him a meal, but Spud ran on by. Digger Bob had hardly recognized him. But it was confirmed: Spud was here in the gulch, back so soon from Salt Lake. Digger Bob hadn't seen a little girl with him.

Lee Cameron's worst fears eased, but still he struggled to keep in front, to be first, to snatch her from the demon's jaws before the crazed mob started shooting, one more feeble voice on the side of sanity.

They wound their way snakelike up the sharp, slippery switchbacks and rounded the base of the cliff beneath the Ervin Camp. The torches hissed and smoked in the raindrops and cast distorted shadows on the rock face. They came upon the Ervin camp suddenly from around the curve of the mountain. It lay before them against the jagged rock of the north slope under a starless storm-blackened sky. The silver mist of a new moon frittered eerily through the cloud layer and barely speckled the buildings. The yawning entrance to the mine tunnel showed blacker still. All was quiet.

Worley had been sitting atop the lookout rock and saw the torchlight procession moving inexorably forward. He ran to awake the sleeping Hump but Hump was already gone. Worley fled to higher, safer ground.

The campfire still burned when they reached the camp, Lee Cameron stood in the firelight at the front of the procession with a bitter Rob Glenby. The Chinese girl, Mai Ling, stepped from among the towering men. "Mr. Sime is in there." Trancelike, they followed her diminutive black form.

She led them down a narrow path and into the gaping adit. Down into the earth, like soldier ants, they marched. The torchlight rent the darkness like a knife. Cameron followed close on her heels, dreading with each new stride, the horrors he would find ahead.

Ryder reached up to pinch his nose. Cameron's nose twitched too. They were at the entrance to the south stope. A faint wind wafted toward them from an air shaft deep within. Cameron recognized the smell and drew out his handkerchief to cover his nose. Every man who had ever fought a battle knew that smell for what it was. It was sweet and penetrating and made the bile rise in your throat like the smell of wet decaying roses. It was the smell of the battlefield after the battle, the smell of the coffin, the morgue, the funeral and the grave—the smell of decaying human flesh.

It invaded the damp air like a miasma in a swamp. Cameron's chest heaved uncontrollably. Even tough old Ryder coughed and covered his mouth with a rag. No one spoke. Each separate sound echoed: every scrape of boots on gravel; every crackle of torch; every drip of water from wet crossbeams.

The tunnel forked and Mai Ling directed them left, down a deep staired passageway, the south stope. It was then they heard it, a purring sound, like a cat but louder. Mai Ling drew back shivering against the arm of Mayor Thatcher and she would go no farther. She pointed, "He's there."

This was the moment Lee Cameron had been waiting for, the moment when he'd hoped that Marie would come forward from out of the shadows. There was nothing.

Cameron and Glenby with Thatcher and Ryder at their heels stepped down with the torches that illuminated each crevice. Their eyes bulged like gargoyles. Rob Glenby shoved a torch into a side hole that had almost escaped their notice. He suddenly straightened and swore. Cameron and Ryder bumped him forward from behind. But he was blocked by a pile of newly-dug earth and some larger stones barely visible in the dim light. They crowded together.

A body lay there in the bloated and blackened contours of death. It was badly decayed, teeth and bone protruding from its face, a few dirty shreds of clothing still clinging to its flesh. Behind it, farther back in the blackened hole, they spied a second skeletal form, alive,

251

stooped over it. Filthy and dishevelled, this was Spud Ervin. He knelt in the dim light of a single lantern, next to his father's corpse. He had removed the stones Worley had placed to cover Sime's body. Frantically, he scraped at the hard-packed earth with a broken bowie knife. Whether he was unearthing his father's body or digging his grave, he alone knew. In the dank gloom, his eyes were hollow black holes. His temples protruded like elbows from cavities at the sides of his skull. His skinny lips worked feverishly, mumbling continuously, a shrill lunatic plea to his dead sire that reverberated eerily against the narrow sides of the tunnel like the feeble breath of a sinner against the the black draperies of the confessional.

"I sniped it, Pa! I sniped it back....I stashed it in my pocket...Pa. Yours and mine, the richest piece a paper in all Varina! You called it right, the Cleopatra, the Mother Lode, and what a fine breeder she is, big-titted and swollen! Milk fer a whole damn litter! We're rich, you an' me. I'll make you proud, Pa! Gold's safe in the bank.. If I kin trust those snivelin' Mormons... An' I'm gonna get hitched, Pa, ...sire some fine foals! She's a handsome lady, Pa, bodied like a thoroughbred and tempered like one too with blood runnin' hot an' eyes full a fire... Cat claw in a woman boils my blood, Pa, like that Chinee slave girl of yours....like Cleopatra herself." He rambled incoherently.

Lee Cameron, Rob Glenby, and Ryder stood for a moment transfixed. They caught a few more words and Spud ended with a maniacal peel of laughter. Spud Ervin was not aware that he was being watched. And the men watching him recoiled, not from fear, but from an excess of horror and pity.

Cameron scanned the scene: Marie was not here. But the realization brought him no peace. Where could she be? Spud Ervin, in his frenzy, could have killed her. He could have buried her in any one of the numerous side tunnels but there was no sign that any of the other tunnels had been used. Did Spud Ervin know where she was? Could Spud Ervin remember, accept responsibility for or explain any of his own actions? If questioned, could Spud Ervin even understand what was asked and construct an intelligible answer? Suddenly, Lee Cameron's anger melted away and a powerful fear made his whole body shudder: he realized that he may never find his daughter. He prayed with all his heart that his little girl had never encountered the awful fate that his imagination conjured.

Thatcher broke the silence. "Ervin, come out of there." It was a command, but gently proffered.

Spud Ervin didn't move. He seemed not to have heard. Cameron thought back to the younger, more confident Ervin, the dandy with his

252

watch fob and new Stetson, the boaster with his bevy of friends, the lustful, envious youth. Thatcher repeated his summons more forcefully. "Spud, you want we should come in and get you?" No reaction.

Finally, Ryder issued an ultimatum in his gruff marshal's voice "I come in, I flatten you first, boy."

Spud Ervin turned his head at the word 'boy'. He stared dumbly. When he saw his spectators, he stepped back like a curious animal, not belligerent or afraid, but alert, all senses fine-tuned to what the presence of these strange creatures could mean. If he sensed a threat, he showed no sign and resumed his digging.

What human connections he had once, were gone. Family, what little he knew of it, was extinct except in his imagination. The friendships of his earlier youth, had dissipated with his prosperity. Even the men whose wages he paid, had left him at the first sign of impotence. Ghostlike and inhuman, he was trying to resurrect the bones of a dead man, to wrench love and sympathy from a corpse.

Burnwell and Thatcher stepped back appalled. Ed and Bill Lamb pushed forward to fill their places. Cameron and Glenby remained anchored to the ground. Hank Ryder drew his gun. Others strained to see in the smoky torchlight, through the narrow opening over their shoulders. With his single hand, Spud scratched rythmically at the earth. It came away in tiny clumps. His fingers were bloody and dirty. It was a useless, futile effort but it consumed his whole concentration. Like a miser counting his gold, like his father before him, he pursued his obsessive task. Grain by grain, spoonful by spoonful, he exposed the gruesome sight.

"That's Sime's body. I know the plaid of 'is shirt. Wouldn't buy a second one. Wore it for months at a time. I sold it to 'im!" Ed Lamb had craned his neck for a look. He knew Sime Ervin well. For three years, he had delivered supplies once a week to the Ervin camp. Others shoved forward pinning Cameron and Thatcher to the damp hard wall.

Ryder pushed ahead and laid a hand on Spud's shoulder. Spud smacked it back as he would a ticklish fly, but with swift and decisive violence. Ryder hit him, a glancing blow, on the side of the head with the flat edge of his gun butt. Spud staggered. Mayor Thatcher stepped forward, drew the guns from Spud's holster and waistband and took a crinkled paper from Spud's pocket. Spud did not object. Thatcher, motioned to Cameron and the two of them bent down to lift Spud and take him away. Suddenly, Ed Lamb pushed through and landed a hefty blow on Spud Ervin's jaw. Spud fell backwards. Ed's store lay in ruins and the sight of Spud Ervin hadn't inspired any mercy in the tough trader. Cameron and Thatcher reached to lift Spud again.

Now Spud's temper flared, "Don't you touch me!" and he jumped up but it was a blind lashing-out, not at his captors or at Ed Lamb who had assaulted him, but at the sudden intrusion into his imaginary world and the rude interruption of his insane conversation. The corpse of his father stretched half-buried in the tunnel. He arched his head back and sucked the fetid air and howled like a hungry wolf and his legs collapsed under him.

Cameron understood the sounds of utter despair. Ryder grasped Spud firmly by the right biceps just above the stump. Glenby braced his good arm behind his back. With his arms pinned, they lifted him to walk him away but he jerked free and flung himself backward toward the body, begging, imploring the dead man for the simple acknowledgement Sime had never bequeathed in life.

Ryder and Thatcher stepped forward a third time and lifted Spud easily. He had stopped resisting but neither did he walk. His body collapsed. His last effort had been too great and he had no strength left. His eyes closed. He dropped his knife. They dragged him out the length of the tunnel, pushing their way through the angry gauntlet of miners. Curses and threats bounced like bullets off the granite walls. News of the discovery of Sime Ervin's body had sped quickly from tongue to tongue. Outside the tunnel, the crowd seethed. They had not witnessed Spud Ervin's pathetic performance in the mine tunnel and they had little patience now. The cold rain only sharpened their anger like a whetstone on a steel blade.

Lee Cameron relished the freshness of the mountain air after the deathly stench of the mine. His eyes scanned the blackness. His head spun and dry heaves wretched his stomach. Cameron walked behind Spud Ervin and began to back away when he heard Rob Glenby's rasping voice. Glenby had witnessed Clem's fiery death. Like Ed Lamb and Bill Lamb and most of the other men here, he was very angry. Gentle Glenby who had cared for Clem, slapped Spud Ervin hard across the mouth with the back of his hand to gain his attention. For a moment, Spud focussed a dazed look on Glenby's impenetrable face. "This man's kid is missing. Where is she?..." Glenby struck again squarely across Spud's mouth. Spud laughed like a banshee. Glenby repeated, "Where's Cameron's daughter?"

The answer, if it was an answer, was incomprehensible and Rob Glenby struck out a third time. His knuckles split and blood spurted from a gash in Ervin's lip.

Cameron grabbed Glenby, straining to pin Rob Glenby's arms to his sides.

"Don't you want your daughter back?" Glenby was a big man and

Cameron used every ounce of his remaining strength to subdue him.

"Not this way. You don't shoot the dying!" He said it softly and clung hard to Rob Glenby. Suddenly, he realized that tears were streaming down his face.

Spud stood meekly now still babbling to himself and glaring into the hypnotizing flames of a torch. At the mention of Marie, the points of his lips had turned up momentarily, but that was all. Any meaning retreated to the inner sanctum of his being. He tried one last time to reach out and caress the flame but his knees crumpled and caved in.

Ed Lamb waved a carbine over his head and shouted, "There 'e is boys, the rattler in the hen's nest!"

Cameron watched hatred take hold of these men, his own companions and friends of the last few months. He had to remind himself that there were good people in Varina, kind people who would care for a lost child. Even notorious Charlie Slade or the Chinese, Fu Ling, or Vince Benson or chatty little Behnke would not harm Marie.

Hoots and yells broke the night. A rock struck Spud on the jaw and snapped his head around. Rough men grabbed him. Ryder, with Thatcher and Cameron, stood by to fend off some of the blows. Judge Burnwell protested in vain. He tried to strongarm his way to the prisoner but the crowd trampled him into the mud. Ryder lifted him up. Even the tough Marshal was white-faced and shaken but he sensed the explosiveness of the mob and shouted to Cameron and Thatcher. "You ain't gonna counter that mob! Them's was vigilantes! We all were. It may be cruel but it's a kind of justice an' it works an' it's all you're gonna muster tonight!"

Thatcher was not to be silenced that easily. Shivering, rainwater pouring in a stream off the brim of his hat, he pleaded in vain. Nobody listened. The swift and implacable justice of the hangman held sway in the cold rainy night. Spud Ervin would be tried by these citizens of Varina for the immolation of their city, the murders of Dan McGillicuddy and Sime Ervin, the shootings of the Chinese, the death of Clem and whatever other wrongs had been laid to his hand this day. The entire congregation was jury. Burnwell was the thin almost non-existent voice of defense; Lamb was an eager prosecuter; and this whole mob of humanity was executioner. There was no burden of proof. The liturgy of law was too slow. This justice was immediate. But it would preserve at least some trappings of civilization.

Rough hands hoisted Spud Ervin up onto a wagon. He huddled against the rude wooden planking. Thatcher sat on the drivers seat in front of the hostile crowd and Ed Lamb called the first witness, Fu Ling. The Chinese shook visibly and stammered in broken English but his meaning was clear. It was what the crowd wanted to hear and it condemned Spud Ervin.

The rain stopped. A thin arc of moon peeked out from behind the clouds and a brisk wind picked up. In the chill air, the mood of the mob grew steadily darker. An eagerness to have it over and done sprung up like a fungus from wet ground. In the thin light of the moon, bodies swayed visibly as a unit toward Ed Lamb. When Burnwell stepped forward to cross-examine, a torch waved in front of his face and licked the front of his vest. He jumped back, slapping at the waistcoat that covered his protruding belly. Suddenly, the wagon lurched. Thatcher felt the move, and, grabbing the startled Chinese, jumped to the ground. Spud Ervin slammed against the boot and crumpled into the box.

In the inky darkness, someone had lifted the blocks that anchored each wheel, detached the double-tree and shaft, and heaved, or perhaps the blocks had slipped in the mud of the rainy night. The wagon moved, downhill toward the switchback where the trail turned eastward and descended steeply around the face of the cliff above the chasm. Not one hand lifted to stop it or turn it from the steep dizzying drop and the rocky floor of the gulch below. Men dove back headlong from the crunch and splash the advancing wheels. They rolled ahead, slowly at first, then faster, swaying, lurching, bumping over rocks, picking up speed. The wagon careened down the road, bounced hard over the sharp lip of the precipice and like an eagle launched itself onto the updrafts. For a second it seemed to fly, then hover, then like a stricken, fallen angel, it arched down crashing into the yawning blackness. There was a rush of wind and a scraping as the wagon tore against trees and outcroppings, some ear-splitting cracks as the axle split and wheels spun away, a final crash.

The quiet hovered like a shroud. The last splintered boards groaned once more like a hollow tree toppling in a storm and settling into its final bed. The men on the rim heard nothing human, no cry of pain, no groan of agony, not even an animal moan. They could see nothing. The dim light of their torches could not penetrate the abyss.

Chapter 39

Some turned their heads away. Not so Lee Cameron. He stood for a moment, with his hand on Thatcher's shoulder, stunned. Someone tossed a torch down over the rim and it sparked briefly in the wet brush, then sputtered out. He and the marshal peered over the edge but the blackness was complete. They could barely spy the arced outline of a wheel.

Shaken and silent, the mob turned back toward their smoking town and the dark and tortuous walk home. There was no blame. There was little remorse. Mayor Thatcher shook his grey head in dismay that the course of law had been diverted. Marshal Ryder stared impassively and Lee Cameron had to concede that the night had wrought a kind of justice, quick and violent, like the times and the crimes that engendered it. Varinans were honest, hard-working men. They were men of action all: soldiers; gold seekers; merchants; wagon masters; men of resource, resolution and vision. Just as they had diverted a creek to scour out their gold, they had bent the law to their own immediate requirements. When the gold was gone, the creek would flow back into its comfortable bed. When the violence calmed and tempers eased, reason and law would resume their even sway.

Thatcher lingered a while and Lee Cameron lingered, and with them, Rob Glenby. They stood on a flat rock staring out into the darkness. The wind rose and the glimmer of moonlight squeezed through the seams in the clouds. It barely outlined the three tall figures against the blackness of the depths below. Thatcher shoved his cold hands into his pockets and kept shaking his head as if he could somehow shed the image of what he had just seen like a wet dog shakes and sheds water. Cameron had his own regrets. His head hung down; his shoulders hunched. He wrapped his arms tightly around himself, every nerve straining to its limit like the strings of a finely-tuned fiddle. He had never felt such pain. It wasn't physical. It was an ache and a throb and a vicious stab at his heart and pounding at his brain and there was no respite. The old feelings of inadequacy and rejection resurged but with a new urgency. He had lost his beautiful child. He had failed Emma. Only the sight of Rob Glenby sustained him. Rob Glenby's pain was worse. Clem was dead.

But Rob Glenby wasn't dwelling on his pain, "We'll find your girl." There was determination in his voice.

Plain and resolute, the words made Cameron think of his far-off days with Emma in St. Louis, of his war years, of his lonely gambling life. Like Glenby, he would have to muster the will to try again. He answered Glenby doubtfully, "Will we?"

They walked woodenly back away from the cliff, stumbling down the rutted trail, Thatcher in front with the lantern, Cameron next and Rob Glenby, behind. At Highland, they stopped and slept in the open in a rough pile of hay. The damp hay provided some warmth and it was the first time Cameron had slept in days.

When they awoke, Glenby was sitting next to Cameron and the sun was high. Glenby was coughing. Cameron's every muscle seemed to flap loosely against his bones and a throbbing pounded at his temples. Thatcher insisted they stop to eat before going on. It was a crude meal, cornmeal and water scraped together from what was left after feeding the hungry refugees of the fire, and fried in a greasy skillet, but it renewed their strength.

They entered Varina about noon from the Highland Road and looked down on the devastation. Thatcher's nostalgic words summed up their feelings. "She wasn't quite civilized an' she was vain an' she was greedy but she kept our bellies full an' our beds warm. She was a damn good lay." A plain man's words, they lacked the full-blown magnetism of a politician. Thatcher didn't usually mumble. "She needs a good scrubbin' and a whole new wardrobe. We owe 'er that much. Varina...you're a pretty woman."

Cameron and Glenby nodded quietly. Half the town was a charred ruin. Chinatown had disappeared completely. A stench arose from the burned debris and the bloated flesh of animals. But the graves on Outlaw Bar still stood beyond the creek, untouched, sentinels over a larger graveyard.

A few hardy souls were sifting through the rubble. Cameron recognized Behnke, the barber, and Dad Long. Behnke was actually smiling—he'd found an unbroken bottle of his famous scent. Dad Long was sorting boards—what could be salvaged and used from what must be destroyed.

Cameron left Thatcher and Glenby at the corner of Jefferson and headed for the Queen of the Nile Saloon and Emma. What would he tell her? He had no idea. She had probably heard the news of the night's events by now. The battle was over and he didn't know whether he had won or lost. He just wanted to feel her touch, smell the warmth of her body and rest his weary head against her shoulder.

"Cameron, you find 'er?" It was Charlie Slade.

Lee Cameron stopped short and finally muttered, "No... and he added, "I thought you were leaving?"

"I don't have a horse. Tendon's bowed an' she's cut pretty bad...but she'll mend with time." Slade let the subject drop and fell into step beside him.

The saloon was crowded when they arrived. Men, women and children had jammed in for shelter from the rain. Now they spilled out onto the steps in the warm noon sunshine. Inside, people slouched over tables and chairs and Cameron stumbled over their blankets and belongings.

"Captain Cameron, I been lookin' for you." It was Rachel and her voice was cheerful. Rachel didn't wait for a greeting, "The missus is at the Thatcher's, over on Jefferson. Me an' Mrs. Pauline took the powder grains out best we could. It hurt some, Mr. Lee. She's a brave lady...I put lard on like we done in slave days, after whippin's...an' I come here to find you. Rachel bit her lower lip and stared—she knew the answer to the one question she couldn't ask.

"Tell her I'm fine, that I'm still trying... and Rachel, thank you."

The black girl's chin quivered as if she were fighting back tears and the pain in the girl's jet eyes touched Cameron. There was community in suffering. Rachel knew what loss was, to lose a mother, a brother, a child, a husband. Her people had lost loved ones on the mere whim of an overseer or worse to the rake of the cat-o'-nine-tails. She lay a hand on his arm, human to human, and he did not pull away. Captain Leland Cameron C.S.A. began to understand the injustices of the cause he had fought for.

"By the blessed saints, Lee Cameron, ye disappear like the sunshine in an Irish bog whenever a man be tryin' to find ye." Cameron turned abruptly. Patrick Lysaght glared out from under his corniced brows and he was laughing.

"Lysaght!" He had no tolerance left for the blustery old Irishman.

"Aye, I be lookin' all over the town like to found me pot o' gold at the end of me rainbow, an' here ye be gamblin' and drinkin' when ye should be attendin' to our budding family." The old voice cackled gleefully from behind the hermit's length of beard. Whether it was said in criticism or good humor, Cameron didn't care. He shoved rudely by Lysaght and nearly tripped over the dog. But Pat Lysaght was not to be put off so easily and accosted his back. "I'm too old to be a father unless it were to a strapping young swain that can lift the years from me shoulders.... I cannae be nursemaidin' to ribbons and skirts and high button shoes!"

Cameron turned on the old man with a rush, "What are you saying, man?"

Lysaght was never at a loss for words. "That it's fine parents ye be, losin' a wee pretty one like that in a time of mortal peril."

"Tell me Lysaght! Do you know where Marie is? Lysaght, say so!"

The old eyes fairly popped out from above the wrinkled cheekbones. Bits of moisture sputtered from the white whiskers and the glaring eyes stared accusingly like God in judgement. Lee Cameron had provoked the old Irishman's ire. "Aye, Captain Leland Cameron, the wee pretty one is up the mountain at me humble cottage." He raised his voice to a scolding shout. "Ye've shirked your God-given, paternal responsibilities by leavin' her like the lowliest urchin to fend for her poor self in the burnin' streets...."

Cameron didn't wait for Lysaght to launch a lecture. He was out the door and on his way running up Garnet Creek, Lysaght's words ringing in his ears.

Emma spotted him from the Thatcher's porch and ran to meet him. The side of her face was in bandages but he hardly noticed. In his enthusiasm, he yelled from a distance, "She's fine! Up at Lysaght's."

They clasped together in relief and joy. It was an embrace; it was a release; it was the tension of days, of years, draining away. They had won; they had overcome. Their little family was in tact. Knowledge of Marie's precious human presence was all that mattered. They were dirty; the trappings of their lives were in ashes. But they were infinitely happy to be alive.

Together they set out on foot up the rocky trail. Cameron did not tell Emma what gruesome events had bloodied these places. She had never walked here before and every new vista, every crag, every fossil's imprint, every trembling shadow of bristlecone and lodgepole on the great red face of the mountain, elicited her awe. At the Ervin camp, four men were lowering a basket over the precipice to the wreckage below. Emma questioned him then, and he told her briefly what had happened—that Spud Ervin would never threaten her again. She uttered one word. "Tragic." That was all.

They pushed on past the Ervin camp and the dangerous precipice. When the last outcrop of rock still blocked Lysaght's hut from view, they began to hear voices, the shrill and happy voices of children. They rounded the bend in the trail and there was Marie, kneeling on the stony ground with all twelve of her classmates, in the small clearing in front of Lysaght's dugout. Each one had a small stick and his own patch of soft earth. They were practicing their letters and prattling away happily. Mrs. Wood and righteous Mrs. Baird stood close by.

"Cameron! Emma!" Tilton called then and motioned them to be quiet. He walked up to them with a mild limp. "Brilliant little girl you have there, Emma, penning fine letters like others two years her senior." He turned to Cameron. "And Lee, thank you from us all for telling us to find Lysaght. Great man! Loves children!" He looked back at Emma, "What happened to your face?"

Chapter 40

Two days later, they buried Clem. Clem's funeral was simple. It was held in the nearly completed Church and Brother Luke, an itinerant preacher, presided. It was a simple ceremony, attended ony by Glenby, Cameron and Emma, and Charlie Slade. They lay Clem to rest in a lonely grave up high on the divide overlooking the Madison Valley, the Spanish Peaks and the racetrack, in the high-mountain sunlight where he could look down on the horses he loved so much. Charlie Slade stayed for the burial and then headed out for Corinne, Utah, and a warmer, more lucrative place to spend the winter.

The freight wagons began to arrive on the third day, from Helena with woolens for clothing and white canvas for tenting; from Bozeman City with potatoes, turnips, corn and hay. Bannock sent barrels of nails and and new stoves. Word of a huge mule train en route from the Mormon settlements, arrived over the wires. With luck, it would beat the snows on the Pleasant Valley Divide. Riders went out from Varina to speed it along. Father Manno's mission sent pemmican and squash. Help came from as far away as Oregon in the form of a small herd of beef cattle that pushed over the divide only a few days ahead of the deep snow. Varina's neighbors were far flung, but in adversity they came together, the thirsty gold seekers, the greedy, the lawless, the Union blues and Confederate greys, the vanquished and the victors.

And Varina's citizens bent their backs to the building. They cleared the burnt timbers and carried away buckets of sodden debris. They poled tents for temporary shelter. They hammered and nailed, mortised and pegged. They rebuilt their flumes, raised walls and lay on sod and hay for roofing. They cut timber in the mountains, dragged it to Holter's Mill in Ramshorn Gulch, and carted it the eight miles to Garnet Gulch and Varina. All this they did in great haste because winter was coming and tents were flimsy insulation against the storms of high-altitude winters. Already Warren Street shone with new colors: the white of the tenting and the yellow of raw pine lumber.

Within a week, Lee Cameron recognized the spidery form of Dawson driving a freight wagon up Warren Street. Dawson halted his mule team in front of Lamb's store and began to fling down sacks of potatoes. Cameron walked over to help with the unloading.

Dawson grinned widely at him, took off his hat and wiped his sleeve over his sweaty brow. "These here potatoes I grew misself! Got another whole cellar full!"

Cameron caught the hint of boyish pride in Dawson's voice. He smiled back. "I took your advice.... I bought it, the Sedgewick place! Be there come spring soon as the snow melts."

Dawson took a look around him. "You waitin' here, in these jack-legged shacks when you got a home you kin be proud of?"

Cameron gaped open-mouthed. "You mean go now?...For the winter! No fuel, no food, we'd starve!" And how would Emma react to such a hurried departure?

Dawson shrugged, "What you got left here? I'd help you out an' maybe we'll have a mild winter.

"I'd have to ask Emma."

"That you do. But explain it right. Explain that Three Forks is lower down, warmer. Mountains screen out the northers. Elk winter in the valley on my very own range and on your own too. They know where the winter is gentle an' where the grass grows thick. Tell 'er Dawson grew more corn an' potatoes than Mother an' Jenny an' the boy can eat. Tell 'er flour's cheaper in Bozeman City than it'll ever be in Varina after the fire. Tell 'er Jeb an' me'll ride you an' her an' yer kid back with us to Three Forks, an' you be nice and snug in yer very own home. Just lemme know so's I can call off the dogs."

"What about the sickness?" Cameron hadn't forgotten that the Sedgewicks were dead.

Dawson tilted his head. His blue eyes shot fire, straight as an arrow. He chewed his unlit pipe for a moment in silence. "You been there. You ain't dead. They was my next-door neighbors.... I ain't dead....I'll be leavin' day after tomorrow, nine o'clock. You make up your mind."

Cameron spoke to Emma that night at supper in front of everybody. There was no privacy—the three of them shared a tent with

Midge and Gertie. Rachel, Jimmy and Dad Long had come to join them from the tent next door.

Dad Long reacted immediately. "Yer own good land, Captain Lee, settle it before someone else decides to squat."

Emma surprised him. She was eager to go. "If I left St. Louis with Dubois, whom I didn't love, I can leave Varina with you, Lee Cameron." The words were plain and quiet and open for all to hear. There was no fear of criticism, nor heat of emotion yet the simple words touched Lee Cameron exquisitely, like the erotic fingers of a passionate lover. He took her hand and pressed it hard against his lips.

She smiled a contorted smile because some powder grains still stiffened the left side of her face. "I'm going to like Mr. Dawson. He must be a very intelligent and practical man."

Quiet Jimmy Long spoke then, his brown face long with worry. "Captain Lee, I got to ask you for Rachel to stay here by me. She knows 'er figures an' 'er letters and she the only one can write the invoices for the pipeline."

Cameron had never even thought of taking Rachel with them although she had been with Emma since her childhood. Jimmy Long was still living in slavery days, when a black man left children, husband, family and home to follow his master.

"She's a free woman, Jimmy. You take good care of her."

"Don you worry about us, Captain Lee. My first spiggot's up, just east of Brewery. Folks says wooden pipes don't last but my pipes is runnin' from out Sunshine Creek, right under these streets. Folks can drink from my spiggots an' we ever have another fire, we have enough water to dowse it. Folks is payin' me prime dust for pure water!" Jimmy Long was a smart man. The skin on his back was as welted and scarred as Lee Cameron's soul. It was luck, the luck of the draw, the luck of the gold strike, the luck of survival in a bloody and brutal war, the luck of a man's birth and the color of his skin, that had determined the past but the past was ended.

Cameron left immediately to find Dawson. Dawson was sitting on the steps of the burned-out California Hotel puffing his pipe and watching people carry bags of his potatoes away from Lamb's store.

Cameron shouted from the street. "We're coming with you, Dawson!"

Dawson didn't say a word. He took his pipe from his teeth, retracted his spidery legs and leaped down the steps in one stride. Before Cameron could blink, his long fingers clutched Cameron's palm in a viselike handshake.

Cameron added, "I'm going to ask Glenby to come with us."

"By all means." Dawson looked up and shook his bony skull from side to side as if in disagreement. "I was just thinkin'," he was just now framing his words, "Rob Glenby, a Union man, residin' in a nest of Rebels!"

"You'll be livin' next door to one!"

When Cameron invited Glenby to come, Glenby shook his shaggy head. "Clem's the one should've gone with you, not me. I'm too old. You got a wife an' kid an' I'd only be a club in a diamond straight." Glenby did seem older these days, with more white in his hair and more lines at the edge of his grey eyes. But he'd acquired an easy-going resignation very quickly. He was not sad. He had begun to rebuild.

"I'll miss you." It was the closest Cameron could come to showing the real affection he felt for his friend.

"No you won't. Sides, come spring, you'll be right back here trying to buy that mare off'n me." Glenby grinned with the satisfaction of a bear licking the honey from his paws. He was keeping the black mare, the best horse he'd ever owned.

"Slade didn't take her?" Cameron smiled wryly. During the night he had retrieved his stash of gold, what he had dug during the week on Pat Lysaght's claim, from the grave on Outlaw Bar. He would take it with him to another graveyard—graveyards made good hiding places.

Glenby's brown eyes flashed more than innocent curiosity. "What's Charlie Slade gonna do with a lame horse?"

The grey eyes fairly twinkled with delight. "He give 'er to me, papers an' all. I gave 'im a nice dun. I'll nurse 'er good this winter, rest 'er some, come spring I got me the finest mare in Montana Territory... I just might breed 'er." Glenby knew he had Cameron rivetted. He shoved his hat far back on his head, his hands in his pockets and looked off into space. "Need a top stallion though...." His savy eyes looked at Cameron from narrow slits under hooded lids. "You know any?"

Cameron could be cagey too, "Me? Maybe." He could afford to buy the horse now, but, like Slade, he couldn't take a lame horse with him. Best to let Glenby nurse her through the winter. He waited.

Glenby kicked a pebble in front of his boot and cleared his throat. "I hear them Nez Perce, have some good horses over near the Lapwai, funny lookin' poker-dotted beasts, but strong-boned an' sturdy." He watched the stone roll away. "Might get a good stallion from them.... An' they'd trade for a fancy gun like McGillicuddy gave you...Or the Crows. Now they got some really fine stock too, but you get a stallion from them, they'd probably steal 'im back."

Cameron's handsome face lit up. "Rob Glenby, you're one hell of a horse trader, but I'm a gambler.... I'll find that stallion, but you give me the foal. That's as fair a stud fee as I know, where I come from, unless I decide to buy the horse from you at your Shylock price."

"You serious? You southern boys always did appreciate a good horse." He held out his right hand and Lee Cameron grasped it warmly. But Lee Cameron knew he'd revealed too much—Glenby knew he wanted the horse and would drive an even stiffer bargain in the spring.

That evening, by the light of two oil lamps, Lee and Emma Cameron unrolled the old parchment scroll that was McGillicuddy's genealogy. They had to squint to read the finely penned script. It described a history of ancestral combat, and religious strife, a great, great uncle who had lost arm and leg at Waterloo, a theft of land title by the protestant Bishop of Limerick. One McGillicuddy had fought with distinction in the Spanish Navy. But most male heirs had died, like McGillicuddy, "without issue". The Camerons unfolded more and more of the curious document and were near its tightly-coiled core, when a new white paper popped out. When it fell to the floor, Cameron picked it up. It was the Cleopatra deed. Cameron gave the deed to Mayor Thatcher first thing in the morning.

The considerable Ervin wealth and property reverted to the city of Varina, Thatcher and Burnwell as custodians, who sold the town lots and mines at auction and dispensed the money to citizens for rebuilding. A new arrival bought the Cleopatra. He was a big bear of a man, brash and boisterous and he scratched and squirmed uncomfortably in his brand new suit of clothes. Judge Burnwell signed over the Cleopatra deed to one Augustus Terry and sent him to Behnke for a good clean shave. Terry bought a whole case of de-lousing lotion and used it on his mule.

Two weeks after the fire, the Camerons and Dawson were loading what was left of their belongings into a freight wagon outside of Lamb's store, when Pat Lysaght came riding into Varina. Cameron stopped what he was doing because he had never seen Lysaght on a horse and Lysaght pulled a heavily laden pack mule behind. He slumped loose in the saddle, his knees crimped, toes down, stirrup shoved back hard against the heel of his boot. Here was one Irishman who had never learned to ride a horse. He looked diminished astride the large animal, like a crumpled, discarded newspaper.

Emma was leaning over the back of the driver's seat as she pinned a tarp over the contents of the wagon. Marie played on the boardwalk close by. Lysaght ignored Cameron, took off his tattered hat and addressed Emma.

"Mrs. Cameron," he began in his most melodious tenor tones, "ye cannot be leavin' us?"

Emma looked up from her packing and pushed her hair back from her face, but Lysaght didn't give her time to respond. "I've waited sixty years to come back to civil-eye-zay-shun, livin' like a hermit on the bare cold shoulder of the mountain off the spare fruits of the land, and now in me twilight years, you would deny an old man the precious company of Varina's most beautiful woman."

Emma straightened impatiently with her hands on her hips and shouted down from atop the wagon. "No more speeches, Patrick. Look at my face! The beauty's gone, I've no patience for blarney and too much to do!"

"Tis the spirit of saint and siren...." He turned annoyingly to Lee Cameron. "Where ye be takin' her, Captain Cameron?"

"To Three Forks, Lysaght. I've bought a ranch."

"A ranch and ye did not tell me?" The shaggy brows knitted together in a surly frown.

"You weren't here, old man."

Lysaght's voice rose in volume, but the melody was lost. "Ye be takin' the lady and the girl child to a ranch?.... This fairest of fair and her bairn who deserve no less than a castle! Lee Cameron, are ye mad?"

Cameron, Emma and Dawson broke into laughter.

Lysaght's frown deepened; his eyes bulged. "Tis not comedy, Captain Lee, ye must not leave until I return." Like an aging and disapproving parent, he shook a bony index finger.

Cameron softened his tone. "We're packed and ready to go. We leave as soon as Dawson there gives the word."

"Twenty minutes! Ye must wait twenty minutes for an old man!" Lysaght swung his heels backward. His weight fell forward and his nag wobbled on down Warren. The mule tettered behind.

Dawson was frowning. "Who's Methusallah?"

"Patrick Lysaght, from County Galway, first friend I had in Varina....For him, Emma and I have to wait." Cameron snickered and their eyes followed the old man down Warren.

"Well I don't. The Mother is waiting." Dawson cracked his whip and his team pushed forward into the yoke. His wagon began to move.

"We'll catch you at the ford."

"You better....You can't cross the Madison alone an' neither can I."

Lysaght was back in ten minutes. His eyes shone like hot coals and the skin on his face was as white as his beard. He was not happy. "I be bankin' me riches and comin' to live in town. The good Judge calls it settlin' me estate." He snorted at that as if in derision, but he resumed his affable tone. "Mr. and Mrs. Tilton have offered me a room for a small fee."

Cameron was dumbfounded. After Lysaght's dogged insistence that he could never leave his mine, after all the struggles with Sime Ervin, after his lifelong search for gold, Lysaght was coming in, like an old stallion to the corral, whose life's battles had been fought and who finally submits to a rope. And Pat Lysaght was going to live in a household run by a woman, Mrs. Tilton, the printer and school master's wife. Did Tilton know how difficult Lysaght, who had lived only with one other man in the last thirty years, could be? Cameron looked hard at the old man. "Why?"

Lysaght rubbed his bulging eyes, "'Tis the children, God bless 'em. Such a short time they were with me, they turned this old Gaelic heart...I'm going to build them a proper schoolhouse." The old blue eyes focussed hard on Cameron. "My pretty Miss must be properly schooled?" Lysaght pursed his crinkled lips, narrowed his eyes and folded his arms across his chest and issued his next sentence like the judgement of King Solomon. "The school is for Missy Marie." The owl-like stare levelled Lee Cameron.

Emma tried to soften the blow. "Patrick, you're very generous. Marie will learn her letters and her figures I promise you. My mother taught me and I shall teach her."

Lysaght ignored her. "Ye deal the cards, ye cannot teach the numbers and letters."

Emma was indignant. "If I knew no numbers, Patrick Lysaght, I could not deal the cards."

Lysaght raised his pitch to a searing scream. "Ye be takin' me pretty Miss away!" He sounded angry and a brilliant redness crept up from the top of his snowy beard to the wispy white curls on his head but pain etched the lines in his old brow.

Lee Cameron was fast loosing patience. "Lysaght we're movin' out. Ed Dawson is waiting at the ford. We'll come back to visit."

Pat Lysaght was undaunted. "The mountains are hard on a man, harder on the weaker sex and even harder on a wee girl child."

Emma took offense at this. "I am not sitting here today because I am weak, Patrick."

"McGillicuddy fathered ye! Ye'd be scrubbin' floors without 'im!"

Emma flushed with anger. "I ran a business, Patrick Lysaght. I can add and subtract faster than a crooked gambler and I can read and write better than you!"

Lysaght glowered too with real Irish rage. The pitch of his voice heightened and every whisker of his white beard quivered with the trembling of his lips. He stared at Emma while he shouted stridently at Cameron, "Ye be takin' the woman and the wee one into the wilds in the dead of winter, man!"

"We're going to a fine stone house and barn in a warm valley."

Lysaght's pitch heightened more to a shrill staccato soprano. "I've lived in the wild, man, I know. Years I've spent in the mountains livin' on the game of the forest and icy water and some days with not a bone in my pot or a dry stick in my stove, like the prophets of old, like their forty hungry days in the desert, me flesh thinnin' and hangin' on me bones like drapery curtains and shakin' with cold. You're stomachs shall howl like starvin' wolves." He wrenched out the last words, "God damn ye!" turned on his heel and hobbled away.

This was not the way that Lee Cameron had wanted to leave Varina, with the curse of the Gaelic Almighty called down upon his head. He plucked Marie from the boardwalk and hoisted her up next to her mother, climbed into the driver's seat and whipped up his team. As they pulled away from Varina, he gathered his wife and daughter closer to his side with a quiet comment. "Mr. Lysaght loves us, Marie. He loves us too much. We're the family he never had."

Dawson was waiting at the ford.